VALIANT MEN AND
DESIRABLE WOMEN . . .

RENNO—Born white but raised among Indians, he is elected Sachem of all the Iroquois. But his leadership could be shattered by a rival's lies or an enemy's deadly tomahawk.

ANNE—An impetuous beauty, she would escape a cruel captivity only to face the terror of war fighting at the side of her beloved.

BEATRIZ—An irresistible Spanish enchantress, she turns men's desires into weapons that can destroy the Great Sachem.

ADRIENNE—A colonel's loyal wife, she would play a dangerous game of seduction to trap an enemy spy.

ALAIN DE GRAMONT—A White Indian whose soul was bought for French gold and whose heart burns with a vicious hatred of Renno and his people.

SHARE THE DRAMA OF WAR AND
THE THRILL OF ROMANCE

The Colonization of America Series
Ask your bookseller for the books you have missed

The White Indian Series
Book IV

THE
SACHEM

DONALD CLAYTON PORTER

Created by the producers of
Wagons West, Children of the Lion,
Stagecoach, and Saga of the Southwest.

Chairman of the Board: Lyle Kenyon Engel

BANTAM BOOKS
TORONTO • NEW YORK • LONDON • SYDNEY

THE SACHEM

A Bantam Book / published by arrangement with
Book Creations, Inc.

Bantam edition / April 1981

2nd printing .... March 1981	*6th printing .. December 1981*
3rd printing ...... April 1981	*7th printing .. September 1982*
4th printing ...... April 1981	*8th printing ...... April 1983*
5th printing .... July 1981	*9th printing ... February 1984*

Produced by Book Creations, Inc.
Chairman of the Board: Lyle Kenyon Engel

ISBN 0-553-24476-0

Published simultaneously in the United States and Canada

PRINTED IN THE UNITED STATES OF AMERICA

H   18 17 16 15 14 13 12 11 10 9

THE SACHEM

Chapter I

Father and son walked silently in single file through the wilderness that was their natural habitat, the deep forest they loved. In the lead was Renno, the white Indian, adopted in infancy by the leader of the Seneca. Now a renowned war chief, he moved with the ease of one totally at home in his environment. Behind him, slightly shorter, his build massive, walked Ghonka, Great Sachem of the entire Iroquois League of Six Nations. Ordinarily Ghonka would have led, but he had given that place to his son as a sign of his complete trust.

The pair had gone hunting together, enjoying a rare respite from the duties that kept them occupied in the main town of the Seneca. Since the day was dark and the sun cast no shadows, it was easy to find game. The larders of the nation were full, so this was a day

1

devoted to sport for its own sake. For a while both men could put aside their concern over the new war that threatened to break out between the English colonies, who were their allies, and the forces of New France, aided by the treacherous Huron and Ottawa who lived to the north.

The scent of the pines was pungent, and from time to time both stopped simultaneously when they heard a faint rustling sound in the underbrush. But this was not a day to bring down rabbit or other small game. With luck they would encounter a deer and with greater luck they could find the tracks of an elk or even a small herd of buffalo. The excitement of the chase lay in not knowing what rewards they might claim.

It was early afternoon now, and they had been walking since daybreak, maintaining the same steady pace. It did not occur to them to halt, and they banished all thoughts of food and water from their minds. That, of course, was the Seneca way. No other nation's warriors were as self-disciplined as the Seneca, and none of the Seneca better exemplified the high standards of the tribe than the Great Sachem and his war-chief son.

Instinct, honed by the experience of over three decades of wilderness living, caused Renno to turn suddenly to his left. He snatched his tomahawk from his belt and, with blinding speed, took aim and instantly let fly at the center of a thick patch of snarled bush.

At the same moment an arrow grazed the side of Ghonka's face, then buried itself in the trunk of a tree directly behind him, where it quivered. Drawing their knives quickly, the pair ran toward the bush. They stopped short when they saw the body of a warrior, a tomahawk in his chest, his blood soaking the ground. Both noted the acorn suspended on a rawhide thong around the brave's neck.

"Huron," Renno said, making the word sound like a curse.

It was extraordinary for the Huron to send a scout

so far into the land of the Seneca, especially at a time when the two nations ostensibly were at peace. Renno suspected that the warrior had been sent to determine what war preparations the Seneca might be making. Through sheer luck he had encountered the Great Sachem and the war chief, both easily identifiable because of the feathers that adorned their scalp locks.

"He was young," Ghonka said. "An older, wiser warrior would not have tried to kill the Great Sachem. This one could not resist the opportunity. For all eternity he will regret his foolishness, for he will be mocked in the afterworld by his ancestors."

Renno dropped to one knee. He retrieved his tomahawk, which he carefully cleaned, and then, swiftly and expertly, he took the scalp of the man he had killed. That was his right according to the inviolable laws of the wilderness.

"The sachem and war chiefs of the Huron," Renno said, "must have known their scout might be discovered."

"But they took the risk. That means it was more important that they learn what the Seneca do to make ready for a new war."

A sudden thought struck Renno. "It may be," he said, "that he was sent by the great enemy of Renno."

"It may be," his father agreed somberly.

Both were silent. Only a man as daring as Colonel Alain de Gramont, a French officer who had spent more than a quarter of a century living and fighting as a Huron, would have had the courage to send a scout to spy on the leaders of the mighty Seneca. If Gramont—known to the Seneca as Golden Eagle—was active again, it might be a sign that new, serious troubles were brewing, perhaps even with the French high command in Quebec.

Ghonka never wasted time in needless speculation. "The Seneca are grateful to the unseen manitous who watch over them for giving them this warning. The Seneca will be even more alert."

Later, when they returned to the town, Renno would be expected to double the number of sentinels who kept guard over the land of the Seneca day and night. Neither he nor his father would rebuke those who had allowed the Huron to make such a deep penetration. Their obvious failure would be rebuke enough.

Ghonka glanced up at the sky. "There is still time to hunt."

Renno nodded. "Game, not warriors." Without another word they resumed their walk, leaving the body of the Huron for the vultures.

Renno was in no way surprised that he received no word of thanks for saving his father's life. Seneca relied on one another for protection against their foes. But for a fleeting moment he had seen the deep pride in the Great Sachem's eyes as they returned to the hunt. Ghonka rarely offered praise for work well done, but his expression had indicated that his son's performance had filled him with joy. No warrior, Renno above all, could have asked for a greater reward.

Boston, the capital of Massachusetts Bay and the largest city in Great Britain's North American colonies, was a thriving post and commercial center in 1702, but in some ways it was still a small town. The view of the common from the crest of Beacon Hill was idyllic and pastoral. Cattle and sheep roamed freely, seamen from England and other colonies strolled with local girls, and citizens of every class enjoyed the fresh air and sunshine.

The tranquillity of Boston was deceptive, however, and no one knew it better than the two middle-aged men in blue, scarlet-trimmed uniforms who sat before a roaring fire in a second-floor office at the colony's military headquarters. The aristocratic Major General Andrew Wilson, commander in chief of the Massachusetts Bay militia and the proprietor of a large estate in the western part of the colony, frowned and shook his head. "Our worst fears have been realized in Europe," he said. "That's why I asked you here. There will soon be hell to pay on this side of the Atlantic, too."

His visitor, Brigadier General Austin Ridley, head of the Virginia militia and owner of a fleet of merchant ships, knew what his host meant. "The French have ignored the warnings of Britain, Austria, and the Netherlands. Louix XIV, damn him, has put his grandson on the throne of Spain."

"Correct," Andrew Wilson replied. "Philip of Anjou is now King of Spain, but he hasn't renounced his rights to the throne of France. That's why England has declared war."

"Along with the Hague and Austria. France can't be allowed to dominate Europe and gain control of the entire New World, no matter how great Louis's ambitions may be. Queen Anne has sent General John Churchill to the Continent with a large army, and he's joining forces with the Austrian commander, Prince Eugene of Savoy."

Austin Ridley nodded thoughtfully. "Able men, both of them, although the French are so powerful it may take years to bring Louis to his knees." He fixed his level gaze on his old comrade. "I suppose it's too much to hope that London is even aware of our predicament?"

Andrew's smile was sardonic. "I've received a vague promise that the Royal Navy will send us a squadron of warships, but the colonies are being ignored. As usual."

It was difficult for the normally self-controlled Austin Ridley to curb his anger. "Good Lord! You'd think that no one in Queen Anne's government has even bothered to look at a map of North America! New France lies to the north of us, New Spain to the south and west. And between them they can overwhelm us in the Caribbean, which is vital to our trade."

Andrew Wilson could well appreciate his old friend's rage. "It appears," he replied, "that the Almighty is giving us a clear choice. Either the English

5

colonies band together in self-defense, or we surrender to the enemies who virtually surround us."

"Never, Andy! Virginia will send one thousand militiamen to war, although I'll grant it will take time to muster that large a force."

"Of course. As I see it, Massachusetts Bay can raise three thousand, and I hope New York will provide another thousand. I believe Connecticut and Rhode Island will bring in five hundred volunteers each."

"With luck we'll get five hundred from Maryland and another five hundred from the Carolinas. Not too small an army, provided we know where the combined French and Spanish forces will strike. We may be forced to outwit them—if we can—by striking first. I feel it would be feasible and advisable to launch a campaign as soon as possible."

"I agree, although it's premature to plan strategy. So much will depend on our Indian allies. You know as well as I do how they'll react to this news."

Austin Ridley's personal ties to the Seneca, leaders of the powerful Iroquois League, were close. His elder daughter, Betsy, was married to Renno, the most renowned of the Seneca war chiefs. Renno, Betsy, and their son and daughter lived in the main town of the Seneca, but they visited the Ridleys in Virginia each year. And no man had performed greater services for the English colonies than Renno, who had become the vital, primary link between them and their Indian neighbors. Enjoying the trust and respect of both, he moved between them and in the process gave each a better understanding of the other.

"I know my son-in-law appreciates the issues and knows what's at stake for the Iroquois if they come under French rule. That was demonstrated in our last major campaign, when the Ottawa and Huron sided with the French, and the Algonquian were persuaded to take the French side, too."

Andrew Wilson smiled faintly as he remembered how badly the huge Algonquian nation had been defeated by a force comprised of the Seneca and their allies, led by Ghonka. "I suspect the Algonquian will remain neutral in any new war," he said. "And I'm certain that Ghonka will live up to his treaty obligations with us."

"From what Renno tells me and from what I've learned about Ghonka myself, I'm sure he will, Andy. There's no more honorable man anywhere, and I know few who are wiser. Ghonka thoroughly understands the fate that awaits his people if the French conquer us."

The Massachusetts Bay commander jotted some figures on a sheet of paper. "What bothers me most," he said, "is that even if the Iroquois stand with us and even if we fulfill our militia quotas, we'll have the devil's own time beating the combined forces of France and Spain in a war that's certain to last for a long time."

"The prospect isn't encouraging," the Virginian replied. "We urgently need help from London. Renno performed miracles when you sent him to England and he persuaded King William to give us heavy support, but with Queen Anne now on the throne, we've got to start from the beginning again."

"I've been wondering whether we might want to send Renno off to the court again. I hesitate because he's no longer a novelty there and because he can so easily slip into our way of life."

"It's true," Austin said, "that his English is now virtually perfect and that he's at home with our customs. Certainly there's no warrior who is more of a complete Seneca than Renno, but he wouldn't seem that way to the Queen and her ministers. They need to be startled, jarred into giving us the aid we need. Otherwise, they'll remain too preoccupied with their concerns in Europe."

"I've had a thought on the subject, Austin. Suppose we sent Ghonka and his wife, Ena, to London? I have the authority to use one of the Royal Navy frigates in

Boston harbor to transport them, and I know the government will make one of its town houses in London available to them."

General Ridley smiled. "There's no doubt that the Great Sachem would create a sensation in London. And he'd be sure to impress Queen Anne and her ministers. They've never encountered royalty like him." His smile faded. "But the language barrier might be too great. Ghonka and Ena speak only a few words of English. How would they communicate with the court?"

"Well, I've had a rather unorthodox idea," General Wilson declared. "I wonder if Betsy would agree to go with her in-laws and act as their interpreter. She could take both of your grandchildren with her. What I don't know is whether Renno would consent to such a plan."

"Oh, he wants his children to learn about their English heritage. Unless I'm badly mistaken, he'd be delighted. So would Betsy. We had promised her a trip to England some years ago, before her marriage to Renno."

"Then you think we should go ahead with the scheme?"

"As I see it," Austin said, "there's everything to gain and nothing to lose."

"Then let's do it." Andrew Wilson slapped the arm of his chair. "We'll ask the Royal Governors of Massachusetts Bay and Virginia to issue a joint invitation to Ghonka, and when the other governors realize what's at stake, I'm certain all of them will sign the letter, too."

"We're placing a terrible burden on Ghonka," Austin said, "and on my daughter, too. The outcome of the war in the New World may depend on whether they can persuade the Crown to give us the warships, munitions, and other supplies we'll need to beat the French and Spaniards. I hate to think of what will happen if their mission fails."

"Ghonka doesn't know the meaning of failure," Andrew Wilson said. "That's why he's our greatest potential asset."

A score of drums throbbed, their beat measured, as the leaders of the Iroquois League marched slowly through the snow in the main town of the Seneca. Leading the procession was Ghonka, the Great Sachem, wearing the full bonnet of feathers and the buffalo robe decorated with porcupine quills that marked his exalted rank.

Behind him came the sachem, senior war chiefs, and principal medicine men of the Mohawk, the largest of the Iroquois nations. Equally solemn were the representatives of the Oneida, the Onondaga, the Cayuga, and the Tuscarora. Out of deference to their guests, the Seneca delegation brought up the rear, a place rarely occupied by the most ferocious of all the Indian tribes.

The three principal medicine men of the Seneca, wearing wooden masks and shaking gourds in time to the drumbeats, were at the head of the delegation. They were followed by the four senior war chiefs, the generals on whom the military reputation of the Seneca depended. Three were in their middle years, and in spite of the bitter cold, their torsos were bare, their faces and bodies smeared with streaks of green and yellow war paint.

All eyes were on the tall war chief whose scalp lock was blond and whose eyes were as blue as the waters of the lake that lay beyond the town palisades. Renno moved with the grace of a wildcat, the muscles in his shoulders and arms rippling. He was a true member of the Bear Clan, whose warriors formed the Seneca elite. The hawk feathers that decorated his scalp lock were a sign to all who knew him that he had a special affinity with the hawk: his eyesight was as keen as that of the fabled bird, and the manitous, the spirits who guided his destiny, had chosen to send a hawk to him at times of great danger.

The crowd came alive as Renno passed, although anyone unfamiliar with the ways of the Seneca would not have known it. No one smiled or waved, and the faces of the onlookers remained impassive. But the senior warriors who had served under Renno stood straighter, proud of their association with him, while the junior warriors, less seasoned in battle, could not hide their awe. The elders nodded almost imperceptibly, remembering their own days of glory, and the mature women glanced surreptitiously at Ena, Renno's mother and Ghonka's wife, who raised her head a trifle higher.

The younger women looked enviously at Betsy, clad in a doeskin dress and moccasins like all the rest, her pale hair in pigtails. Standing erect on her right, with his hands folded across his chest, was little Ja-gonh, doing his best to look serious. Only his younger sister, Goo-ga-ro-no, jumped up and down in excitement when she saw her father, her blue eyes dancing, her blond hair waving. Renno's sister, Ba-lin-ta, now in her early twenties, tried to quiet the child.

Renno's own composure changed momentarily when he saw his family. His eyes met Betsy's for an instant, which was long enough for them to express their deep, mutual love. Then he winked at his son and grinned openly at his overjoyed daughter.

But he sobered again, looking without recognition at his younger brother, El-i-chi, now a senior warrior and his closest companion. He was equally remote when he appeared to look through Walter Alwin, a young man in his twenties from Fort Springfield. Walter had lived with the Seneca for years and, in spite of physical handicaps, had distinguished himself as a junior warrior. Deaf and dumb since birth, he had gained the power of speech during his manhood trials, and although he was still deaf, he participated fully in the activities of the nation. He and Ba-lin-ta, who had enjoyed a remarkable rapport since childhood, stood close to each other, as they always did. It was taken for granted that they would be married whenever Ghonka decided the time was right.

El-i-chi and Walter reacted precisely as Renno did; their eyes were seemingly blank, their faces stern. It was beneath the dignity of Seneca warriors to show their feelings in public.

The Great Sachem arrived at the entrance to the council lodge, where he halted, then stood aside to allow the principal medicine men to precede him into the building. Rattling their gourds in unison, they marched in a circle around the fire that blazed in the center of the building, the smoke escaping through a hole in the ceiling. Each threw a handful of herbs into the fire, the dried plants turning the smoke white, and then they chanted a prayer, asking the manitous to intercede with the gods of the sun, moon, and earth on behalf of all the Iroquois. Neither the medicine men nor the people of the town yet knew why the conclave had been called, but the event was so unusual that they realized that matters of grave concern to the entire League were to be discussed.

When the smoke escaping from the Council Lodge became pure white, Ghonka pushed aside the flap of heavy elkskin and went inside. The other sachems followed, and together they sat in a circle around the fire, with the war chiefs forming a larger, outer circle around them. A group of senior warriors, ten from each of the six nations having been chosen for the honor, surrounded the Council Lodge and stood sentry duty, quivers of arrows on their shoulders, bows in their hands, and tomahawks at their belts. They were unmoving, resembling bronze statues, and all of them well knew that they could never repeat any of the proceedings they might overhear through the log walls. El-i-chi, stationed at the entrance, held a spear in both hands, symbolically discouraging nonmembers of the Council from disturbing the meeting.

The principal medicine men continued their chant. Ghonka lighted a pipe with a coal from the fire, which he plucked from the ground with his bare hand, and after drawing on the pipe, he passed it to the sachem of the Mohawk, who sat to his left. By the time everyone in the Lodge had puffed on the pipe, the prayers of the medicine men came to an end.

Most Indians delighted in oratory, but the Great Sachem was a man of few words. Rising effortlessly to his feet, he folded his arms across his chest. "My brother sachems and war chiefs," he said, "all have been told that our friends, the English, have gone to war again against our enemies, the French and the men of Spain. Are there any among you who would throw the white wampum of our treaty with the English colonies into the fire?"

No one spoke or moved.

"Then it is agreed that the Iroquois will keep their word to go to war at the side of the English colonists."

"It is agreed," the sachem of the Mohawk said solemnly. Everyone else in the Lodge, speaking in turn, repeated the words.

Those who thought the business of the day had been concluded were surprised when Ghonka indicated he was far from finished. "The governors of the colonies," he said, "have invited the Great Sachem to sail to England in a ship-that-looks-like-a-big-bird. It is their wish that he meet the new Queen of the English. She worries about the war in her world. She is ignorant of the problems in this world. It is the hope of the governors that the Great Sachem can open her ears and eyes. It is their hope he can persuade her to send many ships and firesticks, cannon-that-roar-like-thunder and fire powder to the colonies. The colonists are few in number, but their enemies are as many as grains of sand on the beach. The Great Sachem has prayed to the manitous. It is his belief that it is his duty to make this long journey. Do his brothers disagree?"

The sachem of the Mohawk replied without hesitation. "It is the duty of the Great Sachem to visit the

Queen of the English," he declared. One by one the other sachems indicated their agreement.

That seemed to end the matter, but a war chief of the Oneida rose, his expression troubled. "Who will rule the Seneca during the absence of the Great Sachem?"

Ghonka did not indicate his surprise. "The council of the Seneca always rules during the absence of the nation's leader."

The Oneida shook his head, then reworded his statement. "It may be that the Iroquois will go into battle while the Great Sachem is away. Who will lead the Seneca to war?"

All at once a dozen men clamored to be heard, but they deferred to the elderly sachem of the Mohawk. "Our brother of the Oneida has spoken well," he declared. "He who is the war sachem of all the Iroquois has been a Seneca since the times of the grandfathers of our grandfathers. He who leads the Iroquois during the absence of the Great Sachem should be a Seneca!"

Loud shouts of approval greeted the proposal.

Renno knew his shrewd father well enough to realize that Ghonka had anticipated this development, choosing deliberately to let a member of another Iroquois nation make the initial suggestion.

Many of those present turned to Sun-ai-yee, a short, powerfully built Seneca who stood first in the ranks of the Seneca war chiefs. Knowing his name was about to be placed in nomination, the warrior leaped to his feet with greater speed than grace and waited to be recognized. Although it was customary for a new leader to be elected formally before he addressed the Council, Ghonka inclined his head slightly, indicating that the warrior was permitted to speak.

Sun-ai-yee folded his arms across his chest. "Each summer for twenty-three summers," he said, "Sun-ai-yee has painted his face and his chest with the colors of the Seneca and has gone to war. Sun-ai-yee has learned much about the fighting of a war. But he who leads all of the Iroquois into battle should be one whose legs are as fleet as a deer's. He should be a warrior whose sight remains as sharp as an eagle's. So Sun-ai-yee urges his brothers to ask Renno to act as the sachem of the Seneca and lead all of the Iroquois into war during the absence of the Great Sachem."

A faint hint of a gleam in Ghonka's eyes indicated his deep sense of pleasure. Renno was stunned, although his face remained immobile.

"No warrior," Sun-ai-yee declared, "has won more scalps than Renno. In four battles Renno has won victories against the enemies of his people. The leader of the armies of the Iroquois must also negotiate with the generals of the English colonies. Renno knows all of them. He speaks and reads and writes their language. His wife is the daughter of one of their generals. Often he has fought at the side of the colonists. He understands their use of firesticks and the cannon-that-speak-like-thunder. No warrior is better able to lead the Iroquois into battle at the side of the English colonists."

The nomination was so startling that there was a tense moment of silence as Sun-ai-yee sat cross-legged again.

Then the elderly sachem of the Mohawk rose and drew his buffalo robe more closely around him. "Well do the Mohawk remember when Renno first went into battle," he said. "With shame they admit they doubted him because his skin, his eyes, and his hair are pale. The Mohawk are the first to admit they were wrong. Renno is a great warrior. He is truly the son of Ghonka. The Mohawk will follow wherever he leads!"

Leaders of the other nations were on their feet now, clamoring for recognition, and Ghonka had to exert his utmost authority to restore order.

One by one the nations of the Iroquois promised to obey Renno as their leader in battle. The war chiefs, on whom victory or defeat would depend, were even more enthusiastic than the sachems. The medicine men took no active part in the discussion, which would have been inappropriate, but they knew the young war chief was a devout believer in the faith of the Seneca, so they rattled their gourds to show that they, too, approved.

Ghonka said a few words in private to Sun-ai-yee, who hurried out to speak for a moment with El-i-chi.

"The son of Ghonka will speak now," the Great Sachem declared.

Renno stood and moved slowly to the edge of the fire, raising a hand in salute to his father, then saluting the assemblage. "Renno, son of Ghonka and war chief of the Seneca," he said, "has spent more than thirty winters on the earth. Some of the war chiefs who are present at this gathering have fought for almost that long. Renno is not worthy of the honor you have given him."

Many of those present thought he was going to refuse the post, and Ghonka sucked in his breath.

"But a Seneca must accept the responsibilities that are placed on his shoulders," Renno went on. "The gods of his people would spit on him if he failed to do his duty, and the manitous would turn their faces from him. So Renno will do what is required. He will take the warriors of the Seneca into war and will lead the warriors of the other Iroquois nations as well."

Pandemonium reigned in the Lodge as the war chiefs gathered around the young Seneca to grip forearms with him and pledge their loyalty to him.

Sun-ai-yee saw El-i-chi gesturing from the entrance, went to him, and returned to Ghonka carrying a feathered bonnet and a buffalo robe decorated with porcupine quills.

The members of the Council fell silent as the Great Sachem stood before Renno. "It is not often that the manitous show their favor by allowing a father who is still living in this world to see his son follow in his footsteps. Renno, son of Ghonka, you now will act as war sachem of the Seneca and of all the Iroquois nations."

Renno stood motionless as his father placed the bonnet squarely on his head and draped the buffalo robe over his shoulders.

Then the medicine men began to chant again, asking the gods and the manitous to favor their new leader in the battles that lay ahead. They surrounded Renno, shaking their rattles as they danced.

The newly elected war sachem stood with his arms folded, looking straight ahead. He knew his father was rejoicing inwardly, but he himself felt no elation over the unexpected promotion. His obligations would be overwhelming, and he could only hope he could discharge them well.

At last the ceremony came to an end. The sentry detail outside the Lodge was disbanded, and the people of the town, who had returned to their warm lodges and huts, now reassembled outside to watch the leaders parade to the palisade. There the visitors would accept gifts of food and later disperse to their distant homes.

As Renno marched beside his father, he was conscious of people gaping at him in his new regalia. There was no reason for the Seneca to hide their astonishment and pleasure, and there was a buzz of conversation, followed by impromptu cheers, as the Great Sachem and his son walked slowly toward the palisade.

Renno saw Betsy and knew at a glance that she was deeply troubled. She did her best to play the role of a Seneca wife and hide her concern, but she was still a Virginian, and Renno knew she was afraid his promotion would subject him to great personal danger. There was no way he could soothe her now. It would have to wait until they were alone.

That moment would not come for many hours. Renno conferred separately with each of the departing war chiefs, all of whom would return to the town of the

Seneca when he summoned them to the next meeting. Then, after bidding the war chiefs good-bye, he and Ghonka returned to the Council Lodge, where each of the war chiefs of the Seneca pledged their loyalty to the new war sachem. They were followed by the senior warriors, then the junior warriors, and it was late in the day when the rituals came to an end.

Ghonka was not yet ready to return home, however, and indicated with a gesture that he wanted his son to remain for a private conversation. Renno sat cross-legged in silence before the fire, waiting for his father to speak. It struck him as strange that, henceforth, others would be showing the same mark of respect by waiting for Renno to speak.

"It is the privilege of a war sachem," Ghonka said, "to attach two warriors to his person. They serve him in any way he sees fit. They must be men he trusts."

"I have already given the matter thought, and I would like to name El-i-chi and Wal-ter."

Ghonka nodded. "They are good choices."

"I will not be criticized for showing special favor by choosing my brother and one who will become my brother-in-law?"

"You will be applauded because all will know you have chosen warriors you can trust. But if Ja-gonh, your son, were old enough, it would not be wise to choose him for such a place, just as I did not choose you and El-i-chi as my personal warriors."

Never had Renno been more conscious of his father's wisdom.

Abruptly Ghonka changed the subject, as he always did when members of his family were on the verge of showing their feelings. "I need not tell you how to use the Seneca in battle. They will be the soul and heart of your army."

Renno nodded.

"The Mohawk are reliable, always. They defend as well as they attack. Use them freely."

"I will not forget my father's counsel."

"The Tuscarora and Onondaga also are steady in battle and will not panic. The Cayuga fight better on their own soil than elsewhere. The Oneida are a problem. The Oneida become wild men in battle. They lack discipline, although none except the Seneca have greater courage. Use them as scouts and give them special assignments. But never give them a sector of their own to attack or defend. Their war chiefs will not take offense if you are firm and flatter them. Make it plain to them that you are giving them the most dangerous and delicate assignments. Then they will be happy to follow you."

Renno grinned at him. "I will not forget my father's words of advice."

For a long moment Ghonka did not speak. Then he said in a voice that was suspiciously husky, "On the day I found you, during the massacre in the town of the English, you looked at me without fear, though you were only an infant. Ena had just lost a baby, and I knew the manitous were giving you to us as our son. Not once in your life have I been disappointed. You are all that I could ask of the manitous in a son. All, and more."

Never had Ghonka spoken so freely. Renno wanted to reply, but his throat felt so choked he could not speak.

Ghonka rose to his feet quickly. "Let us join Ena and Betsy in the evening meal they have prepared for us," he said. "If we do not go now, the grandchildren of Ghonka, in whom he takes such joy, will be too sleepy to eat and will whine, which will force me to send them to bed without food, and that would pain me. Come."

They walked in silence through the empty streets, the odors of food being cooked in the lodges and huts sharpening their appetites. Each was conscious of the sacrifice the other was making. For the sake of the long-term safety of the Iroquois, Ghonka was allowing himself to be taken far from his home and thrust into the heart of an alien society. There he would be required to perform a near miracle in obtaining aid from a new British ruler unfamiliar with the urgent needs of her New World colonies. Meanwhile, Renno was accepting the crushing burden of responsibility for conducting a military campaign at the side of allies who were badly outnumbered by their foes. Neither father nor son could afford to fail.

But it was not the way of the Seneca to discuss such liabilities. Each man would plan, work, and fight as best he could, with neither ever contemplating the excuses he could make if he failed to carry out his mission.

In spite of the bitter cold, Ena and Betsy, aided by Ba-lin-ta, were cooking the evening meal over a fire in the stone-lined pit outside the Great Sachem's house. Neither Ghonka nor his wife liked the smell of cooked food to linger indoors, so the fire inside the house was used mainly for heat.

Betsy was the first to see her husband, and she straightened, folding her arms across her breasts and inclining her head in a gesture of respect to the new sachem. Ena immediately did the same, and Ba-lin-ta, as high-spirited as she had been as a child, followed their example.

Renno embraced his wife, contrary to Seneca custom, and then kissed his mother, too. Neither woman spoke, as words would have been inappropriate, but Betsy's love and concern for her husband were evident in her eyes, and Ena's beaming expression was proof of the pride she felt.

Ba-lin-ta dared to defy tradition because she was sure that her father, who so often indulged her, would not reprimand her. "The daughter of the Great Sachem greets the new sachem," she said, her voice vibrant.

Ghonka's expression did not change. It was unseemly for a maiden to address someone of her brother's new rank before he granted permission, but just as Ba-lin-ta had anticipated, her father did not rebuke her.

So Renno felt compelled to put her in her place. "The sachem has not granted Ba-lin-ta the right to address him," he said severely, using his new title for the first time. Then his frown vanished, and he relented. "But I know how you feel, and I thank you for it." Without glancing at her again, he followed his father into the house.

El-i-chi and Walter, warming themselves at the fire, immediately jumped to their feet and raised their arms in rigid salute to Ghonka, then to his temporary successor. Little Ja-gonh, already subject to the strict discipline of the nation, did the same. Only Goo-ga-ro-no was free to do as she pleased, particularly as Betsy was not present to restrain her. She hurled herself at Renno, her blond hair streaming, and when he lifted her into the air, she planted a wet kiss on his cheek. Then she twisted toward Ghonka, who took her into his arms. The warriors of the Seneca would have been astonished had they seen the austere Great Sachem chuckle as he and his little granddaughter hugged each other fiercely.

Although the women made no overt mention of Renno's unexpected promotion, they had prepared a special meal in honor of the occasion. The first course was grilled fish, which Betsy had caught in the lake after making a hole in the ice, and it was sprinkled with a wild herb that she had found in the forest, a discovery that had won her distinction among the women of the Seneca because no one else had ever before used that herb in cooking. The main dish, which Ena cooked to perfection, was the favorite of the nation, a venison stew that simmered for hours in a rich gravy, to which corn and beans had been added. For the sake of Ja-gonh and Goo-ga-ro-no, as well as for the indulgence of Ghonka's love of sweets, the meal ended with a corn cake served with liberal quantities of maple syrup.

The feast was consumed in silence, according to Seneca custom. Not until Ghonka lighted a pipe, puffed on it, and handed it to Renno was conversation permitted.

Renno drew on the pipe, then gave it to El-i-chi, who in turn handed it to Walter. Then Ghonka nodded, and Renno addressed the two young warriors. "El-i-chi and Wal-ter will leave the ranks of the braves and will serve the new sachem. Soon the day will come when he will give them work that is worthy of their cunning and their courage."

They both bowed their heads in obedience, taking care to conceal their pleasure.

Now that talk was permitted, Betsy and Ena began to discuss the clothes they would take with them to England. "My English dresses are in Virginia," Betsy said, "and I intend to write to my mother to have some new ones made for me, too. Of course, I shall wear Seneca dress at court."

"That is good," Ena replied. "It is right that Betsy should move freely between the world of the Seneca and the world of the English."

Betsy hesitated. "Would you like some English-style clothes made for you?"

Her mother-in-law smiled and shook her head. "Ena is a Seneca," she said firmly. "No less and no more. She would look foolish in the clothes of another nation."

"Do you think I should have English clothes made for the children?" Betsy asked. "I'm of two minds on the question."

Ena pondered for a time. "Let them travel as Seneca," she said, "because they are Seneca. If they should go to the court of the English ruler, they should go as Seneca. But they should also have the dress of their ancestors to wear at other times. Their hair and eyes are pale, so it would not be right if the English mocked them."

The advice was sensible, as Betsy knew. Her mother-in-law had left the land of her people only once, for a journey to Fort Springfield and Boston, but her native wisdom enabled her to make accurate judgments about the sophisticated world of the eighteenth century.

Ja-gonh and Goo-ga-ro-no were growing sleepy, so Renno and Betsy returned to their own house. The little boy trudged manfully beside his parents, while his sister, already half-asleep, snuggled in her father's arms.

Betsy put the youngsters to bed on their shelflike bunks covered with young pine boughs, then returned to the principal room, where Renno was striking a flint and lighting the candles that were the family's concession to a different and more advanced civilization.

He looked at his wife, smiled, and caressed her. "Put the worry from your heart and mind," he said.

"I know you've been given a great honor, and I'm so pleased for you," she said. "As nearly as I can work it out, you've been given a rank equal to a major general in that of the Massachusetts Bay or Virginia militia. That's wonderful for someone who is just over thirty years old." She hesitated. "I can't help being concerned for you, though. I've always been worried and afraid when you've gone off to war, and this time you'll be exposed to even greater dangers."

"That may or may not be true," he replied quietly. "No two battles are fought in the same way. I have fought in many battles, and the manitous have preserved my life. They continue to watch over me."

Even though she already had spent several years living as a Seneca, she had not acquired her husband's blind faith in the spirits who guarded him. "I can't help wondering," she said, "if it wouldn't be better for the colonies and better for the Iroquois if you were sent to London in Ghonka's place."

He shook his head and said gently, "The governors of the English colonies have chosen him as their emissary. I know from my own experience there that the court of the British monarch is complicated and has many devious paths, like the maze in the royal gardens. It would be wrong of us to question the wisdom of the governors, who must have reasons for wanting the Great Sachem to represent them."

"I suppose you're right," she replied, sighing. "But I can't help wondering, then, if I could stay here at home with you instead of leaving you to struggle alone in your new post. Do you suppose that would be possible?"

Renno hesitated for no more than an instant before he put the temptation behind him. "When the time is right, I will lead the warriors of the Seneca against the French, the Spaniards, and their Indian allies. So there is little you could do. I know your thoughts will be with me from England, just as they would be if you were here. Besides, Ghonka and Ena will need you as their interpreter. Only you can guarantee the success of Ghonka's great mission."

Betsy walked to the entrance, pulled aside the flap of animal skin, and walked out into the night, where she stood staring up at the stars that shone in a clear, cold sky. Occasionally she rubbed her arms, but otherwise she stood still.

When she did not return, Renno followed her, came up behind her, and placed his strong hands on her shoulders. She turned to face him. "I try to be a good Seneca wife. I know your mother suffers fears, just as I do, but she manages to hide them. I wasn't brought up in such a stern society, and at moments like this I fail you." Tears glistened in her eyes.

"That's not true," he replied as he took her in his arms. "For me you are the only woman on this earth." He kissed her.

Betsy responded, and as they returned to the house, his arm around her waist, she consoled herself with the thought that at least she was able to refrain from telling him about her forebodings. She had the feeling that, during her long absence from the land of the Seneca, he would be subjected to strange dangers, unlike any he had ever faced.

The preparations for the journey came to an end at last, and a messenger from Massachusetts Bay brought word that the ship assigned to transport the Great Sachem and his party to England now awaited them in Boston. The courier also brought Betsy a letter from her parents, telling her they would meet her in Boston with the new wardrobe that had been made for her and the children.

Renno assigned a party of fifty warriors to escort his parents, his wife, and his children to Fort Springfield. Betsy was dry-eyed throughout the last night she and Renno would spend together for many months and was equally composed the following morning, when hundreds of Seneca marched with the party across the frozen cornfields to the edge of the forest that lay to the east.

There, in a brief ceremony, the war chiefs repeated their pledge of loyalty to Renno, promising to obey him in all things. The customs of the people were observed to the letter as Renno and Ghonka exchanged salutes. Then Renno raised a hand in farewell to Betsy and to Ena, each of whom inclined her head stiffly. The suggestion of a smile touched the corners of his lips when he returned the solemn salute of Ja-gonh, and he unbent only long enough to kiss Goo-ga-ro-no, swathed in furs, who was strapped to her mother's back. A few moments later the departing travelers and their escorts vanished into the deep woods.

A Seneca wasted no time or energy on matters of the heart, and as Renno returned to the town, surrounded by his war chiefs, he spoke crisply. "Let the word be sent to the sachems of the Iroquois. Let each of them send to me the numbers of senior warriors and junior warriors who are available for a campaign against the enemy. Also, let them say the number who will carry firesticks and the number armed only with bows and arrows."

"It will be done as the sachem directs," Sun-ai-yee told him. "I have already obtained the numbers from all the towns of the Seneca."

Renno's grunt indicated his satisfaction. "We will study them together in the house of Renno. I will write to General Wilson and to General Ridley. You and I will be ready when they ask us to join them in a council of war."

"There is much we must learn before that meeting, Renno."

"You speak words of truth, Sun-ai-yee. We will send a messenger to the cousins of the Tuscarora who live in the land that the English colonists call South Carolina. They will tell us which of the Indian nations that lie to the south will join the forces of Spain."

"It is even more important to know whether the nations of the north will join forces again with the French."

"I have given much thought to that problem, and I will take care of it in my own way," Renno promised.

They spent the entire morning analyzing the strengths of the Seneca and determining how many might be spared for a campaign far from home, as well as how many would be needed to defend their own land from the hated Huron, the Ottawa, and the ever-treacherous Erie. The other war chiefs were called in to contribute their own thoughts, and it was early afternoon before Renno crossed the town to the house of his parents.

There Ba-lin-ta, now in charge of domestic arrangements, had been keeping hot the remains of the previous night's stew, and El-i-chi and Walter had curbed their own hunger and waited patiently for him. If Ba-lin-ta had expected a less formal atmosphere during the absence of Ghonka, she quickly learned better.

Renno's manner was as severe and formal as that of his father. The meal was eaten in silence, and only when he went through the ritual of lighting a pipe was conversation permitted.

"Tonight," his sister said, "we will eat buffalo steak that has been softened in the juice of grapes seasoned with herbs." She smiled at Walter, knowing the dish was one of his favorites.

"Use only a portion of the steak," Renno told her, "because only you and I will be here to eat it."

El-i-chi and Walter, who had learned to lip-read, exchanged quick, surreptitious glances but waited for Renno to explain.

His manner became more relaxed. "I have wondered what assignment I would want if I were in your places," he told them. "Now I have decided. You will leave this very day for Quebec, the capital of New France. There you will learn all you can about the preparations for war the enemy is making. Concentrate most of your attention on the Huron, the Ottawa, and the Algonquian. Do not neglect the French themselves, of course. But I am certain General Wilson has his own means of obtaining information about them. Your principal concern must be the plans of their Indian allies."

Walter was openly delighted, and El-i-chi said, "We are honored that you give us such great responsibility."

Ba-lin-ta, in spite of her lifelong training, was not one to conceal her feelings. "Will they be in great danger?" she demanded.

"All warriors take risks," Renno replied stoically.

The woman turned to Walter, but he silenced her with a quiet glare. Obviously Renno had taken his disability into account, and he didn't want Ba-lin-ta to persuade Renno to give the task to someone else.

"You must disguise yourselves," Renno said. Unlike the Huron, whose spy scout Renno had killed, the

Seneca took meticulous precautions during spying missions.

"How will we do that, Renno?" the always practical El-i-chi asked.

The young sachem shrugged. "I leave such matters to you."

"Then," his brother replied, "we will wear the war paint of the Huron, but will not disguise ourselves in any other way."

"That is a good choice," Walter said. "The language of the Seneca and that of the Huron are the same. Their ways are our ways." Since Walter's hair and eyes were dark, and his tan as deep as Renno's, he would have no difficulty in passing himself off as a native Indian.

Ba-lin-ta was still upset. "What will happen if you are caught by the enemy, Wal-ter?" she demanded.

He hoped his shrug indicated disdain.

"When the Huron capture an enemy spy," Renno told her, "they test him in the trial by fire."

"They kill him then!" she exclaimed.

She was being deliberately difficult, and her brother sighed. It was only natural that she should be concerned for Walter, but she was going too far. But then the reason for her attitude became plain.

"If I had known before the departure of the Great Sachem that Wal-ter would be in grave personal danger," Ba-lin-ta said, "I would have asked his permission for us to be married without delay. Now, instead, I must appeal to the new sachem."

She was clever, Renno thought, but not quite clever enough. "There is no time for a marriage now," he said. "Wal-ter and El-i-chi will leave as soon as they can obtain jerked meat and parched corn from the warehouse, put their weapons in order, and coat their bodies with grease to ward off the cold."

Walter wished Ba-lin-ta would stop pushing, but he well knew she could be as aggressive as her brothers when she chose, that nothing he might say or do would influence her.

"Renno," she demanded, "will you approve our marriage when Wal-ter returns?"

"I cannot think of family matters when I am organizing the Iroquois for the biggest war we have ever fought." Renno sympathized with her, as he did with Walter, and he wasn't so far removed from his courtship of Betsy to have forgotten the feelings of those who wanted to marry. But he could not allow anyone, including his own sister, to take advantage of his new position.

Walter caught her eye and spoke slowly, taking care to make himself understood. "Wal-ter will wait," he said flatly. "Ba-lin-ta will wait. When the sachem believes the time is right, they will marry."

To the surprise of all three men, Ba-lin-ta bowed her head in submission. At last she was subjecting herself to the self-discipline she had been taught all of her life.

She was unable to restrain herself completely, however, and had to participate in preparations for the departure of Walter and El-i-chi. She gave them a pot of grease to smear on their bodies, and while they cleaned and loaded their pistols, sharpened their tomahawks, and selected arrows for their quivers, she went to the storehouse for the emergency rations of meat and grain they would carry on their trek through the wilderness. She also obtained a quantity of war paint in the Huron colors.

When the pair was ready to leave, they went to Renno at his house for final instructions.

"Use every means at your disposal to find out whether the Huron and Ottawa will go to war against us. Learn how many warriors they will send into the field. Find out if the Algonquian will break their vow of neutrality. Count the number of French ships at anchor in the harbor. You will not find it easy to count the number of French soldiers. Find out what you can about them, but, as I said before, that is not your main concern." The young sachem paused, then spoke with great deliberation. "He who acts as the eyes of the Seneca is of no use to his people if his sight is taken from him. Act with caution. Take no scalps unless you must. Show the greatest courage by keeping your knife in its sheath. And do not linger in the wilderness. When you have learned what you need to know, return with the speed of the hawk in flight. The war will start when the snows vanish."

It did not occur to Renno, either then or after they left, that he was also displaying courage. He was sending two young men dear to him into grave danger, and if they failed to return, he would live with his sorrow for the rest of his days.

Chapter II

Quebec, the capital of New France, was a city unique in North America. The men who ruled a vast realm in the name of King Louis XIV were far from home, but they nevertheless demanded the comforts to which their noble birth entitled them. So the great Citadel, that sat high on a bluff above the lower city, overlooking the warships and merchantmen that rode at anchor in the chilly harbor, was commanded by men who had brought their civilization with them. They carried their silver and chinaware, crystal and wines to America, along with their mistresses, their chefs, and their tailors.

Certainly no one lived in more regal splendor than the new lieutenant general commanding the armies of New France, Michel, Marquis de Rochement. Exquisite lace trimmed the collar and cuffs of his gold-trimmed uniform, the cushions of his thronelike chair were covered in the purest of silk, and all his furniture had been imported from one of his family's many manor houses. Scorning a wig, he nevertheless took care to dye his hair so the gray at his temples did not show. He also took care to import the finest cognac, which he enjoyed sipping with the young woman, gorgeously gowned, who had recently followed him from the court at Versailles. But his love of luxury did not make him weak. Some of his predecessors had been fops or fools, but the Marquis de Rochement was neither. A competent soldier and an able administrator, he had been given his difficult post because he had earned it.

A huge log fire burned in the hearth of the spacious sitting room, and when the wind died away, there was no sound in the chamber but the ticking of the handsome enameled clock that stood on the mantel. General de Rochement was relaxing for an hour or two before dinner by playing chess with his mistress, and as he demanded that his women have brains as well as beauty, he was giving his complete attention to the silver chessmen that gleamed in the firelight.

An aide tapped discreetly on the door, then opened it and stood apologetically in the entrance. "Forgive the interruption, General," he said, "but Alain de Gramont has arrived and awaits an audience with you."

The marquis continued to study the chessboard. "Who is here?"

"Colonel de Gramont, sir. The officer who went into—into retirement after the disasters of the last campaign against the English colonies. The officer who commanded the Huron tribe and has lived with them for so long that he is more Indian than they are." Clearing his throat nervously, the aide added, "You sent for him, sir."

At last the marquis remembered. "Oh, yes." He reached out to pat the pale, delicate hand of the young woman who sat opposite him. "The next move is mine, but I'm afraid it will need to be postponed. I'll send for you when the interview is finished."

The woman smiled, flashing her beautiful eyes at him, and obediently withdrew through a door that led to the marquis's private apartments.

De Rochement sighed inaudibly. "You may show in the colonel," he said, his expression hardening.

Alain de Gramont walked with his customary swagger, although the white and gold uniform he had elected to wear for the occasion was tarnished and shabby. His boots were cracked, the helmet he carried under one arm had lost its luster, and the wig he wore to hide his Huron-style scalp lock was almost absurdly old-fashioned. But he was still lean and lithe, though in his middle years, and his deep-set eyes had lost none of their intensity. He stood stiffly at attention, his salute precise and sharp. "Your servant, General," he said.

The marquis waved him to a chair and wasted no time on trivialities. "I've been hearing about you ever since I arrived in Quebec. At every planning conference I've held to consider our coming campaign against the English colonies, one person or another has mentioned your name."

"That's flattering, sir."

"It shouldn't be," de Rochement replied rudely. "Your talents are regarded as unique, but you have your critics—those who say you were outsmarted by the Massachusetts Bay militia and particularly by the Seneca. There are those who hold you responsible for the loss of Fortress Louisburg, which was supposedly impregnable."

Alain de Gramont had lost none of his self-confidence. "It wasn't impregnable, General," he said, "and incompetents have used me as a scapegoat."

"Then you deny the charges against you?"

"Most of them have no foundation, sir." Gramont sat back in his chair. "I freely admit, however, that the Seneca tricked me once again and defeated my Huron in the climactic battle."

The marquis studied him. "Frankly, I'm curious about you. How does it happen that a French aristocrat has voluntarily spent the better part of his adult life living with a tribe of primitive savages?"

"Many years ago, General, when I came to New France as a young officer and was given command of a wilderness outpost, my wife and child were murdered by the Seneca in a senseless raid. I've used every means at my disposal since that time to obtain vengeance against them. I'd give my soul to trample on the white Indian, Renno, who was responsible for my defeat at Louisburg." His eyes burned in his lean, stonelike face.

"Obviously you've been thinking about our coming campaign," de Rochement said.

"There's been little else on my mind, General." He did not mention that he had already sent a Huron scout to spy on the Seneca and that the scout had failed to return.

"Will the Huron march with my troops?"

"That depends on the progress of the war," Gramont replied without hesitation. "The warriors became disillusioned when the best regiments from France couldn't stand up to the English colonial militiamen. The Huron will need to see proof that you can succeed before they'll join you."

"And the Ottawa, as I understand it, will make no move without the Huron."

"That's correct, sir." Although Alain de Gramont had been disgraced, he knew the French needed him desperately, so there was good reason for his self-confidence.

The marquis was not one to hesitate. "If I gave you a post of authority and restored your commission, precisely what steps would you take?"

Gramont concealed his elation. "We're playing a subtle game for high stakes, General. Without the assistance of the Iroquois, the English colonies can be defeated handily. And the Seneca are the key to the alliance. As long as they remain the allies of Massachusetts Bay, Virginia, and New York, the other Iroquois will stand beside them. If they defect, the entire alliance will fall apart."

"Granted." De Rochement drummed impatiently on the arm of his carved oak chair.

"I have devised a weapon, sir, that will penetrate to the heart of the Seneca and destroy them."

The general looked dubious.

"Their weakness is the young warrior I mentioned a few moments ago—Renno. He's the adopted son of their chief, and—until now—he's been accepted as a Seneca in spite of his blue eyes and blond hair. If the Seneca can be persuaded to turn against him, they'll become so confused they'll give up their treaty with the English colonies."

De Rochement's air of impatience vanished as he listened intently.

"With your permission, sir, I would send the Singer to the land of the Seneca to sow doubt and dissension."

The marquis exploded. "A singer? You dare to mock me—"

"I'm sorry, General," Alain de Gramont interrupted, "but you don't understand Indians. I do. The Singer is a storyteller of great and extraordinary talents. The Seneca would welcome him warily, but it wouldn't be long before they'd be listening to him—and believing every word he tells them."

"Do you seriously believe this—this storyteller could cause the Iroquois alliance with the English colonies to come apart?"

"More than that, General," Gramont said earnestly. "Once the Seneca drop out of the alliance, I can promise you that the Huron and Ottawa will join forces with us, immediately and without hesitation."

The marquis weighed the offer. "I suppose there's nothing to be lost. Do I gather you would travel with this man and direct his activities?"

Gramont smiled. "I'd lose my scalp if I set foot in the land of the Seneca. I have other plans for myself. As I see the overall strategic situation, General, the southern flank is the soft underbelly of the English colonies. They will keep part of their armed forces in reserve for fear you will launch an attack through New England or New York. But it seems to me they can be defeated—decisively—by an attack of French and Spanish forces striking from the southern sector."

De Rochement came to life. "That view coincides with my own thinking!" he exclaimed.

"I haven't finished, sir." Gramont knew he was on sure ground now. "A French and Spanish expeditionary force cannot win a campaign alone. You'll need an alliance with some of the strong Indian tribes of the area—the Creek, the Choctaw, some of the smaller nations like the Pensacola and the Natchez."

"That's sound thinking. You make a great deal of sense, Gramont."

"Do you have anyone on your staff capable of negotiating with those tribes, General?"

The marquis was taken aback. "I can't think of anyone offhand," he replied.

"I offer my services. Every Indian nation in the south will accept me as one of their own because of my knowledge of their languages and customs. Give me enough ammunition. Blankets, trinkets, and cash. Gifts of muskets and pistols, bullets and gunpowder. They'll flock to our cause. While the Singer corrodes the Seneca alliance with the English colonies, I'll be making treaties with new allies who will march into battle with us."

De Rochement, deep in thought, made no response.

"If you wish, sir," Gramont said, becoming deferential, "I'll return for your answer at your convenience."

The marquis waved aside the suggestion. "I find that your double-barreled scheme appeals to me because it is both daring and unorthodox. King Louis and the

War Ministry in Paris except me to perform miracles with inadequate forces. You offer me a hope of victory."

Alain de Gramont tried in vain to look modest.

"Your commission as a colonel will be restored to you without delay, and your pay will begin as of tomorrow morning. Succeed in what you've outlined to me, Gramont, and I guarantee you a brilliant future. His Majesty will be delighted to receive you in a public audience at Versailles, and you don't need me to tell you how generous he can be when he's pleased." Suddenly de Rochement scowled. "If you fail, however, may the Lord have mercy on your soul. Not even your Huron warriors will be able to protect you from King Louis's vengeance—and mine."

It was quiet, almost too quiet, at the Ridley estate outside the growing town of Norfolk in Virginia. Brigadier General Austin Ridley and his wife, Mary, had sailed to Boston in one of the Ridley brigs to see Betsy off to England. They had been accompanied by their son and daughter-in-law, Ned and Consuelo, who planned to pay a visit to Renno in the land of the Seneca before returning home. Ned, now a lieutenant colonel in the Virginia militia, was eager to discuss the coming military campaign against the French and Spaniards. And Consuelo, who had shared so many hardships in the West Indies with her husband and Renno, was cheerfully making the journey through the deep snow of the wilderness because she, too, was eager to see Renno again.

The only Ridley still at home was Betsy's younger sister, Anne, now in her teens. "Beauty runs in the family," Ned had observed, and he was right. Anne was a striking blonde with green eyes, her figure was supple and slender, and she was as buoyant as she had been as a child.

She sat now on the front porch in the watery winter sunlight, enjoying unexpectedly mild weather as she filed and shaped her fingernails. There was no sign of buoyancy in her at the moment, and she looked bored.

Her companion, similarly engaged with a nail file, was an equally pretty redhead of about her own age. Hester MacDevitt was, technically speaking, an indentured servant of the Ridleys, a girl who had come to the colonies a few years earlier and still had two years to serve before she would be free. For all practical purposes, however, she was already a member of the family. She and Anne had become intimate friends, sharing their most secret thoughts with each other, and Austin and Mary had long made a point of treating Hester as a relative rather than as a member of the large household staff.

"Last night was dreadful," Anne said.

"Horrid," Hester agreed. "You'd think that two young men who have traveled to half a dozen European ports and all through the West Indies as mates on Ridley ships would have some sophistication. Or at the very least would be lively."

"They were dead sticks," Anne said. "I simply couldn't help yawning in their faces."

"Well, at least they left early, which was the best part of the entire evening," Hester said, then giggled.

Anne examined her fingernails critically. "I wish papa and mama had taken us to Boston with them. That Harvard College graduate who visited Ned last year was quite dashing."

"Oh, I can understand why they couldn't take us," Hester declared. "General Wilson and your father are going on to a meeting of militia commanders in New York Town, and they'll be terribly busy."

"Well," Anne said, sniffing, "Ned and Consuelo could have taken us with them to the land of the Seneca."

"Have you ever gone there?"

"Once. About a year before you came to live with us, Hester. I was still a child, of course, but I remember it vividly. The young warriors put on an exhibition of tomahawk throwing and shooting arrows for me. It was exciting."

"Between us," Hester said, a trace of a Scottish burr still evident in her accent, "I thought Ned was rather rude."

"It was his idea of humor," her friend replied, "to say the warriors of the Seneca could tolerate an invasion by the Erie better than they could stand a visit by you and me. He thinks he's being amusing when he says we're too pretty for our own good."

"All I need to do is look in the nearest pier glass to know I'm pretty," Hester said, sighing as she placed her nail file in an apron pocket. "But what good does it do me? The only eligible men who come to Norfolk are sailors." There was scorn in her voice.

"Did you ever know any interesting boys in Glasgow before your parents lost their money and died?"

"I was a bit young for boys, so I don't remember any too clearly. All I know is that there's a dearth of men here."

"Consuelo tells me constantly that we must learn to be patient, that sooner or later all sorts of fascinating men will come into our lives."

"It's easy enough for Consuelo to talk," Hester said. "She has a husband."

Anne was silent for a time. "How I envy Betsy in London! What a marvelous time you and I would have there!" She smoothed back her long blond hair. "But what's the sense of complaining?"

"You're right. We do keep busy most of the time. And I'm grateful I have a home with your family. Some people could make life miserable for an indentured girl."

Anne sympathized with her. "I know how you feel. I just wish we could find something really useful to do. It isn't just the lack of interesting men that makes Norfolk so dull. What bothers me is that there are so few challenges here. Aside from chores there's so little to *do*."

The English mansion that stood between the Strand and the River Thames was known as the Albemarle Rooms. More like a gentlemen's private club than a gaming establishment, it was frequented by expensively dressed bluebloods who ate from carved joints of smoking beef, drank pints of ale, and gossiped about the latest open quarrel at court between the hot-tempered Queen Anne and her volatile consort, Prince George of Denmark. Officers on leave from General Churchill's army could not put the war out of their minds, and after a few rounds of cards, they clustered in some of the private rooms to discuss the latest developments in Churchill's drive to link forces with the regiments of Prince Eugene, which were marching from Austria to meet him.

Dice rattled incessantly in some rooms, and those who sought greater quiet took refuge in the chambers where card games were in progress. It was no accident that a large crowd had assembled in a room where young Kenneth Robinson, Lord Symes, was engaged in a game of high-low and a grim-faced stranger, whose silk breeches and tailcoat, gold-buckled shoes and satin waistcoat indicated that he was a man of considerable wealth.

Most of those gathered in the room sympathized with Lord Symes, still handsome in spite of the deep smudges beneath his eyes caused by dissipation. Some had been friends of his late father, one of England's largest landowners, while the younger crowd, who called him Ken, knew him as a fine horseman, superb marksman, and accomplished swordsman. Still in his twenties, he could have been holding a commission in one of Churchill's regiments. Instead, he sat in the Albemarle Rooms, an unlighted West Indian *segaro* clenched in his teeth and an untouched glass of claret beside him as he tried desperately to recoup at least some portion of the fortune that he had lost at the gaming tables in recent years.

"It's as well that Bert Robinson isn't here to see

what the boy has done to his fortune," an elderly earl muttered.

"Damned shame," a viscount replied. "He's frittered away a king's ransom."

The dealer, coatless, his shirt-sleeves rolled above his elbows, sat on a high stool between the two players, every few minutes repeating his litany of, "High or low, gentlemen. Low or high. Place your bids!"

"I've known many men who have had a lust for gaming," the earl said, "but none were afflicted with the disease as badly as young Robinson. Nothing else on earth matters to him."

Except for one estate, which the late Lord Symes had left to his yet unborn grandchildren, Kenneth had gambled away his entire inheritance. He was in debt to his landlord and his tailor, his physician and the innkeeper at whose establishment he ate most of his meals. Yet despite these circumstances, Kenneth could have denied the earl's accusation. The truth was that he had come to hate gaming with his whole heart, and he loathed himself.

But there was no escape. Tonight was his last chance to win enough money to pay off his creditors. Otherwise, even though he was a viscount, he stood in grave danger of being sent to debtors' prison. With no means at his disposal, no way to earn money, he would stay there until he rotted.

"High or low, gentlemen. Low or high. Place your bids!" the dealer said.

Kenneth Robinson braced himself, then fingered his dwindling pile of cast-iron chips. "I bid high," he said, speaking distinctly, "and I wager one hundred sovereigns."

His opponent smiled. "I accept the challenge," he declared, his round face inscrutable.

The conversation in the chamber halted, and several more gentlemen inched their way inside the door.

Kenneth reached out, his hand steady, and took a card from the deck the dealer held out to him. He drew the jack of spades, which he held high, as protocol required, before dropping it onto the table, face up.

His opponent hesitated for a moment, and there were several in the crowd, the old earl among them, who suspected that he was reaching inside the lace cuff of his shirt. Then the man drew, and there was a gasp as he showed the king of hearts.

Kenneth blanched, threw aside his *segaro,* and for the first time took a sip of claret. His chances of winning had grown smaller, but he managed to control the sense of panic that welled up within him, threatening to overwhelm him.

"High or low, gentlemen. Low or high. Place your bids!"

The stranger's smile was bloodless. "I bid low," he said, "and I wager five hundred guineas."

The onlookers were stunned. There were many present who lived comfortably for a full year on an income of no more than five hundred guineas.

Kenneth counted his remaining cast-iron chips and was slightly surprised to discover that they were worth precisely five hundred guineas. Apparently his opponent had counted them and wanted to finish him off with a single blow. Hating himself, despising gaming, Kenneth nevertheless knew he had to take this final risk. "I accept the challenge," he said, relieved that there was no tremor in his voice.

The stranger had the privilege of drawing first but, with a slight but courtly bow, deferred to his foe.

The old earl wondered if there was more to the gesture than met the eye. If young Lord Symes drew first, the other would have the chance to beat him—if he was truly cheating.

The dealer, impassive as always, extended a new deck of cards. Kenneth hesitated for a second, then drew the eight of diamonds. The card was neither low nor high, so he had at least a chance of winning.

The stranger waited for an instant, and again the old

earl wondered if his fingers crept too close to his drooping lace cuffs. Then he drew swiftly and held up the deuce of clubs, the lowest card in the deck. There was an excited babble as everyone in the room seemed to be speaking simultaneously.

Kenneth counted out the last of his chips, pushed them in the direction of the dealer, and rose. The conversation in the room died away as everyone watched him. He drank his glass of claret and bowed to his victorious opponent. Then he turned and made his way out of the chamber, his eyes unseeing.

He walked down the stairs, and a lackey in the vestibule handed him his hat, cloak, and walking stick. Kenneth found a shilling in his pocket, and although tuppence would have been a generous tip, he handed the silver coin to the man. Now he was totally penniless.

He wandered out into the cold night, then walked aimlessly, his steps taking him closer and closer to the river. Suddenly a pair of footpads loomed up ahead of him, both carrying heavy clubs. Reacting instinctively, Kenneth drew a sword from his walking stick. "Don't take the trouble of trying to rob me, lads," he said. "I don't have a ha'penny to my name."

His gleaming sword rather than his words gave the pair cause for reflection, and they silently vanished into the shadows.

Continuing to walk, Kenneth paid no attention when an attractive young harlot called to him softly from a doorway. He was sensitive to beauty and had spent large sums on women in the past, but now he couldn't afford the services of a common whore.

At last he came to the bank of the Thames, and for a long time he stood there, unmoving, wondering whether to end his miseries by throwing himself into the water. No, suicide was a coward's way, and he had already heaped enough disgrace on an ancient and honorable name.

Leaving the river, he walked to his lodgings in the

shadows of Whitehall, the royal palace. His small parlor was chilly, so he lighted a fire in the hearth. Feeling wide-awake in spite of the late hour, Kenneth sat and looked into the flames. By noon the news of his complete collapse would be common knowledge, and then his creditors would descend on him. He would be unable to give them any satisfaction, so they would go in a group to a magistrate and obtain a warrant for his arrest. Within seventy-two hours, at the most, the bailiffs would come for him, and he would be sentenced to a term in debtors' prison that would last "until such time as full restitution is made," which in effect would be for the rest of his life. Very well, then. He would die of starvation in a stinking hell of human misery.

Before that inevitable fate overtook him, however, he could perform one deed that would exonerate him faintly in his own eyes. He would write a letter to Queen Anne, giving up the title of Viscount Symes. He would meet his end as plain Kenneth Robinson. That knowledge gave him a feeling of very slight satisfaction.

A tap sounded at his door, and Kenneth was startled. Day was just breaking, but his creditors were already hounding him. He went to the door and, to his astonishment, saw the round-faced, husky, middleaged man who had been his opponent at the gaming table.

"I trust I don't intrude, milord," the man said.

There was no one on earth whom Kenneth less wanted to see, but his breeding enabled him to say, "Not at all," and usher the visitor into the parlor.

"Would it be convenient for us to have a little talk, milord?"

"If you wish," Kenneth said wearily, wondering why the man who had won his last penny would bother to come here for the purpose of gloating.

Bowing from the waist, the stranger said, "You may call me Mr. Hawkins." He removed his hat and cloak, meticulously folding the cloak before placing both on a table. Moving to the fire, he asked, "Do I have permission to sit?"

"Of course."

Mr. Hawkins took the chair nearest the fire. "You had a run of bad luck tonight," he said.

"Extraordinarily bad luck." Never had Kenneth known worse, and the sly smile he saw in his visitor's eyes made him wonder if the man had cheated him.

"For your sake, milord, I regret that your finances have become so strained. It's my understanding that your total debts are in excess of twenty-nine hundred guineas."

Kenneth was startled. "You're well informed about my affairs, sir."

"My colleagues and I have made it our business to learn all there is to know about you, milord. It may be that your situation isn't as bad as it may seem to you."

"Oh?" The thought flickered through Kenneth's mind that the man spoke strangely careful, precise English.

"My colleagues are in a position to offer you sufficient assistance to take care of your problems, milord. They will give you the sum of three thousand guineas to pay off your debts. They will provide you with transportation to the New World—to New England, specifically—so you will have the opportunity to begin life anew there. And they are prepared to offer you wages of one hundred guineas per month—a most liberal sum, you must admit—if you will represent them in the colonies."

"I find the generosity of your colleagues overwhelming," Kenneth said. "Who are they, sir? And what services could I perform that would be worth a ha'penny—to anyone?"

"Allow me to proceed one step at a time, milord. You've acquired a reputation in London as something of a wastrel, if you'll forgive the observation. But vast expanses of saltwater cleanse reputations. As Viscount

Symes you would be accepted in the highest circles in the colonies. You'd be welcomed eagerly there."

For whatever the man's reason, Kenneth felt certain, he and his "colleagues" had been responsible for draining him of his remaining funds and placing him at their mercy. "Why am I worth a fortune to you and your associates, Mr. Hawkins?" he demanded sharply.

The man's smile was thin. "You yourself are worth nothing to us, milord. But your title is valuable, and your background is impressive. You may have heard that England is now at war with France—"

"I don't appreciate your humor, sir. Would to God I had accepted a commission when General Churchill offered it to me."

The visitor remained unruffled. "Few people on this side of the Atlantic appreciate the value of England's North American colonies. My colleagues are deeply interested in them—and their military preparations. We want to know how many militia regiments and battalions are being raised, especially in Massachusetts Bay, New York, and Virginia. We want to know the quantity and quality of their arms. We want to know how many merchant ships are being converted into privateers, and what cannon they carry. We want to know the state of the alliance between the English colonies and a group of powerful Indian tribes known as the Iroquois League. In brief, we want any and all information pertinent to their war proceedings."

Color drained from Kenneth's face as a deep feeling of anger shook him. "You're asking me to become a French spy!"

"Those are your words, milord, not mine." Smiling blandly, Mr. Hawkins held his hands in front of him, his fingertips touching. "My colleagues prefer to use no labels. I will give you a name and address here in London, and you'll be expected to write regular, detailed letters of all that you learn. You need know no more than that."

46

Kenneth wondered whether to run the scoundrel through or choke him to death.

"If you kill me," the stranger said calmly, "you'll suffer far worse than a debtors' prison. Some of my colleagues are waiting for me, and if I fail to appear at a certain place at an appointed time—which is approaching rapidly—you shall be apprehended by constables and charged with the cold-blooded murder of one who was fortunate enough to win from you at the gaming table. In short, milord, you'll be hanged for your pains."

Kenneth's tormentors had thought of every angle, and he realized he was trapped.

Mr. Hawkins drew a watch from his waistcoat pocket and glanced at it. "I must hurry, or the constables soon will be pounding at your door. Accept my offer, and within an hour you'll receive three thousand guineas to pay off your debts, as well as pay, in advance, for six months and your passage on a ship that sails tomorrow for Boston. You'll also receive a slip of paper containing the name and address of the person to whom you'll write here in London. Memorize that name and address, then destroy the slip of paper. Refuse the offer, and you'll be on your way to prison before the day is out. Some of my colleagues have taken the trouble of insuring that they are among your major creditors, and they shall present themselves to the magistrates the very moment the law courts open their doors. Surely you need no time to consider this matter, milord." He stood abruptly.

Kenneth rose, too, barely able to curb the impulse to smash the round face in front of him.

"If I am harmed even slightly," Mr. Hawkins said, "we shall show you no mercy. Accept my proposal, milord, and be thankful that you have friends who are so concerned for your welfare."

Kenneth knew he had no real choice. Although his title went back to the time of William the Conqueror and among his ancestors had been any number of rogues and scoundrels, he reflected that they had been patriots. He would be the first Lord Symes ever to betray his country. Hating himself for his weakness, he muttered, "Damn your soul, sir, I accept."

The mansion on Milk Street used by the government of Massachusetts Bay to house distinguished visitors was filled to capacity. Generals Wilson and Ridley conferred at length with Ghonka on the mission taking him to London and on the war strategy that would be employed in the New World. Participating in the meetings with the leaders were Colonel Jeffrey Wilson, who had succeeded his father as commander of the western Massachusetts Bay militia regiment, and Lieutenant Colonel Ned Ridley, the head of a newly formed battalion of Virginia sharpshooters, generally acknowledged as the most effective military unit in the English colonies.

Betsy had ample time to renew her friendship with Jeffrey's wife, the lovely red-haired Adrienne. The generals' wives, joined by Ena, had happily gone shopping to buy presents for their grandchildren. Betsy and Adrienne were content to sit in one of the mansion's parlors, drinking tea and talking. Goo-ga-ro-no and Ja-gonh, known as Marion and James in the colonies, were happily playing with Adrienne's children, and Betsy, now attired in one of her new silk gowns, discussed her London wardrobe in detail with the friend who had spent considerable time as a French Huguenot refugee in England and had been helped there by Renno and the man who had become her husband.

One afternoon they were joined by Consuelo Ridley, who had been busy buying bolts of wool and linen for her maternity wardrobe, and Adrienne greeted her warmly. "I'm so glad you're here," she said. "There's something I've been wanting to discuss with Betsy, and since you know European ways as well as I do, I'm sure you'll give me your moral support."

"This sounds quite mysterious," Betsy said, smiling at Adrienne, then at her sister-in-law.

"Not at all, but it is rather delicate." Adrienne hesitated for a moment, then took the plunge. "London is unlike any place you've ever seen."

"I don't doubt it for a moment," Betsy replied, laughing.

"I'm not talking about the size of the city. Or its theaters and taverns or shops. What I have in mind is the atmosphere, the moral atmosphere."

"I begin to see what you mean," Consuelo said.

"Well, I certainly don't," Betsy declared.

"You're still in your twenties," Adrienne told her, "and you're even more beautiful than you were before you had James and Marion. I'm sure you don't even think in such terms when you're in the land of the Seneca, but look at you right now. You're positively ravishing in that silk gown. I can guarantee you that you'll have every man in London at your feet."

"Unfortunately," Consuelo added, nodding sagely.

Betsy was bewildered. "I'm afraid I don't understand."

"You'll be a challenge to every nobleman, every officer in the Royal Navy and Army, every member of the gentry who meets or sees you. I promise you that you'll be overwhelmed with invitations to supper, the theater, and other entertainments. You'll be invited to dinners at town houses and country estates. You'll be besieged with requests to show you London and the countryside."

"That sounds rather pleasant." Betsy was still confused.

Adrienne sighed and turned to Consuelo. "You're her sister-in-law. I wish you'd tell her."

"I shall. Betsy, many of the men you meet will try to seduce you."

"But that's absurd!" Betsy cried. "I'm a married woman!"

The other women laughed helplessly. "Oh, dear," Adrienne said. "She's even more naive than I feared."

Consuelo spoke earnestly to her sister-in-law. "In Madrid, in Barcelona, and in Seville, young married women are continually propositioned."

"Just as they are in Paris and in London," Adrienne said. "Most single girls of quality are still virgins, so only the cads challenge them. But every married woman is regarded as a fair target. The moral standards of Europe and the New World are different. Here a married woman is respected, at least by most men. There she is considered the perfect partner for an assignation, and so many are compliant that the men have become spoiled. They're actually surprised and hurt when they encounter a lady whose virtue is unassailable."

"I find that hard to believe," the shocked Betsy said. "After all, I'm the mother of two children—"

"As if that mattered," Consuelo interrupted. "You're lovely, so they'll want you. And there are many who will go to any lengths to get you."

"Then they'll fail," Betsy said primly.

"Don't underestimate them, dear," Adrienne told her. "They can be very clever and very subtle. They plan a campaign carefully. And—above all—they see nothing wrong in the game they're playing. They regard it as a sport, and a conquest becomes a great victory."

Betsy shook her head. "Renno," she said, "would take the scalp of any man who dared to make approaches to me."

"Indeed he would," Consuelo agreed, "but Renno will be more than three thousand miles away. Ghonka and Ena won't grasp the significance of what will be happening. You'll have to rely only on yourself."

Betsy couldn't help taking offense. "I love Renno, and I have no interest in any other man!"

"We know how you feel," Adrienne said. "And

we're not questioning either your loyalty to him or your virtue. All we're trying to tell you is that you'll be subjected to influences and pressures unlike any that you've ever encountered."

"You spent the better part of your life in Norfolk, where life is simple. In the land of the Seneca it is even less complicated. Boston is the largest town you've ever seen." Consuelo was empathic. "So beware!"

"We don't doubt that you'll be able to handle the crass sort of man who openly makes advances to you," Adrienne said. "They can be rejected easily and quickly. You'll need to be on guard against those who pose as friends. Those with whom you form an honest and honorable platonic relationship."

"Just keep in mind," Consuelo added, "that most every man you meet, regardless of whether he is married or a bachelor, will have the aim of bedding you."

"But that's horrible," Betsy said. "Both of you make the Old World sound like a jungle."

"It *is* a jungle," Adrienne said solemnly. "It is far worse than any wilderness you'll find here. The beasts of the European jungles wear many disguises."

"We're not suggesting that you become a hermit in London," Consuelo said, "or that you hide behind your children and Ghonka and Ena. Enjoy yourself in a dazzling civilization. Go to the theater. Attend lectures and concerts. Have a good time at dinner parties, which can be stimulating and pleasant. But be wary. Always."

"All we're suggesting," Adrienne declared, "is that you use your common sense and don't allow your values to become warped."

Betsy was supremely self-confident. "Never fear," she said. "I won't lose my head. I can't imagine circumstances or situations that would cause me to forget what is important to me."

There were more arrows in Alain de Gramont's quiver than even the Marquis de Rochement knew.

Coaching the storyteller known to the Huron as the Singer and simultaneously acquiring information on the Indian nations he intended to bring into the French camp, he devised another scheme to ensure the downfall of Renno. For more than two years he had known of the presence in Quebec of a man whose talents he could use to good advantage, and now the time had come to exploit them.

Attired in his dazzling new white and gold uniform, Colonel de Gramont walked from the Citadel on the heights of Quebec to a modest cabin in the artisans' quarters of the lower town. Rarely had a visit given him a greater sense of pleasure.

The bearded man who came to the door of the cabin was a house painter in his mid-twenties. He blinked in surprise when he saw the resplendent figure who confronted him.

"Monsieur Vigniere?" Alain asked politely.

The man shifted uneasily in the presence of such high authority, and he nodded.

Without further ado Alain brusquely entered the dwelling, threw his cape and gloves onto a chair, stood in front of the fire burning in the hearth, and rubbed his hands together. Vigniere was even more apprehensive as he closed the door and waited for the visitor to address him.

"You are fortunate, Vigniere, that your French relative taught you to speak our language without a noticeable accent." Alain's tone was casual.

"What do you want of me, Colonel?" There was a note of hysteria in his voice.

The confrontation was developing precisely as Alain had anticipated, and he allowed himself the luxury of a stiff smile. "Your real name," he said, "is Eban Friendly. You are a native of England and a British subject. You were a sign maker by trade, but you became too ambitious for your own good, and you were convicted of forgery. You were sentenced to fourteen years as an indentured servant, and you were sent to Massachusetts Bay."

The man tried to interrupt, but Alain gave him no chance to speak. "Soon after your arrival in Boston, Mr. Friendly, you escaped. You made your way here, and you presented yourself as a Frenchman. You made only one mistake in the three years you have lived here. You told your story to a Huron half-breed woman who lived with you for a time."

"For God's sake, Colonel, don't send me back to indentured life in Boston!" Eban Friendly's voice was ragged.

"France and Britain are at war, my dear sir. We have no traffic with the enemy. But you are in danger of being arrested as an espionage agent for the English colonies, and the penalty for such activities in time of war is death. Only a hair's breadth separates your neck from the guillotine, Friendly."

"I am no espionage agent, Colonel!" The man was close to tears. "I'm a simple house painter. I can take you to people for whom I've worked. I've even painted some of the officers' quarters in the Citadel."

"To be sure. And there you may have had access to military secrets you could have sent along to your employers in Boston."

"Never, Colonel! I swear it! I—I know nothing about military matters—"

"Sit down!" Alain ordered sharply, cutting off the flow of words.

Friendly lowered himself to a bench near the fireplace.

"Do what you're told, keep your mouth shut, and never tell a soul, Friendly, and you won't be harmed in any way. Understand?" Alain de Gramont was in complete control of the situation by now.

The man could only nod dumbly.

Suddenly the officer's manner changed, and he became benign. "Follow my instructions to the letter, and you will be well paid for your efforts. There can be little work at this time of year for a man who paints houses, so you have ample time to concentrate on the task that I shall present to you. Do the work well, and you shall be paid a gold louis for your efforts."

"I'll do anything, Colonel!"

"You are an accomplished sign maker?"

"I—I was, sir, until trouble overtook me."

"Ah. Do you regard yourself as an expert forger?"

Friendly didn't quite know what to reply.

"We shall soon find out. I shall supply you with parchment, sealing wax, and an exact replica of the royal seal of the late King William the Third of Great Britain. The replica was made for me by a Huron wood-carver who didn't understand the significance of what he was making. I shall supply you also with the wording and design of a document that I want you to forge. You will create a masterpiece, Friendly. Do I make myself clear?"

"Y-yes, sir." The man was dazed.

"You will have forty-eight hours, no more, in which to do this work. You will be paid your gold louis promptly. Then, in my presence, you will burn the replica of the British royal seal to ashes in your hearth. Thereafter, you will banish the incident forever from your mind, never mentioning it to any living person. In return you will be able to maintain your masquerade as Vigniere, a French house painter who now makes his home in Quebec. The secret of your background will be safe, and you will not be molested or disturbed by anyone. If you fail to forge this document to my complete satisfaction, however, or if you ever breathe one word of this matter to anyone, you will go to the guillotine as an espionage agent for the English colonies."

"I'll do the job for you, Colonel. Whatever it is you want me to write, I swear to you it will be perfect. And then I—I'll forget the whole thing. I won't even know you the next time our paths cross."

"Make certain they don't cross again, and all will go well for you." Alain took a roll of parchment, a stick of sealing wax, and a carved wooden seal from a pocket of his cape, then removed several sheets of folded paper from a tunic pocket. "Here are the words you will copy, using black ink, and the design you will duplicate. You will save these papers until I return in two days. Then, all papers except the one I take away will be burned along with the seal."

"I'll do it perfectly, Colonel," Friendly babbled. "I swear it! You'll see."

Donning his cape and gloves, Alain left the cabin, certain that the man would exert every effort to do his will.

For the next forty-eight hours he waited impatiently, almost sorry he hadn't commanded the forger to perform his task in half the allotted time. Then he returned to Friendly's house and, as he had anticipated, found that the job had been completed.

As the man had promised, he had done superb work. The document he had prepared with the royal seal stamped in the bottom corner would not only fool the untutored Seneca, but would impress any English colonials who might see it. Only someone familiar with papers coming from Britain's royal court might realize that the supposed decree issued by King William III was actually false.

Alain paid the forger the gold louis he had offered him for his efforts, then watched as the wooden seal and the various papers burned in the hearth. "I won't trouble you again, Vigniere," he said. "Forget that you ever saw me or did this work for me, and you'll be safe here for the rest of your days."

Not until he returned to his new quarters at the Citadel and examined the document again in detail did Alain laugh aloud. What had been prepared for him was an imitation decree, supposedly issued by William at the request of the First Lord of the Treasury, the head of his Cabinet. It stated that the white Indian known as Renno, senior warrior of the Seneca—as he had been at the time of his visit to London—and adopted son of Ghonka, the Great Sachem, had been awarded a vast estate and manor house in Cornwall, formerly the personal property of the monarch. The gift had been made "because of services rendered by Renno wherein he put the interests of the Crown ahead of all others, including those of his own Indian nation."

That damning phrase had been inspired. Not only would it cause the Seneca to lose faith in Renno, but it would create doubts regarding his loyalty in the English colonial hierarchy. He would be thoroughly discredited, unable to function as a leader of the Iroquois.

First the Singer would sow doubts, and then, at the appropriate time, the false document would be produced. All that remained now, before Alain de Gramont went off on his own tour of the lands of the southern Indian nations, was to determine when and how the false document would make its appearance. This method of attack was better than assassinating Renno or killing him in battle. He would continue to live but would suffer disgrace for the rest of his days.

Chapter III

A Spanish galleon sailing from Cadiz to South America put into the port of Havana, the capital of New Spain, on the island of Cuba, and somewhat to the surprise of the imperial viceroy's court, two passengers who debarked were received without delay by the viceroy himself. Ordinarily appointments had to be made with him many weeks in advance.

Still stranger things took place. The middle-aged man and exceptionally attractive, dark-haired young woman were given a house a short distance from the viceroy's palace. Because of the disparity in their ages, it was assumed that the woman was the man's mistress. Thereafter, streams of visitors, many of them coming from the North American mainland, called at the house, and some were closeted there for hours at a time. Nothing concerning the nature of their business was known, and the viceroy's court was intrigued.

The mystery deepened when the viceroy sent two of his own spirited mares to the newcomers' stable. Thereafter, the young woman appeared every morning, wearing man's attire, and rode through Havana to Philip II park, a large expanse of green. There she spurred her mount to a wild gallop, and those who observed her remarked to their friends that she was a superb horsewoman. One day she appeared carrying a brace of pistols in her belt, and after affixing a target to a tree, she fired at it with both of her weapons. Discreet snoopers reported that she could shoot as well as she could ride and that she rarely missed her target.

One afternoon a tradesman making a delivery left the front gate of the house open, and two ladies driving in a carriage caught a glimpse of a pair dueling in the yard. They halted their coach and saw the woman, again in man's clothes, at practice with the gray-haired man. According to the story told by the ladies, which no one was in a position to confirm, the woman was an expert duelist, scoring point after point at the expense of her opponent, who was obviously no novice.

It was almost impossible to keep secrets in the closed society of a colonial outpost, and after several weeks it became known that the visitor was a grandee, Don Diego de Bernardo. To the astonishment of the court, the young woman proved to be his daughter, Beatriz, rather than his mistress. She dressed in feminine attire only when the pair paid a weekly call on the viceroy, who invariably received them in private behind closed doors.

Troop transports brought two new regiments of infantry to Havana in preparation for the campaign that would be fought against the English colonies, and as luck would have it, the wife of the colonel commanding one of the units knew a great deal about the de Bernardos. "Don Diego," she told a group of enthralled ladies, "may be the most sinister man in Spain. He has served the Crown as an intelligence operative for many, many years, and it has been said that he has traveled all over the world. One thing is certain. He always appears in places where trouble is expected."

"Now that the young French duke has taken our throne, does this Don Diego work for him, do you suppose?" one of the ladies asked.

The colonel's wife smiled smugly. "There can be no doubt of it. Don Diego is totally loyal to any man who sits on the throne of Castile and Aragon. I have no idea what he actually does, of course. I think it unlikely that my husband knows, but even if he did I am sure he would not tell me. All I know for certain is that Don Diego is efficient and ruthless. I should hate to be his enemy!"

"The young woman really is his daughter?" one of the other ladies inquired.

"Yes. She is so pretty—and so deadly. She has had a number of suitors in Madrid. One of my husband's captains, who will inherit an ancient title and considerable wealth, was one of them. But she is completely devoted to her father and his work, and she has no interest in any man."

"Why does she ride and shoot and engage in swordplay, always dressed as a man?"

"I daresay she finds male clothing more comfortable when she engages in strenuous physical activity. My husband's young captain says that Don Diego started giving Beatriz lessons in riding, shooting, and swordsmanship when she was very young. She is so expert that she is superior to most of her suitors, and that may be one reason they became disheartened. When she chooses, though, she can be very feminine."

"We have seen her coming and going from the viceroy's palace, and it is plain that when she takes the trouble to primp a bit, she is exquisite."

"She is like a diamond, my husband's captain says," the colonel's wife replied. "Brilliant, but hard and cold. The man who can tame her will win a rare prize, but there does not seem to be any such man."

Beatriz de Bernardo guessed accurately that she and

her father were the objects of great speculation, but she was indifferent to the talk. She had far more important matters on her mind.

Six or eight times each week she sat down with various men who came to Havana from the mainland for the express purpose of reporting to Don Diego. The visitors represented every level of Spanish society. Some were intelligence agents in the service of the new monarch, some were New World hunters and trappers, and a few were farmers and planters who had settled in Spanish Florida or along the western coast of Mexico. Some were patriots, while others expected to be paid for the information they brought, and Beatriz, after quizzing them exhaustively, learning all they could tell her, paid them handsomely from a private fund.

She took extensive notes on everything that was said to her, sorting and compiling the information until she had learned everything of consequence about the leaders of the English colonies and their Indian allies. At no time did she forget the instructions her father had drilled into her from childhood: the purpose of a spy master is to gain information.

For three months she devoted herself exclusively to her work, giving her father written, detailed summaries of her findings. Then, one night when she joined her father for a glass of wine before dinner in the parlor adjoining the dining room, she dressed as if it were a special occasion. She had used cosmetics on her beautifully chiseled face, she was wearing a low-cut gown of red silk, trimmed with lace, and somehow she had managed to affix a black lace mantilla to her short black hair. High-heeled shoes made her appear several inches taller.

Don Diego grinned at her, the wrinkles in his lined face deepening, and poured a glass of wine for her. "Tonight we are celebrating?" he asked.

"Indeed we are. I have instructed the cook to prepare pigeon stuffed with shellfish and beefsteak in a sauce of flaming brandy."

"Truly a celebration." He raised his glass to her. "May I know what we are celebrating—and why?"

"Of course, Papa." His sense of humor always amused her. "Our work here is done. If you approve, we are ready to go to the mainland and set up our headquarters in that little village near the mouth of the Mississippi River. This is the last time I shall wear such clothes for many months."

"Your studies are complete?"

She sat gracefully and took a delicate sip of wine. "There is nothing more to be learned from here, as you will see in the report that I have left on your desk. The time for action has come."

Don Diego sat opposite her, looking her up and down slowly, and then sighed. "Perhaps you should wait for me here until my work on the mainland is done."

"I would die of boredom," Beatriz replied quickly. "I would spend my days gossiping with empty-headed women and my nights fending off advances from foolish young men. Besides, why should I be denied the pleasure and excitement that awaits us on the mainland after all of our long preparations?"

"I sometimes wonder if I was right to have given you so many years of rigorous training in my special line of work. If your mother had lived, may the saints bless her memory, your life would have been so different."

"My life is what it is, not what it might have been," she replied, a hint of steel in her voice. "And I refuse to be prevented from the sharing of the rewards for all of our drudgery in Havana."

"You should be marrying an eligible man and making me a proud grandfather."

"There will be ample time for me to marry. I have yet to find any man who doesn't bore me. Take me with you, Papa!"

"Life on the mainland will be rougher than anything you have ever experienced. There are no cities in New

Spain or New France. Most of the country is virgin, untamed wilderness."

"I hope you have not forgotten," she said tartly, "that last year you prepared me for wilderness living by sending me off to the Pyrenees for five months. When I failed to shoot game, I went hungry. When I could not find a stream, I went thirsty. I made my own clothes out of animal skins, and when I felt ill, I found herbs that cured my ailments. I not only survived, but I thrived there. So the New World mainland holds no terrors for me."

Don Diego procrastinated by drinking more of his wine, but eventually he capitulated. "Very well. You may accompany me," he said. "But when our work in America is done and we return to Madrid, I shall choose a husband for you if you fail to select one for yourself. You are twenty-two now, Beatriz, and I cannot allow you to spend your whole life assisting me. You must settle down into respectability."

The woman's response was deceptively meek. "I shall obey you, Papa, as I do in all things. And if I find no husband in Madrid—which is probable, because I have yet to meet anyone there who excites me—I shall marry anyone you choose for me."

Don Diego knew she had no intention of keeping her promise.

"Besides," Beatriz said, "you need me on this journey. I have already initiated ventures about which you know nothing as yet."

Don Diego immediately put aside personal matters. "What have you done?"

"As you know from my summaries, one of the key English colonial leaders is a General Austin Ridley of Virginia, whose troops are superior marksmen and adept in wilderness living."

"Go on."

"You also know that General Ridley's daughter is married to a white Indian of the Seneca nation whose reputation indicates that he is exceptionally resource-ful. He commands a loyal following of warriors."

"What actions have you initiated?" he persisted.

"I have it from one of our agents, who has just come here by way of Florida after visiting Boston and Norfolk, that the daughter of General Ridley is currently en route to Norfolk, where she will visit her family. I have paid a substantial sum of good Spanish gold to have this young woman kidnapped and brought to the headquarters we will establish on the delta of the Mississippi River.

"Her father and her husband will be distracted. They are certain to conduct an extensive search for her." Beatriz's smile was as cold as her dark eyes were hard. "The Indians who will abduct her are under strict instructions to leave no tracks. So the search conducted by General Ridley and the Seneca will be long and fruitless. During that time the Virginia sharp-shooters and the fierce warriors of the Seneca, whom all the tribes of North America appear to fear, will be immobilized. We shall—by means of this simple move —buy time for the forces of Spain and France to conquer the English colonies. We shall accomplish what it would otherwise require many regiments of trained troops to achieve."

Don Diego's chilly smile matched his daughter's. "I have trained you well," he said.

"All this will be done at the cost of but a single life," Beatriz replied proudly.

"Ah. You intend to dispose of the young woman who will be abducted."

"Once we know her husband and father are search-ing for her instead of making war against us, she will have served our purpose. Perhaps we will allow her to live long enough to write them letters saying she is well, if that should suit our purposes. Then, of course, we can dispose of her because she will be of no further use to us."

The majordomo came to the door to announce that

dinner was served. Beatriz rose, took her father's arm, and walked daintily into the dining room, satisfied with herself. Had she known that the information extracted from the agent was faulty and that Betsy was on her way to London, not Norfolk, Beatriz de Bernardo would not have been so pleased.

El-i-chi and Walter, wearing the war paint of the Huron, spent several days at towns of the Ottawa and Algonquian, then marched eastward to one of the principal towns of the Huron. There they indicated that they were residents of a distant village, and their speech, their manners, and their familarity with the nation's customs caused them to be accepted without question.

They spent the better part of a week with the Huron and then went on to Quebec, where they found it far more difficult to obtain information. It was a simple matter to count the warships and merchant vessels in the harbor, to be sure, but their attempts to penetrate the Citadel failed. El-i-chi, who had taken part in a Seneca attack on the fort when he had been a junior warrior, was determined to try again, even though Walter reminded him that Renno had advised them to concentrate their efforts on the Indian allies of the French.

Then, one afternoon when they were loitering in the lower town a short distance from the main gate, several officers in the white and gold uniforms of French regulars emerged from the fort. They were so engrossed in their conversation that only one, a colonel with piercing eyes, took any notice of the two Seneca. He glanced at them for only an instant and, not recognizing them as warriors he knew, looked away again.

El-i-chi's expression remained bland, but Walter could tell that he was deeply agitated. The moment the French officers vanished from sight El-i-chi spoke. "We will leave this place now," he said in a low, urgent voice.

Without seeming to hurry, they made their way to the waterfront. There El-i-chi walked along the snow-crusted bank of the mighty St. Lawrence. As they passed piers, where boats were tied up, El-i-chi appeared to be searching for something.

"See the mountains of ice on the river," El-i-chi said.

Puzzled, the younger man nodded. Large ice floes were indeed floating downstream, drifting toward the open Atlantic. Navigation on the St. Lawrence at this season of the year was difficult.

"We must cross the river, and crossing will not be easy," El-i-chi said. "We need a boat that is strong. We need one that has paddles, not sails. We do not know how to use the sails of the white men. We must be able to reach the south bank safely if we are to begin our homeward journey." He still did not explain to Walter why they were leaving Quebec without delay, and Walter did not ask.

El-i-chi's dark eyes gleamed with pleasure when he saw a sturdy canoe of the Huron, its paddles lying inside the shell. "We have found our boat," he declared.

Walter hoped they could handle the craft, which had places for at least four warriors. It was far larger than their needs dictated, but they were in no position to choose.

The senior warrior looked up at the gray, dull sky where thick clouds obscured the winter sun. "Soon it will be night," he said. "We will wait."

They retreated inland a short distance so they would be relatively inconspicuous, and then, seeking shelter from the sharp winter wind, they squatted beside the wall of a log warehouse. The raw cold was penetrating, and both, attired only in shirts and trousers of stout buckskin, became uncomfortable but did not complain.

When it was almost dark, El-i-chi and Walter stood, then moved swiftly toward the pier.

They climbed into the craft, cast off, and, with

El-i-chi in the stern to guide the light craft, put out into the St. Lawrence, where the current was swift and strong. It was beyond the capacity of two men to fight that current successfully, so El-i-chi sensibly allowed their craft to drift eastward while making certain that they inched their way little by little toward the far bank. Both strained, and in spite of the extreme cold they began to perspire.

The ice floes were hazardous, sometimes looming up only a few feet from them, and they had to exert all of their skill and strength to avoid being crushed by these miniature icebergs. Just as they made out the south bank a short distance ahead, a huge ice floe bore down on them. Walter, who had spent the first half of his life on a Fort Springfield farm, demonstrated that he truly had become a Seneca. Wielding his paddle superbly, he swung the prow away from the onrushing floe, which grazed the canoe but did not damage it.

Paddling in unison with extra effort, they were able to send the forward part of the craft up onto the south bank. Walter leaped ashore and began to pull. El-i-chi quickly joined him, and they beached the canoe, deliberately leaving it in the open, where it could be found later by its rightful owners. There was no need for a discussion of the matter: both knew that if the Huron were able to regain their property, they would regard the theft as merely a mischievous act. Neither of the Seneca wanted to be the object of a vengeful hunt.

They were tired and wanted to rest, but instead they started off through the forest to the south at the rapid trot that every Seneca warrior learned in his youth. It was a matter of great pride that they could maintain the swift, even pace for hours without faltering.

El-i-chi did not deem it safe to call a halt until they reached a hollow protected on three sides by large boulders. By this time they had been trotting for hours, but they took great care not to show their weariness as they squatted in the hollow and helped themselves to several strips of jerked venison and a few handfuls of parched corn, which they kept in pouches attached to their belts. If necessary, they could subsist on such fare for many days.

Sustenance was their first consideration, and not until they finished their frugal meal did El-i-chi speak. "Did you notice the officers of the French who came out of the great fort?" he asked.

Walter shrugged. He had paid little attention to them.

"One was a colonel."

The junior warrior spoke slowly and carefully. "I do not know how to tell one rank of the French from another," he replied.

"His name is Gra-mont," El-i-chi said, hatred in his voice. "The Indians call him Golden Eagle. He was sent from the fort of the French in disgrace when the Huron he commanded lost to the warriors of the Seneca. Now he has returned. Renno will want to know this."

"Why is this chief so important?"

"Golden Eagle is the best of all the French chiefs. Also, he is sly and cunning. He knows the ways that a warrior thinks, so he has great value to the French." El-i-chi paused for a moment. "He is the enemy of all the Seneca. He is the great enemy of Renno. Golden Eagle's spirit would be happy in the afterworld for all time if he carried the scalp of Renno on his belt."

"We will tell Renno as soon as we get home."

"We will travel as swiftly as the deer that flees from the hunter," El-i-chi agreed. "The other news that we bring to Renno is good. We have learned that the Huron do not plan to make war at the side of the French. The Ottawa do not plan to make war at the side of the French. We have seen with our own eyes that the Algonquian have learned it is not wise to fight the Iroquois again. They will remain neutral. But it is bad—very bad—that the colonel named Gra-mont has joined the French again. When he wears the helmet of a French chief, there is sure to be trouble for the Seneca."

Walter shook off his weariness. "We will rest later," he said. "Let us take to the trail again so we may carry the word to Renno more quickly."

Ned and Consuelo Ridley were quartered in Renno's own house, and although living conditions were primitive, they did not complain. Vividly remembering the hardships they and their host had endured on their long, fearful journey through the wilderness several years earlier, they enjoyed the fire that warmed them, the comfortable bunks nestled inside solid log walls, and the hot, delicious meals that Ba-lin-ta happily prepared for them.

Still an expert shot, Consuelo went hunting for wild turkeys with some of the warriors, and fished with Ba-lin-ta. While she enjoyed herself, Renno and his brother-in-law discussed every potential aspect of the coming military campaign.

"My father and General Wilson feel the greatest threat to our security lies to the south," Ned said. "The Carolinas are thinly populated, and an enemy attack in strength might destroy them. As you and I know only too well, the Spaniards have a strong base at St. Augustine. What's more, French and Spanish traders have been very active on the Mississippi River and the lands that lie to the east of it. They could land a large expeditionary force there without our knowledge."

"Also," Renno replied, "the Indian nations of that part of North America have no ties to the Iroquois. They live so far from us that we have never made alliances with them or fought wars against them. The French and Spaniards have much money and many firearms. It might not be difficult to persuade the warriors of ignorant nations to join them. There are many Indians who do not realize the French and Spaniards would rob them of their freedom after the victory was won."

"Assuming that the French in Quebec adopt a defensive stance, which we'll be better able to judge after El-i-chi and Walter report back to you, how would you proceed, Renno?"

"It seems to me," the young sachem declared, "that we would be wise to send an army of Iroquois to visit the nations of the south. We would exchange the white wampum of peace with those who wanted friendship and send arrows into the hearts of those who would oppose us."

"Suppose you came across a large contingent of French or Spanish troops?"

"I would want a force of marksmen from the English colonies to join my expedition," Renno said promptly. "Enough troops to fight effectively, but not so large an army that they would march slowly. I would want militiamen from Virginia and Fort Springfield, men who know the wilderness and could find their own food. We would march together, and we would march swiftly. Only a very large force could defeat us."

Much to his surprise, a delighted Ned laughed aloud. "You've just outlined the strategy that my father, Ghonka, and General Wilson worked out the day before the Great Sachem sailed to England. I wanted to hear your independent thinking before I presented you with their views."

"The manitous," Renno said solemnly, "have made it possible for us to think with one mind."

"You're not obliged to adopt the plan," Ned said. "Ghonka took great care to point out that you're in command of the Iroquois now, so you'll make the final decision."

"Depending on what El-i-chi and Walter tell us," Renno said, "we will do what all of us have decided. Enough Iroquois warriors will be left behind here to make sure that our enemies to the north will not attack our towns while we are gone, and I know General Wilson and the colonels of Rhode Island, Connecticut, and New York will leave most of their battalions at home."

"So General Wilson indicated."

"We will be gambling, Ned, but it is a good gamble. The sachem who takes no risks does not win wars."

They were interrupted by a senior warrior, who wasted no words. "Sachem of the Seneca," he said, "one of our sentries has just captured a Huron in the forest beyond our sentinel lines. He claims he was coming to pay a visit to this town."

Renno was tense. "What does a warrior of the Huron want with us? We must put him to the test of fire to squeeze the truth from him."

"He is not a warrior, sachem. He is a storyteller. He told the sentries he has already visited the lands of the Mohawk and the Onondaga."

"A storyteller." Renno's manner changed, and he relaxed. "Bring him to me, and I will judge him."

Ned waited until the warrior went off, then asked curiously, "What's this all about?"

"Principal medicine men and storytellers are free to travel where they please, even into the lands of their nation's enemies. There are few who make such journeys, but it is the custom of all nations to show them hospitality and do them no harm."

"I'm familiar with medicine men, of course, but I know nothing about storytellers," his brother-in-law said.

"I was reminded of them when I went to the theater in London," Renno declared. "The English call such people—entertainers. The people of a town gather and listen to them. Some sing songs of days long gone. Others tell tales of the gods and the manitous and of wonderful deeds performed in the days of our fathers' fathers. The best of them bring joy to those who hear them, and the people give them furs, beads, and pottery. Most are harmless, so they are allowed to wander where they wish. They lead a strange life, but some become wealthy, and a few—like Nin-ko-wur of the Oneida—become famous. For many years Nin-ko-wur came here when the leaves on the trees became green, and everyone in the town went to hear him. I was only a child when I last heard him, but I still remember some of his stories."

"I'm glad Consuelo and I are here. Watching this man's performance will be a new experience for us."

"First I must decide whether he is truly a storyteller, Ned. If he is, you will hear him. If he is not, he will die in the trails as a spy."

Two Seneca sentries approached the hut. Between them walked a very thin Indian in his late thirties. His shirt, trousers, and moccasins were gaudily embroidered with multicolored beads, he wore no identifying paint, and his scalp lock was far broader than that of warriors.

One of the sentries carried the man's backpack of buffalo skin, and placed it on the ground. "Sachem Renno," he said, "we have already examined this man's property. He carries wampum and necklaces, skins of the fox and many clay cups. Some were made by the Mohawk and some by the Onondaga."

Renno nodded in silence, noting that the Huron carried only a light bow and arrow and a thin knife, weapons he could use to kill and skin the game he needed for sustenance. They would be useless in combat with a heavily armed brave, however.

Folding his arms across his chest, Renno met the man's steady gaze and inclined his head a fraction of an inch, granting him the right to speak.

"The Singer hails the sachem of the Seneca," the Huron said in a deep, resonant voice.

"What is the name of the singer?" Renno demanded.

The man looked puzzled. "The Singer has had no other name for more winters than he can remember."

"Prove you're a singer." Renno was brusque.

The Huron turned to one of the sentinels. "Give to the Singer his reed-that-makes-music."

The sentry rummaged in the backpack, then handed him a hollow reed with holes on one side, an instrument that reminded Renno of an English flute.

Raising it to his lips, the Singer blew on one end, his fingers playing back and forth along the holes. The sounds that emanated from the instrument were loud and clear, and although their tones were strange, even Ned realized that the man was an expert musician.

Removing the instrument from his mouth, the Singer launched into a lifting chant about a manitou who caused the Seneca and Huron to remember they were brothers.

Renno was satisfied that the Huron was a genuine storyteller but still wanted to take no needless risks. "The sachem," he said, "grants the Singer the right to stay in this town for one night. If he wishes then to visit other towns of the Seneca, our warriors will take him to them."

The man's quick smile was unlike the stone-faced expressions of most Indians. Raising his arm in farewell, he left the hut so rapidly that the sentinels had to scurry after him.

A short time later, as news of his arrival spread, a sense of excitement began to grow. Junior warriors built a large bonfire in the fields beyond the palisade, women and girls changed into the clothes they wore on holidays, and even the stolid warriors applied fresh paint to their faces and bodies. The evening meal was served earlier than usual in the lodges and private dwellings, and people hurried out to the fire to obtain the best vantage places.

By the time Renno arrived, escorting Consuelo, Ba-lin-ta, and Ned, virtually everyone in the community except the sentries on guard duty had gathered. The sachem and his party took seats of honor in the front row.

The Singer began his performance by playing on his instrument. No one in his audience could recognize any of the melodies he played, but the beat was strong, almost hypnotic, and soon the Seneca were either keeping time with their hands and feet or swaying back and forth. The Singer had captured his audience.

Putting aside the instrument, he sang a song about the way the world had been formed by the gods of the sun, moon, and earth. Even Renno was captivated as he translated the words in a low tone for Consuelo. At the end of the song the Seneca put aside their habitual reserve and shouted lustily.

Waiting for the applause to die away, the Singer began again, his melodious voice rising and falling as he sang:

In the beginning all nations were brothers.
The Huron and Seneca, Ottawa and Mohawk were brothers.
Then the men with white skins came. They were evil.
The French were evil.
The English were evil, the English were evil, the English were evil.

As Renno translated for Consuelo, the thought occurred to him that, although the Singer had mentioned the French once, he was stressing the theme that the English were evil:

The men with white skins corrupted the souls of the nations.
The men with white skins turned the Iroquois against their brothers, the Huron and the Ottawa.

The theme made Renno distinctly uncomfortable, and Ned, who was able to understand without an interpreter, was scowling, too.

But most of those in the audience were entranced, drinking in every word avidly.

> *The evil English are clever. They give blankets*
> *and firesticks to the Iroquois.*
> *They buy the friendship of the Iroquois.*

Was it possible that this Huron was trying to influence the Seneca and turn them away from their allies? Renno was uncertain.

> *The evil of the English takes many forms.*
> *Just as he who kills a buffalo dresses in the*
> *skin of a buffalo,*
> *So the evil English dress in the skins of the Seneca.*

Renno did not realize that these words might apply to him personally until he became conscious of the gaze of a number of the older women and several of the junior warriors.

He was being ridiculed by an Indian for being a white-skinned Seneca. Except for one time in his youth, when a former Seneca medicine man had prevented Renno from marrying his daughter, his people had always accepted him, taking his blue eyes and pale hair for granted. Now doubts about him were being sown.

The Singer repeated the verse about the evil English dressing in the skins of the Seneca and then ended his performance with the chant that the English were evil. The applause and cheers echoed through the forest.

The Singer was conducted to a hut where he would spend the night under guard, and as the people of the town returned to their dwellings, they stopped to shower him with gifts.

Renno was silent as he returned to his father's house with his party and was not surprised when they were soon joined by Sun-ai-yee. Consuelo and Ba-lin-ta diplomatically withdrew to Renno's house, and the three men sat cross-legged before the fire.

"I don't like it," Ned said. "I wouldn't have believed

the Huron were clever enough to play a sophisticated trick. But there can be no doubt the Singer was trying to turn the Seneca against the English colonists. And against Renno!"

"That thought came into my mind," Renno said, "but I believed it was my imagination."

"It was not," Sun-ai-yee said firmly. "Many in the crowd—warriors and women and even elders—looked at Renno when the Singer told that the evil English dress in the skins of the Seneca."

Sun-ai-yee rubbed his belly, a sign that he was deep in thought. "It would be well," he continued, "to order the sentries to take the Singer out of the land of the Seneca. He should not sing his songs to the people of the other nations of the Iroquois, either."

"I do not agree," Renno said, his voice vehement, although his face remained expressionless. "The people of all the nations of the Iroquois know what I have done in battle. They know what I have done on my missions to England, to New Spain, and to Quebec. My deeds speak for themselves. I won my promotions fairly, and I have taken many scalps."

Sun-ai-yee pondered at length. "Renno is right," he said at last. "Sun-ai-yee is wrong. Even if the Singer is sent from the lands of the Iroquois, the words he has sung here still will be repeated, and all of the Iroquois will soon know them. And if the Singer is silenced, the people of the Iroquois will believe Renno has something to hide. They will believe he truly is guilty of evil."

"I have served the Seneca and through them the Iroquois all my days," Renno said quietly. "I cannot believe that one Huron storyteller could turn all of the people of the League against me."

"That is true," Sun-ai-yee declared. "There is great anger in my heart against the Singer and those who sent him here. Sun-ai-yee wanted to take his scalp when he sang his hateful words. But I did not. It is best now to forget him and put this night behind us.

Soon the weather will become warm, the warriors will march into the wilderness, and the Huron singer will be forgotten."

"I hope you're right," Ned said. "But I also hope you'll be wary. This could be just the beginning of a campaign to disrupt the Iroquois League."

"We will be wary," Renno replied. He then added firmly, "The manitous have given their sacred pledge that the people of the Iroquois will be one people for all time, until the earth crumbles and is no more. The strength of the manitous is greater than that of Huron magic."

Lacking faith in the spirits that guided the destinies of the Seneca and the other Iroquois nations, Ned was dubious but kept his thoughts to himself. Perhaps the French were responsible for the appearance of the Singer, knowing that the disruption of the Iroquois League would be the most telling blow they could strike against the English colonies. He hoped the spring weather would come soon, before the alliance was further shaken.

On Renno's order, the Singer was once again allowed to roam freely. His mission accomplished, he vanished into the wilderness of his own land.

Ned and Consuelo left the following day, retracing their path to Fort Springfield and Boston, then returning to Virginia by ship.

Less than a week later El-i-chi and Walter came home, and Renno immediately called a meeting of the nation's leaders to hear their report.

El-i-chi spoke at length on behalf of his companion and himself. It was their joint opinion, he declared, that the Huron and Ottawa were too afraid of the Seneca to become the active war allies of the French. The Algonquian, ordinarily peace-loving in spite of their size, had learned a lesson in the last war and probably would remain neutral.

He stated that he and Walter had seen six warships and eleven merchantmen at anchor in Quebec, eight of

the latter French and three of them Spanish. Pressed
by his brother, he described the ships of the French
navy in greater detail.

Renno deduced that two were frigates, three were
sloops of war, and one was a bomb ketch. He would
write to General Wilson immediately.

El-i-chi braced himself. "Golden Eagle—the Huron
warrior the French call Gra-mont—works again for
them," he said.

Sun-ai-yee stiffened, and the other war chiefs stared
intently at the senior warrior who had brought the
unwelcome news.

"How does El-i-chi know this?" Renno asked sharply.

His brother told the story of what he had seen at the
Citadel gate in Quebec.

"You do not know what work Golden Eagle does
for the French now?"

"I know only that he wore their uniform. A new
uniform."

It would be necessary to alert all members of the
English colonial high command at once, Renno knew.
The return of Golden Eagle to active duty meant that
serious trouble loomed ahead. As Ghonka had ob-
served during the siege of Louisburg, the services of
Golden Eagle were equal to those of two regiments of
French infantry.

All at once the thought flickered through Renno's
mind that Golden Eagle well could have been responsible for the performance of the Singer. After living
with the Huron for many years, the Frenchman well
knew the ways of Indians, and he was capable of
perpetrating such a sly, devious trick.

Perhaps it would be wise to write Ned about his
suspicions, but he dismissed the idea from his mind as
rapidly as it occurred to him. The Singer had not
injured the Iroquois alliance and had not succeeded in
doing him personal harm, either. Missing Betsy, their
children, and his parents, particularly the sage guidance

of his father, he knew he had to rely on himself and consequently had to concentrate all of his attention on the campaign that would begin in the near future.

The three warriors of the Biloxi tribe were in a quandary. They had accepted many gifts from the emissary of the Spanish lady in Havana, including warm woolen blankets, cooking pots of iron for their families, pistols and knives of fine Spanish steel for themselves. Now they had made their way without incident all the way from their own land near the mouth of the Great River to the land called Virginia.

The task assigned to them had seemed so simple. They had been instructed to abduct a handsome young woman from the home of a Virginia sachem named Ridley, cover their tracks without fail, and bring her unharmed to the village of the French and Spanish traders on the delta of the Great River. All they had been told about the girl was that she was very pretty, and they knew they would be punished if they killed or maimed her.

They had learned the location of the Ridley home from the emissary of the Spanish lady, and for two days they had kept watch on the house from the deep woods beyond the gates. Aside from people who appeared to be servants, they had seen only two persons in and around the house. Both were young women, and both were attractive. One had pale hair, the other had red hair, and they appeared to be about the same age.

The Biloxi had heard them speaking to each other as they sat on an outside extension of the house in strange chairs that enabled them to rock back and forth. Presumably they addressed each other by name, but the Biloxi could not understand one word of their strange language. So they had no idea which was named Ridley and was the girl they had been told to abduct.

The problem seemed insoluble, and the trio pondered at length, uncertain how to proceed. Then the senior warrior in charge of the party found the ideal solution: they would kidnap both of the young women. His subordinates were in enthusiastic agreement.

Observing the movements of the pair carefully, they ascertained that the girls slept in separate, adjoining rooms on the second floor of the house. The next day the Biloxi made a strong ladder of intertwined vines. That night they watched the lamps in the house being extinguished one by one, and after it had been dark for a time, they climbed onto the portico above the entrance. The leader waited outside on the portico roof, and the others separated, each silently prying open a window and crawling into the bedchamber of one of the girls. The task was simple.

Anne Ridley awakened to find a cloth gagging her mouth while her arms were being bound behind her back. She still suffered occasional nightmares, having been captured by the Pimlico tribe as a child, and for a few moments she thought she was dreaming. By the time she became alert to the reality of the situation, it was too late.

Her wrists were bound securely behind her back, and a dark warrior who smelled of stale grease was motioning her toward the window. She balked, and he produced a knife, which he jabbed into her back, drawing blood. Afraid the Indian would kill her if she failed to obey him, Anne slowly climbed out of the window onto the portico roof.

Meanwhile, Hester MacDevitt woke up while a cloth was being stuffed into her mouth, and thinking her attacker's intent was sexual, she fought him furiously. She managed to rake his face with her nails and drive a knee into his groin, which caused him to gasp, but her physical strength was no match for his, and he subdued her after a brief, vicious struggle.

She, too, had her wrists tied behind her back, and her

only satisfaction was that of seeing the thin streaks of blood on the Indian's face. Treating her roughly, he shoved her toward the window, then pushed her through it onto the portico roof, where she saw Anne.

The senior warrior studied the girls for a moment, then said something to his subordinates in a low tone. One turned back to the bedrooms, while the other helped the leader, each throwing a helpless girl over his shoulder and descending to the ground. The young women, barefoot and clad in their nightgowns, were forced to walk rapidly to the forest.

There the third warrior joined his comrades, grinning as he displayed shirts, doeskin trousers, and shoes that he had found in another room in the house. The Indians had no way of knowing that the clothing belonged to Betsy Ridley, their intended victim. At the leader's direction they plunged deeper into the forest before he halted, then slashed at the fabric of the nightgowns with his knife.

Both girls believed they would be raped, but to their astonishment, their bonds were cut, and the senior warrior threw the clothes to them.

They dressed hastily, aware of the hatred in the narrowed eyes of their captors, who gripped their knives and guarded them closely.

Exchanging swift glances, Anne and Hester communicated silently, agreeing that it would be foolhardy to make a break for freedom. These grim braves meant business, and an attempt to run away might mean serious injury or even death.

As soon as the pair were clad again, the march was resumed. Their captors were so confident of themselves that the girls' wrists were not bound again. The leader preceded them as he made his way through the forest, his sense of direction unerring, and the other two brought up the rear, keeping a close watch on the prisoners.

The warriors set a rapid pace, and ultimately both

girls grew weary. Whenever one of them stumbled or faltered, however, a knife was brandished close to her face. Both somehow mustered the strength to keep going.

As Anne's initial fear subsided a little, she tried to think clearly but was utterly bewildered. These Indians were shorter and darker than the Pimlico, and perhaps it was significant that they wore no war paint, making it impossible to distinguish their tribe. Whatever their motive for kidnapping, they seemed to know what they were doing, and Anne knew enough about Indians to realize they were well satisfied with themselves.

Only when the girls were so exhausted that they could scarcely place one foot in front of the other did the senior warrior call a halt in a small clearing near the bank of a brook. The gags were removed for the first time, the captives were allowed to drink from the stream, and they were given dried meat and parched corn to eat. Too tired to talk, they made no protest when one end of a length of rawhide was tied to an ankle of each, the other end of the leather rope held by a stake driven into the ground. One of the braves kept them under observation as they dropped off to sleep.

Anne and Hester were still being watched when they awakened. They had no idea how long they had slept, and they knew only that the sun had risen.

Anne, in command of herself, addressed the leader in the tongue of the Pimlico, which she could speak fluently. "Who are you?" she demanded. "Why have you taken us from our home?"

The Indians were able to understand her, even though they could not speak the language of the Pimlico, and it surprised them that this white girl was able to communicate with them.

Before he replied in the tongue of the Biloxi, the senior warrior thought carefully. "The women with pale skins," he said slowly, "will be taken to a far land. If they do what they are told, they will not be harmed.

81

But if they try to run away or make a loud noise, they will be sent to join their ancestors, and their scalps will hang from the belts of the warriors."

Hester could not understand a word that was being said, but Anne, able to make out the meaning of the senior warrior's words, interpreted rapidly for her.

"But why have they abducted us?" Hester demanded. "There must be a reason!"

Anne translated the question, but the short, wiry leader folded his arms across his chest and looked off into space, making it plain that he did not intend to reply.

The prisoners were given food, then allowed to drink from the stream, and the march was resumed. The senior warrior again set a blistering pace, and many hours passed before he allowed the captives to rest for a short time. They did not halt until long after night had fallen.

As they were about to go to sleep that night, Anne said, "I don't think this was a random abduction. For whatever their reason, these Indians—whoever they may be—came to Norfolk for the express purpose of kidnapping us."

"I've been thinking, too," Hester said. "I wonder if they could be enemies of your father—or of Ned. I know very little about Indians, but I can't think of any reason they would bother to abduct you and me."

"I suppose we'll find out eventually," Anne murmured, "if our feet don't fall off first."

The better part of a week passed before one of the braves vanished into the forest, then returned with the carcass of a deer across his shoulders. That night the Biloxi and their prisoners had a hot meal.

Fortified by the food, Hester became bolder. "These men don't seem too bright," she said. "Perhaps we can plot our escape."

Anne shook her head. "Don't underestimate them. For years now, Renno has advised me never to try to outsmart warriors who might be enemies. It isn't a question of courage, Hester. Their standards aren't our standards, and I'm afraid the leader of this band meant what he said when he threatened to kill us if we try to run away. Besides, I—I'm not sure I could find my way back to Norfolk without help."

"I know I couldn't," a crestfallen Hester said reluctantly. "One part of this wilderness seems like another. I never knew North America was so huge."

They made their way across mountain ranges and traveled through valleys, sometimes following the course of swift-running rivers as they marched across plains. Gradually the weather became somewhat warmer, and by noting both the weather change and the position of the sun when it set, the girls realized that their captors were heading southwest.

Their feet first blistered, then became callused. They wore out their shoes, and one of the braves fashioned moccasins for them out of buckskin. Another shot a wild turkey with his bow and arrow, giving them a welcome change of diet, and sometimes they ate fish from the rivers. Regardless of whether the sun shone or rain fell, one day was like another, and in spite of their efforts to keep count of the passage of time, Anne and Hester were no longer certain how long they had spent on this endless march through the forest.

Only the leader spoke to them, and he addressed them infrequently. The warriors were surly and tireless, apparently bending all of their efforts toward a single goal, that of reaching their destination safely. On one occasion they remained in the same place for twenty-four hours, lighting no fires during that time. Their captives suspected there might be other Indians in the vicinity.

The girls discussed that possibility. "If we really knew that people might be near," Hester said, "we could take the chance of calling for help."

"Renno has told me that most Indians have never seen people with skin our color. Of those who have, some tribes are actively hostile. We might be worse off if we fell into the hands of enemies, and there's no way of knowing what they might do to us. As things stand right now, we aren't being injured or molested. We're being fed—not as much as we might like, but enough. We have chances to rest. I wish we wouldn't be forced to walk so far every day, but we're in no position to complain.

"You're probably right," Hester said. "We'd best leave well enough alone."

The senior warrior was relieved that his prisoners were causing him so little trouble. Perhaps, when he delivered them to the emissary of the Spanish lady, he could ask for a special reward. He would enjoy making a personal slave of the maiden whom the Spanish lady didn't want.

Chapter IV

The mansion, one of the most imposing private homes in London, was located only a short distance from the royal palace, Whitehall. Built during the latter years of King William's reign, the mansion was used to house distinguished official visitors. Scarlet-clad troops of the Royal Household Cavalry stood sentry duty at the gates, the large staff of servants wore the Queen's livery, and every effort was made to insure the comfort of guests of the nation.

Not even in Virginia had Betsy known such splendor, and she was amused when she compared her handsomely appointed suite with the simple quarters she shared with Renno in the land of the Seneca. Her children had bedchambers, a playroom, and a private dining room across the corridor. Their activities were supervised by a governess who made it her business to acquaint them with many aspects of life in England.

Just as Adrienne Wilson had predicted, Betsy was

instantly a social success. She received more invitations
to dinners and suppers than she could accept, and she
attended the theater frequently. She was relieved that
the escort provided for her was Sir Edward Carlton, a
handsome bachelor in his early thirties who was a
member of the Whitehall staff. Carlton was courteous,
friendly, and charming but, contrary to the dire predictions of Adrienne and Consuelo, refrained from making advances to her.

Only Ghonka and Ena were impervious to the luxury that surrounded them. The Great Sachem was
treated as a head of state, and the extensive grounds of
Whitehall were closed daily when he went for long
walks. Exercise was important to him, and every effort
was made to meet his desires and needs.

To be sure, he and Ena had to learn new ways, too,
the most difficult being that of eating in the English
manner at a table. Ena, more malleable than her husband, soon learned to use forks and spoons, but
Ghonka scorned such implements, cutting his meat
with his own knife and, whenever possible, eating with
his fingers.

His patience was being strained because, in spite of
the cordiality of his hosts, he had not yet met Queen
Anne. She and Prince George, her consort, currently
were living in seclusion at one of her country estates,
leaving the day-to-day operations of the government in
the hands of her principal minister, Lord Godolphin,
while she concentrated her own efforts on the prosecu-
tion of the war with France. Ghonka's initial audience
with her had to await her return to London.

In the meantime Betsy was becoming familiar with
the intricacies of life in court circles. She quickly
learned that the most influential couple in the realm were
General John Churchill, recently raised in the peerage
with the title of Duke of Marlborough, and his wife,
Sarah, who was Queen Anne's intimate friend. Marlborough returned to England from the Continent,

where his army and those of the Austrians and Dutch were skirmishing with the forces of France, and although he had not yet fought a major battle with the enemy, he was given a conqueror's welcome.

Betsy, Ghonka, and Ena watched from the portico of the official guest house as the commander of Britain's armed forces took part in a parade designed to stimulate the public's war fervor. Three regiments—one of cavalry and two of infantry—marched in the parade, and the Great Sachem studied the troops closely, noting every detail of their bearing, uniforms, and, above all, the arms they carried. The Duke of Marlborough, resplendent in scarlet and gold, rode in an open carriage beside his wife, both of them bravely ignoring the raw, chilly wind that swept across London. Again and again the general raised a hand to the visor of his helmet as he acknowledged the cheers of the huge crowds lining the streets.

A surprise was in store for the trio on the portico of the guest house. As Marlborough's carriage rolled past them, the duke ordered his coach halted for a moment. Then he stood, looked at Ghonka, and drew his own dress sword, saluting with a flourish. No one appreciated protocol more than the Great Sachem, but what impressed him even more was the general's quick, infectious grin.

"It would be good," Ghonka told his wife and Betsy, "to fight at the side of that warrior."

Soon after breakfast the next morning, while Betsy was in the nursery playroom with her children, a servant came to the door, apologizing for interrupting her. "Sir Edward Carlton begs the indulgence of an urgent interview with you, ma'am," he said.

Patting her upswept hair into place, Betsy lifted her long skirt and petticoats and hurried down to the small sitting room where the visitor awaited her.

Sir Edward rose to his feet as she approached, his eyes appreciative as he studied her, and then he bent low over her hand. Although Betsy had become accustomed to having her hand kissed, the gesture still made her uncomfortable.

"I'm sorry to disturb you so early in the day," Sir Edward said, "but the Duke of Marlborough intends to call on Ghonka within the hour. I hope he hasn't gone off for his walk around the palace grounds."

"No, I believe he was intending to leave shortly, but I'm certain he'll change his schedule. What brings the duke here?"

"I have no idea, and I wouldn't dare ask," Sir Edward said, smiling. "John Churchill does what he pleases, when he pleases. All I know is that I was called to his town house and was told to inform the leader of the Iroquois that he'll have a visitor this morning."

"I'm glad, and I know Ghonka will be pleased, too." Betsy knew that her father-in-law was becoming increasingly irritated because there had been no opportunity for him to initiate the mission that had brought him so far from his own home. "You'll stay for the meeting, Sir Edward?" she asked politely.

"I was hoping you'd ask me. Please convey the importance of his encounter to Ghonka. Queen Anne is likely to take any advice the duke and duchess give her."

Betsy excused herself, then hurried up to the suite occupied by Ghonka and Ena, telling them of the impending visit. The Great Sachem received the word calmly. "It will be good to smoke a pipe with the brother of Ghonka," he said, making it plain that he regarded himself as the equal of England's military leader. Donning his feathered bonnet and buffalo robe, he went directly to the sitting room downstairs.

Sir Edward, who was never at a loss for words when alone with Betsy, was distinctly uncomfortable in the presence of the burly Seneca, who disdained small talk and sometimes sat in unmoving silence for long periods. Ghonka felt no need for conversation, and preferring the floor to one of the room's dainty, gilded chairs, he sat cross-legged on the rug near the coal fire burning in the hearth. There was no sound in the chamber but the interminable, steady ticking of an enameled clock on the mantel.

When they heard the sergeant in charge of the sentry detail call his men to attention, the Great Sachem rose effortlessly, then waved the servants aside as he went to the front door himself, opened it, and stood on the threshold.

General John Churchill, Duke of Marlborough, was as tall as Ghonka. He had a slightly rolling gait and outdistanced the three aides who followed him, attempting to match their steps to his.

Ghonka raised his arm in the traditional Indian greeting. "The Great Sachem of the Iroquois welcomes the Great Sachem of the English to his house," he intoned.

He and Betsy were stunned when Marlborough replied in the tongue of the Seneca. "The Great Sachem of the English greets his brother."

Ghonka rarely showed surprise, but he made no attempt to hide his astonishment and then laughed aloud. They gripped forearms in the Indian manner, then shook hands.

Marlborough, grinning broadly, bowed to Betsy. "You're Renno's wife, of course. Tell Ghonka that my aide-de-camp taught me that little speech with some difficulty, and I practiced all the way here from my own house. I've now exhausted my Seneca vocabulary."

They moved into the principal reception hall, where coal fires burning in twin hearths removed the chill from the room, and Sir Edward was startled, as were the duke's aides, when Marlborough lowered himself to the rug and sat cross-legged opposite Ghonka.

Betsy was surprised, too, but tried to recover her equanimity. "May we offer Your Grace some refreshments?"

"It's too early in the day for wine," he replied. "What do you usually drink at this hour?"

"Ghonka is very fond of the apple juice that's served in this country," she said.

"Perfect," the English commander in chief declared. "Apple juice it will be. And I want both you and Ghonka to know how eager I've been to meet you. How well I remember Renno's visit to London. It's said that I'm a fairly good judge of character, and I've rarely met a young man who impressed me as he did when he came here to get help from King William for the colonies."

Betsy inclined her head, then translated for her father-in-law.

"Renno has his chance to prove whether he is truly a sachem," the imperturbable Great Sachem declared.

Servants soon appeared with pitchers of cider, which they poured into silver goblets, and Marlborough raised his cup. "I drink to our coming victories," he said.

After Betsy translated his words, Ghonka raised his own goblet. "May our belts grow heavy with the scalps of our enemies!"

The aides and Sir Edward were embarrassed. Always sensitive to the feelings and reactions of others, Marlborough realized that his subordinates could not understand why he was treating this savage Indian with the courtesy that he ordinarily reserved for such peers as Prince Eugene of Savoy. "Gentlemen," he said brusquely, not bothering to spare their feelings, "be good enough to withdraw so we can confer in private." The aides, accompanied by a reluctant Sir Edward, went off to an anteroom.

Betsy understood the general's motives and was relieved. Occasionally, in her dealings with the English, she had suspected that they were snickering at Ghonka and Ena behind their backs. But the commander in chief was demonstrating genuine respect for his New World colleague.

Marlborough inquired at length about Renno, expressing his confidence that the young sachem would live up to his new responsibilities. Then he asked searching questions about the military situation in America. Ghonka responded by outlining the strategy that he, General Wilson, and General Ridley had devised.

The duke nodded. "Your thinking is sound," he said, "provided your warriors are resolute and the militia who march with them are flexible. One factor in your favor is that King Louis will be able to send precious few French and Spanish regiments to the colonies for at least another year. He and his Bavarian allies are beginning to muster a huge army in central Europe, obviously hoping to capture Vienna. We're pretending to be ignorant of his aim. The more troops he assembles, the more will fall into our net. When the time is ripe—perhaps a year or more from now—we intend to hit the French from three different approaches simultaneously. We could attack them now, of course, but our forces aren't yet equal to his. Prince Eugene and I aren't making the mistake of placing too low an estimate on the worth of the French divisions. There are no better troops anywhere on earth."

"When you meet them in battle you will win?" the Great Sacham asked.

The duke shrugged. "If the Lord wills it and if our artillery is strong enough."

"It is always wise to rely on the manitous and on the aim of your warriors' arrows," Ghonka replied.

"Your situation is difficult at best, too," Marlborough said. "The combined forces of the French and Spaniards in America are already greater than those of our English colonies, but Queen Anne will be reluctant to send more troops to the New World. She'll also claim she can't spare any arms and other supplies."

Ghonka faced the problem realistically. "Then my mission will fail?"

The duke shook his head. "No, but it won't be easy

to accomplish." He looked at Betsy, then asked, "May I speak very candidly?"

"Of course, Your Grace."

"Queen Anne is a typical Stuart. There's no one on earth more stubborn or harder to convince. I intend to initiate my own campaign to sway her, and my wife will do the same. I can only hope she'll have an open mind by the time she and Prince George return to London."

Carefully, Betsy translated the statement into the language of the Seneca. Ghonka was silent.

"We're leaving London early tomorrow so I can say good-bye to the Queen before I rejoin my troops," Marlborough said. "So we'd very much like both of you and Ghonka's wife to join us for dinner today. The duchess's attitude can be critical because she has a greater influence over Queen Anne than anyone else— when she wants to exert it. I'm convinced of the need for a total victory in the New World, and I want my wife to feel as I do."

The arrangements were made for later in the day, and the duke took his leave, accompanied by his aides.

Not until Ghonka and Betsy were alone did the Great Sachem speak his mind. "England is a strong country," he said. "England is a great country, but it is also a strange country. In none of the lands of the Iroquois would a woman be the sachem, taking advice from another woman."

Sir Edward Carlton returned early in the afternoon to escort the party to the town house of the duke and duchess. Betsy had changed into a trim-fitting gown of watered silk for the occasion, and Sir Edward was quick to compliment her. "You look lovely," he said. "And I commend you for your boldness."

"In what way am I being bold, sir?"

"Sarah Churchill was once pretty, but her looks faded as she matured. In fact, some people hold the opinion that the only woman in the British Isles who is homelier is the Queen. So most of the ladies who visit her go out of their way to look a trifle dowdy in her presence."

"Oh, dear. Perhaps I should change," Betsy said.

Sir Edward smiled. "On the contrary. Her Grace will admire you. Many people don't realize that she shares one of her husband's more admirable traits. She enjoys the company of people who are honest and don't resort to subterfuge in their dealings with her."

The modest Churchill house, to which a new wing was being added, stood near the Thames, overshadowed by the magnificent palace of the Earl of Somerset, who had been a royal favorite almost a half-century earlier. Under his own roof the Duke of Marlborough wore conservative civilian attire and allowed his wife to bask in the limelight. Sarah Churchill, known to foreign envoys as the most powerful individual in Great Britain, was short and plump. She wore a dress of yellow satin, trimmed in green, that clashed with her ruddy complexion. A diamond choker was conspicuous at her throat, and she wore many jewel-studded rings.

Betsy realized the meeting might determine the outcome of Ghonka's mission and consequently was apprehensive. But the duchess quickly put her fears to rest, chatting so volubly with her and with Ena that the young woman had to devote herself exclusively to the task of interpreter.

Ena, who never lost her dignity, enjoyed the company of this talkative woman and responded in kind, talking more freely than she had in her conversations with anyone else since she had come to England.

The men were left without the services of a translator, so the duke took Ghonka, trailed by Sir Edward, to see his collection of weapons. The Great Sachem was fascinated by the swords of different kinds that had been used over the centuries, and he handled pistols and muskets with an easy familiarity. He was thunderstruck when he examined a crossbow, the principal weapon of English armies before it had been replaced by the first, primitive firearms.

In spite of the language barrier, Marlborough and his guest repaired to the extensive garden behind the house, each armed with a crossbow and a number of metal-tipped arrows. They pinned a target to the thick trunk of an elm tree at the far end of the garden.

Neither had ever used a crossbow, and they were grimly silent when initially they completely missed the target. Ghonka soon realized that it was necessary to plant his feet wide apart and take aim from the waist rather than from shoulder height, as was his custom with the conventional Seneca bow and arrow. Marlborough observed him carefully, and soon he, too, began to acquire the knack.

They retrieved their arrows, then started again, both laughing boisterously and clapping each other on the back when one or the other actually hit the target. Sir Edward had gathered that no man ever touched the person of the Indian chieftain, and certainly no English officer would have the temerity to become unduly familiar with the commander in chief. But watching them as they cavorted like carefree boys, shouting loudly whenever one of them hit the target, Sir Edward knew they were kindred spirits. It was possible, he mused, that all men who reached their rank had qualities in common that were lacking in lesser mortals.

The duke and Ghonka were so engrossed in their sport that the duchess had to send the majordomo to fetch them when dinner was served. They had developed a real camaraderie by the time they came to the table, their eyes glowing.

The meal was elaborate. Betsy accepted the wines that were served with each course, but Ghonka and Ena, unaccustomed to alcoholic beverages of any kind, preferred fruit juices and cold water.

For a time the talk at the table was general, dealing mainly with the reactions of the visitors to London. Then Sarah Churchill became impatient and turned to Ena. "I know why we must defeat the French in

Europe," she said, "but I'd like you to tell me why a victory in the New World is important."

Ena stopped eating and folded her hands in her lap. "The wife of Renno has two babies," she said. "They are free to grow up in the land of the Seneca. The boy will hunt and protect us from our enemies. The girl will grow crops and make a home for her family. They will be free to live as the Seneca have lived since the beginning of time. They will be free to visit the family of Renno's wife in the colony called Virginia. If the Iroquois and the English colonists win the war, no one will try to take their freedom from them. If the French win, the son and daughter of Renno will become slaves. Some of the English colonists will be killed. Others will be driven into the Great Sea. All will perish. When they die, all freedom in the wilderness will die."

Everyone at the table fell silent as Betsy translated. Then the duchess turned to her. "Would you like to add anything to what your mother-in-law has said?"

"You are married to a soldier, Your Grace," Betsy said simply. "My husband, like his father, is a soldier, too. They fight for the same principles that His Grace of Marlborough fights to preserve. We are separated by the Atlantic Ocean, but we are one people, sharing the same ideals. Louis of France would destroy those ideals by destroying us. If he wins the English colonies, he will become so powerful that not even the combined armies of England, Austria, and Holland will bring him to his knees. All of America and all of Europe will be forced to accept him as their master."

"Well said," John Churchill murmured as he sipped his wine.

His wife looked hard at Ena, then at Betsy. "I never trust men when they speak of war, not even the husband I love and respect. They thirst for glory, and I always suspect they actually enjoy the excitement of planning a campaign and the danger of fighting a battle. Between you, in these few moments, you've convinced me that your cause is our cause."

Ena, believing she had done all she could, calmly began to eat again, handling her knife and fork as though she had used them all her life.

"Queen Anne," the duchess said, "knows nothing about the colonies, even though Lord Godolphin has tried to tell her that our growing trade there is important. I shall do everything I can to persuade her to listen without prejudice when she meets Ghonka. I shall tell her what Ena and Betsy have told me, and I hope she will heed their advice. She is a monarch, it is true, but she is also a woman, and I trust that she will be touched, as I have been."

Color rose in Betsy's face. The Duchess of Marlborough had become an ally, so there was reason to hope that the campaign to secure Queen Anne's support for the English colonies would be won.

Sir Edward Carlton watched the radiant young woman who sat across the table from him, his diplomat's smile masking his real feelings. He had wanted her since he had first seen her, but he had proceeded with great caution, maintaining an impersonal air even when being cordial. Now that there seemed to be at least a chance that the cause that brought her to England might be successful, she would become more relaxed, which would give him the opportunity to pursue his own campaign.

There was no doubt in Sir Edward's mind that he would win her. There was a ruthless will behind the charm that had already carried him to a high place in the Queen's service, and he was confident that the day would come when he would be given a government ministry of his own. He was equally certain the day was not far distant when this lovely young innocent, so naive that she apparently enjoyed her place in life as the wife of a savage Indian, would succumb to him.

Sir Edward had known many women, but this one was different. She was more beautiful than all the rest, just as she was far more ingenuous. He found that combination irresistible.

The Ridley family returned to Norfolk only twenty-four hours after the abduction of Anne and Hester. The frightened household servants knew only that the two young women had not come down to breakfast and appeared to have vanished. The ladder of vines that the Biloxi warriors had fashioned was still hanging from the portico, and a swift examination told Austin and Ned Ridley that the kidnappers had been Indians. No colonist had ever made such a ladder.

General Ridley summoned his staff to a conference, then sent messengers to every Indian tribe in the area, particularly the Pimlico, to seek information. Meanwhile, Ned set out alone to track the abductors. Almost as at home in the wilderness as Renno, Ned followed a clear trail for several miles as he plunged deeper and deeper into the endless forest. Then, suddenly, the tracks vanished.

He remained in the wilderness for several days, heading first in one direction and then in another before he had to admit defeat and return home. His mother and Consuelo were sitting in the parlor when he entered the house wearily, and both looked at him in tense, anxious silence.

Ned shook his head. "The trail grew cold very quickly," he told them. "I have no idea where they've been taken." Pausing only long enough to kiss his wife, he walked down the hall to the library, where General Ridley made his office.

Austin looked up from the papers on his desk, the expression in his son's eyes telling him what he did not want to learn.

Ned came to the point at once. "There was a clear trail as far as Little Bend on the Elizabeth River, sir," he said as he sat. "Five people in the party. Two must have been the girls. The others were men who wore moccasins. Indians, probably, after seeing the ladder we found, but I had no way of making a positive identification. Only Renno can sometimes distinguish warriors by the marks of their moccasins."

His father nodded. "You lost the trail at Little Bend, Ned?"

"Yes, sir. There are sand bars there, as you know, so the river can be crossed by wading it at this season. At the far side there were no tracks of any kind. I scoured the length of the river for more than two miles up and down Little Bend. Every spot that could have been crossed on foot. But the tracks stop at the water's edge on the near side."

"How do you account for that?"

"I can't be sure, sir. My only theory is that after crossing the river, someone in the party bringing up the rear made it his business to obliterate the tracks of those who marched ahead of him. It's a laborious, nasty job, but both of us have seen it done."

"They wouldn't need to be erased for more than a short distance," General Ridley said. "A full regiment scouring the area would find it difficult to pick up the place where the tracks resumed."

"A full regiment," Ned said with a sour smile, "would create too damn many tracks of its own."

His father sighed and nodded.

"You've had no luck, either, sir?"

"None," Austin said, his voice flat. "The Pimlico know nothing, and neither do any of the smaller tribes. All of their sachems and medicine men swear they have no reason to provoke us into fighting a new war by abducting my daughter, and I believe them. They know that with the French threat hanging over our heads we'll tolerate no nonsense from them."

"What puzzles me," Ned said, "is why the warriors of any Indian nation would bother to abduct Anne and Hester in the first place. They might take Anne and then make demands of some kind on you and me as ransom, but we've had no such demands. As for Hester, she has no value of any kind to them."

"I've tried to figure it out, too," his father replied, "and the more I think about it, the more confused I become. The entire incident makes no sense."

"The question now is what to do next." Ned was grim.

"I've discussed the problem by the hour with my staff," Austin said, "and I have literally no idea how to proceed."

"We've got to assume the worst, sir. It may be that the girls will be murdered because some disgruntled braves have a warped idea of obtaining revenge for imaginary insults and slights. Or the abduction could be a prelude to the start of a war against us by some Indian tribe."

"One guess is as good as another right now. We can't institute a major search because we don't know where to begin looking for them. They could be somewhere within a day's march, or they could have been taken deep into the interior."

"I hate this feeling of helplessness."

"My own feeling," Austin declared, "is that this abduction is a prelude to war. More often than not, as both of us know only too well, Indian tribes don't bother to issue a declaration of war. They simply launch sneak attacks on towns or outlying villages. And we don't have enough men in the brigade to provide adequate protection for the entire Virginia frontier."

"But we can retaliate, sir. Quickly and with great force, after an attack takes place."

"Are you suggesting that I call the troops to active duty, Ned? Remember that a full-scale mobilization will take the men away from their civilian pursuits. They're needed on their farms and in their shops, and I don't believe it is justified to put the entire brigade into uniform simply because my daughter has been abducted."

"I wasn't thinking in terms of the entire brigade," Ned said. "It would be enough, I think, if your adjutant put my battalion on an alert. Within twenty-four hours we'd be in a position to mobilize three hundred of the finest sharpshooters in the colonies. I'm not boasting when I say that my men can destroy an army of a thousand braves of just about any tribe—with the exception of the Seneca."

General Ridley thought at length, absently opening and closing the lid of the ink jar that sat on his desk. "Very well," he said at last. "You shall have your alert. Whatever the motives for the abduction, Virginia isn't going to be trapped in a surprise attack."

Had Beatriz de Bernardo known of the decision, she would have been dismayed. Not only had the wrong victims been kidnapped, but the results were the opposite of what she had intended. Instead of creating a state of confusion, the move by the Biloxi was increasing Virginia's preparedness for the coming war.

Kenneth Robinson hated Boston, the traitorous and unsavory task he was compelled to perform, and his own weakness, which was responsible for his dilemma. His French employers had kept their word, giving him the funds they had promised him, and he had been able to pay off his gaming debts. By accepting that money he had compromised himself, and if he failed to keep his end of the bargain, the puppet masters who controlled him could ruin him by reporting him to the British authorities. He would be placed on trial and then executed as an espionage agent.

Because he was Lord Symes, every door in Boston had been opened to him, and in the two weeks he had spent in the town, he had dined with the governor of Massachusetts Bay, owners of merchant fleets, distinguished attorneys, and other prominent colonial citizens. The weather was raw and cold, and at the same time the provincial atmosphere was stifling. He could take credit only for avoiding the gaming tables at the private clubs where he had been entertained.

During his stay in Boston, he had picked up enough

tidbits of information about the war plans of Massachusetts Bay to send a preliminary report that would satisfy his employers temporarily. As he well knew, however, the data he had gleaned lacked substance. He needed to learn the size and disposition of the Massachusetts Bay militia, the largest military organization in the English colonies, and even more important, how and where they would be deployed when they went into the field.

His discreet inquiries revealed that such information was available only in Fort Springfield on the Connecticut River, at the western end of the colony, where Major General Andrew Wilson made his home and headquarters.

Drinking far more than was good for him in order to stifle the waves of guilt that threatened to overwhelm him, Kenneth nevertheless remained a dashing figure, and his colonial hosts did everything in their power to grant any wishes he expressed. When he announced casually that he would like to visit Fort Springfield so he could taste life on the edge of the wilderness, arrangements were made quickly. A letter was dispatched to General Wilson, who replied cordially and promptly that he would welcome Lord Symes as his guest.

The success of the maneuver was absurdly simple, and after spending almost three weeks in Boston, Kenneth set out for the town at the far end of the colony. Living conditions on the road were deplorable, he soon discovered. After riding a rented horse all day on rutted, snow-littered roads, he stayed at inns where the meals were barely edible and the sleeping accommodations primitive. He dreaded what lay ahead.

To his astonishment he found that the Wilsons' home was as spacious and as comfortable as any country house he had ever visited in England. He was greeted cordially by his hostess, Mildred Wilson, and her daughter-in-law, Adrienne. General Wilson and his son, Jeffrey, were attending a conference of intercolo-

nial military leaders in New York, but the visitor
nevertheless was urged to stay until they returned.

The food was delicious, his bedchamber was large
and comfortable, and when he expressed a desire to
visit the fort, manned by troops of Colonel Jeffrey
Wilson's regiment, the doors were opened to him without delay. Still drinking far too much, Kenneth began
to enjoy himself for the first time since his arrival in
the New World. Adrienne's hospitality was largely responsible.

Mildred was recovering from a bout of the ague, a
common ailment in a land where the snow was piled in
deep drifts, so the burden of entertaining the noble
guest fell on Adrienne. While still performing her
household duties and carefully supervising the activities of her small daughters, Patience and Margot, she
took the time to make certain that Kenneth was occupied and at ease.

Relishing the attention, Kenneth was fascinated by
the vivacious, red-haired young beauty who spoke English with a trace of a French accent. That accent
upset him until he learned she had been a Huguenot
refugee, driven from her native France by the bigotry
of King Louis XIV. Sympathizing with her, he recognized the irony of his own position. He was working
against his will for a monarch whom all freedom-loving
English people despised.

Adrienne gave a small supper party in the visitor's
honor, and it did not matter to Kenneth in the least
that the other guests were frontier colonials with no
knowledge of London. Adrienne's presence made the
evening a delight for him, and he eagerly anticipated
dining with her at noon and again in the evening each
day.

It dawned on him, after several days at the Wilson
house, that he was infatuated. Perhaps the absence of
female companionship since he had left England was
responsible, and he warned himself not to create complications that might embarrass his charming hostess

or endanger his mission. But the large quantities of rum and brandywine that he consumed at the table and after meals numbed his sense of the proprieties. It was not difficult to convince himself that Adrienne Wilson was developing a personal interest in him.

One evening, when they dined alone, he was even more conscious of her as a woman than he had been previously, perhaps because she was wearing a sophisticated, low-cut, form-fitting gown. Downing several tumblers of rum with his meal, he convinced himself that Adrienne was flirting with him. It did not occur to him that she was naturally high-spirited and that she was making every effort to make him feel at home here.

After the meal they adjourned to a small sitting room, where Kenneth built up the fire already burning in the hearth. The atmosphere was conducive to intimacy, and he realized he badly wanted this woman.

Adrienne knew he had been drinking large quantities of liquor, but so far he had been able to handle it, so she did not hesitate to wave him to the crystal decanter of brandywine that stood on a table at one end of the room. "Help yourself," she said. "We may not have brandywine in the house much longer."

"Why is that?" He poured himself a generous drink.

"The English have never learned the secrets of distilling brandywine. It comes only from France and Spain, and all of our trade with them has been cut off since the start of the war. We could still get it by way of the West Indies, of course, but Jeffrey and his father refuse to deal with the enemy, even indirectly, and I endorse their stand. There are times I wish I were a man so I could fight the French, too!"

Kenneth raised his glass to her. "I can't imagine you as a man." Adrienne smiled. "You grace the world far more as a woman," he went on. Adrienne was beginning to feel uncomfortable.

"I hope you won't think I'm being overly inquisitive," Kenneth said, taking another large swallow of his drink. "But perhaps you can satisfy my curiosity. What do people in this remote corner of the world do for excitement and pleasure?"

Relieved at the change in subject, Adrienne laughed as she flipped back a long lock of auburn hair. "I've lived in Paris and London, but life on the frontier is very different. The greatest satisfaction comes from doing one's work well. My husband and his father are always busy. Managing this estate and directing the militia take up most of their time."

"I can see that it would. But what about you?"

"Well," she said, "my children keep me occupied. So does helping my mother-in-law operate a large household. We do a great deal of official entertaining."

He drained his glass and returned to the decanter for another drink. "That's all well and good, but there must be times when you seek pleasure for its own sake."

She failed to grasp the point he was trying to make. "We invite friends here for meals, and we go to their houses. In the summer we have picnics and roast meats and fish out of doors."

"That doesn't sound very exciting to me." Kenneth downed his fresh drink, not realizing that he was no longer steady on his feet. "Surely you must engage in an occasional romance to add some spice to frontier living."

Adrienne was shocked. "You must be joking, sir," she said, in an attempt to evade the meaning of his leading remark. "I'm a married woman."

"Having lived in two of the world's most cosmopolitan cities, you must know that married ladies avail themselves of certain—ah—privileges and opportunities."

Her eyes turned cold. "I don't regard such encounters as being privileged, sir."

He was unabashed. "That's a pity."

"Furthermore, you surprise me. Is it your idea of

pleasure to seduce married women?" Adrienne felt she had been insulted and wanted to strike back at him.

Kenneth laughed wryly. "At one time, not too long ago, I found far more excitement than I wanted at the gaming tables. My present vocation is thoroughly distasteful. In fact, it sometimes makes me ill."

It hadn't occurred to her that a prominent nobleman might have a vocation. "What is your profession?"

The drink had made him reckless. "I wish I could tell you, my dear. But it happens to be very secret. You might even call it a state secret." He placed his empty glass on the table beside him with such force that he cracked it. "So an occasional drink to help me forget and an equally occasional romance, with a lady who is lovely and charming, are my only remaining pleasures."

Adrienne froze as he started to move toward her, too late realizing she should have cut him off before. She knew, also, that he was too intoxicated for her to appeal to his honor and reason, so she tried to evade him.

But Kenneth was too quick for her. Grasping her wrist, he tried to pull her to him.

Frontier living had given Adrienne great physical strength. Although his grip was firm, she managed to wrench free. Then she shoved him so hard that he half fell into a chair behind him, and before he could recover, she fled from the sitting room. Racing up the broad central staircase, she ran to her own bedroom suite and bolted the door behind her.

He had enough sense not to follow her, and gradually she grew calmer. Her first instinct was to tell her mother-in-law, then ask Lord Symes to leave. But, as she thought about the incident, she began to wonder what lay behind it. His talk of his "vocation" being a "state secret" intrigued her. And why did he feel compelled to drink excessively in order to put that work out of his mind?

There would be ample time in the morning to tell Mildred what had happened and then ask him to go elsewhere. Adrienne was afraid she was being cowardly, that she was reluctant to create a scandal, and she wondered if she was simply using her curiosity about him as an excuse to avoid an ugly scene. She didn't know.

She slept poorly that night, and in the morning she followed her usual routine, having breakfast with Patience and Margot in their nursery, then paying a short visit to her mother-in-law, to whom she made no mention of the previous night's incident.

As she was returning to her own quarters, she heard rapid hoofbeats and, looking out of the nearest window, saw Lord Symes riding off at a gallop on his morning constitutional. It was apparent that he was suffering no ill effects from his indulgence, and she had to admire his horsemanship. Not even Jeffrey, who had owned his first pony at the age of two, was a better rider.

Reasonably certain that the wayward guest would spend at least an hour in the saddle, Adrienne hurried to his room. Perhaps she should be ashamed of herself for snooping, but she rationalized that if she found something, she could ask him to leave the house for reasons other than the advances he had made to her.

His clothes were hanging neatly in an oak wardrobe, his saddlebags were empty, and she could find nothing of interest in the chamber. Then, as she was about to leave, she caught a glimpse of a leather-bound book he had taken from the library on the ground floor. A portion of a folded paper lay beneath it. She picked it up, unfolded it, and was stunned by what she read:

Fort Springfield

Total garrison: approx. 3 officers, 70 men.

On duty at any one time: 1 officer, 20 men.

Armaments: 5 small cannon, all six pounders

that seem to be in working order.

Morale: high.

Garrison carry inferior, old-fashioned muskets.

Attack from river side risky. Better to launch surprise

assault from rear. Could be accomplished easily by

force of 100 to 150 French regulars.

Adrienne's hand shook as she read the words a second time. Obviously he had made a detailed study of the fort's defenses. Why? The key phrase was his reference to "French regulars."

Her mind reeled at the implications. Unlikely though it seemed, she was forced to conclude that Lord Symes, the holder of an ancient, honorable, and distinguished English title, was an espionage agent in the employ of the French. She had discovered far more than she had wanted to find.

Now Adrienne faced a terrible dilemma. If she and her mother-in-law asked the man to leave, he would be free to continue his espionage activities elsewhere. Only Jeffrey and his father would know how to handle this situation, so it was her duty to figure out a way to keep him here for an additional seventy-two hours until they returned.

Before she could allow her mind to dwell on that difficult task, however, she had to copy his notes. She went to her sitting room for more paper, copied the document, and then carefully refolded it, placing it beneath the book where she had found it.

Only now could she concentrate. A man of any sensitivity would depart without delay after his advances had been angrily rebuffed by his hostess. She could not allow that to happen. Somehow, she would have to persuade Lord Symes that her rejection had not been as final as he had thought. With great reluctance Adrienne came to the conclusion that she would have to play a game for the next three days. She would have to dangle herself as bait to keep him here until Jeffrey came home. She realized she might be in danger and would have to be very careful. Lord Symes was risking his life to obtain military information for France, and there was no way of knowing how violently he might react if he learned that she had discovered his secret.

She could not take the chance of sharing what she had gleaned with her mother-in-law. Mildred Wilson was a direct, forthright woman who well might show her contempt for the visitor. And if Lord Symes felt cornered, he might injure the women or the two little girls.

Bracing herself for what lay ahead, Adrienne deliberately chose a provocative dress to wear at dinner, then devoted great care to applying make-up. She even went so far as to affix a small, black velvet beauty patch to one cheekbone, then placed another above her cleavage, calling attention to it.

Her insides were churning, but she managed to look serenely lovely when she met Lord Symes in the sitting room before dinner.

Kenneth bowed stiffly and, giving her no chance to speak, launched into an address that he had been rehearsing. "Mistress Wilson, I hope you have it in your heart to forgive me before I take myself elsewhere. My only excuse for my behavior last night was that I was under the influence of drink, but even that is no excuse." He paused for breath.

Adrienne interrupted quickly. "I'm the one who must apologize, milord."

She took him by surprise, and he could only murmur, "You, ma'am?"

"I have been living in the wilderness outpost for years, milord, and I had forgotten how people behave in a more advanced society. I freely admit you startled me, sir, but I reacted far too strongly, and in the wrong way. On reflection, I should have been flattered. In fact, I truly am flattered."

Noting her low-cut gown and her use of make-up, Kenneth moistened his lips, wondering if it was possible that she was opening the door she had slammed in his face.

"You've given me food for thought, milord. Now I hope you'll be patient and give me time to readjust my thinking, my whole approach to life."

He bowed so she would not see his grin.

Adrienne's heart pounded. He would no longer think of leaving for another place of residence. Her greatest danger, which she could not minimize, was the possibility that she might encourage him to go too far. It would not be easy to skirt the edge of the water without getting her feet wet.

"Perhaps," she said delicately, "we could dissolve our misunderstandings in a glass of sack." She well knew that sack was less alcoholic than rum, and she was determined not to allow him to become intoxicated in her presence again.

"Allow me to do the honors." He went to the table in the corner and filled two glasses almost to the brim with sack. With a flourish he handed her one before raising his own glass. "Permit me to drink to you— Adrienne." He called her by her given name for the first time.

She managed to return his steady gaze. "I prefer that we drink to us—Kenneth," she replied. She could feel the blood rush to her face and felt certain he would assume she was proposing an assignation.

He smiled as he drank.

"I beg only one indulgence," Adrienne said. "I must have enough time to—to alter my thinking."

"How much time do we have?" he demanded.

She knew she had to lie. "I don't expect my husband to return for at least another week. The—the step I am contemplating taking is quite bold, and I know I'll need at least a few days to acquire the courage for it," she said coquettishly.

"To be sure." Believing he had already won her, he could afford to be generous.

To Adrienne's infinite relief, her mother-in-law felt well enough to join them at the dinner table for the first time since Lord Symes had arrived. In spite of her presence, however, and the need to converse politely with her, Kenneth had eyes only for Adrienne. She, in turn, realized she had to maintain the façade she had just created, so she flirted with him subtly, reverting to a manner that had been second nature to her before her marriage.

Mildred Wilson pretended to be unaware of what was taking place, but after the meal, when she retired to take a nap, she summoned her daughter-in-law to her chamber for a private chat. "I could scarcely believe what I was seeing, Adrienne, but you were offering personal encouragement to Lord Symes!"

There was no way that Adrienne could explain the situation. "You're mistaken, Mother," she said, speaking as calmly as she could.

"I think otherwise," was the grim reply.

"If I'm being rather animated in his presence, I have valid reasons for my behavior. I must ask you to trust me, just as I know that Jeffrey trusts me."

"You ask a great deal of a woman who loves her son and her grandchildren. And who has loved you since the day you first came to this house."

"I assure you I shall give you no cause to lose faith in me. Just as I hope you know that I love Jeffrey, no one else, and will continue to love him for the rest of our lives."

"Then why were you favoring Lord Symes with those smoldering, lingering glances?"

"You've lived in the New World far longer than I have." Adrienne did her best to make her lame excuse sound convincing. "You've forgotten that everyone in London flirts at meals. It's a harmless pastime, and it's universal. Lord Symes is a man of the world, and I want him to feel at home here."

"Not too much at home," Mildred said dryly.

"I beg you to have faith in me," Adrienne replied, cutting the conversation short by leaving the room.

She maintained her air of bravado until she reached her own suite, and there she collapsed. So many hazards confronted her in the days immediately ahead that she didn't know whether she could cope with them. She had to keep Lord Symes's hopes of conquest alive until Jeffrey came home and took charge yet, simultaneously, to discourage Kenneth from drinking too much, for fear he might become unmanageable. Now a new complication was added, that of her mother-in-law's suspicions.

Somehow, Adrienne knew, she had to carry the game through to the end. She remembered Jeffrey telling her that one well-placed spy could do more harm than could thousands of enemy troops in battle. She couldn't go off to war, but what she was doing could be a major contribution to the victory that was essential if the English colonies were to maintain their freedom.

Chapter V

A lain de Gramont could do no more in Quebec, so
he set out toward the south, accompanied by an
escort of several senior warriors. He himself wore his
familiar Indian attire of a war chief, but he intended to
travel close to the land of the Mohawk, so he and his
companions did not wear the paint that would immediately identify them as Huron. The party traveled rapidly, avoiding encounters with other Indians, and
reached the upper portion of the Hudson River without
incident.

There Alain called a halt and, giving one of his followers strict instructions, sent the warrior off to the
nearby main town of the Mohawk, carrying the forged
document meant to disgrace Renno.

Obeying his orders to the letter, the warrior, masquerading as an Oneida, presented the impressive-looking document to the sachem of the Mohawk. "This writing of English words," he said, "was carried into the land of the Oneida by a man with pale skin. He was an enemy of the Oneida, and he was killed. Before he died he said this writing has great meaning to all the people of the Iroquois League. The Oneida know no men with pale skins who can tell them the meaning of these words. But the Mohawk know many. So the Oneida give this writing to the Mohawk so they may learn the meaning of the black scratches."

No one in the town could read English. The sachem pondered for a time, then sent a delegation to Fort Albany, where the lieutenant colonel who commanded the garrison translated the document.

The Mohawk were stunned. "Are these writings true?" the war chief in charge of the party asked.

The militia officer examined the paper carefully. "All I know is what is written here," he replied. "I have never seen a royal decree, but the seal appears to be authentic, and I reckon this is the way a Crown decree would read. That's all I can tell you."

The sachem of the Mohawk was deeply disturbed when the delegation told him the contents of the document and the reaction of the militia officer. He promptly sent messengers to the Oneida, Onondaga, Tuscarora, and Cayuga, and their sachems came to the land of the Mohawk for a parley. It was difficult for them to believe that Renno was a traitor who placed the interests of the English ahead of those of the Iroquois, but the damning evidence in the document spoke for itself.

The Mohawk chieftain addressed his colleagues with feeling. "Renno is the son of Ghonka. Also, Renno has performed many great deeds for the Seneca and his Iroquois brothers. It may be that he had good reasons for accepting the gift of land and a house from the sachem of the English. So it is right that we hear what he will say when we show him this writing. If we are satisfied with his words, we will make no change, and he will lead us to war. If we are not satisfied we will elect another to take his place."

The other sachems agreed, and accompanied by their war chiefs, they traveled to the land of the Seneca. They sent no advance word of their coming, and only the drums of the sentries stationed deep in the forest announced their approach to the main town of the Seneca. A surprised Renno and his war chiefs assembled hastily and went out to greet the unexpected guests.

The leaders of the Iroquois nations were courteous, observing the amenities expected of fellow Iroquois, but Renno thought he detected a cool detachment in their manner. He had been on friendly terms with them since boyhood, subsequently fighting beside many of them in battle against common foes, and their attitude puzzled him.

The sachem of the Mohawk was blunt. "It is the wish of all the Iroquois that their leaders smoke a pipe in a Great Council," he said. "Let only the sachems and the war chiefs gather. Let there be no medicine men or senior warriors who hear the words that will be spoken."

Renno and Sun-ai-yee exchanged a quick glance. Only on rare occasions were the principal medicine men excluded from a meeting of the League's leaders. Obviously a grave military problem had arisen.

No time was wasted. A fire was lighted in the Council Lodge, and Renno instructed the senior warriors who would stand guard duty outside the building to close their ears. The leaders filed into the Lodge, where Renno lighted a ceremonial pipe, and there was an ominous silence as the leader passed it solemnly around the chamber.

Then the Mohawk sachem rose to his feet. "A writing of the English sachem who has now gone to join his ancestors has come into the hands of the Mohawk," he said, producing the forged document.

115

Without further ado he recited the translation that he had taken care to memorize.

Renno was shocked, although his expression remained unchanged. He stood and reached for the paper. He read it slowly, then himself translated it again, word for word.

"What says the sachem of the Seneca to this writing?" the Mohawk leader demanded sternly.

"The words written here are lies! King William of England gave firesticks to Renno. But he gave Renno no land. He gave Renno no great house."

"Can Renno prove his words?" the Onondaga sachem asked.

"It is not easy to prove that which never existed," Renno replied. Composing himself, his mind racing, he turned back to the Mohawk. "How did this writing come into the hands of the Seneca's brothers?"

The Mohawk leader described the visit of the supposed Oneida senior warrior.

Here, perhaps, was a clue, and Renno seized it. Looking at the Oneida sachem, he demanded, "Who is the senior warrior who took this writing from the man with pale skin?"

The Oneida leader was troubled. "I do not know this warrior," he said flatly.

Renno felt a surge of self-confidence. He appeared to be on the right track. "Who carries in his belt the scalp of this man with pale skin?"

The Oneida could only shrug.

The young Seneca looked at each of the Oneida war chiefs in turn. One by one they repeated their leader's shrug. Obviously none of them had ever seen the scalp of the white man who was allegedly killed.

Renno continued to speak softly. "Did the warrior of the Oneida who had this writing take it first to his sachem?"

"No." The Oneida sachem was increasingly troubled. Sun-ai-yee could not refrain from interrupting.

"Why would this warrior take the writing to the Mohawk rather than to his own sachem? This is very strange."

None of the Oneida could offer an explanation.

The elderly sachem of the Tuscarora rose to his feet. "Ghonka has served his brothers well. The son of Ghonka has served his brothers well. Ghonka would not betray the Iroquois. Renno would not betray the Iroquois."

Heartened by the support, Renno nevertheless wanted no doubts about him left in the minds of the League leaders. "No man knows the name of the warrior who brought the writing to the Mohawk. No Oneida has heard of the man with pale skin who carried this writing, and although it was said that he was killed by the Oneida, no one has seen his scalp."

Sun-ai-yee rubbed his belly vigorously. "This man with pale skin has never existed," he said, "and the warrior who went to the Mohawk was not a warrior of the Oneida."

The sachem of the Cayuga, who had never dealt with the English settlers and whose domain had never been invaded by the French, was thoroughly bewildered. More naive than any of the other leaders, he asked plaintively, "Why would a scribe make false writings?"

Rather than reply directly, Renno preferred to allow his colleagues to grope their way to the truth, and he said, "Renno lives in the land of the Seneca. The wife and children of Renno also make their home here. The skins of Renno, his wife, and his children are pale. If they wished to live in a great house in the far land of the English, they would have gone to that place many winters ago. If Renno wished to accept great wealth from King William, why would Renno linger here? If he and his family had wanted to join the English, he would have gone to their land. But he is here. He will stay here." For the first time he raised his voice. "Renno is a Seneca! His wife and children are Seneca!

They bow their heads to the sachem of no other nation!"

He sat abruptly, cross-legged, his back straight and his head high, making it clear that he had spoken his final word.

The sachem of the Mohawk was left in charge of the meeting. "Who would try to sow the seeds of hatred in the hearts of the Iroquois against their brothers?"

There was a long silence before Sun-ai-yee spoke contemptuously. "The French," he said, "who are the enemies of the Iroquois. Those who have fought at Quebec and at Louisburg know the treachery of the French, who fight not only on the field of battle but in many other ways."

The sachem of the Oneida finally saw the light. "The warrior who went to the Mohawk was not one of my nation. He was an ally of the French. He was a Huron or an Ottawa. He brought the false writing so the nations of the Iroquois would not go to war against the French!"

Renno was several steps ahead of his colleagues but made no further comment. El-i-chi and Walter had brought him the news that Golden Eagle once again was in the service of France. He was the only man clever enough to have devised a forgery that, if successful, would have destroyed the unity of the Iroquois and at the same time destroyed the reputation of the young Seneca who was his most hated personal foe.

There was no need to mention Golden Eagle to the assemblage. Before the pending war ended, Golden Eagle's and Renno's paths would cross, and the French officer-Huron war chief would pay for his treachery. Renno silently called on the manitous to hear his vow: he would not rest until the scalp of Golden Eagle dangled from his belt. He prayed that the manitous would grant him the favor of allowing him to meet Golden Eagle in fair, open battle so the issue could be settled honorably.

The Mohawk sachem held the false document high

over his head for a moment, then cast it into the fire. Everyone present watched in somber silence as the paper turned brown, flared, and then burned to ashes.

"It was agreed," the Mohawk leader declared, "that Renno would lead the warriors of the Iroquois into battle. Is it still agreed?"

The response was a loud, prolonged shout that startled the sentries on duty outside the building.

"Is there any sachem or war chief present who does not agree?' the Mohawk persisted.

No one moved or spoke.

"The Iroquois hope," the Mohawk continued, "that Renno will not bear hatred in his heart for those who doubted him."

"Renno does not hate them because he could not hate his brothers," the young Seneca replied firmly. He stood, indicating that the meeting had come to an end. "Now Renno and his brothers will eat smoked fish and roasted venison. Today we feast together, just as later we will fight together."

André Cooke believed he was the only white man in North America who had no wish to take sides in the war that England and France would fight in the New World. The young hunter and trapper who had spent a full decade living alone in the wilderness, sometimes taking his furs down the Mississippi River, sometimes carrying them overland to distant Virginia, had good reason for wanting to remain neutral. His late mother had been French and his late father had been English.

Not that anyone was forcing him to fight on one side or the other. He visited a civilized community no more often than once each year, and for long months at a time he was alone, living in the snug, secure cabin he had built for himself in the vast timberlands, near the bluffs, high over the east bank of the Mississippi. He was at home in the wilderness, relishing his successful, constant battle with the elements. He and the Indians who lived some miles from his cabin enjoyed a mutual respect, and they created no problems for him, although a sense of restlessness had pervaded the tribe in recent months. Unaffected by the growing conflicts among both the Indians and the Europeans, André continued to shoot game and catch fish, take berries, nuts, and herbs from the forest, grow vegetables in his garden, and make his clothes from animal skins. His needs were few. Self-reliant and proud, he was the master of himself and his environment.

No two days were alike, and when he awakened one morning, he was pleased that he sensed a hint of spring in the gentle breeze. Washing in the brook that ran behind his house, André dressed in his buckskins, combed his hair and full, dark beard, and decided to catch some fish in the Mississippi for his breakfast. Carrying his musket, a knife, and the carefully balanced tomahawk he had fashioned for himself, he strolled in the direction of the great river.

Suddenly he halted, all of his senses alert. There were people somewhere in the forest ahead. Perhaps the strangers were warriors of a friendly tribe, but he had to find out for certain; a man who lived alone in the forest learned never to take needless risks.

André advanced again stealthily, making no sound, then climbed a sturdy maple to obtain a better view. Only a short distance ahead he saw three short, wiry warriors, darker than the Indians of his own neighborhood. Since they wore no war paint, he was unable to identify them, so he guessed they were members of a distant nation. They appeared to be making a raft and were patiently lashing logs together with vines. It was a fair guess that they intended to float down the Mississippi on it.

A shock shot through André when he realized there were two young women seated on the ground a few yards from the Indians. One was blond, the other red-haired, and both were fair-skinned. Their clothes were torn and ragged, there were bramble scratches on their arms, legs, and faces. They both slumped wearily, looking miserable. His manner became grim when he saw a length of rawhide tied to an ankle of each, the opposite end attached to a stake driven into the ground. These girls were obviously the prisoners of the braves, and he decided he must help them.

He studied the warriors more closely. All were heavily armed. Aware that there might be still more braves in the party, he decided to act swiftly.

Devising a plan, he put it into operation without pausing to weigh the odds against him. He drew his knife, took careful aim, and threw it at the back of a warrior who was kneeling and tying a vine around a log. The blade sank deep into the Indian's flesh, and he slumped forward, then lay motionless on the ground.

His companions were alarmed and, snatching the bows and arrows that lay on the ground beside them, looked around wildly for their unseen, silent foe.

Taking his tomahawk from his belt, André let fly again. Few warriors could match his skill with such a weapon, and the razor-sharp blade cut into the second brave's neck, virtually decapitating him. Now the odds were even.

Unfortunately, the leader of the expedition had located his foe and, bracing himself, notched an arrow in his bow. Before he could shoot, however, the sound of musket fire echoed through the still forest, and the leader slumped to the ground, a bullet hole in the middle of his forehead.

André leaped to the ground, then ran toward the girls.

Frightened, Anne Ridley and Hester MacDevitt huddled together. When they saw the bearded, buckskin-clad figure racing toward them, they were afraid they were falling into the hands of a new tormentor.

He shouted to them in French, and they looked at him blankly. He tried again in English. "Are there any more warriors in this party?"

Anne was too terrified to do more than shake her head.

"André Cooke at your service, ladies," he said, smiling. "You have nothing to fear from me." Retrieving his knife and tomahawk, he slashed their bonds. "Perhaps we should leave this unpleasant scene of carnage to the vultures. Will you come with me?" Not waiting for their reply, he turned away.

They followed him into the forest for a considerable distance before he paused long enough for them to introduce themselves. "Talk can wait," André said curtly, and did not halt again until they reached his cabin, where he offered them gourds of plump, fresh berries and a platter of dried, salted fish.

They ate ravenously, although still uncomfortable in the presence of this tall, lean stranger who had saved them. "How far are we from Virginia?" Anne asked between mouthfuls.

"Virginia! The great river you saw just now is the Mississippi. How long have you been on the trail?"

"More weeks than we can count," Hester told him. "We've each worn out shoes and two pairs of moccasins."

"Who were these braves, and why were you their prisoners?"

"We can't answer either question," Anne replied. "My father is Brigadier General Austin Ridley of Norfolk. They abducted us from his house one night. We couldn't understand what they wanted, and they rarely spoke to us."

"They didn't abuse us, really," Hester added, "but they never gave us a chance to rest. We spent every day on the trail, and every night we were tethered to prevent our escape." She smiled as she looked around the sturdy, simply furnished two-room log cabin and the neat vegetable patch beyond it. "Did you make all this?"

"Of course. This is my home." He explained that he earned his living as a hunter and trapper.

Anne eyed him warily. "You spoke to us in French at first, I believe."

He understood her fear. "I am both English and French, so I am neither."

"Well, we're English colonists and proud of it!" she said emphatically.

André shrugged. "Everyone is entitled to loyalties." He took a kettle from the hearth and filled three large chipped mugs with a dark, steaming brew. "Acorn tea," he said. "It's an acquired taste, but try it."

Hester made a face when she took her first sip but forced herself to drink.

Anne drew a deep breath. "Sir," she said, "if you'd be kind enough to escort us back to Virginia, I'm certain my father would pay you a substantial reward."

"Impossible," he replied curtly. "I'd lose too much of the hunting and growing season. Besides, I have no use for any man's money."

"I'm not sure we could find our way alone through the wilderness," she said.

"You couldn't. And you'd stumble into the warriors of a dozen or more tribes who would take you home with them as their permanent captives."

"Then whatever are we to do? My family has no notion of what has become of us, and they must be frantic. We've got to return home."

"I'll think about the problem," he said as he stood. "Can you use firearms?"

"Of course," Anne replied. "I grew up on the frontier!"

"What about you?" he demanded, turning to Hester.

She shook her head. "I've never in my life aimed a weapon or pulled a trigger."

"I see." He loaded a pistol and an extra musket, then handed them to Anne. "I'm taking you at your word. I very much doubt that anyone will come near the place. If there should be visitors, though, use these only if you must. I'll return about dusk, if not earlier, and when I approach, I'll give an owl call. Like this."

He gave a credible imitation of the bird. "That way you'll know me and won't fire at me."

"You—you're leaving us here alone all day?" Hester was stunned.

"I have three mouths to feed, so I need fresh meat for my table. Please don't be foolish enough to start off alone toward Virginia while I'm gone. There are more dangers in these forests than you can possibly imagine."

"Having spent far too long in the wilderness," Anne said tartly, "we've developed lively imaginations."

"Good. Then you'll do nothing rash."

"Indeed we won't. And before you go off, sir, thank you for saving us. We had given up all hope of rescue."

He nodded in stiff embarrassment, then hurried away, quickly vanishing into the forest.

The girls looked at each other. "Well," was all that Hester could manage.

"Our savior appears to be a rather strange man. And a hermit."

"I think he's handsome," Hester said.

Anne smiled. "How can you tell what he's like behind that bushy beard?"

"Well, I do like his house."

"I've never seen a better made cabin," Anne admitted. "No air or rain will seep in here. And he seems to have a knack for making furniture."

"He's also a good farmer. Have you noticed the garden out there?"

Anne nodded, then sighed. "It's very odd. For almost longer than I can remember, I've been praying for our freedom. Now that we've been freed at last—or appear to be—I have no idea how to use my time. All I know is that we can't just sit here until Master André Cooke returns."

"I'm going to sweep and tidy the place. He may be a clever carpenter, and we know he's a deadly shot. But he keeps a messy bachelor's house." Hester found a broom of dried straws tied in a bundle and went to work.

Anne went out into the garden, carrying the musket and pistol André had given her, and quickly found work to keep her occupied. There were pea vines to be tied, and weeds and small rocks to be removed. After spending several hours tending the garden, she discovered a latticework fence that their host had devised to keep out rabbits and other small animals. It needed mending in several places, so Anne rummaged in a shed behind the cabin, found some strips of wood, and figured out how to plait them. The fence soon was in perfect repair.

She kept so busy that it was early afternoon by the time she returned to the cabin and saw that it was now spotless.

"I'm sure Master Cooke won't begrudge us some of this," Hester said, showing her a bowl of soft, yellow soap.

They went to the brook, where they took turns bathing and washing their hair. Their clothes were so ragged and filthy they could not don them again. In a cupboard in the inner room of the cabin, they found trousers and shirts of buckskin, which they put on, although they were far too large.

After they dressed Anne said, "Stay here. Keep the pistol, and fire it into the air if anyone disturbs you. I'll be within earshot."

"Where do you think you're going?"

"Into the forest to find some additional food for supper. You know I'll be careful and won't go far. I just want Master Cooke to know that we're earning his hospitality."

Hester stayed behind and spent two hours scrubbing a frying pan, a pot, and the kettle.

Anne returned with her pockets filled. She brought tuberous roots that she said were delicious when cooked in the coals of a fire, and several yellow pieces of a wild fruit that had a semisweet taste. Her triumph was a handful of herbs. "We'll use these with some of the dried meat in the larder and make a soup."

They were so busy that dusk came before they realized it, and they were startled when they heard the hooting of an owl. Hester hastily lighted two candles that she found.

A few moments later André appeared, carrying the carcass of a deer across his shoulders. When Anne offered to butcher it, André accepted. "All right," he said, "but don't cut the skin. You'll need it for the start of new wardrobes. The clothes you're wearing don't fit you too well."

"They were all we could find," Hester said, then laughed merrily for the first time since they had been abducted.

André looked around the house without comment, hurried out to examine the garden, and, when he returned, sniffed and looked at the soup bubbling in the pot. "You've been active," was his only comment.

Anne was spearing chunks of venison, affixing them to thin metal rods that fitted into a holder above the fire, and did not look up. "You saved us when we were in despair," she said. "We've chosen our own way to show you we're grateful. You'd best wash up," she added briskly, giving him no chance to reply. "The soup is ready to serve."

They ate in a strangely relaxed silence for a time, then André said, "I've been wondering all day what to do with you two, and I know of only one solution. I'll add another room to the cabin. Until it's done, you'll use my bedchamber, and I'll sleep in here."

Anne could not conceal her dismay. "I've been hoping you'd reconsider and take us to Virginia."

"I need furs, bales of them," he said, his voice stern. "I've got meat to smoke and lay in store for winter. And I have crops to grow. If I have a productive, successful season, there's a chance I might be able to leave late in the autumn or early in the coming winter. Otherwise, I'll have to wait until the next year."

"Surely you could send a message through your Indian friends," Anne replied impatiently. "They could tell my family we're here."

"The Indians around here are becoming unpredictable," André said. "There's no telling what they'd do if they knew there were two white girls here."

"You mean we'll have to stay here with you in the wilderness all that time?" Anne cried, ignoring Hester's attempts to silence her.

"I don't look forward to it any more than you do," André replied in a matter-of-fact tone. "My privacy has been destroyed, my cabin has been invaded by females, and I'll have both of you to support in addition to myself."

"We'll do our part," Hester said with sincerity.

"You're already doing more than is necessary," he declared. "That doesn't concern me."

"What does?" Anne demanded.

He stopped eating and glared at her. "The same things that bother you. Like it or not, the three of us will have to learn to live together under one roof. I'd be making false promises if I told you that travelers heading for the English colonies sometimes come this way. I've spent five years here, and I've yet to see another white man in the area. Besides, even if some came along, I'm not so sure I'd trust them to escort two pretty girls through hundreds of miles of forest."

"Are you telling us we can trust you?" Anne raised an eyebrow.

André tried to control his anger. "If I had wanted a wife, I'd have gone to Boston or Quebec to find one. When I've needed a woman, I've gone to Havana or New York Town. I know the difference between ladies and trollops. You'll be safe here, but don't provoke me. One of the reasons I've chosen to live alone is because I have a nasty temper. I tend to become ugly when I'm badgered."

"If you're asking me to keep out of your path, I'll be glad to oblige you!" Anne retorted. "I'll remember, as

I have no doubt you will, that we aren't staying here through our own choice. But we'll do what's required of us. We'll keep your house and tend your garden. We'll gather wild vegetables and fruits, and we'll cook your meals. Bring us animal skins, and I'll cure them. Then Hester will make them into clothes. We're not helpless, and we're not afraid of work. You aren't the only one who requires privacy. So do we."

"Then we should get along," he said, growing calmer.

She was still annoyed. "Speaking for myself, you needn't be afraid I'll work my wiles on you—if I have any. I'm not interested in becoming either your wife or your mistress, and I'm quite sure Hester feels as I do."

Hester was too embarrassed to speak.

André started to reply, thought better of it, and finished his meal in silence. Then, announcing he intended to get some wood for the fire, he left the cabin. The girls started to clean the dishes and cooking utensils.

"Have you lost your wits?" Hester asked in a harsh whisper. "This man not only saved us from those dreadful warriors—and whatever horrid fate they were planning for us—but he's taken us into his own home and given us refuge. Why are you going out of your way to antagonize him?"

"Why is he antagonizing me?" Anne demanded. "We'll pay our way here through hard work, and he knows it. It's his—his superior attitude that angers me. All that talk about privacy. And about wives and trollops. I just wanted him to know that I'm not interested in him either as a husband or a lover."

"You needn't be so vehement about it. He was wonderful—this very day—when he killed those three braves, risking his own life for us."

"I'm showing my appreciation in the only way I intend to show it," Anne said with asperity, pouring water from a bucket into the soup pot, then briskly scrubbing it with a pine cone.

Hester was bewildered by her friend's attitude. She seemed to be going out of her way to be deliberately rude to a man who was treating them with kindness and generosity.

Hester realized, however, that there was a difference in the way André treated the two of them. She didn't know him well enough to understand his personality, but it was obvious that, while he was being courteous, even slightly impersonal, in his dealings with her, he was actually abrasive whenever he addressed Anne.

Life in this remote wilderness cabin, although far better than the captivity they had been forced to endure, might be very difficult in the months ahead.

Queen Anne, the second daughter of James II, had been a homely child and now, in her late thirties, had become an exceedingly plain woman. Her figure was ungainly and thick in her taffeta gown, and the gems that sparkled in her rings and bracelets accented the awkwardness of her movements. Her Majesty was renowned for her clumsiness, if for little else. She had the long Stuart jaw and protruding teeth of her royal ancestors and unfortunately also had inherited her mother's deep-set eyes and poor complexion.

George, Prince of Denmark, her consort, was equally unattractive. He was a lumbering bear of a man, quickly bored by the routines and protocol of court life. His principal interests were food and drink, and his few friends said privately that he preferred quantity to quality in both. His duty required him to attend his wife's audiences and levees, but it was no secret in palace circles that he and Queen Anne, both hot-tempered and stubborn, quarreled frequently and violently about trifling matters. Prince George wanted no influence at court and, consequently, had none.

Lonely and neglected during the reign of her father

and that of her older sister, Mary, the wife of King William III, Queen Anne leaned heavily on the woman she regarded as her only true friend, Sarah Churchill, the Duchess of Marlborough. Cynics claimed that the duchess's sole motive for the association was the desire to promote the interests of her husband, but they were mistaken. John Churchill was well able to advance himself, and his wife had developed deep sympathy for the ungainly woman who had received no training for her exalted post.

One of the drawbacks of Sarah Churchill's friendship was that of attending all official functions at Whitehall because the Queen liked to gossip with her in private about those who made their obeisances at court. Today, however, the duchess looked forward to the first reception held by the monarch since her return to London.

Queen Anne and Prince George, tardy as always, entered the smallest of the audience chambers at Whitehall a half-hour behind schedule. As usual, they ignored the salutes of the scarlet-clad officers, the deep bows of a score of gentlemen, and the curtsies of a number of ladies as they mounted the two steps of the dais and seated themselves on their thrones. Only the duchess was at ease as she moved quickly to the dais.

"Good morning, ma'am, good morning, sir," she said briskly, then climbed the dais and addressed the Queen in a low, confidential tone that the courtiers could not hear. "The first audience is important, you'll remember."

Queen Anne's expression was vague. "Who is it I'm seeing?"

"An American Indian chieftain, his wife, and their daughter-in-law, who will act as their interpreter. He's the head of six Indian nations who are our firm allies in the New World. He's a king in his own right, and he'll be offended if you fail to treat him as an equal."

Her Majesty sighed. "Very well, Sarah."

130

The duchess remained close at hand so she could intervene if trouble developed. She nodded to the royal chamberlain.

"Your Majesty," he called, "I have the honor to present Ghonka, the Great Sachem of the Iroquois League."

The courtiers gaped as a tall Indian wearing a feathered bonnet and an elaborately decorated robe of buffalo skin came into the audience chamber. Several of the ladies tittered nervously when they saw that he was followed by two women, one a middle-aged Indian and the other, although also attired in a dress of doeskin, a young and attractive white woman.

The smiles faded quickly, however, as Ghonka walked the length of the carpet that stretched from the entrance to the base of the dais. His manner was dignified, his bearing was majestic, and he exuded the confidence inherent in a man of great authority. The courtiers, some of whom had served three monarchs and many of whom had known European kings and queens, were quick to sense the Indian's regality.

The duchess glanced meaningfully at Queen Anne. Her Majesty stood, gathered her full skirt, and descended to the carpet, then walked toward her guest.

The ladies and gentlemen were astonished. Only the reigning kings of major nations were accorded such honors. The room became very still.

Ghonka was the first to break the silence. Raising his arm in a stiff greeting, he said in his deep voice, "The Seneca and the other nations of the Iroquois League send their greetings to our sister."

Betsy promptly translated for her father-in-law, her voice firm.

The duchess nodded encouragement to her own monarch. Queen Anne cleared her throat. "We greet our brother," she replied.

Sarah Churchill joined her and presented Ena and Betsy. Ena inclined her head, so the Queen did the same. Betsy, to the relief of the court, curtsied gracefully, and immediately became the principal object of interest to those not familiar with her relationship to these Indians.

"Bring chairs for our guests," Her Majesty ordered.

The chamberlain repeated the order, and uniformed servants hurried into the chamber with armchairs.

Rather than return to the dais, the Queen deliberately seated herself with the party at the foot of the throne.

Prince George, who had been totally ignored, heaved himself to his feet, sighed petulantly, and moved toward the party. Ghonka promptly stood and took hold of his forearm in a grip of iron.

As the consort sat, he surreptitiously rubbed his arm where Ghonka had gripped it, and Betsy noticed that the duchess was amused.

Queen Anne struggled to make conversation. "We trust you are enjoying your stay in London."

Ghonka's reply was succinct.

Betsy elaborated on it in her translation. "The Great Sachem is grateful for Your Majesty's hospitality. He wants you to know how much we enjoy the house you have put at our disposal. But he feels the ways of the English are strange."

The Queen was intrigued. "In what ways are they strange?"

Ghonka spoke at greater length.

There was no way Betsy could translate his words diplomatically, so she did not try. "When the weather is cold, the women of the English wear dresses that expose their skins to it. People ride in carriages for short distances when it would be better for their health if they walked. Many good things to eat are disguised by rich sauces that ruin their taste. Many war chiefs of the English preen in front of pier glasses instead of going off to fight their enemies." She paused for a moment, then forced herself to continue. "The Great Sachem also finds it odd that a woman should be the

Great Sachem of the English while her husband does nothing."

The courtiers were shocked, but Queen Anne was delighted, and her cackling laugh echoed through the chamber. Now the ladies and gentlemen laughed, too.

Ghonka's face looked as though it were carved of stone, his expression unchanging. Then he spoke again, his voice sounding monotonous to those unaccustomed to the subtle nuances of the Seneca language.

Betsy was heartened by the response to the earlier part of his statement, so she translated more boldly. "The enemies of England prepare for her destruction. Thousands of warriors gather in France and Spain. They are building many large ships of war. They forge new cannon. They plan to kill all who stand in their path. But in London the people celebrate holidays. War chiefs drink the water that makes them dizzy, and they flirt with ladies. Everyone eats at inns and taverns where there is too much food. Theaters and concert halls are filled with people who give no thought to the danger they face."

Queen Anne looked stricken, and several generals and admirals in the throng were scowling.

Still not raising his voice, Ghonka made a few final remarks with somewhat greater emphasis. "If the people of England fail to arm themselves and go into battle against their foes," Betsy translated, "they will deserve to become the slaves of the French."

Admiral Sir Thomas Becknett, the First Sea Lord, and Major General Lord Grey, who was the Duke of Marlborough's deputy and happened to be home on leave, further startled the assemblage by applauding.

Sarah Churchill whispered something to the stunned monarch.

"What brings my brother to England?" Queen Anne asked.

Now Ghonka became eloquent, describing the situation in the New World at length and pleading for

Britain's assistance so her colonies would have at least a chance to win the war.

Queen Anne was ashen-faced. "My dear," she said to the duchess, "perhaps you can explain our new situation to our guests. It pains us too much to talk about such matters." She stood abruptly, bringing the audience to an end.

Sarah Churchill led the visitors to a private ante-chamber, and there Sir Edward Carlton, who had been present during the audience, quickly joined them.

Ghonka could not understand why the Queen had terminated the interview without replying to his request, and Betsy was completely bewildered.

"I should have anticipated this," the duchess said. "Her Majesty was embarrassed. For better or worse, her reign has entered a new era. King William had his troubles with Parliament, but he was a strong, competent leader even though he was married to a Stuart. Anne, poor soul, *is* a Stuart and consequently is unpopular. The House of Commons is very jealous of the prerogatives it has won, and within the past week notice was served on Lord Godolphin, the head of the Cabinet, .that the Ministries must be responsible through Parliament. That means the powers of the Crown are being severely limited."

Ghonka could only shake his head when Betsy translated for him. The Great Council of the Iroquois had a voice in the government of the League, but the Great Sachem allowed no interference with any major decisions that he made.

"What do we do now to win this country's support for her colonies?" Betsy asked, taking her own initiative.

"First, you'll have to see Sidney Godolphin. He'll decide what aid should be sent to the colonies, and then he'll seek Parliament's approval. When it has been granted, Queen Anne will sign the necessary orders and decrees. Her new position is delicate, and she can do nothing on her own."

Ghonka folded his arms across his chest when the statement was translated. Only Ena knew he was disgusted and angry.

"My husband is currently in Holland," the duchess said, "and I shall write to him immediately. Rest assured he'll send a strong letter to Lord Godolphin, urging that aid be given to the colonies."

"When can we see Lord Godolphin?" Betsy asked.

Sarah Churchill exchanged a significant glance with Sir Edward, then sighed. "Unfortunately, he's a man who places little trust in his subordinates. He does more work than he should, so his calendar is crowded. I've heard that it requires a month to set an appointment with him."

"More like two months," Sir Edward declared.

Ghonka's patience was legendary, but he thought the English were procrastinating deliberately. "The Great Sachem is not a beggar who waits many moons for a handful of parched corn," he said scornfully.

Betsy was afraid he would call off the mission at once and insist on returning to the New World without any assurance that Britain would give assistance to her colonies.

"Perhaps I can be of help," Sir Edward said. "I've known him for years, although I can't claim to be his friend. He has no real friends. I can force my way into his office by virtue of my position on the palace staff, and perhaps I can convince him it's paramount in the national interest for him to see Ghonka without delay. He's competent, honorable, and proud of his appointment as First Lord of the Treasury, so I'm certain he'll respond favorably when he realizes the colonies' needs are desperate."

Ghonka's anger cooled somewhat.

Betsy finished the translation, then turned to the diplomat, her eyes glowing. "You're being wonderful, Edward," she said impulsively. "I don't know how to thank you."

At the appropriate time she would learn the thanks

135

he wanted, he thought, and then smiled. "I make no promises, but I'll do my best. Dine with me this evening, Betsy. I'll make it my business to see Godolphin today, and perhaps by tonight I can give you a specific date for the appointment with him."

"We're so grateful to you," she said, and if she had known him better, she would have kissed him.

Sir Edward knew about the problems of the New World colonies and those of their savage allies, but it was only the personal gratitude of this lovely young woman that was of interest to him.

Adrienne Wilson's agony of suspense came to an end when her husband returned home, saying that his father would remain in New York for a few more days. Jeffrey was introduced to Lord Symes, whom he greeted cordially, and when they started to chat, Adrienne saw that her mother-in-law was eager to take her son off for a private conversation.

It was essential that she herself speak with him first, so she unhesitatingly interrupted them. "Jeffrey," she said, "you and Lord Symes will have ample time to talk at supper. There are some matters I need to discuss with you."

Jeffrey was surprised by her unexpected bluntness but excused himself and followed his wife to their private sitting room.

Adrienne clung to him. "I thought you'd never come home!" she exclaimed.

He realized her customary self-possession had deserted her, and he held her at arm's length. "What's gone wrong?"

"Everything." The words tumbling out, she told him in detail about Lord Symes's visit, including his drinking, his advances to her, and the notes she had discovered in his room. "To make matters still worse," she concluded, "I've flirted with him in order to make sure he would stay here until you returned, and your mother is convinced that I'm interested in him."

Jeffrey was not concerned about her fidelity and grinned at her. Then, as he sorted out her story, his smile faded. "Calling a nobleman of Lord Symes's standing a traitor and a French spy is a serious matter. Can you prove it?"

Adrienne went to her oak jewelry box, unlocked it, and withdrew the copy she had made of his notes regarding Fort Springfield.

Jeffrey studied the paper for a long time. His attention was riveted on two sentences: *Better to launch surprise assault from rear. Could be accomplished easily by force of 100 to 150 French regulars.*

"What do you think?" she asked anxiously.

"This is damning, there's no question about that. But it wouldn't be enough evidence to convict him in a military court-martial, and I daresay the civilian courts would be even more lenient. After all, he is a man of consequence."

"I'm sure he's guilty," Adrienne said. "I can't tell you how often he's said his work is distasteful to him and is responsible for his drinking. You can't imagine how difficult it has been to keep him fairly sober to prevent him from lunging at me. No wonder your mother has been suspicious of me."

Jeffrey nodded and continued to think.

"You—you aren't displeased with me?" Adrienne asked.

He took her in his arms and kissed her. "You're not only the best, most faithful wife on earth, but you've performed a great service for Massachusetts Bay. If you're right about Symes's espionage activity, you're a heroine. And even if you're mistaken about him, you deserve great credit."

She relaxed, content to nestle in his arms.

"I'll set my mother straight as soon as the matter is settled," he told her.

"What will you do?"

"I intend to confront him. Right now. I wanted to change into civilian clothes, but that will have to wait."

She knew he would have preferred that she remain in their private quarters until the issue was settled, but she accompanied him when he went back down the stairs. To their surprise they found visitors in the parlor with Mildred and Lord Symes. Reverend Obadiah Jenkins, the Fort Springfield clergyman, and his wife, Deborah, were among their closest friends. Jeffrey was pleased that his wife would be distracted while he attended to the unpleasant business at hand.

"Milord," he said to Symes after exchanging greetings with the guests, "will you walk with me in the yard?"

The request was abrupt, and the weather was too chilly and raw for a stroll, but Kenneth accepted gracefully. Alert and inwardly uncomfortable, he walked into the open with the militia officer.

Jeffrey led him to a place behind the storage sheds, where they could not be seen from the house. "Milord," he said, "I want to dispose of a nasty matter as quickly as possible. I accuse you of being an espionage agent in the pay of the French."

Kenneth felt as though the earth had opened beneath him, then closed again. His immediate problem was similar to that which he had faced so often at the gaming table: he had to keep his wits collected and bluff. Forcing a tight smile, he said evenly, "I'm not sure I appreciate your sense of humor, Colonel Wilson."

"This is no jest. I make the charge in earnest, milord."

"You are mistaken, sir, and I demand either proof or an immediate retraction."

Jeffrey took his wife's copy of the notes on Fort Springfield from his pocket and handed it to the nobleman. "The original of this document is in your possession, I believe."

Kenneth's blood ran cold as he read the paper, but his expression was one of amused scorn. "Do you call this proof, Colonel Wilson? Really, sir!"

Jeffrey's eyes narrowed. "What do you call it, milord?"

"The expression of an innocent pastime. Circumstances made it impossible for me to accept a commission on the Duke of Marlborough's staff, but I've been interested in military affairs for many years. I've made similar notes about every fortress I've ever visited in England, including castles where the sounds of battle haven't been heard in hundreds of years." Playacting superbly, Kenneth chuckled indulgently.

Jeffrey was positive that Lord Symes was lying and that his aloof manner was a pose. "How do you explain your reference to one hundred and fifty French regulars?"

"If it requires an explanation, which is absurd, I was using an example for my own amusement. You'd require far better proof than that, Colonel, before any court in Her Majesty's realm would condemn me to be hanged!"

He was right, of course, and Jeffrey realized he had been placed on the defensive. He was so sure of the man's guilt, however, that he regarded it as too dangerous to allow Lord Symes to wander where he pleased in the colonies. The man had to be immobilized, at least long enough for confidential warnings to be sent to the militia leaders of the other colonies.

A way of solving the problem came to Jeffrey's mind. "Do you also deny, milord, that you made sexual advances to my wife?"

"Surely you're enough of a man of the world to realize I meant her no insult. We live in the eighteenth century, Colonel Wilson, and pretty women can't be kept by their husbands behind locked doors." This lesser charge was so frivolous that Kenneth felt vastly relieved.

But Jeffrey regarded him coldly. "On my wife's behalf and my own, milord, I resent your actions. You have dishonored us, and I demand satisfaction."

Kenneth well knew he was one of the most accomplished swordsmen in England, and he had no desire to wound this bumbling colonial. "I shall leave your house at once," he said, bowing.

"Not so fast!" Jeffrey had resolved his dilemma. He had practiced swordplay since he had been a boy, and he hoped he could inflict an injury just severe enough to incapacitate the man for a few weeks. It would take no longer than that to warn the militia commanders to take steps to prevent an enemy espionage agent from learning about their defense installations. "I've already told you, milord, I demand satisfaction!"

There was no way out, and Kenneth realized it. Very well, then, he would inflict a harmless scratch and take himself elsewhere. Obviously he would learn nothing more about the state of military affairs in Massachusetts Bay, so he would go without delay to Rhode Island, Connecticut, and New York. "I am at your disposal, Colonel."

"If you'll be good enough to wait here, I shall return in a few moments." Jeffrey hurried off toward the house.

Kenneth paced up and down nervously. He was tempted to kill this interfering provincial in the duel, but that might confirm the suspicion that he was a French agent, and General Wilson might well order a full-scale investigation. A slight scratch that drew blood would be quite enough, and then Kenneth would put Fort Springfield behind him.

At least he had learned a valuable lesson in this remote frontier town. There was no way he could be detected if, henceforth, he wrote no notes, kept information he gleaned only in his head, and then committed the data to paper just once, when he wrote to the spy master in London. By proceeding with caution, he could remain in the service of the French until they felt he had satisfied his debt to them and released him from his disgraceful obligation.

Jeffrey approached, carrying a leather case that contained dueling rapiers. Obadiah Jenkins accompanied him.

The clergyman was distressed. "Jeffrey," he said heatedly, "you've asked the wrong person to witness your duel. I disapprove of the vile practice on moral grounds. Adult men who live in a civilized age should know better than to settle their disputes with blades that can kill! All disputes, no matter what they may be, can and should be resolved peacefully." Obadiah Jenkins knew well of what he spoke. In his youth he had accidentally killed a man in a duel and had never completely forgiven himself. He did not wish to see Jeffrey make the same mistake.

"I'm sorry to involve you, Obadiah, but you happened to be on hand, and this is a duel that simply can't wait." If the fight were postponed, Jeffrey was afraid Lord Symes would disappear, and the opportunity to stop him from doing more mischief might be lost permanently.

Reverend Jenkins appealed to Kenneth. "Surely you're a man of reason, milord."

Kenneth knew there was no way his opponent would put off the engagement, so he had to make the best of the situation. "You heard Colonel Wilson. I'm afraid my honor leaves me no choice but to proceed with this matter."

The clergyman looked even more unhappy.

Jeffrey opened the case of dueling swords, offering the challenged party his choice of weapons. The sabers appeared to be identical, and Kenneth took one, felt its balance, and was satisfied. He bowed from the waist.

"The proper form, I believe," the desperate clergyman declared, "is to inquire whether you will be reconciled. Will you, gentlemen?"

"I will not," Jeffrey said firmly.

There was no need for Kenneth to reply. The colonel was taller by an inch or two and appeared to have a slightly longer reach. He was strong and agile, in the physical prime of life, but the Englishman had no doubt that he would win the engagement. He was tempted to leave a permanent scar on Wilson's face, but he put the thought aside. Such an act of vengeance might be satisfying, but it would serve no useful purpose. All he needed to do was inflict a slight scratch on the lout's arm.

"Stand apart, gentlemen." Obadiah Jenkins was trying to make the best of his impossible dilemma. "On guard!" Both men took the duelist's stance.

"You may begin," the clergyman said lamely, then quickly retreated toward the wall of a storage shed.

Steel clashed against steel, and Jeffrey knew at once that he had more than met his match. Lord Symes's touch was light and sure, and the way he handled a blade indicated that he was an expert. Jeffrey quietly cursed himself for having been too confident. Having studied under a master-at-arms in London, he had acquired skills far superior to those of other men in the colonies, but his foe was even more accomplished.

The only way to win the engagement was to strike boldly and swiftly, utilizing his greater physical strength. He slashed wickedly, but his opponent's blade rose instantly, warding off the blow.

Kenneth was content to remain on the defensive for a few moments in order to convey the impression that they were roughly equal. It would be a mistake to advertise his expertise.

Jeffrey thrust repeatedly but was incapable of touching the nobleman. Lord Symes seemed to anticipate each blow and gracefully evaded it.

Kenneth toyed with the colonial for several minutes, then tired of the sport. Parrying neatly, he went onto the offensive, trying to pink Jeffrey in the arm. To his own surprise, the thrust missed by a hair.

The incomplete blow told Jeffrey he was certain to lose if the duel was prolonged. He felt a sense of desperation, but by refusing to go onto the defensive, he inadvertently adopted a surprising, unorthodox tactic. Kenneth had to draw back against the continued thrusts of his opponent. He was losing his ground.

Jeffrey thrust again, demonstrating more power than skill, and his blade penetrated Lord Symes's left shoulder. Kenneth fell back, lowering his sword and grimacing as a spasm of pain shot through him.

"The fight is ended," Reverend Jenkins announced, adding bitterly, "I hope you young butchers are happy."

"Blood has been drawn," Jeffrey said, "and I've won fairly, so I am satisfied." He bowed, wiped his sword on the ground, and placed it in its case.

Kenneth continued to stand, blood seeping through his shirt and coat.

"Are you badly hurt, milord?" the clergyman asked. "Here, let me see your wound."

With great difficulty the silent, mortified Kenneth managed to remove his coat. Even worse than the injury itself was the knowledge that he had lost the engagement to a rank, bungling amateur.

Reverend Jenkins examined the wound. "Here, hold a handkerchief to your shoulder and press hard," he said. "I'm no physician, but it appears you've suffered nothing worse than a nasty flesh wound. I'm afraid it will take time to heal."

"I will be leaving the Fort Springfield area at once," Kenneth said, through clenched teeth.

"You shall not, milord." Obadiah was firm. "Obviously you cannot remain here as the guest of the Wilsons, but you need to be examined by a physician, and judging by the blood you're losing, you'll do no extensive traveling for many days to come."

"I'm fine," Kenneth muttered, but even as he spoke he staggered.

The clergyman caught hold of him before he fell. "I insist you come to the rectory where my wife and I can look after you. It's the very least I can do for you after my inability to prevent the duel."

Kenneth, in no condition to argue, allowed himself

to be helped toward the front of the house, where the Jenkins's dilapidated carriage was standing.

Jeffrey felt a grim sense of satisfaction. Before the day ended, his letters of warning would be on their way to the commanders of the colonies' militia. If Lord Symes truly was a French espionage agent, as he believed, the man would be effectively neutralized.

Leaving Jeffrey to explain the situation to his wife and mother, Obadiah took the injured visitor to the carriage, then hurried into the house to fetch his wife. They drove home without delay, and less than an hour later the young Fort Springfield physician examined the patient and bound up his wound.

"Milord," he said, "you're fortunate. If the blade had penetrated a fraction of an inch to one side, you might have lost the use of one arm permanently. As it is, you'll need to rest for several weeks. I'll see you regularly and change your dressings. You'll do no physical exercise of any kind, and until I tell you otherwise, you'll try to immobilize your shoulder."

"But I can't stay here," Kenneth protested.

"Indeed you shall," Deborah said firmly. "Dueling is stupid, as I hope you've learned, but it would be an even greater stupidity to disobey the doctor's orders. It will be no trouble to have you here. My husband, our children, and I will enjoy it. We live simply, and I just hope you won't find our ways too plain."

"I—I'm grateful to you, ma'am, and to the reverend," Kenneth said huskily, suddenly overwhelmed by the kindness of these people. It had been a long time since anyone had shown concern over his well-being.

The Jenkins's small son and daughter were presented to him, then Deborah hurried off to the kitchen to prepare a small supper of soup, cold meat, and bread, leaving the disabled guest comfortably propped in the only easy chair in the parlor.

Obadiah helped the visitor to his seat at the table when supper was ready. Then, to Kenneth's surprise, the entire family bowed their heads, and the clergyman prayed for his swift, complete recovery. Obadiah ended his prayer on a note familiar to his wife and children. "Lord God," he said, "we thank you for this food, for allowing us to live together in harmony, and for protecting us from evil."

Kenneth heard himself joining in the "Amen." No one had ever before prayed for him, and he couldn't remember when he had last heard grace said at the table. In spite of the pain that throbbed in his shoulder, he was beginning to enjoy his stay with these direct, honest, and uncomplicated people.

How they would despise him if they knew he was working for the enemy. How he loathed himself.

As soon as supper was finished, Obadiah helped Kenneth to the guest room. He was given a drink of bitter laudanum that the physician had prescribed to dull the pain, and then he sank into a feather bed beneath a worn but marvelously warm comforter. As Kenneth became drowsy he thought again about how these simple, hospitable people had taken him into their home without question, and although their resources obviously were limited, they were sharing everything with him. There was obviously much more to life in these colonies than he had thought when he had first arrived in Boston.

Chapter VI

Alain de Gramont studied Beatriz de Bernardo critically as they sat beside a camp fire on the lower reaches of the Mississippi River, eating wild ducks that he had brought down that same day. At first glance, in her man's attire, she resembled a youth, but he was struck by her provocative sexuality, which her masquerade could not conceal.

Beatriz, for her part, had conceived an active dislike for this high-ranking French officer who wore a loincloth and war paint and shaved his head on either side of his long scalp lock. As she had commented earlier to her father, he was little better than the savages with whom he was traveling.

"Do not judge him too quickly," Don Diego had told her. "The French do not promote fools and barbarians to the rank of full colonel."

It was the Frenchman's arrogance, so similar to her

own, that caused Beatriz to bristle. She was willing to grant that he was an authority on the New World, where he had lived for so many years, but she could not tolerate the thought that he would be in charge of their joint enterprise. Her father, whom she admired above all other men, was wise, shrewd, and competent, and she had assumed that he would be giving the orders. Instead, the half-naked Frenchman had calmly taken command.

"We mesh well," Alain said. "I know more about the natives of North America than any other white man in the world. You have the funds that will buy them firearms, knives, blankets, and the rum for which they're acquiring a taste. So, between us, we should win a great many tribes to our cause."

Beatriz eyed him coldly. "Do you have any specific plans, Colonel, or is it your intention to wander aimlessly from tribe to tribe?"

The wench was being deliberately insulting and needed taming. "I always plan every move I make," Alain said brusquely. "We'll concentrate our efforts on the major nations. The Creek and the Chickasaw in particular. I hope we'll also find it opportune to visit the Shawnee and the Osage, who live far to the north. Neither of these tribes is large, but they are ferocious warriors. We'll also seek the support of some of the smaller tribes, like the Pensacola and the Natchez."

Beatriz exchanged a superior, amused glance with her father. The names of these Indians meant nothing to either of them.

Alain saw her look and promptly decided to put her in her place. "You may have lost us the help of the Biloxi. I have the distinct impression that your mistake is causing them to shy away from us."

Beatriz was furious, and her manner became icy. "I rarely make mistakes, Colonel."

"Well, you've made a bad one." It pleased Alain that he had put her on the defensive. "Your idea of kidnapping General Ridley's daughter, the wife of

Renno, was ill-conceived. You should have killed the woman; you should have made it appear that she was murdered by other Iroquois. That would have caused a rift between the Seneca and other members of their League. As it is, the entire enterprise was botched. We have no idea whether the young woman was even actually abducted. All we know is that three warriors of the Biloxi have disappeared without a trace, making the leaders of the tribe doubtful of joining in any enterprise with us."

"I am sure the warriors will appear one of these days and will have their captive with them. Then you will see how our enemies become immobilized."

"Well, I don't share that certainty. There is nothing even to suggest that the Seneca and the colonial armies have become distracted in their search for the woman." Realizing he needed the active, continuing cooperation of this woman and her doting father, Alain softened slightly. "However, what's done is done. Even if the Biloxi refused to join us, their loss isn't critical."

Beatriz recognized his reasons for backing down a bit, and she was conscious of the need for cooperation, too, so she smiled at him. Nevertheless, her eyes remained unyielding. "And even if *this* plan fails," she said, *"we* will not."

Don Diego decided to intervene before an open quarrel erupted. "How do you intend to win these tribes, Colonel?"

"Indians may be primitive, but they are far from stupid," Alain said. "If we're too crass in our offers of bribes, they'll reject us because they'll feel we've demeaned them. Keep in mind that most of them have never seen Europeans—or colonials, either, regardless of whether they're French, Spanish, or English. But the news of our fabulous weapons has spread to every nation. There isn't a warrior on the entire continent who hasn't heard of our muskets and pistols. All of them will accept me as a Huron war chief, Don Diego, and before we open active negotiations with each nation, I shall put on a shooting exhibition for them. I guarantee they'll be more than impressed. They'll be overwhelmed. Then we'll strike our bargain with them."

Don Diego nodded. The scheme was clever, and he had to admire the Frenchman's approach. But Beatriz had her own thoughts. "Is your marksmanship equal to the test, Colonel de Gramont?"

There was no doubt in Alain's mind that she was being deliberately insulting. "I'll let my musket and pistol answer your question, Señorita de Bernardo."

Her smile was enigmatic. "We shall see. For now, I will bid you good night."

He knew she had something in mind, but as she rose effortlessly and went off to the tent that had been erected for her, he knew only that she felt a measure of contempt for him.

"My daughter," Don Diego said as he, too, stood, "is very competitive. Do not take her attitude personally, Colonel."

Alain watched him as he went to a tent near that of Beatriz. They were an odd pair, and as he wrapped himself in his blanket on the ground, he hoped that Spain had chosen the right representatives for the difficult mission. Its success would depend as much on the de Bernardos as it would on his own efforts.

Thirty-six hours later the trio, accompanied by Alain's Huron and several Spanish servants whom Beatriz had hired in Havana, reached the main town of the Creek nation, one of the largest in the area. The visitors were welcomed with ceremonial speeches that, after the Indian fashion, lasted for hours. Alain replied on behalf of the guests, and he, like his hosts, spoke interminably.

Don Diego did not understand a word of what was said, but he was infinitely patient and managed to look absorbed throughout the slow proceedings. Beatriz made no attempt to hide her bored expression, and only her great self-control prevented her from fidgeting. Occasionally Alain glanced at her and had to admire her discipline: although it was plain that her thoughts were elsewhere, she sat as still as the Indians.

After the speeches ended and the medicine men of the Creek danced around the visitors, shaking gourds, chanting, and stamping, Alain de Gramont announced that he wanted to show the Creek the weapons of the white men. "This is a long firestick," he said, holding up a musket, "and this is a small one." He indicated his pistol.

The warriors started to crowd around him, but he waved them back. "Let all see what the firesticks can do," he declared.

A strip of yellow wampum, about eight inches high and almost as wide, was suspended at eye level from a tree branch. A silence fell as Alain walked about one hundred feet from the target and marked a line in the dirt with his foot. He then raised his musket and fired.

The shot nicked the lower left-hand corner of the wampum. The warriors filed up to it, examined it, and then marveled.

Advancing to a distance of fewer than fifty feet, he made another mark, then took aim with his pistol and fired again. The bullet passed through the strip of decorated leather on the right side near the top. Again the Creek were impressed.

Suddenly Beatriz de Bernardo was on her feet. Removing her hat and lifting her head proudly, she was making it plain to the Indians that she was a woman. Picking up her own musket, she walked with it to the line farther from the target. Bowing to Alain, her manner casually ironic, she raised the weapon and aimed.

The Creek watched in puzzlement. Never before had they seen a woman use arms of any kind. Beatriz squeezed the trigger, and the sound of the shot echoed across the Creek town. All at once the warriors were screaming and shouting. The bullet had made a hole in the center of the strip of wampum.

Alain de Gramont was startled. Never had he seen such expertise, and he tried to convince himself that it had been accidental, that the woman had enjoyed phenomenal good luck.

Beatriz handed her musket to her father, strolled to the closer line, then bowed again to the Frenchman. He raised his hand in salute and couldn't help grinning at her. In spite of her hostility to him, he was forced to admire her cool courage.

Still unconcerned, Beatriz fired her pistol. There was pandemonium when the Creek saw that the bullet hole in the leather strip was less than an inch from her previous mark.

The stunned Alain was gracious. "I never thought I'd encounter anyone who was my equal as a sharp-shooter, but you're much better than I."

Beatriz had won, so she could afford the luxury of a genuine smile.

She and Alain were escorted in triumph to a cooking fire, where quarters of buffalo were roasting, and the pair were treated as the guests of honor at the feast that followed.

Don Diego looked somewhat uncomfortable, sitting cross-legged on the ground as he ate chunks of smoking, dripping meat with his fingers. But his daughter, flushed by her victory, entered into the spirit of the occasion with gusto, looking and behaving as though she felt completely at home.

Alain and the sachem engaged in a lively conversation, with several of the senior warriors occasionally adding a few words. Neither Don Diego nor Beatriz could understand a word, but they sensed from Alain's complacency that he was making a satisfactory arrangement.

Not until later, when the trio gathered in the hut that had been assigned to Beatriz, was he able to explain. "I have promised the Creek two hundred and fifty muskets and two hundred and fifty pistols, along with ammunition and powder for the weapons," he said.

"That is a big order," Don Diego replied. "But, if I must, I shall send to Havana for one of my supply ships that is already waiting in the harbor to bring us what we need. I hope the Creek will be generous in return."

"They'll provide us with one thousand of their best warriors in the campaign," Alain said with deep pleasure. "They don't realize they won't have been trained in the use of firearms and will have to rely on their bows and arrows. But that doesn't matter. They're already convinced they will be invincible in battle."

The Spaniard was delighted and beamed at his daughter. "This is even better than I had hoped. I am sure you are responsible, my dear."

Alain's pale eyes gleamed. "She is, but in a manner that you well might not have anticipated. Indian women never go to war. So the Creek are convinced that the accurate shooting they witnessed was due exclusively to the magic of the firesticks. It's their attitude that if a mere woman can achieve such marksmanship, it will be simple for them to do the same." He chuckled quietly, convinced that he had scored in the duel the woman appeared to be waging with him.

Beatriz scowled for a moment, annoyed because her expertise had not been recognized by the Indians. Then the humor of the situation struck her, and for the first time she laughed merrily.

Alain joined in the laughter, hoping they had started to establish a bond. It would be difficult to work closely with her in the months ahead if she continued to treat him with suspicious reserve and hold him at arm's length.

A short time later, night having fallen, he and Don Diego went off to their own nearby hut. The Spaniard stumbled twice, unaccustomed to making his way in the dark, and Alain couldn't help wishing that the authorities in Madrid had assigned the liaison post to someone experienced in the ways of the New World. The de Bernardos, because of their apparent lack of wilderness knowledge, could prove to be handicaps.

While Don Diego prepared to retire, Alain sat outside the hut. He had no desire to talk further with the Spanish agent, so he lighted a pipe, deciding he would smoke it before he went indoors and rolled up in his blanket.

After a time he sensed someone moving slowly toward him, and in an automatic gesture he placed a hand on the hilt of his knife. Then he saw Beatriz and let his hand drop to his side again. She did not speak. Instead, she halted several feet from him and looked at him. Fortunately for Alain, he could see in the dark as easily as could any experienced Indian warrior. There was no need for her to speak. He could read the invitation in her eyes and was taken completely by surprise. Then Beatriz turned away and walked back toward her own hut, her hips swaying provocatively.

In the many days that Alain had been acquainted with her, he had never seen her indulge in such a feminine gesture. He followed her, wondering what had changed her opinion of him. She had to have some ulterior motive for seeking a rendezvous with him.

Alert, eager, and slightly bewildered, he followed her into the hut, and she allowed the animal skin covering the entrance to fall into place. Then, standing just beyond arm's reach, she slowly unbuttoned her shirt, removed her man's breeches, and in a few moments was totally disrobed.

Alain de Gramont needed no additional invitation. He threw aside his loincloth, and when he advanced toward her, Beatriz melted into his arms.

It was plain from the outset that she was sexually experienced. She responded to his kisses and caresses with a greater passion than his own, and he had to struggle to keep the initiative. It appeared that, as in all things, she wanted to be the conqueror.

But the Frenchman, still in the best of physical condition, refused to allow anyone to dictate to him, especially in lovemaking. His physical strength was greater, and ultimately he managed to master her.

Even in his moment of victory, however, Beatriz got the better of him. Her passion soared to a sustained frenzy, and he found it difficult to satisfy her. His own determination was as great as the girl's ecstasy, and only when she had succumbed did he collapse, too. They remained locked in an embrace, perspiring heavily, their breathing uneven.

Little by little they grew calmer, and Alain murmured to her. He was astonished when her steady, even breathing told him that she had already fallen asleep. Extricating himself, he donned his loincloth and returned to his hut. Only then did he realize that neither had spoken a single word before, during, or after their lovemaking.

Beatriz had performed brilliantly, as she apparently did in everything she undertook. But he couldn't help suspecting that she had experienced nothing other than erotic desire and the release that had followed. He had known many mistresses over the years, and only this young woman had been totally mechanical, filled with sexuality yet devoid of any other feeling.

Until this evening she had never indicated by as much as a look or a gesture that she was interested in him as a man. He had a hunch that she still had no real feelings for him. Her only purpose in going to bed with him must have been to attempt to gain domination over him and to place him in her debt. He guessed that sex was only one of the many weapons in her arsenal.

Very well. She had warned him. He would continue to bed her whenever she gave him the chance, to be sure, but henceforth he would be on his guard. The mission in which they were jointly engaged was of paramount importance to him. He had been given the opportunity to return to a place of favor with the

155

French high military command, and he intended to win recognition as the architect of the plan that would bring the territories of Great Britain in the New World into the domain of Louis XIV. He would be promoted to the rank of general, and a grateful monarch would be certain to elevate him to the peerage. He would accept the assistance of Beatriz de Bernardo and her father, and he would utilize their services in any way that might be of benefit to his grand design. But he would not share the ultimate glory with them. He alone would receive the dazzling honors that would be showered on the victor.

The walls of Fort Albany on the bank of the Hudson River were thick, studded with cannon and as impregnable as any fortress in the New World. One hundred and fifty New York militiamen were on duty at all times, peering out into the wilderness behind the settlement for any sign of trouble. These troops were assisted by a force of fifty Mohawk warriors, constantly on the prowl in the forest, prepared for the arrival of an expedition from Quebec. The fact that no one had learned any such mission might be sent against Fort Albany in no way lessened the vigilance of the defenders.

The room on the second floor of the wooden fort contained only a large, round table of unpainted pine, plain chairs, stools that militiamen had made in their spare time, and, on one wall, a map of those portions of North America that had been visited by explorers. Virtually the entire territory west of the Mississippi River was a blank, and as the French and Spaniards were believed not to have established any bases there, that section of the continent was being ignored.

Major General Andrew Wilson, commander of the Massachusetts Bay militia, was the senior officer present and the chairman of the conference. Directly to his right was Henry Patterson of New York, the only other major general, and beyond him were Brigadier General

Austin Ridley of Virginia and the leaders of the other colonies' militia. On General Wilson's left sat Renno, who interpreted for the other Iroquois sachems beyond him. Of all the Indians present, only he was comfortable sitting in a chair.

"First, I want to bring everyone present up to date on actual military developments," Andrew Wilson said, moving to the map. "We have received word that a full regiment of Spanish troops from St. Augustine has marched to the west. They are currently in camp on a fine bay that rests on the Gulf of Mexico." He pointed to a spot where, many years later, the city of Mobile, Alabama, would be located. "The Spaniards have been joined by a contingent of French regulars that had been stationed in the West Indian Islands. I'll let the sachem of the Iroquois pass along news that has just been received by the Seneca."

Renno said a few words to his fellow sachems, then addressed the militia commanders. "Indian nations friendly to us have sent messengers to inform us that the Creek have moved into the fold of the French and the Spanish," he said.

The militia leaders looked at each other in dismay, and General Ridley addressed his son-in-law. "The Creek of the East or the Creek of the West?"

"The Creek of the West," Renno said. "The eastern branch will remain neutral, we are told by the Tuscarora. They want no war with the Iroquois. They are wiser than their cousins. But the threat from the Creek of the West is very serious. The messengers bring word that one thousand Creek will join the regiments of French and Spanish troops. That is only the start. Three whites are busy trying to recruit all of the major tribes of the area. One is a Frenchman who dresses as an Indian and wears the war paint of the Huron. Only one man fits that description—Colonel Alain de Gramont, whom my brothers know as Golden Eagle." His jaw jutted forward. "I look forward to meeting him again in combat. The others are a Spanish man and a

157

Spanish young woman. It is said that she rides and shoots with the skill of a man, although these reports well may be exaggerated. All we know for certain is that Indians of the region call her the she-devil."

"What is important here," General Wilson interjected, "is that other tribes will be bribed or otherwise persuaded to join the forces of the enemy. All of this activity, combined with the failure of the French and their allies to mobolize in Quebec, has convinced a number of us that the major attack of the French will be launched from the southern sector."

"Consequently," General Patterson added, "we must dispatch an expedition in sufficient strength to prevent our foes from gaining their objective."

"At the same time, however," Andrew Wilson declared, "we can't allow ourselves to forget that the southern maneuver may possibly be a feint. We don't know. Therefore, we're required to keep the bulk of our own forces at home to protect our colonies and the lands of our Iroquois allies. Does anyone question this overall strategy?"

There was a long silence after Renno translated for the Iroquois, and one sachem after another shook his head.

"I agree without reservation," Austin Ridley declared, "but the expedition we send off to smash the enemy must be powerful enough to accomplish that goal. A token force can't do the job."

"All of us have the primary desire to protect our own borders," General Patterson said. "I believe it will be fair if we ask for volunteers to form the expedition. Only if the numbers fall short of what's needed should General Wilson and Sachem Renno make additional assignments."

A brief recess was called and the Iroquois withdrew to a far corner, where they sat on the floor in a circle and debated their problem. Meanwhile, the militia commanders remained at the table and held their own private talk.

Then General Wilson called the Iroquois back to the table. "It has been decided," he said, "that Massachusetts Bay will send one-third of her entire army, a full regiment, on the expedition. I have the honor to inform you that my son, Colonel Jeffrey Wilson, has volunteered the services of his frontier regiment."

Austin Ridley cleared his throat and smiled at his son-in-law. "I reckon this will be something of a family expedition. Lieutenant Colonel Ned Ridley's battalion of riflemen has volunteered, too."

"That makes about five hundred militiamen in all," General Patterson of New York said. "If you need more, I'll supply you with one of my regiments."

"And I'll send a battalion," the Connecticut commander said promptly.

"I'll send two batteries of artillery," the head of the Rhode Island militia declared.

"It would be too difficult for your artillery to transport their cannon through the wilderness," General Wilson replied. "As for New York and Connecticut, we'll keep your offers in mind, gentlemen, and I thank you, but we want a force familiar with the wilderness so they can move swiftly. What do you think, Renno?"

"I will march with the men from Massachusetts Bay and Virginia myself," the young Seneca said, "and I will bring one thousand of my warriors."

The contribution was so large that the militia leaders were deeply impressed.

"It has been agreed," he continued, "that I also will lead four hundred Mohawk and one hundred Oneida, who will act as scouts. All of the nations of the Iroquois will join in protecting our lands from invasion by the French, the Huron, and the Ottawa while we are away from our homes."

The matter was discussed exhaustively, and it was agreed that a total expedition of two thousand of the finest fighting men the colonies and the Iroquois could provide would be sufficient. Other forces would be designated to help them if necessary and would be dispatched quickly if word was received that assistance was required.

The Iroquois could not imagine such a situation. "An army led by one thousand Seneca will sweep away the enemy like grains of dust," the sachem of the little Cayuga nation said in awe.

"Only one question remains," General Wilson said. "The appointment of an overall commander of the expedition."

"If you please, sir," Renno interjected, "we will not want or need any one man to be in command. Ned Ridley is my brother-in-law. Jeffrey Wilson is my old friend. All of us fought together at Louisburg. Each of us knows the minds of the others. We will work together, but no one man will be in command, and in that way my warriors and the troops of Massachusetts Bay and Virginia will not become jealous of each other."

General Patterson thought the solution was brilliant. Rivalries between the colonies long had been a major stumbling block to effective cooperation and military coordination.

After further discussion it was agreed that the three separate units would meet at a designated point on the Ohio River and, for the sake of speed, would travel down that river and subsequently down the Mississippi on rafts that the men would construct for the purpose.

Austin Ridley had arrived just as the conference was beginning, and as soon as the meeting was adjourned, he went privately with his son-in-law to a small, secluded guard room.

"I know what you're going to ask, sir," Renno said. "Seneca messengers have gone to fifteen Indian nations to inquire whether Anne has been seen. Every sachem has sent me the same reply. No one knows what might have become of her. Or of Hester Mac-Devitt."

His father-in-law straddled a chair, resting his chin

on the top rung of the straight back. "Mary is worrying herself into her grave," he said.

"I'm sure she is, and I can't blame her for feeling as she does. It's a terrible situation."

"You haven't mentioned the subject to Betsy in your letters?"

The young Seneca shook his head. "There's no need for her to be concerned, too. She'll find out soon enough when she returns from London, if Anne and Hester haven't been located by then."

"What do you think has happened to the girls?"

Renno preferred not to speculate, seeing no need to cause the loving parents of Anne and Betsy more grief. It was possible that the girls had been enslaved by some remote tribe and would never be seen again. It was also possible they had been killed. "You know the forest, sir," he said. "All I can tell you is that the search will continue under the direction of those who will take my place in the land of the Seneca when I go off to the war. I will receive messages from them and will send them messages. We will not stop searching for Anne and Hester."

"If I ever get my hands on the swine who abducted them—"

"There will be no need for you to raise your hand," Renno said, interrupting him. "Ned and I will learn their reasons before we kill and scalp them."

Austin Ridley was a strong, self-contained man, but his face contorted and there was a suggestion of moisture in his eyes. "Renno," he said huskily, "when you and Betsy were married, I had my doubts about your future together because your ways of life were so different, or so I thought at the time. I was mistaken. You have the same sense of honor, the same principles, the same values. You aren't my son-in-law. You and Ned are my sons."

Sir Edward Carlton was diligent and persistent, motivated by a recognition of the colonies' need for assistance, as well as by his desire to seduce Betsy. Thanks to his efforts, an appointment was made for the Great Sachem with the First Lord of the Treasury only a few days after Ghonka had been received at court by Queen Anne.

Certainly Sidney Godolphin was no fool. A competent administrator with a clear understanding of national and foreign issues, a wily politican and a keen judge of human nature, he had risen to his position as First Lord, and thus head of the British government, through his own efforts. Consequently, he was intrigued by what he might learn from the Seneca chieftain who had created such a sensation at Whitehall.

Unprepossessing in appearance, the middle-aged Lord Godolphin was short, his eyes deceptively mild, and he put on no airs. In an age when other men wore gaudy clothes, he dressed somberly, and his second-floor office in a massive government building a short distance from Whitehall and the Houses of Parliament was modest, small, and simply furnished. His only luxury was an oversized hearth in which a log fire kept out the chill of London.

He and Ghonka sat in front of the fire, facing each other, while Betsy occupied a chair, set back slightly, so the two leaders could look at each other with their view unhampered.

The Great Sachem's manner was crisp. Judging the First Lord correctly, he knew the man's time was valuable, that this was not an occasion for long speeches. So his opening comment was both pungent and provocative. "Does the sachem of the English wish to defeat the evil Louis of France?"

Lord Godolphin's thin lips parted in a startled smile, and his eyes lighted. "My one aim in life is to defeat the tyrant who would deprive the free people of this nation and her allies of their liberties. I have no other goals, I seek no greater wealth than I already possess, and I want no new honors. All I want chiseled on my tombstone are the words, 'He destroyed Great Britain's worst enemy.' Does that answer your question, sir?"

As Betsy translated his words, Ghonka warmed to him. This was a man with whom he could deal. "The Iroquois are the enemies of the French, too. The English colonies are the enemies of the French. Like the people of England, they prize their freedom."

The First Lord realized that this grave savage was truly his peer. "What is your situation?" he asked.

The Great Sachem replied at length. The English colonies and the Iroquois who were on their side were badly outnumbered by the French and by the Spaniards, as well as by Indian enemies. Also, the French and the Spaniards had more ships of war in the New World than the English, and their armaments were superior. Most important, they were in a position to attack from the north or the south.

Lord Godolphin fingered his coat lapel in a nervous gesture that indicated he was concentrating deeply. "In other words, sir, the French have the option of taking the offensive. Perhaps taking a multiple offensive."

Ghonka shook his head. "The English colonies and the Iroquois will attack first. The enemy must be overwhelmed before he can gather his full strength."

"That is a brilliant strategy!" Lord Godolphin exclaimed. "Who is responsible?"

Betsy replied on her own initiative. "It was devised by Ghonka and the leaders of the colonial militia at a meeting held in Boston just before we sailed for England."

The First Lord looked at the Great Sachem with increasing appreciation. The strategy was almost identical to that which the Duke of Marlborough and Eugene of Savoy were employing in Europe. "You are wise," he said. "The regiments of the French are the finest soldiers in the world. The only way to beat them is to catch them off balance."

They were finding a common ground, Ghonka knew,

and he was convinced that the key to the success of his mission lay in the Englishman's obvious hatred of Louis XIV and his desire to conquer the world. "The Seneca grieve," he said, "because the French will win the war in America."

Betsy was so stunned by the totally unexpected, pessimistic statement that she was speechless.

Ghonka repeated the comment, indicating with a gesture that he wanted it translated at once. Hesitating for a moment longer, Betsy reluctantly translated the remark.

Lord Godolphin was equally surprised. "We cannot afford to be defeated. Great Britain's future lies in the continuing development and expansion of her New World colonies. If they fall to the French, Louis will become even wealthier and more powerful. We cannot win in Europe unless we also win in America."

Ghonka was pleased. He had maneuvered the First Lord into a corner from which there was no possible escape. "Then the English must act at once. They cannot continue to do nothing and leave the task of defeating the French and the Spaniards to the colonies and the Iroquois."

Lord Godolphin became aware of his visitor's shrewdness and smiled broadly. "What are your needs?" he asked bluntly.

"It is not easy for the English to fight two wars at one time," Ghonka replied. "That is difficult for any nation. The Seneca know this. In the time of Ghonka's father and his father before him, the Seneca had to fight such wars. They defeated their foes. Now all the other Indian nations fear them, and many will not fight against them."

Godolphin was conscious of the lesson he was being taught. "What do you need to ensure that we will win the war?" he repeated, his voice betraying the strain he was under.

"It is not fitting that one who comes from a far land should tell the sachem of the English what aid he should send." Ghonka folded his arms across his chest, his bearing proudly regal. "Also, it is not the way of the Seneca to beg."

Godolphin knew the hard bargaining was under way. "We cannot spare any troops," he said flatly. "Every man who wears the Queen's uniform and has been trained as a soldier is serving under Marlborough. The French army is the largest, best equipped, and best trained on earth."

"The colonies and the Iroquois do not ask for more warriors." Ghonka was equally emphatic. "Our warriors have the strength of the bear, the cunning of the fox, and the courage of the great cat that lives deep in our forests. The war chiefs of the Iroquois are men of wisdom. None is a better leader than the son of Ghonka."

As Betsy translated his words, her heart pounded. Her father-in-law rarely praised Renno.

"The war chiefs of the colonies also are wise. They beat the warriors of the French at Louisburg. They can win again.'"

Relieved that he was not being requested to send any of the regiments so badly needed in Europe to the New World, Godolphin became more expansive. "I believe we can help you in many other ways."

"That is good to hear," the Great Sachem said gravely. "Even the most courageous of warriors cannot fight armed enemies with their bare hands. The men of the colonies need many firesticks. The Iroquois, who also have learned to shoot these firesticks, have too few of them. There is a need, too, for the large firesticks-that-speak-like-thunder."

"Our arms and munitions plants are already working day and night to manufacture firearms, ammunition, and gunpowder," Godolphin said, then made his first formal commitment. "But we will send as many muskets and cannon to the colonies as we can." He interrupted the conference to pick up a small silver bell, which he rang briskly.

A subordinate came to the door immediately. "You wanted me, milord?"

"Get me a full set of the arms production figures as of the first day of this month. Then give me a close estimate of Marlborough's needs. Keep in mind that he won't be fighting a major battle for a good many months. I want the figures no later than this afternoon."

The aide was dubious. "I—I'm not certain I can make the estimates that quickly, milord."

"Then I shall replace you with someone who can." The First Lord was unyielding. "I must have them without delay. Meanwhile, I want at least a half-dozen merchantmen diverted from other activities to carry a major shipment of arms to the colonies. We'll work out the details later."

The aide hurried away and closed the door behind him. Lord Godolphin turned back to his visitor. "Does that satisfy you?"

After Betsy translated for him, Ghonka shook his head. He had already achieved his major goal, but his eyes were still hard and firm. "The colonies also need ships that will fight the many ships of the French and Spanish," he said.

Lord Godolphin hesitated. "As it happens, I've been of the opinion that we're going to win the war in Europe on land rather than at sea. We have a smaller navy than the combined fleets of France and Spain, but we're better armed and our seamanship and gunnery are far superior to those of the enemy. And we're engaging in an extensive shipbuilding program that will give us even more of an edge. The Admiralty may protest, but I can certainly give the colonies greater protection at sea."

Ghonka nodded, waiting to hear more.

"I always keep an eye on the development of trade between our North American and West Indian colonies, as well as what we ourselves are importing from both regions. So I regard it as vital that we keep our sea-lanes open. Can you be specific in giving me the needs of the colonies?"

Betsy translated his words, then took her own initiative again. "The Great Sachem is a soldier, not a sailor, milord. The land of the Seneca lies far inland from the Atlantic Ocean. So, in preparation for this meeting, the governors and military leaders of the colonies prepared a list of their needs. Naturally, these are their minimum requirements." She handed Godolphin a sealed document.

He broke the seal, unfolded the single sheet of paper, and studied it. Then he sat back in his chair and smiled. "This is a very modest list," he said. "You're sure this is all the colonies are asking?"

"Quite sure, milord," Betsy said.

"They want only two ships of the line, three to five frigates, and no fewer than a dozen sloops of war, together with several bomb ketches—the precise number having been left to the discretion of the Admiralty. Britain would be a poor nation indeed if she couldn't meet those needs, and we would deserve to lose the war. Tell the Great Sachem that I pledge a minimum of three ships of the line, five frigates, and fifteen sloops of war. I'll leave the bomb ketches to the Admiralty to determine."

His generosity was breathtaking, befitting a man whose nation was the world's leading maritime power, and Betsy was so relieved she didn't know whether to laugh or weep.

Ghonka remained impassive but acknowledged the support being offered by inclining his head for a moment.

"We'll need approximately one month to assemble the Royal Navy squadron, load the merchant ships with arms, and arrange for the squadron to escort them across the Atlantic. The French wouldn't dare attack that strong a fleet."

"Thank you, milord, on behalf of all the colonies and the nations of the Iroquois," Betsy said impulsively.

Ghonka had learned just enough English to make out what she was saying, and then he added a definitive word of his own. "The sachem of the English," he said with slow emphasis on each word, "is the brother of the Great Sachem of the Iroquois." He could offer no greater compliment.

Lord Godolphin was deeply touched, and after shaking hands with Ghonka, he took the initiative in grasping the Seneca's forearm. For the first time Ghonka's composure was shaken, and he grinned.

Suddenly the thought occurred to Betsy that the mission had been completed. "Now we can go home!" she exclaimed joyfully.

"Let me urge you to wait until the flotilla of warships and merchantmen sails to the New World," Lord Godolphin said. "The French have agents in England, you may be sure, and they would know if you sailed on an unescorted ship. They would like nothing better than to take the leader of the Iroquois captive and hold him as a prisoner until the war ends. The Royal Navy can provide Ghonka with the safety he requires."

The suggestion was sensible, and Ghonka, who had no need to prove his courage to anyone, was prudent enough to accept.

Betsy conquered her feeling of disappointment. She would have to remain in England for another month, but at least she knew now when she would be going home. The spring would be well advanced by the time she and the children reached the land of the Seneca with Ghonka and Ena, so it was too much to hope that Renno would still be there. She knew he would be on the march with his warriors as soon as all necessary preparations were made.

Sir Edward Carlton was waiting for Betsy and Ghonka in one of the reception rooms, and Betsy offered him her warm thanks for the assistance he had rendered. Delighted that the mission had succeeded, he promptly asked her to dine with him that same evening.

"I'm sorry," she said, "but I want to celebrate in our own way with Ghonka, Ena, and my children. You don't know how much this aid from Great Britain means to us—and to everyone in the New World."

"Through you I've gained a fairly good idea," Sir Edward replied. "Unfortunately, I'm required to go to the country tomorrow with Queen Anne and Prince George. I'll spend the next week out of the city, but I hope you'll go to the theater with me and have supper afterward on the day I return."

Betsy accepted without hesitation. She was deeply in the debt of this man who had done so much for the colonies and the Iroquois, seemingly with nothing to gain for himself.

The Seneca party spent the evening in the house they were using, and Ena offered prayers of thanks to the manitous, to whom she attributed the success of the mission. At the end of each prayer, after the Seneca custom, Ghonka, Betsy, and the children repeated the final lines with her.

The English servants in the house were startled. These extraordinary guests had broken many precedents during their stay, but even the imperturbable butler and the worldly housekeeper found it incredible that the Indian couple, the young white woman, and the two small white children should spend several hours chanting in unison.

The next day Betsy began her final shopping, prior to the voyage. Accompanied by Ja-gonh, who wore English attire and was instructed to speak only in the language of that nation in public, she went to the shops of a number of swordsmiths. After visiting several, she found what she was seeking, a double-edged, razor-sharp knife made of the best Sheffield steel.

"Papa will like this very much," Ja-gonh said.

Betsy nodded, then asked the swordsmith, "Do you have any others of the same quality that are smaller?"

"Indeed, milady."

The man returned with a large tray of knives, the longest of them only half the size of the weapon she had just selected for Renno. She looked at them carefully, then took one that was about four inches long. "I'd like two of these, if you have them," she said.

"Of course, milady. They're also gifts for your husband, I presume."

She shook her head and smiled. "No, they aren't. As a matter of fact, I'm giving one to my son and keeping the other for myself. Here, James."

Ja-gonh took the knife she offered him, inclined his head in thanks, then slipped it into his belt. In true Seneca fashion his face remained unchanged, and only the slight gleam in his eyes indicated his joy.

"You may wrap mine with the knife I'm taking to my husband," Betsy said to the astonished swordsmith. After she returned to the house, she would replace the more cumbersome knife that she, like all Seneca women, carried at all times, strapped to one leg.

The man muttered to himself as he packed the blades. Never had anyone purchased a weapon from him for a young child, and although it had been fashionable some years earlier for ladies to carry poniards no longer than their thumbs, he had never encountered any member of the fair sex who intended to keep a four-inch knife. He could not imagine the use for which she might intend it.

The following day Betsy splurged on dresses for herself and Goo-ga-ro-no, using the funds her mother had given her. Reckless and lightheaded because the mission had been so resoundingly successful, she went to one of London's leading dressmakers and ordered a low-cut gown of green velvet for herself, along with a green velvet dress for her daughter. There would be few opportunities to wear the gown in the time that remained in London, but she would take it with her on future trips to Virginia, where her family would enjoy seeing her and the little girl in the latest London styles.

By the time Sir Edward Carlton returned to London from his sojourn in the country with the Queen and Prince Consort, the gown had been delivered, and she decided to wear it on her celebratory evening with him. During her stay in England, she had carefully noted the appearance of other women, so she piled her pale hair high on her head in a manner currently in vogue, used more make-up than was her custom, and even affixed a green velvet beauty patch to one cheekbone.

When Sir Edward came for her, he thought she looked as dazzling as the smile with which she greeted him. He hoped he wasn't fooling himself, but she seemed genuinely pleased to see him, and he realized she had dressed with great care for the occasion.

Sir Edward had obtained seats in a private box for a performance of Ben Jonson's *Epicene,* or *The Silent Woman,* one of the most popular plays in every company's repertoire. Betsy had never seen it and was delighted by Jonson's dry, caustic wit as well as by the brilliance of the performances.

Sir Edward was attentive, and soon after the play began, he ordered special drinks—a mixture of light rum, brandywine, and sack—which she found delicious. Sir Edward sent for two more rounds before the play ended.

Slightly giddy and still thinking about the play, Betsy failed to note that Sir Edward's hands lingered at her shoulders when he held her silk cloak for her. Taking his arm as they left the theater, she realized that others in the audience were staring at her openly.

"Why are they ogling me, do you suppose?" she asked innocently.

"My dear Betsy," he replied, chuckling, "you really are unique. You're the only beautiful woman I've ever known who appears to take her beauty for granted."

His comment startled her. In Norfolk, which had been a tiny village during her formative years, everyone was struggling for survival and had had no time to discuss anything as ephemeral as beauty. And in the land of the Seneca, no one was ever rude enough to mention a woman's appearance.

Sir Edward helped her into the carriage and sat close beside her. "I defy you to tell me you don't know you're ravishing!" He was challenging her deliberately.

Betsy felt the color rise to her face. "I suppose I've always known I'm rather pretty," she admitted, "but in my family we took such matters as one's physical attributes for granted."

Sir Edward took her hand. "Surely you must realize that there aren't three women in all of England as lovely as you are."

Not wanting to appear ungracious, she refrained from withdrawing her hand. "I've honestly never thought about it."

"Well, I have. Frequently. I've been under your spell ever since our paths first crossed."

She accepted the compliment and discovered she rather enjoyed it. As much as she and Renno loved each other, he rarely mentioned her beauty.

The carriage passed down Fleet Street, and when they came to the Strand, it drew to a halt in front of a gray stone building that looked like a private dwelling. Betsy was surprised, thinking they were going to a public place for dinner.

"This is one of the most exclusive dining places in London," Sir Edward said as they mounted the stone steps. "I'll tell you more about it when we've made ourselves comfortable."

They were greeted by a majordomo in elegant livery, who bowed low, then led them up a broad marble staircase to the second floor, where he opened a door.

"Your Portuguese wine has been cooling, Sir Edward," he said, "and the supper you ordered is being prepared. Pull the bell rope if there is anything else you should wish."

When the man withdrew, Betsy saw they were standing in a sumptuously furnished chamber resembling a parlor. A Persian rug covered the hardwood floor, two exquisite tapestries were hung on the walls, and heavy drapes of damask silk had already been closed to keep out the London chill. A cheerful coal fire was lighted in the grate, and in front of it was an oversized divan on which silk pillows were scattered.

Sir Edward took Betsy's cloak, and again his hands grasped her shoulders. "This may be the most exclusive establishment in town, much like a private club," he told her. "One pays an annual fee for the privilege of belonging, and it has no name. It is called Thirty-seven Strand, after its street address."

"Is this a cloakroom of some sort?" she asked.

He smiled. "No, my dear Betsy, this is our private dining room. All rooms here are private, and all meals must be ordered well in advance."

"How elegant." She wandered from table to table, admiring the statuettes, porcelain boxes, crystal, and other bric-a-brac, all of it as handsome as anything she had seen at Whitehall or at the royal guest house where she and her family were living.

A discreet tap sounded at the door.

"You may come in," Sir Edward called.

A uniformed servant entered with a tray, on which stood a cut-glass decanter filled with white wine and two matching glasses. The man withdrew at once, taking care not to glance in the young woman's direction.

Sir Edward filled the glasses, handed her one, and raised his own. "To the loveliest of all colonials," he said.

Betsy's cheeks burned, and she thought it only polite to toast him in return. "To the most kind and thoughtful of English gentlemen, who has done so much for the cause that brought me so far across the sea."

He bowed. "I wish I could have done more."

"That would be impossible," she said. "We couldn't have succeeded without your help."

Sir Edward waved her to the divan. She seated herself, and as she sank onto the cushions she was conscious of her neckline, which was far lower than that of any other dress in her wardrobe.

"I hope you won't forget me when you return to the New World," he said.

"How could I? Your friendship and attention have made you dear to me, and I shall think of you—often —as long as I live."

"That's good to know," he said, then added lightly, "I wish I had some token of your regard that I could cherish for the rest of my own days."

The significance of his hint was lost on her. "You sound as though we'll never meet again. I hope you'll come to America someday." Waving at the surroundings as she allowed him to refill her glass, she couldn't help giggling. "You'll find the land of the Seneca quite unlike all of this."

He returned her smile but shuddered inwardly. Certainly he had no intention of going to the crude colonies, much less marching far into the interior to a town made up of mud huts. "It may be that you'll return to England one day."

"I think I'd like that," she said. "Thanks to you, I no longer feel like a total stranger here."

"The pleasure has been mine," he said, then added, "I wish I could do more for you."

"I can't think of anything I want. Yes, I can. I've eaten nothing all day, and I'm starved!"

Sir Edward refilled the wine in her glass before pulling the bell rope that brought the servant to the room.

Their meal was unlike any that Betsy had ever eaten. They started with oysters poached in a rich sauce, followed by a clear, pungent soup laced with sack. The fish course was grilled sole. Then came the masterpiece, squares of beef that had been cooked inside squabs, which then had been discarded. Their salad greens were coated with oil and vinegar, a combination that Betsy had never before tried, and even though she could eat only small quantities of each course, she was so full she had to refuse dessert.

A different wine was served with each course, and Sir Edward kept Betsy's glass filled. She had no idea how much she was drinking, but she was not concerned. She was celebrating the success of Ghonka's mission with a friend who had contributed a great deal to the outcome, and it didn't matter that her head was spinning. In fact, she enjoyed the unusual sensation.

A tug at the bell rope brought the servant to the room quickly, and he removed the supper table. After the man retreated again, Sir Edward splashed generous quantities of brandywine into two large glasses, then seated himself on the divan beside Betsy, so close to her that their shoulders touched. She had grown too careless to be alert to the intimacy and did not draw away from him.

He continued to chat with her until he saw that she had consumed the better part of the potent brandywine. The time to act had come. "Dear Betsy," he said, "I want to make a confession to you, and I hope you won't think any less of me for it."

"You may say whatever you please, Edward," she replied, "and I assure you that you'll stand high in my regard."

He placed their glasses on a low table, then took hold of her shoulders, facing her squarely. "Soon after you came to England," he told her, "I fell in love with you."

She was so startled that she didn't know what to say.

"I tried to rid myself of the feeling," he continued in a husky voice, "but I've failed." His face was only inches from hers.

175

Betsy found it difficult to think straight but made an effort to get rid of her dizziness. "You know I have a husband and children and that I love all three of them."

"I do know it, but that hasn't helped."

She had never known an unrequited love, but she felt great sympathy for this man whom she had regarded as a friend. "I'm so sorry," she said, "but I've given my heart to one man, and I'll never change. I know you'll recover and find someone else. Someone who is truly worthy of you."

Sir Edward felt that his maneuvers were succeeding, and he tightened the knot. "I ask only one favor. Let me kiss you, so I'll have that memory forever."

Betsy hesitated for a long moment. She had no desire to be kissed by him, but the gesture was a small return after all he had done to help her and to further the cause that had brought Ghonka to England. In her muddled state of mind, she thought that no harm could result.

Smiling slightly, she nodded, then raised her face to his. Sir Edward instantly swept her into his arms, his lips gentle at first as they sought hers. Then, his grip tightening, he eased her backward onto the divan, and his kiss became bolder, more demanding. Betsy was too surprised and confused to react. Slowly it dawned on her that, in spite of herself, she was beginning to respond to the man's advances.

Still kissing her, his tongue probing delicately, Sir Edward began to caress her.

This was too much! Betsy realized that it was his intent to seduce her, and she tried to free herself. But there was no escape from his lovemaking. Utilizing his greater strength, he pinned her to the divan. Continuing to kiss her passionately, he managed to draw one side of her gown from her shoulder, and his hand closed over her breast.

That gesture had the opposite effect of what he wanted. The shock of being touched by this man cleared her mind, and a sense of revulsion swept over her. He was not giving in to the impulse of the moment. On the contrary, his seduction had been carefully planned. This private dining chamber. The large quantities of wine she had unwittingly consumed. The seemingly innocent request for a simple kiss.

Even as she understood the situation, she realized she was in danger and knew she had to rely on cunning to free herself. So she forced herself to relax, allowing him to believe he was succeeding in arousing her.

Sir Edward loosened his grip, holding her in one arm, and with his free hand he fumbled with the other shoulder of her gown. Betsy allowed him to do as he pleased for the moment. Meanwhile, her hand slowly crept down to the hem of her dress. She lifted it surreptitiously, then took hold of the hilt of the newly purchased knife that was strapped to her calf.

Her seducer had no idea of what was in store for him until he felt the point of the blade pressing into his chest. The sudden stab of pain was so intense that he drew back instinctively and was horrified when he saw a small patch of crimson spreading on the front of his white lawn shirt.

Betsy held the knife firmly in place, exerting only a slight, continuing pressure. "Release me at once, sir, or I swear I'll drive this steel into your heart."

He saw that her eyes were cold and contemptuous, her mouth tight. Evidently this astonishing young woman meant what she had said. He pulled back farther, shrinking toward the far end of the divan, still gaping at her.

Betsy struggled to her feet and quickly rearranged her gown. Still gripping the knife and prepared to use it if he touched her again, she looked at him with loathing. Adrienne and Consuelo had told her what to expect in London, and she would not have found herself in such an embarrassing predicament if she had remembered their warning.

"I am a woman of the Seneca," Betsy replied icily.

"No matter whether I am at home in my own land or traveling in far places, I have the means to protect myself."

"If I had known," he said ruefully, "I would have made my plans accordingly."

It occurred to her that he failed to realize he had confessed his scheme. "Be good enough to order a carriage for me," she said.

"I'll take you home."

"I prefer to go alone." She was polite but uncompromising.

He shrugged, then tried to arrange his waistcoat in a way that could conceal the bloodstain on his shirt. Not looking in her direction again, he left the room.

Betsy hastily repinned her hair, donned her cloak, and, concealing the knife beneath it, left the chamber. She hurried down the stairs and found Sir Edward speaking in a low voice to the majordomo, who remained serene. This was not the first time, and would not be the last, either, that a lady exercised her prerogative and upset her escort's assignation plans. "Your carriage will be here in a moment," he murmured, bowing to the rigid-backed young woman.

While Betsy waited, she took no further notice of Sir Edward. Then, when the carriage arrived, she walked to it, her bearing majestic. Sir Edward, ever mindful of proprieties, mastered his hurt pride and gave the coachman her address as if nothing untoward had happened. Then he paid the man and bowed the young woman into the carriage.

"Good night and good-bye, Sir Edward," Betsy said. "We shall not meet again." She would not forget the incident and the lessons it had taught her, but she knew that, when her shame and embarrassment subsided, she would be able to put it behind her. Her future belonged to Renno and their children.

Ten days later a messenger from Whitehall brought word that Queen Anne requested the pleasure of

Ghonka's company at a private audience. Betsy accompanied him to act as his interpreter.

An equerry met them at the palace entrance, and as she and her father-in-law, both in Seneca attire, made their way to a private chamber on the second floor, they passed an audience hall in which a large number of ladies and gentlemen had gathered to await their monarch's arrival.

One of the men bowed, and out of the corner of an eye, Betsy saw that he was Sir Edward Carlton. She walked past him without as much as a nod of recognition. Her anger had subsided, her disgust for him had vanished, and she now felt nothing toward him. He had become a total stranger.

Queen Anne awaited her guests in a cozy, simply furnished parlor that in no way resembled the splendor of the palace's public rooms. Rising and greeting them warmly, she escorted them to comfortable chairs near the coal fire.

"You will soon be leaving for the New World," she said, "and I wanted to see the Great Sachem again. I have signed the documents that will provide our colonies with the arms and munitions they need, and I have given my formal approval to the dispatch of a Royal Navy squadron to assist the colonies in our joint war with France and Spain. May our mutual cause flourish."

"We will win the war," Ghonka replied with simple, firm conviction.

"I want you to know, sir, how much your visit has meant to me and my subjects," the Queen told him. "Your rebuke to the people of Great Britain for their careless indifference to the war has spread everywhere. Not only has there been a surge of patriotic feeling, but I've been informed that new volunteers are joining Marlborough's army in such large numbers that the recruiting offices are finding it difficult to process them. Britain is in the Great Sachem's permanent debt."

"Those who fight a common enemy do not weigh their friendship," Ghonka replied with dignity.

Queen Anne smiled. "Perhaps not, but I want you to have a token of my regard." She handed him a small but heavy box.

He opened it and inside saw a pistol with a butt of solid gold stamped with the Queen's coat of arms.

Ghonka inclined his head to her in a gesture of sincere gratitude.

"I'm told that you have become expert in the use of our weapons, so this little gift is no mere ornament."

"It is true that I have learned the use of firesticks. The Great Sachem thanks his English sister for the gift."

He and the Queen smiled at each other, the mutual reserve that had separated them vanishing. Then Queen Anne turned to the young interpreter. "You will accompany the Great Sachem to the New World, I take it?"

"Yes, Your Majesty, I'm going home," Betsy said.

The Queen's eyes softened. "You've made a valuable contribution to the Great Sachem's talks with me and with Lord Godolphin," she said. "I envy your beauty, your talents, and your buoyancy—all the qualities that are lacking in me."

For a fleeting instant Betsy caught a glimpse of the lonely woman who lived behind a royal mask, and she felt sorry for her.

Queen Anne twisted a diamond ring from her hand and dropped it into the younger woman's palm. "Keep this as a symbol of my regard."

Overcome, the surprised Betsy stammered her thanks. The monetary value of the ring meant nothing to her, but it was precious because it was a token of the Queen's regard, and someday she would pass it down to her daughter.

Chapter VII

People who had known Lord Symes in London would not have recognized the Kenneth Robinson who walked slowly down High Street in Fort Springfield, nodding to the many acquaintances he had made during his month's stay with Obadiah and Deborah Jenkins. He had just come from a visit to the physician, who had pronounced his shoulder completely healed, and there was a spring in his step, an expression in his eyes, that old acquaintances would not have recognized.

The past month's sojourn, Kenneth believed, had changed his life. He had not tasted a drop of alcohol during that time and no longer missed it. Utilizing the opportunity that circumstances had forced on him, he had looked back at his past and had taken a solemn vow never again to gamble.

What had given him a new outlook had been his observation of the life led by Obadiah, Deborah, and their children. The clergyman was unselfish, listening to the problems of those who came in large numbers to him every morning. He devoted his afternoons to visits to the sick and the grieving, sometimes riding his gelding many miles through the wilderness to isolated homesteads. Deborah was equally generous, rearing her children in accordance with her own high principles and, no matter how rushed or weary, greeting the wealthy and the poor alike with a warm welcome.

When Kenneth had come to the colonies, he had held all provincials in contempt, regarding them as simple, backward clods. Now he knew better. These courageous men and women fought constantly against heavy odds to create new, free lives for themselves and their children on a harsh frontier. They battled the elements, accepted dangers as a matter of course, and always came to the aid of their neighbors in times of crisis. There was nothing shallow about existence in western Massachusetts Bay.

Contrasting what he had seen and learned the past month with his own dark and frustrating past, Kenneth had been compelled to look into his future. Although he had not confided in Obadiah and Deborah, they had realized he was troubled and had encouraged him in scores of little ways. What he liked best about them, perhaps, was their treatment of an English viscount and the newest penniless immigrant as equals.

Now Kenneth knew what he had to do. There was no turning back, no procrastinating, and he walked still more briskly down the road that led to the extensive working farm of Andrew and Jeffrey Wilson. The next hour would not be easy for him, and it was even possible that he might be courting danger, but he did not hesitate. He had thought of little else for many days.

Jeffrey Wilson, who was leaving with his regiment in a few days, answered the door himself and was surprised to see the visitor who stood on the threshold.

"Colonel," Kenneth said, "I'd like a brief word with you and Mistress Wilson."

"I'll call her," Jeffrey said curtly and waved him into a small parlor.

Kenneth stood still, looking out at the snow melting in the fields where the spring planting soon would begin.

Adrienne accompanied her husband into the room, openly bewildered by the appearance of the unexpected, uninvited guest. Kenneth bowed to her. "Mistress Wilson, I tender you my apologies for my unwarranted conduct. I regret what I did, and I have no excuses to offer for my behavior. I just hope you have it in your heart not to bear me a permanent grudge."

"Why, the past is forgotten, milord," Adrienne replied graciously.

He bowed to her again, then turned to her husband. "May I have a word with you in private, Colonel?"

"Certainly." Jeffrey nodded to Adrienne, who left the room.

"Colonel, you did me a great favor when you wounded me in your duel. I've had an opportunity to think—and think—and I want to reveal some facts to you."

Jeffrey felt anything but cordial but nevertheless waved him to a chair and sat opposite him.

"The notes that Mistress Wilson found in my room indeed were the work of a spy. I was engaged in espionage for France. Thanks exclusively to my own weaknesses."

The astonished Jeffrey wondered if Symes recognized the gravity of his admission.

Giving him no opportunity to reply, Kenneth launched into a crisp recital of his past, his years as a compulsive gambler who had thrown away his inheritance, and his desperate attempt to recoup his losses, which had allowed representatives of the French to take advantage of him.

"Why are you telling me all this?" Jeffrey asked when Kenneth stopped speaking.

"I can no longer work for the French, no matter what the consequences. I'll take my chances that the blackmailers—this Mr. Hawkins and his associates—will ruin me in England. Frankly, all of that seems very far away to me right now. I place myself at your disposal and will submit if you wish to place me under arrest."

"Do you give me any alternatives?" Still not liking him, Jeffrey nevertheless was impressed by his candor and courage.

"I have no reason to return to England," Kenneth said. "For many obvious reasons it is too late for me to apply for a commission and join the Duke of Marlborough's staff. If I can, I want to make a new life for myself here in the colonies. And with that aim foremost in my mind, I volunteer my services as a member of your militia. I'll gladly enlist as a private soldier."

Studying him, Jeffrey was too stunned to reply.

"As you know, Colonel, I am an accomplished swordsman. I am a marksman with both musket and pistol, and I've yet to find a horse I can't ride. I'm also reasonably intelligent, although my past acts might lead you to believe the contrary."

Jeffrey made a swift analysis of the situation. "Lord Symes—"

"If you please, Colonel, I prefer to be known only as Kenneth Robinson. If I earn the right to use a title I've disgraced, I'll think about using it again at some future time."

"Very well, Master Robinson. Ordinarily a man of your education and class would be offered a commission in the militia. But in view of your revelations that you were an espionage agent, I'm reluctant to make you an officer."

"That's understandable, Colonel, and I don't ask it of you."

"There's still another complication. I'm marching

with my regiment into the wilderness later this week. There's no time to give you sufficient military training to justify your joining us."

"Then you reject my application?"

"Yes and no," Jeffrey said. "Certainly I have no intention of forcing you to stand trial as an enemy agent. From what you've indicated to me, none of the data you sent on to the French was of any real value."

"I've told you literally everything, Colonel Wilson."

Watching him closely, Jeffrey took a deep breath. "There is a way in which your services could be utilized—without running the risk that you might change your mind and go back to work for the French."

"Never!" Kenneth was emphatic.

"That remains to be seen, if you'll forgive the observation. As it happens, however, I am sending a small delegation of marksmen to the land of the Seneca tomorrow at dawn. Some of their younger warriors have been training with muskets for the first time and need the help of sharpshooters for the final week or two." He did not mention that his unit, Renno's Seneca, and Ned Ridley's Virginia battalion would meet on the Ohio River, then march together. If Lord Symes was still in the secret employ of the French, there would be little he could tell them.

"Assuming you really are an expert shot—and we can find out fast enough by setting up a target in the back yard—you could be of great help to the Seneca. I'll willingly send you with my delegation, but in a strictly civilian capacity. Their warriors will be going off on a campaign in the immediate future, and if you prove your worth to them, I daresay they'd be willing to take you with them."

"I accept, Colonel," Kenneth said promptly. "But I must admit I don't know anything about savages and have never spoken a word of their language."

"Renno, their sachem, is a white man whose command of English is as good as yours and mine. One of their young warriors, Walter Alwin, came from Fort Springfield, and he also speaks English. I'm sure that they'll help you become acclimated until you can pick up some Seneca essentials."

Kenneth wondered how it was possible for a white-skinned man to be the leader of a major Indian nation, but this was not the time to ask unnecessary questions. "I'm ready to take any test with a musket or pistol—or both—that you care to devise, Colonel Wilson."

"One moment. I want to make it clear to you what you're accepting. The journey to the land of the Seneca won't be easy, but that will be just the beginning. Living conditions there are primitive, but you'll be expected to accept their ways. And if Renno agrees to take you into the field with him, the life you'll lead will be even more difficult. Seneca march at twice the speed that we do, and if you can't keep up their pace, they'll leave you behind."

"I assure you that won't happen," Kenneth said grimly.

"You'll learn, when it is necessary, to subsist only on dry strips of jerked meat and equally tasteless parched corn. Even when you're given hot food—and you'll soon learn to do your share of the hunting— you'll eat with your fingers. If you encounter a hostile tribe, you'll follow Renno's orders. You'll bathe only when you come to lakes or rivers that are suitable for the purpose, and you'll get along on less sleep than you've ever imagined you could."

"You're not frightening me, Colonel," Kenneth said. "I've sunk so low that all I ask is the chance to prove myself. I'm not afraid to live and work with the Seneca."

Even if the man was being honest, Jeffrey reflected, he was setting out on the thorniest of paths. Sympathizing with Robinson's seemingly deep desire to rehabilitate himself in his own eyes and in the eyes of others, he knew the man had his work cut out for him.

Sun-ai-yee was briefing the senior warriors who would march in fourteen days, and Renno left them, wandering alone toward the field where the junior warriors who would accompany the expedition were at musket practice. Ba-lin-ta and many of the other young women were preparing the food the warriors would carry, and everything was in order.

Renno tried not to think about the remote possibility that Betsy and the children might arrive home before he departed. The manitous might regard him as selfish and greedy if he asked them to let him see his wife, son, and daughter before he went off to war, so he carefully refrained from making the request. It would be the gravest of errors to anger the representatives of the gods when he would need their help in the moons ahead.

Strangely, the prospect of meeting the foe in combat no longer challenged or excited him. Like Ghonka before him, he had fought in too many battles for that. He was ever conscious of his ultimate responsibility for the success of the expedition, and he would perform his tasks conscientiously. He would take scalps, of course, whenever the opportunity arose, and he was determined to inflict a stunning defeat on the enemy. But he had been fighting the enemies of the Seneca for more than a decade. He could well imagine how much wearier Ghonka felt after spending his entire life in the service of their people.

The only prospect that aroused Renno was the hope that his path would cross that of Golden Eagle. Twice in the past the wily Frenchman-Huron had eluded him, but if the manitous willed another encounter, he was sure only one of them would emerge alive from their ordeal. And Renno was grimly determined to be that winner.

The junior warriors were firing at targets set up on the far side of the field, their efforts supervised by the delegation of marksmen Jeffrey Wilson had sent from Fort Springfield for the purpose, and Renno paused at a distance to watch them. He paid particular attention to Kenneth Robinson, the only civilian in the group.

He was attired in a new buckskin shirt, trousers, and moccasins that Ba-lin-ta had made for him, for she had felt sorry for him when he had arrived in the town of the Seneca with his genteel clothes in tatters. He moved ceaselessly up and down the line, and Renno had to admire his eye for critical detail. He corrected the stance of one warrior slightly and altered the elevation of another's musket. Sometimes he fired a round himself to illustrate the point he was making. He was both conscientious and tireless.

Jeffrey had written Renno a confidential letter telling him about Robinson's past and his desire to change. Renno had already decided that if Robinson's attempt to reform was genuine, he would take the Englishman with him on the expedition. He and Sun-ai-yee would keep him under surveillance, and if he made one move that indicated he was still in the pay of the French, he would die. The fact that Renno liked the man and was pleased that he was forming a friendship with Walter Alwin would carry no weight. Let him prove he was still a spy, and Renno himself would sink a tomahawk into his head.

Kenneth paused beside Walter, watched him shoot, and then changed the position of his right leg. "You're shooting too quickly." Kenneth mouthed the words slowly and distinctly.

Walter nodded.

"A bullet travels swiftly, so never rush your shot. And never jerk the trigger. Always squeeze it gently. Like this."

As Kenneth was demonstrating, the junior warrior just beyond them was reloading his musket. Ramming home a charge, he raised the weapon to his shoulder and fired. A violent explosion rocked the area, instantly halting the practice.

Renno saw, as he raced toward the scene, that the junior warrior's defective musket had been blown to bits. The young Seneca and Walter were sprawled on the ground. Kenneth bent over the two men. The junior warrior who had fired the shot was dead.

As others hurried to the spot, Renno called to Kenneth in English, "How badly is Walter hurt?"

Walter sat up, still somewhat dazed by the explosion, and said, slowly and with difficulty, "I—am not —hurt. The manitous—preserved me."

Renno stopped short and stared at him. "You knew I just asked about you, but you weren't looking at me to see what shapes my lips took."

As the realization dawned on Walter that he had actually heard spoken words, he was stunned and bewildered, his mind unable to accept the miracle. After a long, painful pause, he whispered, "I—can— hear."

Some of the junior warriors had thrown themselves to the ground to pray aloud to the manitous, asking to be preserved from the wrath of the gods. Renno was so shaken himself that he first devoted his attention to the dead junior warrior, directing some of his friends to remove his body from the field and inform his family of the tragedy. "Before the sun goes down," he announced, "all in the town will attend the funeral of one who has gone honorably to join his ancestors for all time in the land of the manitous."

His immediate order was obeyed, and others continued to cluster around Walter, who rose slowly to his feet. "I—can—hear," he said again and again. "The manitous—have made—a miracle."

"I knew of another case like this," Kenneth told Renno, and Walter, the only other person who knew English, found himself enjoying the unique experience of listening. "The son of the gardener on my father's country estate was deaf. Some gunpowder accidentally exploded not far from him one day, and his hearing was restored. I remember the incident clearly, although I was just a small boy at the time. Unfortunately, I can't recall the reasons my father's physician gave for the effect that the explosion caused."

Renno translated his words for the benefit of the junior warriors who still stood nearby.

"Then the manitous—of the English—make miracles, too," Walter said.

Rejoicing for the young warrior, Renno excused him from work for the rest of the day, then sternly directed the others to resume their target practice. A still-marveling Walter walked beside Renno, returning to the town with him. Suddenly he bolted, offering no explanation, and ran ahead at top speed.

Renno immediately guessed his purpose and destination, so he took his time as he went to the house of his father. Pausing outside the door, he cleared his throat loudly before he pushed aside the flap of animal skins that covered the entrance.

As he had anticipated, Ba-lin-ta and Walter broke their embrace and moved apart, both starting to talk simultaneously.

The girl was ecstatic. "That which could not happen now has happened!" she exclaimed, and any outsider who mistakenly believed the Seneca were an unemotional people would have been startled by her radiant expression.

"For more than ten years Wal-ter has lived with the people of this land," Walter said solemnly. "For the first time he can hear the sweet voice of Ba-lin-ta, who was his voice and his ears."

As they continued to babble in delight, Renno's thoughts were centered on Walter's mother, Ida Carswell, and her second husband, Leverett. She had suffered ever since her son had been born a deaf-mute. When he had gained the power of speech a few years earlier, she had rejoiced, and this new miracle would give her great happiness.

"I think," Renno said, "you should go to Fort Springfield at once and tell this wonderful news to your mother."

"I have been thinking of my mother as well as of Ba-lin-ta," the young man replied, "but I cannot go. For more than ten years I have lived with the Seneca. I have become a Seneca, and I will remain a Seneca. The children Ba-lin-ta and I will bring into this world will be Seneca. I have worked hard, and I have become a junior warrior. Already I carry two scalps in my belt. I took grave risks when I went with El-i-chi to Quebec. Now I have my chance, at last, to prove myself in a great war. If I fight with courage and skill, I may become a senior warrior. If I go to Fort Springfield, you will march without me. I will not be able to fight at the side of my brothers."

Renno understood Walter's feelings. It would not be fair to deny him the right to fight against the enemy.

"I will write a letter to my mother this very day," Walter said. "Then, when the war ends, Ba-lin-ta and I will visit her."

Renno nodded. "Very well. I will send a special messenger with the letter as soon as it is written." Ida Carswell would learn the wonderful news quickly, and the sachem was satisfied. His obligation to an individual was as important as his duty to his nation.

There were tears of joy in Ida Carswell's eyes as she stood in the parlor of the Jenkins's parsonage and thrust the letter at Deborah, her niece. "Read this!" she commanded. Deborah scanned the letter, then embraced her aunt, and they wept together.

Obadiah came into the parlor, and he bowed his head in silence when he heard the astonishing news. Then he murmured, "The ways of the Lord are truly mysterious."

"Is it really possible for an explosion close to Walter's head to have restored his hearing?" Ida asked.

The clergyman spread out his hands. "I'm a man of the cloth, not a physician. Perhaps the explosion jarred or broke an obstruction inside Walter's head. What matters is that he can hear."

"How I wish I could see him!"

"You'll have to be patient, Aunt Ida," Deborah said. "He tells you why he can't make the journey here now. It would be wrong to deny him what he's struggled against such odds to achieve."

The older woman sniffled. "I know I'm being selfish."

"Hardly," Obadiah said.

Ida turned to him. "Is the church open?"

"No, but I can unlock the doors for you. Would you like me to come with you?"

She shook her head. "If you don't mind, I'd rather go alone. Leverett wanted to come with me, too, but I'd rather that he wait until the regular service on Sunday."

"I will make this miracle the subject of my sermon," Obadiah said.

There was no fire in the hearth that stood at one side of the church, and the interior was cold, but Ida Carswell was indifferent to the chill. She had always said her prayers standing or sitting, never having believed in kneeling. Now, however, she made her way to one of the front pews, then slowly sank to her knees as she looked up at the altar.

Her heart was so full that she could not articulate her gratitude. Instead, she clasped her hands together, tears streaming down her face as she continued to gaze with unseeing eyes at the altar.

She had suffered so many hard blows over the years, losing her first husband a short time before her baby had been born, then giving birth to a boy who had been a deaf-mute. She had struggled on her little farm to earn a living for them; she had tried and tried to help Walter overcome his handicaps. And how dismayed she had been, when Ba-lin-ta had first come to

Fort Springfield, to discover that the young woman and her son had instantly found some way to communicate with each other.

Her heart had been broken when, against her better judgment, she had allowed the boy to go off to the land of the Seneca. Her subsequent marriage to a kind and generous man of substance had eased her financial burden, but Walter still had been ever present in her mind.

Ida had never quite believed the story that during his manhood trials, Walter had seen a hawk, the messenger of the manitous, overhead—and suddenly had gained the power of speech. In her privately held opinion his thinking was that of an Indian barbarian. She had attributed his recovery exclusively to the Almighty and had remained deeply disturbed because Walter had insisted on continuing to live with the Seneca.

Now, as she prayed, a crushing burden suddenly was lifted from her shoulders. Her son could hear as well as speak. He had been made whole.

She had finally come to accept that it was right for him to have become a Seneca. She found that she no longer resented his spending his life as an Indian, planning to marry an Indian woman, and rearing their children—her grandchildren—as Seneca living in the wilderness. Divine Providence was demonstrating to her that Walter was following the right path. Never again would she stand in his way or oppose him. Perhaps, in time to come, she and Leverett would visit Walter and Ba-lin-ta in their homeland, something she had always sworn she would never do.

Humbled yet rejoicing, Ida remained on her knees for a long time, long after the tears on her face had dried. Then, her soul cleansed, her heart lighter than it had been in more years than she could remember, she walked out of the church, blinking in the early spring sunlight. Her son was beginning a new, fruitful life, and she was at peace within herself.

The Biloxi were a small tribe living on the lower reaches of the great Mississippi River, the entire nation consisting of no more than fifteen hundred people. So the sachem and the few members of his council were apprehensive. Three of their warriors, lured from their homes by Spanish gifts, had gone off on a secret mission known to no one else, then had vanished without a trace. Their relatives were certain they were no longer alive, and the whole tribe mourned them as dead.

Now a far graver crisis had arisen. The Spanish she-devil responsible for the disappearance of the warriors had appeared in the land of the Biloxi, accompanied by an older Spanish man and the legendary Frenchman-Huron, Golden Eagle. The trio had demanded the allegiance of the tribe in their coming war with the English colonies. The Biloxi were given no choice. Either they would become the allies of France and Spain or soldiers armed with firesticks would destroy their villages, and the powerful Creek would plunder the land, taking as slaves any members of the tribe who survived.

The leaders of the Biloxi were cornered and were compelled to join the alliance. But as soon as the foreign trio departed, the sachem called his war chief and medicine man to his hut. All three sat for a time, passing a pipe of aromatic tobacco.

The sachem broke the silence. "The alliance we have been forced to make is not good."

"It is bad," the war chief declared. "The Creek long have wanted our land. When this war is ended, they will drive us out and take it from us."

"We have no quarrels with the English colonies, whose homes are far from this land," the medicine man said uneasily.

"Our position is even worse than has been said," the sachem announced. "My brothers heard the man who calls himself Golden Eagle say that the Iroquois will be fighting at the side of the English colonists. The warriors of the Biloxi will die if they invade the lands of the Iroquois. Not even the Creek can win in battle against the mighty Seneca! We will invite our own destruction!"

"The words the sachem has spoken are true," the war chief said. "The gods will punish us for our stupidity if we go to war against the Seneca, the Mohawk, and the other great nations of the Iroquois."

"If that is agreed, then we are decided," the sachem said. "But how are we to avoid the vengeance of the French, the Spaniards, and the Creek?"

The medicine man was craftier than his colleagues. "The Biloxi will pretend to stand on the side of the Creek and the French. But when the time for battle comes, the Biloxi will change to the side of the Seneca. Let us select two young warriors of courage and strength, warriors who can run with the speed of the deer or the wind. Send them to the land of the Seneca. Let each of them be taught the words he will say to the Seneca. Let them say that the Biloxi are not the enemies of the Seneca and the other Iroquois. The Biloxi are their friends."

The others nodded solemnly, and the sachem said, "The medicine man speaks words of wisdom."

But the war chief was puzzled. "Why should two warriors be sent to the Seneca? Why do we not send but one?"

"Many evils lurk in the forest," the medicine man replied patiently. "Already three of our warriors who were bribed by the Spanish she-devil have vanished. If the Seneca do not receive our message, the Biloxi will be slaughtered like buffalo in the great-hunt-of-the-time-when-the-leaves-turn. We must make very certain that the Seneca receive word of our allegiance. So it is safer to send two messengers. If evil befalls one, perhaps the other will live long enough to deliver the words to the Seneca."

Again his colleagues approved, and the meeting came to an end. Then, after due deliberation, the sachem and the war chief selected two young warriors as messengers. Ha-lem, the elder of the pair, was a swift, tireless runner, long familiar with the forest. Da-no, several years younger, was a trifle slower but was ruggedly built and could sustain himself in the wilderness for long periods.

The war chief gave them careful instructions, and both faithfully memorized the message to be delivered to the Seneca. "You will travel far," the sachem said, "but let nothing slow your steps."

They both nodded.

"If you should fall into the hands of enemies," the sachem went on, "speak no word of your mission. If the French, the Spanish, or the Creek should learn that we will not be faithful to them, they will burn our villages to the ground. All our people will die, and the Biloxi nation will be no more."

They swore that nothing would wrench the secret from them, and they went on their way at once, traveling separately. Aware of the risks they were taking, both braves moved at a steady trot, and a day and a half later, after carefully skirting land that the Creek used as hunting grounds, Da-no breathed a trifle more easily. Still vigilant, he paused only when it was essential that he sleep for a short time.

Ha-lem was less fortunate. When he was well into the second day of his march, he was surprised by a party of four burly Creek warriors, who took him prisoner in spite of his protests that the Biloxi were the friends of the Creek. Tying his hands behind his back, they forced him to accompany them to a temporary camp set in a clearing, and Ha-lem knew he was in trouble when he saw two tents that he recognized instantly. They were the portable cloth dwellings used by the Spanish she-devil and the older man.

Alain de Gramont, in his Huron attire, was the first to appear, and moments later Beatriz and Don Diego de Bernardo emerged from their tents. "I knew it would be wise to set up a screen," Gramont said,

addressing his companions in Spanish, which neither the captive nor the Creek understood. "I didn't like the attitude of the Biloxi leaders. As I told you, I strongly suspect they intend to betray us."

"It will be interesting to learn what this man will tell us," Beatriz said.

Don Diego studied the prisoner. "He knows that difficulties lie ahead for him. It will not be easy to pry information from him."

"The Creek have their ways," Gramont said, "and the Huron know still others. He will speak." He turned to the captive, addressing him in an Indian tongue that virtually all tribes east of the Mississippi could understand. "Where were you going when you were made prisoner?"

"I was hunting," Ha-lem replied instantly.

Gramont shook his head, folded his arms across his chest, and became harsh. "You were hunting far from your own land, when the land of the Biloxi is full of game. The war chief of the Huron believes you speak with forked tongue."

"The war chief of the Huron may believe whatever he wishes," the young brave replied.

"There are ways to make you more eager to tell the truth."

Ha-lem made no reply, which did not surprise Gramont. No captured warrior would voluntarily violate the creed of his own people to reveal matters of consequence regarding his own tribe. Only torture would persuade him to speak freely.

At Gramont's order the members of his Huron escort cut down a tree and striped its branches, then, at one end of the clearing, drove it into the ground like a spike. They tied the captive to it, with his hands bound behind his back and his ankles made secure to the post.

"It might be well," Gramont suggested to Beatriz, "if you take yourself elsewhere for a time. I'll have two of the warriors escort you to a pond where you can spend the rest of the day fishing for our supper."

"I am not squeamish," she said. "I prefer to remain here. Once he starts to speak, perhaps I can make a contribution to the interrogation."

Ha-lem was already braced for what lay ahead. Every warrior, no matter what his tribe, received rigorous training from earliest childhood to prepare him for the day when he might fall into the hands of his nation's foes. Ha-lem suffered no false illusions. The Creek could be cruel, the Spanish she-devil breathed fire, and the warrior who wore the paint of the Huron looked ruthless. No matter what was done to him, however, he took a vow to keep sacred the trust of his own nation.

He prayed to the gods to give him the strength, endurance, and courage to withstand the trial that awaited him. The certain knowledge that he would die did not frighten him. On the contrary, he knew he would join his beloved grandfather in the afterworld, and their spirits would roam through the forest together for all time, blissfully hunting and fishing.

The Creek went to work on the prisoner first, whittling pointed sticks and, after stripping him, jabbing him repeatedly with them. Whenever a stick broke or its point was blunted, it was sharpened again.

Ha-lem made no sound, staring straight ahead and ignoring his tormentors.

The Creek did not expect him to break quickly and were just warming to their task. The jabbing would continue until the victim could not tolerate more pain.

Beatriz spread a rug on the ground, sat on it, and watched the Creek braves at work. She did not flinch or avert her gaze when the captive's blood began to run, and she retained her composure even when scores of small wounds had been inflicted on his face and body.

Gramont noticed that she was actually enjoying the grisly operation. Her father accepted it as a necessity, as did both the Creek and the Huron. But Beatriz was relishing the experience. Her lips were parted, her eyes shone, and she smiled from time to time as the sharp sticks broke the captive's skin.

"Are you ready to question him yet?" Beatriz demanded impatiently.

"We've just started. He would laugh at us and boast of the courage of the Biloxi."

"But he is enduring great pain," she replied. "That much is obvious."

"Permit me to contradict you. I know the Indians of North America, and you, my dear, do not." Gramont was annoyed and wished he had not become intimate with her. This woman was so cold-blooded that he was conceiving an active dislike for her.

"When will you talk to him?" she persisted.

"We shall judge his resistance at the proper time," Gramont said.

The Creek worked in groups of three, each unit spending several hours torturing the captive before being relieved by another group.

A cooking fire was lighted, and the evening meal was prepared and consumed. Gramont turned his back to the proceedings while he ate, as did Don Diego and the warriors, but Beatriz watched the torturers all through the meal, her appetite unimpaired.

Alain de Gramont was much admired by Huron and Ottawa for his calm reaction to any experience, but the Spanish woman's fascination with the continuing torture sickened him. Under no circumstances could he make love to her tonight. "Go to bed," he told her when night came. "I won't be joining you. I'll keep watch here through the night."

"I should like to stay with you," Beatriz said.

"No!" He realized he needed to find a logical excuse. "The prisoner is less likely to talk in the presence of a woman."

She went reluctantly to her tent, and Gramont remained in the open while the torture continued.

By morning Ha-lem's entire face and body were covered with bloody wounds, and the warriors were probing deeper into the injuries they had already inflicted. Ha-lem tried to remain impassive, but his agony was so intense that sometimes his face involuntarily contorted, and occasionally a deep, animal-like grunt emerged from somewhere deep within him.

Gramont had to admire the Biloxi's courage and stamina. He had seen other warriors beg for mercy and begin to speak freely after enduring far less.

The Creek went on without pause. At times Ha-lem thought he was seeing visions, and at these moments he felt no pain. Gradually, as he hallucinated more and more frequently, he knew he would win the battle. Soon he would be beyond the reach of his enemies.

"Surely you must be ready to interrogate him now," Beatriz said at noon.

Gramont concealed his anger. He had already decided the time to question the captive had come, but he resented Beatriz's insistence on taking command, so he allowed the torture to continue for another hour. Only then did he call a halt.

"Speak, Biloxi!" he ordered.

The wary Ha-lem, his whole body feeling as though it were on fire, clenched his teeth.

"Tell us why you were marching through the forest so far from the home of your nation," Gramont said. "Speak the truth now, and your torment will end. Sweet balm will cover your wounds, and you will be allowed to return to your people."

The Huron was lying. Hearing him from a great distance, Ha-lem still retained enough of his sanity to realize that the moment he revealed his mission a knife would enter his heart. No Indian nation allowed a prisoner to live after he had been tortured.

"If you will not speak," Gramont said ominously, "far worse than you have already suffered is in store for you."

Ha-lem sagged against his bonds, his remaining

strength spent, but he made no sound. Beckoning to his Huron, Gramont nodded in the direction of the captive.

Don Diego could not watch these broad-shouldered Indians at work. Using their knives deftly, they slowly removed whole patches of skin from their victim's body. They were literally skinning him alive.

But Beatriz was entranced, her expression ecstatic as she watched. She was inhuman, Gramont thought. In striving to develop a perfect extension of his will, her father instead had created a monster lacking in all feeling, all humanity.

The pain was so sharp, so intense, so all-encompassing that Ha-lem could feel himself losing his grip on reality. His soul was moving beyond the reach of these enemies, and soon, when his spirit entered the realm of his ancestors, only his battered, lifeless body would remain here.

Don Diego had to clench his fists to prevent himself from calling a halt. Even Gramont felt a twinge of pity for the victim. He could only hope, if he was ever forced to submit to such torture, that he would have the strength and the will to endure it.

Beatriz edged closer to the stake, unwilling to miss any detail of what she was witnessing.

Suddenly Ha-lem gave a deep, hoarse laugh. Gramont instantly signaled his Huron to stop.

"The warriors of the Creek are weak," Ha-lem whispered. "The warriors of the Huron are like women. Only the warriors of the Biloxi nation are great."

His head lolled, and he stared into infinity with sightless eyes as the breath left his body. Gramont knew he had lost.

"I wish you had allowed me to take charge," Beatriz said. "I would have found some way to squeeze the truth out of him."

"He was a man of spirit," Gramont said. He ordered the warriors not to scalp the Biloxi before they buried him.

Beatriz began to pace restlessly. "What do you suggest we do next?" she demanded.

Alain shrugged. "If the Biloxi were sending one messenger somewhere, it may be they'll dispatch another. We'll keep up our screen in the forest, and if we catch another courier, perhaps he'll be more amenable to persuasion than this man proved to be."

"If. Perhaps." Beatriz was scornful. "You have said repeatedly that you do not trust the leaders of the Biloxi tribe. Take their chief as a prisoner and torture him. Or let the Creek attack them and destroy them. Other tribes will learn a lesson very quickly and will beg for the privilege of becoming our allies."

"If that is the policy you wish to pursue," Gramont said coldly, "you'll have to act without me. I will withdraw, and I will inform my superiors in Quebec and in Paris that it is no longer possible for me to cooperate with the emissaries of Spain. That might mean the end of my career, but at least I won't be totally disgraced."

Don Diego was alarmed by the threat. "Not so fast, Colonel. Surely you find some merit in my daughter's suggestions."

"I find none. The capture of the Biloxi sachem by the Creek would be an unwarranted act, a breach of faith, and would be an attack on the Biloxi. You regard all Indians as savage barbarians. What you fail to realize is that they have their own strict codes of conduct. We merely suspect that the Biloxi are reluctant to become our allies. We have no proof of treachery against us. Without that proof they must remain untouched. A single act of bad faith on our part will guarantee the ultimate success of the English colonies. Every Indian nation, large and small alike, will race to join an alliance with them. We'll be seen as the betrayers."

Beatriz stubbornly started to argue with him, but Alain cut her off. "You waste your breath," he told her. "If I asked the Creek to attack the Biloxi or capture their sachem, they'd rebel. They would desert us and enter the ranks of our enemies."

"People will do anything when the bribe is big enough," Beatriz said contemptuously. "If we give them enough firearms and knives, enough iron pots and trinkets and other rubbish, they will do anything we ask of them."

Perhaps one tribe could be bought for a time, but without a sense of purpose, without the promise of a bright future, no nation would remain loyal on a permanent basis. Beatriz could provide the gifts, but only he could provide the sense of purpose. "I have no control over your activities," Alain replied. "You may deal with the Indians in any way you see fit. But I will part company with you. Today. And I will make my report to my superiors accordingly." He was refusing to yield in any way.

Beatriz glared at him, and Don Diego warned his daughter with a sharp glance that she was going too far. This strange, high-ranking French officer, who preferred to live as an Indian, was their vital link to the native tribes of the continent. Without his continuing cooperation, it would be impossible for them to forge the alliances on which the long-rang French-Spanish strategy depended, and their own mission inevitably would fail.

Beatriz was so angry that Don Diego realized he had to intervene. "Please do not be hasty, Colonel," he said, his manner conciliatory. "I know of no one more talented than my daughter, but she lacks our experience in dealing with people. I am content to leave the direction of establishing Indian alliances in your hands."

Beatriz was furious with her father, but she had accepted his authority in all things for so long that she backed down. "I disagree with you, Alain, so I want my opinion known for the record. But I must do as my father wishes. You will remain in charge."

"Very well." Alain de Gramont spoke gruffly but

was privately relieved. With his own position confirmed, the chances of forging a series of strong alliances were vastly improved. What he wanted, ultimately, was the command of all French forces in the New World; that post, combined with the influence he exerted over the Huron and Ottawa, would make him the single most powerful man in the history of New France.

Obviously, his brief affair with Beatriz de Bernardo had come to an abrupt end, and that was to the good, too. How long she might remain useful to him as a subordinate remained to be seen, but he realized he was dependent on her and her wily father for the supplies and arms they were providing. Their own alliance was shaky, but it had to be maintained. No matter how great the dislike he was developing for this impetuous young woman, he was obliged to continue to cooperate with her, at least until such time as she outlived her usefulness.

Warriors assigned to the expedition came from every part of the land of the Seneca to the main town and made camp in the fields beyond the palisade. They were joined by the Mohawk contingent, four hundred strong, and when the one hundred Oneida who would act as the army's scouts also arrived, Renno was ready to march. No ceremonies were held because that was not the Seneca way. The warriors said farewell to their families in private, and then virtually everyone in the town gathered to watch the expedition leave.

Ba-lin-ta demonstrated that she was a true woman of her nation. Her face expressionless, she raised her hand in a simple gesture when Renno took his place at the head of the main column, and she said good-bye to El-i-chi in the same manner when he moved up to a place beside his brother.

Only when the junior warriors fell into line was her composure somewhat shaken. She looked hard at Walter, but she remained self-controlled even when he returned her gaze for a long moment. Both took care not to betray emotion, although they realized they might never see each other again. Their destiny was in the hands of the manitous now, and Walter's survival depended on the will of the gods.

Kenneth Robinson took his place in the line beside Walter, an arrangement the latter had requested and that Renno had approved. Until Kenneth learned more of the language of the Seneca, Walter could act as his interpreter. Equally important, if the Englishman was still in the pay of the enemy, the harm he could do would be relatively limited as long as he marched with the junior warriors.

Renno had reservations about Kenneth's ability to maintain the blistering pace set by the Iroquois on the trail. "If you cannot keep up with us," he had warned Kenneth, "we shall have to leave you behind. I cannot allow one outsider to hold back fifteen hundred warriors."

Kenneth had nodded but had made no reply. Unsure of what was in store for him, he nevertheless was determined to do whatever was required.

The Oneida, all of them senior warriors, fanned out in the forest far ahead of the main column, and directly behind them came one hundred senior warriors of the Seneca, who comprised the vanguard. These two groups were responsible for discovering the presence of any foes in the wilderness and, in addition, had the task of shooting enough game to enable the army to eat. Every man carried enough emergency rations to last for several days, but the Iroquois tradition prevented the warriors from carrying substantial quantities of food. No matter how large a force they sent into the field, they lived off the land. This made it possible for them to travel far more rapidly than any similar force of white men.

All of the Iroquois in the war party had long been accustomed to the pace that Renno set. They moved at a rapid trot, and they took it for granted that few halts would be called. There was no conversation in the ranks, and almost without exception the warriors were so light-footed, so familiar with the wilderness that they made no sound.

Kenneth was astonished by the phenomenon. Fifteen hundred British redcoats moving through the forest would be heard for miles. These Indians ran like ghosts. Watching Walter and those who were ahead of them in the line, he tried to emulate them and enjoyed increasing success. He learned to tread lightly, never stepping on dried, fallen branches, never stirring up piles of leaves.

Thanks to the weeks he had spent with Obadiah and Deborah Jenkins, as well as the self-training program he had followed since coming to the land of the Seneca, he was in good physical condition. He estimated that the column remained on the move for more than eight hours before Renno called a halt long enough for the men to relieve themselves and drink cold water from a lake. But Kenneth soon discovered that the halt lasted for no more than a quarter of an hour. "How much longer will we be on the move today?" he asked Walter.

The junior warrior's bland shrug was that of a Seneca, not an English colonist. "When the sachem decides it is time to rest and eat," he said, "then we will halt."

As the day wore on, Kenneth became progressively wearier. His calves ached, his feet were sore, and he found himself wishing he could stretch out on the ground and take an hour's nap. But the Indians with whom he was marching appeared as fresh as they had been at dawn, and he marveled at their stamina. He could do whatever they did, he told himself, and he became grim as they continued to trot for hour after hour.

It was long after nightfall when the column at last came to a field where the Oneida scouts and Seneca vanguard had built cooking fires, and Kenneth was astonished when he saw sides of venison and buffalo roasting. He dragged himself to the bank of an icy river to drink and barely had the strength to join Walter beside a campfire. Sinking to the ground, he massaged his aching legs and feet.

Walter grinned at him. "Be glad this wasn't a forced march today," he said.

"You mean we might have marched still longer?"

"Every warrior of our people," Walter replied proudly, "is required to march for two days and two nights without rest before he may join our war party. Years ago, when I was still a child, Renno marched for four days and four nights without rest. He was being pursued by Huron, and he escaped from them."

Kenneth shook his head in wonder. It was beyond belief that any man could have such endurance.

When the meal was ready, the warriors hacked chunks of smoking meat from the sides of venison and buffalo, then sat cross-legged on the ground and ate with their fingers. Kenneth had to do as they did, and he found to his surprise that he had never enjoyed food so much.

He was still eating when Renno strolled through the encampment, accompanied by Sun-ai-yee and El-i-chi. Seeing the Englishman, Renno came to him and Walter. "You are still in our company," Renno said, a hint of approval in his tone.

Kenneth's grin spoke more loudly than words.

"Each day the task will grow lighter for you."

"Once I build up my endurance," Kenneth replied, "I hope you'll allow me to go out with your hunting parties from time to time."

Renno paid him the supreme compliment. "Tell me when you are ready, and you will go with the hunters." Any doubts he might have entertained about the Englishman's stamina and desire to participate in the campaign had vanished.

Chapter VIII

A nne Ridley had been taught to shoot by her father and brother at an early age, but her natural impulsiveness and her lack of patience had made her less than an enthusiastic hunter. Now, however, when bringing down game had become a necessity, she was gradually growing more adept at the sport under André Cooke's tutelage. Goading and prodding, he taught her to wait near a salt lick used by deer, neither speaking nor moving for hours She was learning how to stalk game, how to shoot at a wild duck or goose on the wing, how to aim with care.

Hester MacDevitt, who had never before used firearms, was a far more apt pupil than her friend. She had no bad habits to forget, and she was eager to learn the sport. André was delighted with the progress she showed and began to utilize the girls' naturally competitive spirits in order to spur Anne to achieve better results.

"Today," he told the pair early one morning at breakfast, "I'm putting you to a real hunting test."

Anne sighed loudly, her wordless complaint an attempt to annoy him. Hester said nothing, but her friend's reaction caused her to smile. Anne unfailingly did her best to unnerve and distress the man who had given them refuge, and Hester knew that Anne was being perverse only because she was developing an interest in him.

"Yesterday," André continued, ignoring the interruption, "I saw a small herd of buffalo heading toward the valley that lies about five miles off to the east."

"At the beginning of the Chickasaw hunting grounds?" Anne asked.

"Approximately, yes."

"In your endless lectures to us," she said sweetly, "you've told us again and again that we must never trespass on the hunting grounds of any Indian tribe. You've said that to trespass is to invite an attack by angry warriors. So why should this proposed hunting trip today be different?"

André knew she was baiting him, so he tried to remain cool. "Strictly speaking, the valley is located at the border of what the Chickasaw regard as their territory. I can assure you I'm not stupid enough to arouse their wrath by entering their actual hunting grounds!"

"I just wanted to make sure," Anne murmured, looking innocent.

"We're going to shoot only one buffalo," André continued, "for the simple reason that it will be hard enough, after we butcher the carcass, to bring the meat all the way back here. One of you will bring down the beast."

"Which one?" Hester asked.

He grinned. "That's the whole point of today's expedition. We'll approach the herd against the wind, naturally. That way, the sound of gunfire will be deflected. A single shot well might cause a stampede, and because buffalo aren't the most intelligent of animals, they sometimes run right in the direction from which a shot has come. Under ordinary circumstances we'd shoot two, maybe three, but I don't believe in killing for pleasure. Our limit will be one. You'll have an equal opportunity to fire, and your own skill will determine which of you is the winner."

"Why not wait until the time comes and then select one or the other of us?" Anne demanded.

André didn't want to tell her he was trying to encourage her interest in hunting. "I have my reasons, and we'll handle this my way," he said.

Hester decided to put an end to the discussion before the pair began to bicker again. "We'll do whatever you wish, André," she said sensibly. "How soon do we start?"

"Now. It will take us more than an hour to reach the valley."

They made immediate preparations for the outing, and the woodsman noted with approval that the girls had become acclimated to wilderness living. They checked and loaded their muskets, took several rounds of ammunition and horns of powder, and remembered to pack some leftover beans and cold meat for a meal at midday. They had already become far more self-reliant than either of them realized.

They set out at once, with André in the lead, Anne following him, and Hester bringing up the rear. By now it had become second nature for the girls to move through the forest in single file, Indian fashion, because it was the safest way to avoid an ambush by warriors or an attack by a wild animal. Many weeks of living and hunting deep in the virgin forests of North America had taught the girls how to walk silently, how to keep their bearings, and how to be alert to the subtleties of the wilderness. Also, they were becoming adept at reading what André called forest signposts.

After passing in one direction, they could find their way back to the cabin unaided by memorizing the shapes and peculiarities of various trees they passed.

From time to time André halted abruptly, stood still, and listened intently. His companions did the same, freezing, straining their ears, and never breaking the silence by asking questions. When he satisfied himself that all was well and started forward again, they did the same.

They walked steadily at a rapid pace for almost two hours, and when André halted again near the crest of a hill, beckoning and pointing, the girls moved up beside him. Far ahead in a grassy valley, they could see a small herd of buffalo grazing. There were three cows, a bull, and a calf, and both Anne and Hester had become sufficiently wise in the ways of the wilderness to know that the primary target should be one of the cows. The meat of a bull was so tough it had to be cooked interminably to make it edible, and the calf was too small to be suitable game. At André's nod they started forward again toward the entrance to the valley, descending the hill for that purpose.

Anne's manner changed suddenly. She had been indifferent, looking bored on the march, but now there was a gleam in her eyes. André told himself his strategy had been effective: her interest in the hunt was sparked by her desire to get the better of Hester.

They started forward through the thick pines that led to the head of the valley, and both girls removed the safety catches from their muskets. André told himself it was unlikely that he would need to tell either of them when the time was right for them to open fire.

All at once he froze. The two girls were bewildered but did the same. Then André motioned them behind a thick clump of bushes, even though the bushes were laden with brambles. Knowing that something serious was happening, Anne and Hester crouched low as André removed the safety catch from his musket, his face

212

grim. He indicated with a gesture that he wanted the girls to maintain absolute quiet.

Soon they, too, heard human footsteps and moments later saw a file of warriors whose paint identified them as Chickasaw. In their midst, riding on spirited horses, were three white people: a middle-aged man and a young woman in buckskins and a pale-skinned man dressed in Indian attire, who was wearing Indian paint that André did not recognize. He was conversing amiably with one of the Chickasaw who trotted beside him, and it was apparent that the trio were not prisoners but were regarded by the warriors as friends.

André was taking no chances. There would be serious trouble with the warriors if he and his companions were discovered, so he kept his musket trained on the shaved head of the white-skinned Indian, a powerfully built man in his forties.

The older man turned in his saddle and spoke in French. "How much farther must we go to reach the town of these savages?"

The white-skinned Indian replied in the same tongue. "Be patient, Don Diego. Distances mean little to Indians. An extra hour or an extra day on the trail means nothing to them. Concentrate on the offer we plan to make to them in order to establish an alliance."

Anne and Hester knew only a smattering of French and consequently could not understand the conversation, but André Cooke's expression changed, and he scowled.

The party passed beyond earshot. The two girls and André were safe now, but they remained in their hiding place behind the bushes for a long time. When André finally spoke, he confined his orders to a few words. "Forget the buffalo hunt. We'll go home—quickly and quietly."

They followed him as he led them back to the cabin, his pace far more brisk than it had been when they had

213

set out on the hunt. Only when they reached the cabin did he offer an explanation. "A single shot would have told that party there were others in the immediate vicinity who know the use of firearms. We couldn't take the risk."

"Who were those strange people—and what were they saying, André?" Anne could curb her curiosity no longer.

He reported the conversation.

"The French are trying to make allies of the Chickasaw, then," Anne said. "Just as the Iroquois are on our side. That's smart of them, I suppose."

"The French and the Spaniards are working together. The older man spoke French with an accent and was called Don Diego. That's a Spanish name."

"What confuses me is why the younger man was dressed like an Indian," Hester said.

"Well," Anne replied, "you know that my brother-in-law, Renno of the Seneca, is white, but he's completely an Indian."

"Perhaps I've lived alone for too long in this remote place," André said. "There can't be too many white war chiefs, but it would take someone who knows more than I do about the policies of the various nations to identify him. All I know is that I don't like this situation."

The girls looked at him.

"This portion of the wilderness has been at peace for many years," he explained. "The tribes of the area have respected the boundary lines of the others' hunting grounds, and there has been no violence. Now it appears that the war is being forced on the nations of the Mississippi."

They were silent, absorbing what he had said, and then Anne spoke somberly. "It may be that you'll have to take sides, after all."

"That thought has been uppermost in my mind all the way back here," André said. "I believed a war between Great Britain and France would leave me untouched, but the war seems to be coming close to my doorstep."

"So you could become our enemy," Anne declared.

"Never, no matter what I might decide. I don't believe in making war on women."

"Do you have any idea which side you'll join?" Hester asked. "If you join either, I mean."

He looked at her, then stared even longer at Anne. "I've had divided loyalties all of my life, and I suppose one reason I've made my home alone in the wilderness is because I've wanted to avoid making the choice. But—assuming I must—I won't evade my responsibilities. I need a little more time to make up my mind."

The regiment from Massachusetts Bay was the first to reach the rendezvous site on the Ohio River, and the troops went to work at once, chopping trees and fashioning rafts. The battalion from Virginia arrived the following day, reuniting Jeffrey Wilson and Ned Ridley, and the latter's men promptly joined in the task of preparing rafts. A sentry sighted a large herd of buffalo north of the river, only a short distance from the bivouac, so a platoon of Virginia sharpshooters went hunting. Enough of the beasts were slaughtered to ensure ample supplies of meat for many days to come.

The army of the Iroquois made its appearance suddenly, dramatically, with hordes of warriors emerging silently from the wilderness. They established their own camp with an ease and dispatch that the militia envied, staking out ground, cutting firewood, and immediately sending out their own hunting and fishing parties. Unlike the colonials, they erected no tents, intending to sleep in the open by choice, and they built fires only for cooking, needing none for warmth.

They made their camp in such an orderly manner that Renno, accompanied by Sun-ai-yee, was able, within half an hour, to join Jeffrey and Ned for the first meeting of their high command.

Renno was grieved to learn from his brother-in-law

that there was still no news of Anne, but Ned had other news that was heartening. "The day before I left Norfolk," he said, "one of my father's ships put in from England, and the captain said he'd heard a rumor in London—a rumor he couldn't confirm before he sailed—that Ghonka's mission was a success."

The others listened in grateful silence. Renno bowed his head for a moment, and the others knew he was thanking the manitous because his wife, his parents, and his children might soon return from their long journey.

In the days that followed, the warriors went to work, cutting down trees and making rafts, and they were so efficient that the entire task was completed ahead of schedule, enabling the expedition to start down the Ohio River sooner than anticipated. A final meeting was held because Renno had a problem on his mind.

"We are old friends who have fought side by side in the past," he explained. "So each knows the minds of the others. That is why General Wilson did not appoint an overall commander of the expedition. But it may be, when we actually start to fight, that there will be the need for one man to give the orders. Often in battle there is confusion. Let there be but one commander, and the confusion will lessen."

"That's true," Ned Ridley said. "And I reckon it's wise to settle this matter in advance."

"Jeffrey is a full colonel," Renno said. "Let him command us in battle."

His old friend from Massachusetts Bay grinned and shook his head. "You flatter me, but I must refuse. If just one man gives the orders, it must be Renno. Not only does he command the biggest force in our expedition, but he's the best qualified. I'll feel better knowing you'll be in charge, Renno."

"So will I," Ned added emphatically.

That settled the question, and Renno reluctantly accepted.

The leaders ate a predawn breakfast of broiled fish

on the morning the fleet of rafts would be launched, and Jeffrey asked Renno, "Have you decided to allow Kenneth Robinson to remain in your ranks?"

Renno inclined his head. "Robinson has earned that right," he replied. "It was not easy for him to march at a Seneca pace, but he kept up with the warriors. And not once did he complain."

Jeffrey lowered his voice. "Fair enough. But I still worry that he might be working for the French."

"It is possible," Renno said, "but I think not. El-i-chi has wisdom in knowing what lies in a warrior's heart. He has secretly kept watch over Robinson. Not once has Robinson been curious about matters that do not concern him."

"Then you believe he's seriously trying to reform and make something of himself?"

"One who travels forty miles each day in the company of the Seneca could not be other than serious," Renno replied. "There are few militiamen who could do it."

"I know I couldn't." Jeffrey pondered, then smiled. "As long as you're satisfied, keep him in your ranks. But I hope El-i-chi will continue to observe him."

"It will be done," Renno promised.

The voyage down the Ohio to its junction with the Mississippi was swift. The leaders believed they were being watched by various tribes along the way, but no nation attempted to halt the journey of the large force of Iroquois and the hundreds of white colonists armed with firesticks. Occasionally a raft ran aground, but it was soon launched again. The unfortunates who inadvertently had been forced to take an icy bath in the Ohio were teased without mercy by the occupants of rafts that suffered no misfortunes.

The current of the Mississippi was slow, and the rafts moved in single file. Militiamen and warriors alike looked at the deep forest on either side of them and were relieved that they were riding in comfort rather than marching. Each day one group or another traveled on foot, however, in order to do the hunting necessary for the army. At sundown the rest of the warriors and soldiers went ashore to eat and sleep.

As yet the high command had no way of determining whether the French and Spaniards had landed a force of their own somewhere on the Gulf of Mexico. "When we're closer to the mouth of the Mississippi," Colonel Jeffrey Wilson said, "I suggest we find out whatever we can from some of the local tribes."

His colleagues agreed. "One thing is sure," Lieutenant Colonel Ned Ridley said. "The Mississippi is the logical waterway for any invading army to use. If the enemy is preparing a thrust against us, they're certain to travel upstream, just as we're going downstream."

News of the foes' activities came unexpectedly. One evening when the army was eating roasted meat and grilled fish at the overnight camp, a senior warrior of the Oneida interrupted Renno and Sun-ai-yee at their meal. "A messenger who has let it be known that he is of the Biloxi nation came to our sentry post. He seeks the ear of the sachem."

Renno instantly agreed to see the man, and a few moments later the short, swarthy Da-no was escorted to the cooking fire, with several of the Oneida in watchful attendance. Greetings were exchanged, and Renno offered the visitor food.

Da-no ate hungrily, and as he licked his fingers he said, "The warrior of the Biloxi brings words for the ears of the sachem of the Iroquois."

Renno dismissed the Oneida guards, and only Sun-ai-yee remained behind with him.

Da-no immediately repeated the message of the medicine man. "The Biloxi are not the enemies of the Seneca and the other Iroquois. The Biloxi are their friends." He then went on to tell the Seneca leaders in detail about the recruiting being done by a Spanish couple and a French officer who lived and dressed as an Indian. The trio had already won the support of the large Creek nation and were trying to force the Biloxi and other small tribes of the Mississippi basin to join them, too.

A sense of grim excitement surged within Renno when he heard the mention of the Frenchman who masqueraded as an Indian, but his face remained expressionless, and he waited patiently for the messenger to finish his story.

The white-skinned trio had flooded the forest with Creek warriors, Da-no went on, so he had been forced to hide for many days, which had delayed his journey. He prayed to the gods that his brother Biloxi, Ha-lem, had not been captured and killed and that no retribution had been visited on the Biloxi, but he felt certain that, even if captured, his brother would never reveal the intention of his nation to become the allies of the Seneca.

Within the past two days, Da-no revealed, he had had to hide again. He had been making his way through the nearby land of the Chickasaw when the same two Spaniards and the Frenchman had appeared on the trail, escorted by a large band of Chickasaw warriors. They had not been aware of his proximity, and he had been able to conceal himself.

Renno exchanged a wooden glance with Sun-ai-yee. "The sachem of the Iroquois wishes to learn more about the war chief of the French who is also an Indian. What war paint does he wear?"

"The Biloxi have never seen that paint."

Renno remained patient. "What are the colors?"

"One is as purple as deep water, the other is more white than new snow."

That answered Renno's question. There was no doubt in his mind who the Frenchman was. "Da-no will rest. He is the guest of the Seneca," Renno said. After instructing El-i-chi to make certain the Biloxi remained in the camp, he and Sun-ai-yee promptly went to the far side of the bivouac to confer with Jeffrey and Ned.

"I know nothing about the old Spaniard and the

young woman who rides with him," Renno said. "But no man on earth causes more trouble for us than Golden Eagle."

"Is it too late to persuade the Creek to abandon their alliance with him?" Ned asked.

Renno shrugged. "The Creek have given their word."

"They will keep that word," Sun-ai-yee added. "They will remain the friends of France and Spain."

"The Chickasaw are warriors of great courage," Renno said thoughtfully, "and it may not be too late to persuade them it isn't in their best interest to oppose us. Also, we have an opportunity to do away with Golden Eagle and the Spanish man and woman, whoever they may be."

"What do you have in mind?" Ned asked.

"The messenger of the Biloxi will guide fifty senior warriors of the Seneca into the land of the Chickasaw. They will set an ambush and will kill Golden Eagle and the Spaniards. Then their leader will sit with the sachem of the Chickasaw and will reason with him. Our army will wait here until this work is done."

Only Sun-ai-yee nodded in approval.

"You're intending to lead this raiding party yourself!" Ned declared.

Renno nodded. "The manitous would brand me as a coward if I failed to give this assignment to myself. And they would be right. It is my destiny to meet Golden Eagle. Either he will kill me or I will kill him."

"You're taking too great a risk," Jeffrey said. "We can't take the chance of losing the head of this expedition."

Renno could not be moved. "Only a sachem can reason with the sachem of the Chickasaw," he replied. "The sachem of the Chickasaw will open his ears and his mind only if our foes are dead."

Ned realized it was useless to argue with him. "When will you leave on this mission?"

"Tonight. Right now. I want to stop Golden Eagle before he does us more harm." Renno rose to his feet. "Wait here until I return. Sun-ai-yee will command the Iroquois while I am away."

Returning to his own part of the bivouac, Renno quickly selected fifty senior warriors to accompany him. El-i-chi was the first he named, but he rejected the request of Walter and Kenneth Robinson that they join the war party. The delicacy of this mission made it necessary to utilize the services of experienced warriors.

Da-no agreed to lead the party into the land of the Chickasaw. It was clear to him that, regardless of the outcome, the Seneca would extend their protection to the Biloxi tribe.

Stripping to their loincloths and moccasins, the members of the party greased themselves with animal fat, then daubed their green and yellow war paint on their faces and torsos. Renno, whose rank was denoted only by the cluster of feathers he wore at the base of his scalp lock, ordered the warriors to carry only their knives and tomahawks, bows and arrows. It was best not to use firearms on this mission, he decided, because his braves were less familiar with them than with the traditional weapons of their people.

"Do not kill or scalp any warrior of the Chickasaw," he said before they started. "It may be that the chance to take their scalps will come. But do not give in to temptation. It is the hope of the Seneca that the Chickasaw will become their friends, not their enemies."

They started off at their customary trot, with Da-no in the lead, and Renno had to urge him to move more rapidly. The pace of the Biloxi was far slower than that of the Seneca.

The night was dark, with thick clouds hiding the moon and stars, and the warriors moved like wraiths through the thick forest. After they had spent considerable time on the trail, Renno sensed the proximity of a Chickasaw sentry, whom they easily avoided. The presence of the man served notice that the main town of the tribe was somewhere ahead.

Da-no cautiously slowed to a walk, then halted and pointed when they came to the crest of a wooded hill. Renno raised his hand, and the entire party stopped. The young sachem stared into the night, and his extraordinary vision enabled him to see what others could not. Several hundred yards ahead lay a clearing, and beyond it stood the palisade of the Chickasaw town. Several dim shapes were barely visible just outside the wall, and after he studied them for a time, he was able to make out the silhouettes of horses.

His lips tightened. The Chickasaw, like the Seneca, were a nation that owned few horses, so he felt certain that Golden Eagle and the two Spaniards were in the town. He beckoned to El-i-chi, who moved up beside him. "Our enemies sleep in the town of the Chickasaw," he murmured.

The word was passed from warrior to warrior, and the party squatted, each man eating a little jerked meat and a handful of parched corn. The worst of any battle, as the experienced well knew, was the idle period before it began, but the Seneca remained unflustered as they waited patiently for the night to end.

Renno analyzed the situation and knew it would be a mistake to enter the town and search for his foes. The Europeans were the guests of the Chickasaw and consequently were under their protection. No attack should be made on the Chickasaw guests until they left the confines of the town. On the other hand, it was almost impossible for the war party to escape discovery if they had to spend the entire coming day so close to the palisade. Sooner or later the Chickasaw would see them and would raise an alarm.

As Renno saw the problem, he was forced to gamble. If the negotiations with the Chickasaw had been completed, the visitors would be leaving the town early in the morning. He would stay in place in the hope that would happen. If worse came to worst, he and his warriors would retreat into the forest and would wait until the following day, hoping they could conceal themselves for that long a time.

Streaks of dirty gray appeared in the sky, and as day dawned, a light, chilly rain began to fall. The Seneca stoically paid no attention to the weather. After they had eaten, they continued to squat, and without exception, all of them, including Renno, closed their eyes.

The astonished Da-no guessed that they were sleeping, and he was right. He marveled at the self-confidence of warriors who could snatch a period of rest prior to a battle, certain that they would awaken instantly in the event that trouble arose.

The gate of the town creaked open in the distance, and although the sound was barely audible, the warriors were awake and alert. But only Renno stood.

A number of Chickasaw emerged into the open, among them a war chief and several senior warriors. Then a middle-aged white man in buckskins came out of the town and mounted a horse. He was followed by a young woman, similarly attired, and a few moments later Golden Eagle appeared, wearing his familiar Huron attire, and also getting on horseback.

Renno was impassive and unmoving, but his blood raced. The confrontation he had awaited for so long was at last at hand!

The three riders, surrounded by a Chickasaw escort twenty strong, moved onto the trail and headed toward the waiting Seneca. Renno had guessed correctly; the visitors were being taken in the direction of the Mississippi River.

No order or sign was given, but Da-no again was amazed when he saw the Seneca rise simultaneously, some stringing their bows and reaching for the arrows they carried in their quivers, while others took their tomahawks from their belts. It was small wonder, the Biloxi reflected, that no nation was the equal of these disciplined braves.

The Chickasaw and their guests approached slowly,

and Renno could hear the middle-aged man speaking. His head was turned toward the rear, and Renno knew only that he was speaking in Spanish. It was not possible to understand what he was saying.

Continuing to wait, Renno strung his own bow, then suddenly raised a hand. The warriors spread out on either side of the trail, concealing themselves behind trees and bushes. They accomplished the maneuver in total silence; not a single twig snapped beneath a brave's foot.

Da-no wanted to take part in the battle with his new friends but wisely decided not to participate. The Seneca had their own method of fighting, and he might blunder or otherwise interfere with their operation.

Renno's patience was almost inexhaustible. Remaining motionless until the head of the column came within bow and arrow range, he called in a loud, clear voice, "Warriors of the Chickasaw! Do not raise your hands against those who await you, and you will suffer no harm. We are the friends of the Chickasaw. Only the French and the Spanish are our foes!"

One of the Seneca hurled his tomahawk at the Spaniard's mount. The aim was true, the blade striking the beast on the head. As the horse stumbled and fell, El-i-chi sent an arrow into the Spaniard's throat. He pitched forward, his blood dampening the ground as he sprawled on the narrow path.

The Chickasaw stood frozen. It was impossible to determine whether they were stunned or were heeding the order not to intervene.

But Alain de Gramont wasted no time. Grasping Beatriz's reins, he shouted to her, "We've been ambushed. Come with me! Quickly!"

"My father!" she screamed. "My father is dead!"

Renno chose this moment to step into the open. He could have remained concealed and dueled his mortal enemy in anonymity, but his honor demanded that

Golden Eagle know his adversary. Raising his bow, Renno let fly.

In that same instant the Frenchman-Huron recognized him and fired the pistol he already held in his free hand. Renno's arrow grazed the side of his enemy's head. Golden Eagle's bullet missed the young Seneca by inches.

Neither had an opportunity to strike again. Still forcing the grief-stricken woman to accompany him, Alain de Gramont plunged into the forest, spurring his horse to a gallop.

A hail of arrows followed the pair, but they were untouched, and the hoofbeats of their horses receded rapidly in the wilderness.

El-i-chi moved onto the trail, bent down, and scalped Don Diego de Bernardo.

In spite of Renno's deep disappointment over his failure to kill Golden Eagle, his task here was not completed. Raising his arm in greeting, he called, "Renno, sachem of the Seneca, wishes to parley with the sachem of the Chickasaw."

The war chief who had been the leader of the escort came into the open and returned the salute. Numbed by the discovery that the invaders were the dreaded Seneca, he nevertheless realized that their sachem had kept his word. No Chickasaw had been harmed in the assault.

Renno fell in beside him, and the other Seneca followed, with El-i-chi wearing the dripping scalp in his belt and two of the other warriors carrying Don Diego's body.

Men, women, and children came into the open to stare as the grim procession passed through the town, but no one spoke, the sight of the Seneca war paint chilling the people.

The leader of the nation emerged from his house and stood unmoving, his arms folded, as he watched the approach of the party.

Renno raised his arm. "Renno, sachem of the Seneca, comes in peace," he said.

The Chickasaw replied in kind. "Ing-o-lye, sachem of the Chickasaw, receives the Seneca in peace."

The warriors dropped the body of the Spanish agent at his feet. Ing-o-lye's face was expressionless as he glanced down at the lifeless form of the scalped foreigner who, minutes earlier, had been his guest. Then he beckoned, stood aside, and allowed Renno to precede him into his house. They sat cross-legged on the bare ground, facing each other, and the Chickasaw leader took his time preparing a pipe, which he lighted slowly, then handed to his visitor.

It was apparent to Renno that the man was stalling for time, hoping the reason for the intrusion would be explained. It suited the young Seneca to make his point bluntly. "The Spaniard whose body will be eaten by wild dogs was the enemy of the Iroquois and the English colonies."

"It is so," the Chickasaw acknowledged.

"The French-Huron and the woman also are our enemies, but they escaped." Renno concealed his distress. "No matter. The manitous will cause our paths to cross again. Then they will die."

Ing-o-lye made no comment, and Renno decided to drive home his message without delay. "All who are enemies of the Iroquois and the English colonies will die. The army of the Iroquois and the English settlers rests at this moment near the land of the Chickasaw. Their numbers are as great as the leaves that fall to the floor of the forest when winter comes." He paused, then added casually, "Let Ing-o-lye send a messenger who will see for himself that Renno speaks the truth."

"A messenger will be sent," Ing-o-lye declared, then went on hastily, "but the Chickasaw do not doubt that the words of the Seneca are true."

"It is true also that the foreigners came to the Chickasaw to persuade them to become allies in the new war."

The Chickasaw sachem was becoming increasingly uncomfortable. "That was the reason for their visit," he conceded.

"The warriors of the Seneca, the Mohawk, and the Oneida need no help from the warriors of other nations," Renno said loftily. "But any who join the French and the Spaniards become their enemies. The land of the Tusacarora of the South lies to the east of the land of the Chickasaw. The Tuscarora long have coveted the hunting grounds of the Chickasaw. If the Chickasaw join our enemies, the Tuscarora will take and keep those hunting grounds. All of their brothers in the Iroquois League will come to their aid." The challenge was explicit.

The situation was anything but what Ing-o-lye had envisioned the previous evening when he had yielded to the generous offers of Gramont and Don Diego. Now, only a short time later, the Spaniard was dead, and the Iroquois were poised on the threshold of his realm instead of staying in their own lands, many hundreds of miles away.

Ing-o-lye reconsidered his position. "The foreigners told lies to the Chickasaw," he said. "So the Chickasaw are not bound by their honor to keep the treaty they have made." He rose, went to the entrance, and spoke in an undertone to the warrior on sentry duty there. Then he returned, sat, and folded his arms.

Renno thoroughly understood what was going through the mind of his fellow sachem. The promise of firearms and supplies to be delivered at some future time by France and Spain became insignficant in the face of the immediate threat of an invasion by the powerful Iroquois.

There was no conversation, but Renno patiently continued to wait.

The warrior appeared, handed something to his superior, and withdrew. The sachem of the Chickasaw unrolled a strip of wampum, white beads that filled a length of soft leather, the borders edged in red. "The

Chickasaw give their pledge to the Seneca that they will not take up the cause of France and Spain. They swear they will remain neutral in the war."

This was precisely what Renno had been seeking, but he did not take the wampum. "Let the pledge be repeated in the presence of the people of the Chickasaw and the war party of the Seneca," he said.

Ing-o-lye had no choice, so they went into the open, and the promise was made publicly.

Now Renno was willing to take the token. "If the Chickasaw stay neutral, the Seneca promise in the names of their gods that they will remain at peace with the Chickasaw."

This new agreement, made by the leaders of the two nations, was binding on both sides. The full burden of responsibility was carried by the Chickasaw, to be sure. If they changed again when and if French and Spanish arms and supplies arrived, they would be guilty of breaching a sacred covenant and would face the combined forces of the Iroquois nations. No tribe had ever survived such an attack.

Satisfied that Golden Eagle's mischief had been undone, Renno consented to stay for the traditional meal that followed the making of a treaty. He was eager to return to his forces waiting on the Mississippi, but the demands of protocol had to be met.

As the honored guest he was served slices of buffalo liver and a portion of the heart of an elk as well as the more ordinary venison stew. Several of the tribe's young women were assigned to the task of meeting his needs, and all of them flirted with him. Had he shown an interest in one, the woman gladly would have retired with him to one of the houses.

But Renno had no interest in a woman just for the night. Soon, if the manitous continued to show him their favor, Betsy would return from England and would be waiting for him at home. His eyes remained stony, so the young women contented themselves with bringing him more food.

As soon as the meal ended, he and his warriors took their leave. To the surprise of Da-no they returned to their bivouac at the same rapid trot that had brought them inland from the great river. The stern Seneca always were in a hurry, it seemed to the Biloxi, and they maintained their customary disciplined silence on the trail. Not until they came within sight of the camp-fires on the river bank did Da-no summon the courage to ask for the right to accompany the expedition to his own land.

Renno nodded in agreement, then went to join his colleagues.

Jeffrey Wilson examined the contents of the Spaniard's purse, then handed them to Ned Ridley. "The man El-i-chi killed appears to have been called Don Diego de Bernardo, but that's all I can make out. You read Spanish, so maybe you can translate these documents."

Ned read the papers carefully. "Don Diego seems to have been an important personage. He carried a letter from the first minister in Madrid and another from the viceroy of New Spain, both ordering all Spanish subjects everywhere to follow his orders and give him any assistance he needed."

"Yet he died on a wilderness trail in the New World." Jeffrey shook his head and smiled wryly. "El-i-chi carries a very heavy scalp."

Renno realized he had accomplished a great deal on his brief expedition. Not only had the Chickasaw been snatched from the grasp of France and Spain, but a prominent representative of the Spanish government had lost his life. The victories left a sour taste in his mouth, however, because he had not succeeded in concluding his private battle with Golden Eagle. Ordinarily an unerring marksman with a bow and arrow, he had missed his target. He realized at the same time that Golden Eagle, a deadly pistol shot, somehow had missed him, too.

There was only one conclusion Renno could draw.

The manitous had their own mysterious reasons for prolonging the feud. The climactic duel would be fought at some future time, so Renno had to remain patient and await that day. He did not doubt that sooner or later it would come.

Deep in the forest far to the south of the land of the Chickasaw, Alain de Gramont sat near the campfire he had built in a hollow, and he brooded bitterly. He needed no one to tell him that the Chickasaw would renege on their promise to join the French and Spaniards. Renno would see to that. The forces of the Chickasaw, added to the Creek, would have made the allies virtually impregnable, no matter how many Iroquois joined the English colonists.

Damn Renno! How Alain hated the younger white Indian who consistently turned his victories into defeats. He had to admit that the depth of his hatred was responsible for the fact that Renno was still alive. No man was cooler or more resourceful in a crisis than Alain, and in the past he had struck far more difficult targets. He could only guess that his rage, when he had recognized his adversary, had caused his hand to shake. There was no other explanation for missing.

Well, he had to console himself with the thought that he and Renno would meet again. The presence of the Seneca, along with a band of his warriors, this far from his home meant that the Iroquois had divined the overall French-Spanish plan and had sent an expedition to the lower Mississippi region. Fair enough. By the time he made several new alliances, he would be more than ready to meet Renno again.

Night was falling, and Alain was relieved when Beatriz de Bernardo returned from the stream where she had bathed. In spite of his contempt for her, she was vital to his plans; since the murder of her father, she alone could provide the necessary arms, munitions, and supplies to cement future alliances with the tribes of the area.

A glance at the woman told Alain that she had recovered from her hysteria. After her father's death she had ranted and raved like a lunatic until he had forced her to eat some wild herbs he knew would sedate her. She had slept without awakening for nearly twelve hours, and now she was calm, almost too calm.

Seating herself opposite him on the far side of the small fire, she helped herself to a portion of grilled fish and some of the roots he had roasted in the coals. She ate slowly, in silence, and only once did she speak. "For many years my father prepared me for the day when he would be gone and I would work alone. I always knew the time would come when he would die, but it never occurred to me that he would be slaughtered senselessly by savages in a primitive wilderness. That was too much. It was such a waste of a great man."

Alain noted that she spoke without emotion, and when she finally raised her eyes to his, he saw that her face was as blank as that of an Indian warrior. Perhaps she was still in a state of shock.

"I want you to tell me all you can about the white Indian who was in command of the party that laid the ambush for us."

"His name is Renno. How he became a Seneca I don't know, but he has spent his entire life with them. He rose swiftly in their ranks, and today he is a sachem, or national chief."

"How did he rise so high?"

"Well, his father is the Great Sachem of the Iroquois League, but Renno has earned his promotions; I freely admit it. He's competent, courageous, and a natural leader of men. More than ten years ago he became acquainted with the English colonists, and since that time he has become a link between them and the Iroquois. As you know, his wife comes from Virginia, but I know few details about her."

"Would you say he has a weakness for white women?" Beatriz asked.

"Not to my knowledge. If I knew of any weak spot in his character, I would have exploited it long ago. Fate has thrust me opposite him more often than I care to recall, and his good luck is remarkable. You saw that yourself two days ago, when my pistol shot missed him. I rarely miss. I'm the best shot in all of North America."

"There may be one who is better," she replied, but did not press the point. "What is the significance of his presence so near the home of the Chickasaw?"

"It can only mean that the Iroquois have sent an expedition against us. So we'll have to double our recruiting pace. It wouldn't surprise me if the English colonies have sent some of their militia into the area, too. So our French and Spanish troops will need all the help we can provide for them if they're to win a clean-cut victory."

"Are the Iroquois such good fighting men?"

"There are none superior to them, and only my own Huron are in a class with the Seneca. We'll not only need to speed up our schedule, but we'll need to make certain that the arms and supplies we promise are sent promptly from the headquarters our joint forces have established on Mobile Bay."

Beatriz watched him, her eyes hooded. "You sound afraid of the Seneca."

"I fear no one on earth," Alain said curtly, "but the mere mention of the Seneca is enough to frighten most tribes. You can be sure that by now the Chickasaw have abandoned their alliance with us."

"If that is true," she said softly, "then my father surely died in vain."

Something in her tone caused him to stare at her. "You intend—as you've indicated—to go on with your father's work?"

"Of course. I should be letting him down if I did not. Why do you ask, Alain?"

"I'm not sure. There's something in your attitude that I can't fathom."

To his surprise she laughed aloud, and her amusement seemed genuine. "You and I have slept together, Alain, but you do not understand me in the least."

"Correct. I don't pretend to know you."

"That is because of my father's genius. He taught me the art of never revealing my inner self to anyone. Of all the people you have ever known, only I have no weaknesses. You have them, and so does this Renno of the Seneca."

Alain was nettled. "What are my weaknesses?"

"You are arrogant," Beatriz replied calmly. "Too often you reject advice and counsel without weighing the problem at hand from another point of view."

He considered her criticism for a moment, then shrugged. "You may be right."

"I am. And I know this Renno must have weaknesses, too. I want you to remember all you have ever learned about him. Either from you—or in some other way—I intend to learn what holes are to be found in this white Indian's armor!"

"Our first duty," he replied, "is to strengthen the Franco-Spanish regiments by making alliances with as many Indians tribes as we can."

"I will not forget my duty, rest assured of that," she said. "Just as I will not forget my personal obligation, either. All that I am, all that I ever hope to become I owe to my father. His memory is sacred to me."

"I fail to see the connection. What does your debt to your father have to do with our mission?"

"How is it possible that you could be so stupid?" Her voice rose to a shout, and then she regained her self-control again. "Forgive me. I did not mean to scream at you. You would have no way of knowing what takes place in my mind."

"Well, you needn't concern yourself with Renno. Just knowing he has come to this part of the wilderness is sufficient for me. Ultimately our forces and those of Renno and his allies will meet in battle. When we do, take my word for it, I will find him and kill him."

Beatriz's smile was cold and brittle. "Has it not occurred to you that this—this natural leader of men, as you called him, could be immobilized before the armies actually meet on the battlefield?"

"I dislike mysterious hints," Alain said.

"Then I will spell out my position for you," Beatriz said, a note of bitter hatred creeping into her voice. "Renno of the Seneca is responsible for the death of my father. My soul cries for vengeance. I swear to you that Renno will die—before the armies clash. I will see to it myself, and if I must, I will strangle him with my own hands!"

Alain de Gramont was regarded as merciless, but the burning hatred for Renno that he saw in the Spanish woman's eyes caused him to shudder.

Chapter IX

Renno spent a troubled night following his journey into the land of the Chickasaw, and early the next morning, before breakfast, he went to his fellow commanders. "I think the time has come to stop traveling by raft," he said. "We should start marching overland."

Ned Ridley laughed. "I know," he said. "You're afraid the men will grow too soft."

The young sachem remained grave. "No, it is wrong to stay on the water."

"What are your reasons?" Jeffrey asked.

"We know now that Golden Eagle is busy seeking allies in the area," Renno said. "We know that the Creek, at least, have joined the French. It may be that other nations also have become their allies or soon will do so." He paused, then added solemnly, "When I was a small boy, Ghonka often said to me, 'My son, always

235

remember that the forest has eyes.' I have never forgotten."

"You're right," Jeffrey said. "Warriors on the side of the French could be watching us from the bank of the Mississippi, and we wouldn't even realize it because they could conceal themselves so easily behind the thick foliage."

"You and I have been shortsighted, Jeff," Ned declared. "How simple it would be for an enemy to count the rafts, even count the number of men on each barge. With no effort at all they could determine the exact size of our force!"

"Renno," Jeffrey said, "we're indebted to you. We'll destroy the rafts at once, and this very morning we'll resume our journey on foot."

Various adjustments were required, and realizing they were now in territory where enemy warriors might be lurking in strength, Renno sent the Oneida and a band of one hundred Seneca senior warriors ahead as scouts. He instructed them to cover the area from the river to six or seven miles east of the Mississippi, and he made it clear that he wanted to be notified without delay of any signs of other humans they encountered. Now there was no way that Golden Eagle could launch a surprise attack.

The Seneca led the main column, reducing their rate of march to the slower pace of the Massachusetts Bay and Virginia militiamen. So, instead of trotting, the warriors walked, always taking the precaution of fanning out over a considerable area. The Virginia sharpshooters came next, followed by the larger unit under Jeffrey's command, while the Mohawk, also spreading out, brought up the rear and kept it secure.

Renno also ordered that the hunters who provided food for the army use only Indian weapons. Under no circumstances were firearms to be employed for the purpose. Unseen enemies would hear the sound of musket fire and would know that the Iroquois and militia units were in the vicinity.

The first day passed without incident, the force covering approximately twenty miles. This was only a fraction of the journey they could have made by raft on the Mississippi, but Renno was no longer apprehensive. He and his warriors were completely at home in the forest and were prepared to fight without warning.

The Oneida and Seneca scouts, who had rejoined the main column the previous evening, departed again long before dawn in order to scour the area through which the day's march would be made. Sun-ai-yee, who was chafing because of the slow pace, decided to accompany the scouts for a day because, he said, he felt a need for strenuous exercise.

The use of cooking fires had not yet been prohibited since no enemies had been sighted, and Renno was able to enjoy a hot breakfast of grilled fish. Each day he deliberately ate with a different band, and this morning he had elected to sit with the junior warriors. Walter, whose ability to enunciate clearly was improving day by day, couldn't resist showing off to his future brother-in-law and was more talkative than usual.

Kenneth Robinson, who was lean, fit, and heavily tanned, was a member of the group, and although he said little, it was evident that he was proud of his ability to hold his own in this company of Indians.

"You are doing well," Renno said, believing he deserved a compliment.

Kenneth grinned but made no reply.

Vividly recalling his own sojourn in England many years earlier, Renno couldn't help wondering how this sophisticated nobleman, who was accustomed to the luxuries of European civilization, was adjusting to the harsh realities of wilderness living. "Do you think often of London?" he asked.

"Almost never." Kenneth spoke quietly but emphatically. "The man who squandered his inheritance at the gaming tables, drank far too much, and spent time with wenches no longer exists."

Renno could tell he was sincere. "I think I know what you mean."

"The wilderness is the greatest challenge I've ever known. I don't mind admitting to you that I was contemptuous of the New World when I first came here, but the primitive appeals to me. This may sound foolish, but I feel I'm more of a man when I conquer my surroundings."

"You are truly a man," Renno replied, pleased that he had played a role in the nobleman's change of attitude. At the first opportunity he would give Jeffrey a full report.

To Renno's surprise they were interrupted by Sun-ai-yee. "I came to you myself rather than send a messenger," the war chief said. "Two of our Seneca scouts found a house of logs in the wilderness."

"A house?" Renno was incredulous.

Sun-ai-yee nodded. "Three people live there. One is a man, two are women, and all are white."

Renno pondered. "Perhaps they work for the French."

"It may be," the war chief replied. "It is strange that people with pale skins live so far from the towns of their own kind. I did not allow the warriors of the Seneca to attack. The house is surrounded now, and none can escape. I thought you would wish to question them. If they speak the tongue of the English, the sachem can speak to them himself. If they speak the tongue of the French, some warrior in the camp of Virginia or Massachusetts Bay may be able to interpret."

Kenneth had learned enough of the language of the Seneca to pick up the essence of what the war chief had just said. "I can speak French fluently," he said, "and I'd like to make myself useful. Take me with you."

Renno agreed and decided to include Walter in the escort of fifty warriors he would take with him. He conferred briefly with Ned and Jeffrey, telling them about the unexpected development. All agreed that it was best for the main body to wait until the wilderness dwellers were captured alive and questioned before the army moved on.

Sun-ai-yee declared he would lead the party to the house. Renno went with him at once, Kenneth trotting beside them and the warriors of the escort spreading out in the forest around them.

André Cooke awakened at dawn, as he always did, and dressing quickly, he went to the crib behind the cabin to relieve himself. Then he picked up two buckets, intending to fill them with water in the stream, but he took only a step or two before halting abruptly. Alert to every nuance of the forest around him, he sensed that something was amiss. His eyes narrowing, he studied the woods that stood beyond the clearing, and after a time he detected a faint movement.

The water forgotten, he returned to the house, carefully bolting the door behind him, then peered out of a window, taking care not to let himself be seen. He stood motionless for some minutes, his blood chilling, and then hurried to the closed door of the new bedroom he had built for Anne and Hester.

"Wake up!" he called softly as he tapped at the door. "Dress at once, and make no noise!"

A short time later, when Anne Ridley and Hester MacDevitt came into the main room of the cabin, they found him carefully loading every musket and pistol in the house. "What's the matter?" Anne demanded.

André wasted no words. "The house is surrounded by Indian warriors," he replied. "I have no idea how many of them are out there, and I haven't seen them well enough to distinguish their tribe—as if that matters. But there's no question that there are enough of them to cause us trouble, plenty of it."

Anne tapped a foot. "What makes you think they're necessarily enemies?"

"Friendly warriors don't surround a house and stay

239

hidden in the forest," he replied in irritation. "They come to the door and offer to exchange gifts. Look out there for yourselves. Wait!" he called as they started toward the windows. "Take care not to let them see you."

Hester and Anne went to separate windows and peered cautiously past the edges of the animal skins they had hung in lieu of drapes. For a long time neither spoke, and then the latter gasped.

"I saw one! He was naked to the waist and was smeared with paint."

"What colors?" André demanded.

"I couldn't quite see." Anne sounded disappointed.

He waved them away from the windows. "I'll keep watch," he said, placing a musket and a brace of pistols on the floor beside him. "If they start to advance, act quickly. Use the other firearms and keep shooting. We'll try to take as many of them with us as we can."

"You think they're going to attack, then?" Anne asked quietly.

André's smile was grim. "Warriors don't surround houses for sheer sport."

"But why?" she insisted.

"The usual motives. Robbery, probably. They want our guns. The blankets. The frying pan and kettle. Anything of value." There was no need to give the girls additional cause for concern by saying the Indians might be tempted by the desire to gain possession of two female slaves, too.

They accepted his statement with seeming calm. "I see no reason to fight on empty stomachs," Hester said. "I'll get us some breakfast, and with luck we may have a chance to eat it before they attack." She went to the hearth at the far end of the large chamber, threw several small logs on the coals, and began to fry thinly sliced, smoked bear meat.

André sucked in his breath. "Anne," he said, speaking just loudly enough for her to hear. She saw that he was continuing his vigil and was not looking at her. "We may have only a short time to live, and I don't want to die without telling you something. You and I have been quibbling and quarreling ever since you came here, and lately we've been unable to agree on anything. Well, I want you to know the fault is mine."

"No," Anne said. "I must share it with you. Sometimes I've disagreed with you for no reason at all except that I felt cantankerous."

"I'm to blame," he insisted, still watching the forest, "and I've needed all this time to find out why. I guess I can speak openly and freely now because it no longer matters that you come from a wealthy Virginia family and I'm a nobody, a shiftless hunter and trapper who has lived a hermit's life for too many years." He hesitated, moistened his lips, and then said firmly, "Anne, I love you. I know I'd never have the right to ask for your hand, but under our present circumstances that's of little account. I love you."

A lump formed in her throat, making it impossible for her to reply.

"Did you hear me?" he demanded fiercely. "I just told you that I—"

"Yes, I heard," she interrupted. "I—I couldn't speak for a minute. Well, you may as well know that I love you, too, André Cooke. Hester has accused me of it many times, and I've always denied it. But there's no sense denying the truth if we're both going to die."

André turned to her for an instant, then forced himself to keep watch again.

She went to him, placed a hand on his shoulder, and kissed him on the cheek. "That will have to do for the moment," she said.

"I promise you a real kiss after we run out of ammunition," he said, then added bitterly, "I'm afraid that's about all I can offer you in this world."

When Hester came to them with the bear meat and slabs of corn bread she had baked the previous day, she found them silent but strangely content. She had heard them muttering while she had been at work over the fire, and only now, when she saw the expression in her friend's eyes, did she realize they had reached an understanding. How sad it was that they may have waited until too late.

All the same, Hester envied them. She had not loved anyone, either in Scotland or in Virginia, and now she might never have the opportunity. All she could do would be to die courageously.

They ate their bread and meat in silence, then sipped mugs of a fragrant and potent herb tea that Hester had brewed.

Still the Indians in the forest made no attempt to rush the house.

The sun rose, and the trio continued to wait. "Perhaps they're trying to wear down our nerves," Anne said.

"That's possible," André declared. "It would be typical of Indian tactics. They sometimes—" He broke off sharply, then commanded, "Get down! Sit on the floor and don't show yourselves. A warrior is coming alone into the open."

Renno stood by himself at the far end of the clearing and called out in his own tongue. There was no reply, so he went on in English. "Surrender to us, whoever you may be, and I give you the word of a sachem that no harm will come to you!"

"Ah, so he's a sachem." André raised his musket to the sill and rested the barrel on it. "At least I'll have the satisfaction of knowing I've killed their leader."

Something in that distant voice sounded familiar to Anne, and she was troubled. Ignoring André's warning, she raised her head slightly and looked out.

She gasped, then knocked the musket out of André's hands before he could squeeze the trigger. As it fell to the floor with a clatter, she leaped to her feet, raced to the door, and ran out into the open before he could halt her.

Renno's composure deserted him when he saw the blond young woman who so closely resembled his wife hurtling toward him.

"Renno!" she cried and threw herself into his arms.

He stared at her in wonder as he embraced her. "Is it really you, Anne, or are the manitous showing me a vision?"

She was laughing and weeping, unable to reply.

Then Hester emerged from the cabin and walked forward slowly. "Renno," she called, "you've just given us the fright of our lives!"

The young sachem knew now that he wasn't dreaming. When he had been a child, Ena often had told him that the manitous performed magical deeds in the world of the living, just as they did in the afterworld. As always, his mother had been right.

A bewildered André Cooke followed the girls into the open, his musket in one hand. Kenneth Robinson stepped forward, his twin dueling pistols pointed at the bearded hunter. "Drop your musket!" he commanded. "I have you covered!" André obediently allowed his weapon to fall to the ground.

Anne laughed and wept more loudly, and then began to say something. Hester spoke simultaneously, and in the confusion neither could make herself understood.

Renno gestured sharply, then pointed a stern forefinger at his sister-in-law. Anne began to regain her self-control. "This is André Cooke who saved us from our abductors and has shared his home with us, protecting and shielding us. André, this is Renno of the Seneca, the husband of my sister."

A slow smile spread across André's face. "I bid you welcome to my humble house, sir," he said.

Renno extended his hand in the English manner. "On behalf of Anne's parents and her brother—who is only a few miles from this place—I thank you for saving her and Hester."

Kenneth lowered his pistols, feeling foolish, and felt

color rising to his face when he saw the red-haired Hester staring at him.

Renno called out something at length in his own tongue, and all at once the clearing was crowded with Seneca warriors. Of all the warriors present, only Walter Alwin had understood everything that had been said, and Renno summoned him. "Go quickly to Colonel Ridley," he said. "Tell him of this miracle, and bring him here at once!" Walter ran off into the forest.

The last to emerge into the open was Sun-ai-yee, who remembered Anne from a visit she had made to the town of the Seneca. He was introduced to Hester and André. Dazed by the unexpected, dramatic reunion, everyone remained silent, standing motionless.

Hester remembered her good manners. "Everybody has a long story to tell, but there's no need to stand out here in the yard. I have a pot of herb tea on the fire, and I can brew more." She included Sun-ai-yee and Kenneth Robinson in her invitation, and as they moved toward the house, she turned to Renno in embarrassment. "I—I'm afraid we don't have enough tea or food for all these warriors."

"They prefer their own food and drink to that of the settlers," he replied, then called out orders to the warriors. "They will stand sentry duty," he said, and he followed the girls into the house.

Anne and Hester told in detail of their abduction and rescue, lavishing praise on a suddenly shy André, who sat on a bench close to Anne. Then Renno explained how he, his warriors, and a large number of militiamen from the English colonies happened to be in the vicinity. Explanations were still being exchanged when an elated Ned Ridley reached the cabin, and the stories had to be repeated. It was decided that the good news would be sent with the next messenger who carried dispatches to Norfork.

Renno excused himself from the gathering long

enough to tell his warriors to find game for themselves and roast it in the yard. Not only would this session last a long time, but he had the foresight to realize that some important decisions had to be made.

As the men talked, Anne and Hester went about preparing a meal. André's eyes followed every move that Anne made, and Ned and Renno had no need to communicate in order to recognize the affection Anne and André felt for each other.

As they ate, Renno raised the problems that were bothering him. "For whatever your reasons," he said to André, "you chose to live alone in the wilderness, far from your own people. But the war has come to this part of North America, and your isolation is ended." He explained that France and Spain were actively seeking the assistance of tribes all the way to the Gulf of Mexico and that the expedition in which he and Ned were engaged intended to wage a military campaign against the enemy in the area.

Ned told them how Renno had killed Don Diego de Bernardo and reversed the decision of the Chickasaw to become the allies of the French.

"We saw that Spaniard," Anne said, "as well as the white Indian who serves France, and the young woman. They almost stumbled across us."

"That sort of thing will happen more and more often," Renno said. "These forests are no longer safe for anyone. Including you, sir," he said to André.

Ned looked hard at the hunter-trapper. "Do I assume correctly that you have English ancestry?"

André's smile was pained. "My father was English, and my mother was French. I came to the wilderness because I was torn." As he spoke Anne reached for his hand.

"I'm afraid that no Englishman or Frenchman on this continent can enjoy the privilege of remaining neutral in a war that will see one way of life or the other emerge victorious," Ned said.

"I'm well aware of it, Colonel Ridley." André gripped Anne's hand more tightly. "I've thought much about the matter of late. Thanks to what Anne and Hester have said in our many discussions, I've learned this is a war between the forces of freedom and those of repression. And feeling about Anne as I do, I could never go to war against her. So I volunteer my services to the English colonies, Colonel."

"I accept with pleasure, sir," Ned said. He and Renno would discuss the man's relationship with Anne in a private family talk.

"I believe I can be of great service to your cause," André said. "I have lived in this region for many years. No warrior of any nation is more familiar with the territory than I am. I know every inch of land all the way to the Gulf of Mexico, from the Mississippi to the Spanish forts in the Floridas."

"Do you know any of the Indian tongues?" Renno asked.

"Well enough to understand and make myself understood."

"Then, much as Ned might want you in his battalion, I prefer to assign you to our scouts. We have a Biloxi warrior helping them, but he knows only a limited area. We have a great need for one with your knowledge."

"We'll compromise, Renno," Ned interjected. "I'll grant him a commission as a captain of the Virginia militia, and then I'll lend him to you to work with your scouts."

Renno nodded amiably, then sobered. "That matter is easily solved, but we face an even worse problem. We can't allow Anne and Hester to remain in this cabin by themselves. And we can't spare a strong escort to take them back to Virginia, either. What shall be done with them?"

"I've taken it for granted ever since Walter came to me with the wonderful news," Ned said, "that they would stay with the expedition."

Anne beamed at André, then looked at her brother. "Are you suggesting that we march with your army?"

"I don't suggest it," Ned replied. "I insist on it. There's no other way."

Anne nodded, pleased because she and André would not be separated so soon after discovering their mutual love.

But Renno was dubious. "We cannot slow our march because of women in our midst," he said. "I am not certain they can keep up with us."

"Don't worry about Anne and me," Hester said with spirit. "We were forced to come all the way to the Mississippi from Norfolk on our own feet, and we've learned much about the wilderness in the months since we've lived here. We'll be a burden on no one!"

"I'm not concerned," Ned said. "Remember, Renno, how my wife kept up with you and me when we were fleeing from the Spaniards and their Indian allies in Florida."

"True," Renno said grudgingly. "But this situation is different. Many troubles could arise when two attractive young women travel with many hundreds of men."

Kenneth Robinson, who had taken little part in the conversation, suddenly spoke up. "May I make a suggestion, gentlemen?"

Everyone looked at him.

"Assign two men to act as the escorts, guards, and protectors of the young ladies. I volunteer my services because I can deal with the militiamen and know enough of the language of the Seneca by now to handle fundamentals. I recommend Walter for the other position. He has become a Seneca, but he knows English, too."

Hester MacDevitt noted that the Englishman avoided looking at her as he made his proposal, and she was sure he was attracted to her, just as she was interested in him. Certainly he was the most handsome and intelligent-looking man she had ever seen.

Ned withdrew to the open with Renno to discuss the suggestion. "You've had his lordship under observation for many weeks now. Do you feel he can be trusted?"

"I do," Renno replied flatly. "What's more, he was born and reared as a gentleman, which is more than can be said for most of our army. And Walter is a perfect selection because no woman other than Balin-ta exists for him."

"I'll agree, then, because I know of no other solution. You and I are far too busy to act as chaperons." They returned to the cabin, and Ned said the offer was accepted.

Hester smiled at Kenneth, but he remained sober-faced, obviously taking his new responsibility seriously.

Renno looked out at the position of the sun. "The day is far advanced," he said, "and we have already lost a full day's march. There is much to be done before tomorrow, so the time has come to join the army. Tonight," he told André, "you and I will plot tomorrow's march, and then we will meet with the Seneca and Oneida scouts. We will do this every evening."

Ned felt a twinge of sympathy for the hunter-trapper who was forced to leave his home. "I suggest you bury your valuables, lock up your house, and hope for the best."

André nodded.

"How much may we take with us?" Anne asked.

"Only what you yourselves can carry," Renno replied sternly. "Clothes, weapons you know how to use, and small personal belongings. We have no carts and no packhorses."

The warriors on sentry duty quickly dug a large hole in the yard. In it André placed leather boxes containing his cooking pots and utensils, packing blankets, and spare clothing. The warriors filled it in, deliberately planting several bushes and small trees to camouflage it. By the time they were done, it was impossible for anyone to see that the excavation ever had been made.

On the walk to the bivouac, Renno and Sun-ai-yee took the lead behind a small vanguard of warriors, and Ned fell in beside his sister and André. "You two," he said, "seem to have achieved some sort of understanding."

Anne's smile was beatific as she explained that only that morning, when they thought they would die, had they confessed their love for each other.

"I'm delighted for both of you," Ned said, "just as I'll always be grateful to André for rescuing and harboring you. Rest assured I'll send word to papa with the next messenger, though the news may take a while to reach him."

"I believe I know what you're thinking," André replied. "I speak for both of us when I say we'll do nothing rash."

"I'm glad to hear it, and I ask you to go one step more," Ned said. "Postpone a formal betrothal until you've obtained my father's permission. Though Renno and I represent the family, Anne's father must consent to her marriage. She is still quite a young woman, and he must give his approval. I might add that as one of the commanders of this expedition, I can't allow personal considerations to interfere with our campaign."

Anne giggled. "I never knew you could be so stuffy, Ned," she said.

André was quick to understand what Ned meant. "You need have no fears," he said. "I'm relieved that Anne and Hester will have a greater degree of safety than I was able to provide for them alone. As for me, it is hard to give up a way of life I've known for many years, and—on the very same day—to find that I love a woman who loves me in return. But I intend to devote myself to the task I've undertaken for you. I don't believe in half measures—or losing wars."

Here was a man of principle, Ned reflected. He knew that Austin Ridley would welcome him as a son-in-law.

The arrival of the two young women created a sensation at the army camp, and even the quickly disseminated word that one was the sister of Lieutenant Ridley only partly dampened the enthusiasm. While André ate supper with Renno and the scouts, telling them about the terrain they would cover on the following day's march, the girls were served their evening meal at the fire of the Virginians nearest the camp of the Seneca, and they took their food to the open area between the two units to eat. Kenneth Robinson and Walter Alwin ate their own meal nearby, but not until Anne and Hester had rolled up in their blankets for the night did the significance of Kenneth's and Walter's proximity dawn on the troops and the warriors. The Englishman slept about ten yards to one side of them, his loaded pistols and a knife beside him, while the junior warrior rested on the far side, his tomahawk and knife close at hand.

Soon, Kenneth hoped, the novelty of the girls' presence would wear off, and they would be taken for granted. If trouble developed, he knew he would be responsible for stopping it. He had volunteered for the difficult post and was annoyed with himself. He had gained his equilibrium after a long, difficult struggle, and he didn't want the red-haired girl to destroy his sense of balance.

Alain de Gramont translated for Beatriz de Bernardo as she addressed the sachem of the Creek, but there was no need for him to convey the intensity of her feeling. Her clenched fists and her blazing eyes attested to the depth of her emotions.

"Two more major Indian nations and two smaller nations have given their pledge to join us," she said. "Make sure he knows that."

"I've already told him," Alain said, concealing his

annoyance, "but it will do no harm to tell him again."
He repeated her remarks.

The sachem was complacent. "The day is at hand
when the Seneca will no longer be the most powerful of
nations," he replied. "Soon the Seneca will be like the
aged bear who has lost his teeth and whose claws are
crumbling. His roar will frighten no one."

"We want to make sure the teeth of the Seneca are
pulled," Beatriz declared, "and I know of a special
way this can be done. I can guarantee it."

Alain looked at her questioningly even as he translated for her. Apparently she had something new in
mind that she had not bothered to discuss with him.

"No warriors fight well without their chief," she
said. "The same is true in my land. Kill the general
who commands the army of Spain, and his men become sheep who march blindly to their death."

The Creek's eyes narrowed as he listened. So far, he
neither agreed nor disagreed.

"The sachem of the Seneca is a great war chief,"
Beatriz said. "The Iroquois praise him in many songs.
The Algonquian are afraid of him. The Ottawa will not
fight him. Even the Huron fear him."

Alain deliberately omitted her reference to the Huron
in his translation, refusing to denigrate the nation with
which he had so long been associated.

"Renno is truly a great warrior," the Creek said.
"His name is known even in this land, far from the
land of the Seneca."

"Kill Renno," Beatriz said, her voice shaking with
hatred. "Kill him, and the Seneca will be lost without
their leader."

The sachem of the Creek did not appear to be
particularly impressed. "How would this be done?"

Alain translated, then told Beatriz a thought of his
own. "Hundreds of Seneca protect their sachem. What
you suggest is too difficult to achieve."

Beatriz ignored the protest. "The Seneca and the
militia of the English colonies are even now marching

through the forests of this area. No man is safe from those who have the courage to destroy him. Here is what I propose. Send two of the most clever Creek warriors into the forest. Let them hide there. When the Seneca march past that place, let them send their arrows into the heart of Renno."

Alain dutifully translated her thoughts, even though he put no faith in the scheme.

"The Seneca are not stupid," the leader of the Creek declared. "It may be the Seneca would kill the warriors of the Creek before they could shoot their arrows into the heart of Renno."

"That is possible," Beatriz admitted. "But if you will take the risk, I will give you a rich reward. The warriors you send on this mission will be rewarded, too."

The death of her father, Alain thought as he translated, caused her to hate Renno even more than he despised him.

"What gifts will you make?" the Creek demanded bluntly.

"The army of the Creek will be given two great cannon. The sachem of the Creek will receive one hundred Spanish gold *dólares* and may use the money to buy whatever he wishes. He will be given two beautiful slave girls as well. Each of the courageous Creek warriors will be given ten gold *dólares* when Renno is dead."

Alain de Gramont balked. "No Indian nation has even been given cannon! That's directly contrary to Franco-Spanish policy. Not even the English provide their Indian allies with weapons that powerful. What's more, we have never set the precedent of making gifts of gold. Soon every tribe will be demanding money instead of cheap blankets and cooking pots!"

"Tell him my offer," she insisted. "I make it personally, as well as on behalf of the government of Spain."

Alain was dubious, certain she had gone too far, but

he nevertheless translated her offer, his own desire to
see Renno dead overcoming his better judgment.

The Creek's eyes gleamed. "The guns-that-sound-
like-thunder, the gold, and the slave girls will be given
to the sachem of the Creek," he declared, "even if his
warriors fail."

The demand was outrageous, but Beatriz refused to
quibble. "Agreed," she said firmly.

The sachem lighted a pipe, puffed on it, and handed
it to her.

Without hesitation she drew on it, too. The bargain
was sealed, and somehow she would obtain the bribes
from the viceroy of New Spain in Havana. Renno's
murder was worth any price.

The Oneida and Seneca scouts, two hundred strong,
fanned out through the forest, their stealth in no way
hampering their speed as they searched for any signs of
the enemy. Renno led the main column, the bulk of his
Seneca force behind him. Only a few paces to his rear
were Anne and Hester, escorted by Kenneth and Walter. After consultation with Ned Ridley, it was decided
that the young women would be safer with the Seneca,
whose familiarity with the wilderness was even greater
than that of the Virginia sharpshooters. Also, although
the two young women were not told this aspect, Renno
was best able to judge whether they were finding it
difficult to keep up the pace he set, and if necessary, he
could slow the march from time to time in order to
give them a respite.

André Cooke had been a fine instructor, and Anne
and Hester walked quietly, making no more sound
than most of the militiamen. At no time did they talk
during the march, either, but the rule of maintaining
silence was relaxed during the periods of rest when the
column halted. As long as André did not send back
word that an enemy force had been sighted, no harm
was done by allowing them to converse when they

rested. There was no point in making their day-to-day existence more difficult than necessary before the army went into actual battle.

Little by little Kenneth learned about Hester's past, and he found her story familiar. Her family had been comfortably situated, but the demands of her father's landlord, a nobleman with a taste for high living, had bankrupted him. Hester had been left penniless after the death of her parents and, going to London in the hope of earning a living there, had become so hungry, so desperate that she had stolen a loaf of bread. For that crime she had been condemned to a term in Newgate prison and had been released only on condition that she go to the New World as an indentured servant. Her situation had improved immeasurably when the Ridleys had taken her into their home.

Kenneth had been far less frank about his own background. Hester had no idea that he was Lord Symes, and he told her nothing about his passion for gaming, his heavy drinking, or his wenching. It was increasingly important to him that this red-haired young woman with the quick, infectious smile think highly of him. His outlook on life had changed, he had abandoned his intemperate ways, and he saw no reason to rake up his distasteful past.

Certainly he had no intention of revealing that he was a viscount who had inherited an ancient, distinguished title. Hester would be sure to conclude that she was far beneath him and would shy away from him. Well, it was true enough that Lord Symes would not have developed a genuine interest in an indentured servant. If he had thought of her at all, he would have wanted to bed her for a single night. But he regarded himself only as Kenneth Robinson now. His title no longer meant anything to him, and he was seriously thinking of abandoning it. That move would have to wait, however, until the war ended and he decided his future. He knew nothing about farming, and he had no idea how he might earn a living. All he knew now was that he was inclined to take up residence in a frontier town like Fort Springfield. But he couldn't think seriously about sharing his future with any woman until he found some way to support her.

Anne was endowed with the Ridley stamina, and as the column moved forward at a steady pace, Renno had to admire her. She not only physically resembled Betsy, but she had many of Betsy's traits, and just being in her company made Renno realize how much he missed his wife. Perhaps, if the campaign ended in a decisive victory, he and Betsy would be able to spend the better part of their time together again. He also looked forward to being reunited with his children, and it was pleasant to contemplate that he would spend ample time with Ja-gonh, who would soon begin his pre-warrior training.

Glancing over his shoulder, Renno was gratified to note that Hester MacDevitt was still walking briskly. Somewhat smaller boned and less resilient than Betsy or Anne, she was high-spirited, determined to be a burden on no one. After suffering initial doubts about her stamina, he knew now that she would not falter on the trail.

The forest of oak and red gum, cypress and cottonwood grew thicker directly ahead, where yellow pines also were pushing their way through masses of foliage toward the sunlight above. Not even Seneca could move in formation through such a maze, so Renno adjusted his pace accordingly, slowing a trifle.

A ray of sunlight filtered down through an opening in the trees, and Renno was reminded of the way daylight cast a similar beam in the Norfolk church the Ridleys attended. He looked up at the patch of blue, enjoying it as he enjoyed all of nature's many-sided manifestations, and suddenly a chill shot up his spine. He saw a tiny speck that swiftly grew larger. It was a hawk. The manitous who guarded him frequently had sent a hawk as a messenger to guide and inform him.

The hawk swooped low enough for Renno to see it clearly, and an instant later it vanished from sight again, hidden by the treetops. There was no longer any doubt in his mind: his manitous had sent word to him that trouble loomed ahead for him.

Instantly alert, Renno drew his tomahawk from his belt, automatically balancing it as he gripped the smooth oak handle. Still moving at the same steady rate and telling none of his subordinates about the message, he was alert, all of his senses alive to peril. He could smell nothing untoward, hear nothing unusual, but as he systematically searched the trees ahead and those on either side, his skin prickled.

All at once Renno knew. Two alien warriors armed with bows and arrows were cleverly concealed in the branches of adjoining trees, their arrows aimed at him. Reacting instantly, he threw his tomahawk with full force at the nearer of them.

At virtually the same moment a pistol shot rang out directly behind him. Somehow, Kenneth Robinson had become aware of the menace, too, and was firing at the second warrior.

Renno's aim was unerring, and the warrior who had been his target dropped to the ground, already dead. The other brave, gravely wounded and bleeding heavily, also tumbled to the forest floor.

The entire column halted immediately. Walter threw the two girls to the ground to remove them from the line of fire. The Seneca knew what was expected of them; scores of warriors spread out and conducted a tree-by-tree search for more enemies.

Renno ran forward, noting that the two warriors wore the paint of the Creek. The wounded brave, breathing his last, looked up and recognized the feathered bonnet of the sachem. "Renno of the Seneca has escaped the vengeance of the Creek," he said, speaking with great difficulty. "But soon all of the Seneca will die. The mighty Osage and the mighty Shawnee have become the allies of the Creek. So have the Pensacola and the Natchez. All will drink the blood of the Seneca."

Kenneth came up beside Renno, prepared to put another bullet into the warrior's body and end his misery. But Renno raised a hand to restrain the young Englishman, and together they watched the Creek die.

His face showing no emotion, Renno retrieved his tomahawk, then dropped to one knee beside the brave he had killed and calmly scalped him. "You killed that warrior in fair combat," he told Kenneth. "His scalp is yours by right."

Bracing himself, Kenneth drew his knife and crudely cut away the warrior's scalp lock. Lord Symes would have become ill at the mere contemplation of performing such a barbaric act. But the new Kenneth Robinson, frontiersman, thought it was necessary to prove to the Seneca with whom he was serving in war that he was their brother and was not squeamish.

Anne had already hidden her eyes behind her hands, and now Hester had to avert her gaze, too. This charming Englishman whose company delighted her and whose attentions flattered her appeared to be a man of many facets. He was as blunt as any Indian, and although she regarded the practice of scalping as deplorable, she had to admire his courage. She knew he had not found it easy to remove the hair and skin of the dead brave.

Ned Ridley and Jeffrey Wilson came forward together to find out the reason for the halt, and soon Sun-ai-yee, who was commanding the rear guard, also joined them.

For a few moments Renno turned his back to his colleagues, bowed his head, and silently thanked the manitous for intervening on his behalf and saving his life. Then, before speaking to his fellow commanders, he thanked Kenneth for the role he had played. "You have the right to boast about your marksmanship," he said. "I have never seen better."

Facing Ned, Jeffrey, and Sun-ai-yee at last, he told

them what had happened, omitting only the warning appearance of the hawk. That signal had been the private message of the manitous.

Jeffrey looked down at the bodies of the dead, scalped Creek. "There were no other enemies in the vicinity? Just these two?"

Renno gestured toward his Seneca, who were still conducting a painstaking search. "So it seems," he replied, shrugging.

"In that event," Ned said, "they were lying in wait for you, Renno, and for no one else."

"That's what I think," Jeffrey said. "They were assigned the mission of assassinating you. The Creek are treacherous bastards."

"The warriors of the Creek," Sun-ai-yee said, quietly contradicting him, "have been honorable since the time of our fathers' fathers. They are true warriors. They fight well, in the open. They do not hide like serpents before they attack."

"These two did just that," Ned said.

"It may be," Renno said, thinking aloud, "that they were hired to kill me. It may be that my enemy, Golden Eagle, bribed them. Or it may have been the Spanish she-devil." His gesture indicated his indifference. "It matters little. They failed."

Jeffrey understood what he meant. "Repeat what the Creek brave boasted before he died."

"He bragged," Renno said, "that the Osage and the Shawnee, both large nations, have joined the Creek. Which means they have become the allies of France and Spain. He also said the Pensacola and the Natchez have joined them."

"Both are small nations," Sun-ai-yee declared.

"No matter," Ned said, frowning. "Add two hundred warriors here, three hundred there, and the enemy accumulates a very powerful force."

"If the dead brave spoke the truth, and there was no reason for him to lie," Renno said, "we have a need to become cautious. The Creek provide their allies with many warriors. So do the Osage and the Shawnee. Tonight we will sit with André Cooke and hear what he can tell us about these nations."

The march was resumed without further delay. Anne and Hester took care not to look at the grotesque figures of the two dead Creek sprawled on the ground. The war was no longer a mere theoretical enterprise, but had become a deadly reality. Hester, glancing at Kenneth, who wore the scalp of the warrior he had killed in his belt, felt a new respect for him. Obviously he was a man who could take care of himself and help others in a crisis.

When a halt was called that evening, the commanders of the expedition drew apart, taking their principal lieutenants with them and sitting at a separate fire. They were just beginning their meal when the scouts returned for the night, and André joined them, full of apologies for the day's incident.

"I'm to blame," he said. "The scouts and I should have rooted out those two Creek."

"No scouts can be that effective," Renno said. "Any competent warriors have the ability to hide on a trail they know their enemies will follow."

"Thank you for your generosity," André said grimly. "I assure you it won't happen again."

When Jeffrey questioned him about the Osage and the Shawnee, André responded, "Ordinarily, except for an occasional raid on a small tribe like the Natchez or the Biloxi, they stay in their own territories. The French and Spanish emissaries must have promised them the sun and moon in order to persuade them to become their allies."

"What we must do becomes increasingly clear," Renno said. "First, when we draw somewhat nearer the mouth of the Mississippi, we must establish a permanent base. Da-no of the Biloxi tells me again and again that his people will join us. It may be, by the time we reach their land, that they will know where the French, the Spanish, and their allies are gathering.

Then we will send special scouts to learn the size of their regiments, the numbers of their Indian allies, and what arms they carry.

"Right now we know only one fact, and it is not good. We will be badly outnumbered by our foes. While it is true that one Seneca can defeat two warriors of any other nation, and that the militia of Massachusetts Bay and Virginia have proved they are superior to French regulars, we are still taking great risks."

"What can we do about it?" Jeffrey asked, his voice heavy. "The reinforcements offered by Connecticut and New York would be unable to fight in this kind of a wilderness."

"That may be true," Renno said. "But the Iroquois know the wilderness. They will answer our call for help."

"Do you think they would take the risk?" Ned asked.

"The Iroquois," Renno said firmly, "always come to the aid of their brothers. I will send the swiftest of messengers this very night. Warriors will come to us from all the nations of the Iroquois, and they will march with the speed of the wind."

"Until they join us," Jeffrey said, "we'll need to be careful. If we learn that our enemies outnumber us as much as we fear, we'll have to avoid a pitched battle with them until we receive reinforcements."

The meeting came to an end, and Renno immediately went to his brother. "El-i-chi will go this night to the land of the Seneca," he said. "There he will tell all the nations of the Iroquois that many Indian nations have joined the armies of France and Spain. El-i-chi will say that Renno needs much help. He needs it quickly."

"El-i-chi hears the words of the sachem and will do as he commands," the younger Seneca declared. Then, in a rare display of emotion, he clasped his brother's arm. "I will return soon to do battle with the enemy. Renno and El-i-chi will stand together and will take many scalps!"

Boston rejoiced when the Royal Navy flotilla dropped anchor in her harbor, and thousands of her citizens lined the streets to hail Ghonka as a hero. The Great Sachem brusquely acknowledged the applause, then went into conference with the governor and General Wilson. The quantities of arms and munitions sent to the colonies by Great Britain were generous, and supply ships were dispatched at once, under Royal Navy escort, to carry appropriate shares to Providence, New Haven, New York Town, Norfolk, and Charleston. At last the colonies would be well supplied with ships and arms in the event they were attacked.

The squadron that sailed to Norfolk also carried a letter from Betsy. Upon her arrival, General Wilson had informed her that Anne and Hester had been kidnapped, and Betsy wrote at once to her parents, expressing hope that the girls would return home soon.

General Wilson dispatched a detail of the newly formed Massachusetts Bay Cavalry to the land of the Seneca with word that the Great Sachem had returned.

Ghonka was annoyed, although he carefully concealed his displeasure, when he was forced to remain in Boston for the better part of a week. The governor insisted on giving a dinner in his honor, as did the commodore of the flotilla, who held a banquet in the main saloon of his flagship. And General Wilson, not to be outdone, also gave a dinner for him attended by the senior officers of the militia.

Betsy was required to attend these various events, in her familiar role of her father-in-law's interpreter. Always ravishing in one of her English gowns and wearing the diamond ring Queen Anne had given her, she was secretly amused because Ghonka's reticence confined her official duties to a minimum. Invariably he responded to the many toasts and speeches with a single sentence: "Death to the enemies of the Iroquois and the English!"

Betsy had to hide her laughter when wild applause

greeted the Great Sachem's simple, pungent declaration.

At last the party departed, escorted by General Wilson and a detachment of Massachusetts Bay militia. Betsy was relieved because she and her children at last could put aside their English attire and wear the plain doeskins and buckskins of the Seneca.

She was pleased when they reached Fort Springfield and Mildred Wilson insisted they stay for a time as guests. Ghonka and Ena, at Ghonka's request, slept in a tent erected for them on the back lawn. Betsy and her children stayed in the Wilson house, and local friends came daily to greet her and her parents-in-law. She was elated when Ida Alwin Carswell told in detail how Walter had gained the power of hearing. Ghonka and Ena were equally pleased. "May the manitous be thanked," Ghonka said.

Obadiah and Deborah Jenkins came to the house, bringing their children, and while their youngsters, along with those of Betsy and Adrienne, went off to play, Betsy had an opportunity to speak with her friends in private.

"You were right about men in England," she said to Adrienne and for the first time related the story of her experience with Sir Edward Carlton.

"Tell me, Betsy," Adrienne asked, "does the Great Sachem know what happened?"

Betsy laughed. "Hardly. He would have killed and scalped Sir Edward on the spot."

"Do you intend to tell Renno? Not that it's any of my business," Deborah added hastily.

"Renno is a Seneca," Betsy said, "so it wouldn't surprise me in the least if he went charging off to London and sank a tomahawk in Sir Edward's already addled head. Perhaps I should leave well enough alone for now. Someday I'll tell him." She paused, then sighed. "I wish we knew when this expedition might end."

"So do all of us," Adrienne replied. "I've had only

one brief note from Jeffrey, telling me he met Renno and Ned at their rendezvous on the Ohio River, and that was a long time ago. There hasn't been a single scrap of news since then."

"Don't dwell on it," Deborah advised.

"You may be sure we try not to," Betsy said. "I tell myself that Renno will be just fine. He's unique, but he is human, so he's not indestructible!"

Two days later the militia horsemen returned to the Wilson home, accompanied by one hundred Seneca warriors, the commander of the cavalry marveling because the braves had no difficulty in keeping up with the pace set by the mounts.

Ghonka was so eager to return to his own land that he announced he would leave at dawn the next morning. Betsy awakened the children in time for a very early breakfast so that they were ready to leave when Ghonka and Ena said farewell to their hosts. Barges carried the party across the Connecticut River, and Betsy smiled as, surrounded by the warriors of the escort, they plunged into the wilderness.

Little Ja-gonh trudged manfully, taking long strides so he could maintain the pace set by his stern grandfather. Only once, after he simply dropped from exhaustion, did he have to be carried. Even Goo-ga-ro-no, who would be carried on her mother's back when she tired, walked happily between her mother and grandmother, making it plain that the wilderness held no terrors for her.

Betsy knew she herself was content. The great forests had become her true home, and she put London, Boston, and Fort Springfield behind her without regrets. She was returning to her own dwelling in the town of the Seneca, and only the continuing absence of Renno left her less than completely satisfied with the life she had chosen.

Chapter X

The relieved sachem and people of the small Biloxi nation welcomed the expedition of Iroquois and English colonial militia as their deliverers. Although the resources of the tribe were meager, they insisted on giving a feast. Only one sour note marred the festivities. Anne Ridley and Hester MacDevitt, seeing the warriors of the Biloxi, were forcibly reminded of the trio who had abducted them in Norfolk, and the embarrassed sachem admitted that three of his warriors had been responsible for the outrage.

"They took the pay of the Spanish she-devil," the sachem said.

Renno realized he had to be referring to the young woman who was Golden Eagle's companion and was working with him. Certainly she represented a great danger.

After the feast it was permissible to discuss matters of

importance, and Renno and his high command colleagues gleaned vital information from the sachem and his war chief. A combined force of French and Spanish troops, they said, had landed in Mobile Bay and were building a large log fort at the mouth of the Mobile River, assisted by hordes of warriors from the various Indian nations that had formed treaties of alliance with King Louis XIV. Neither of the Biloxi had any idea how many soldiers had landed or how many Indian braves were gathering at the new fort. The little tribe's means were limited, and its leaders had been afraid to send emissaries to learn more.

The situation was further complicated by the request of the Biloxi sachem that the entire tribe accompany the expedition to its own permanent campsite, which was yet to be established. The sachem promised that his three hundred warriors would fight faithfully beside their new friends, but he was afraid the Creek, Osage, and Shawnee would raid his small villages and either kill or enslave the elderly, the women, and children during the braves' absence.

It was impossible to refuse the plea, even though the encumbered expedition would be forced to travel at a far slower pace. So the Biloxi left their huts, taking with them whatever belongings they could carry. At least Anne and Hester no longer were tried to the limits of their endurance as the march toward the south was resumed.

Unexpectedly, Sun-ai-yee was affected more than anyone else by the presence of the Biloxi. A young maiden of the tribe, doe-eyed and with honey-colored skin, took a fancy to the portly war chief the first time she set eyes on him, although he didn't know it. This woman, known as Talking Quail, was slender, with clean-cut features and high cheekbones, and was endowed with a willowy, supple figure. Many of the unmarried braves of her own nation had wooed her without success because she had set her sights higher. Now she concentrated her liquid gaze on Sun-ai-yee.

The first day on the trail, Talking Quail made it her business to become friendly with several of the Seneca, flirting with them until she learned what she wanted to know. The following morning, when Sun-ai-yee appeared at the camp fire for a hasty breakfast, Talking Quail appeared silently and served him a cornmeal and fruit pudding, sweetened with maple syrup.

The war chief could only stare at her. "How did you know this is one of my favorite dishes?" he demanded.

Talking Quail's only response was a dazzling smile.

That same night, when he joined the other leaders of the expedition and André Cooke for supper, Talking Quail appeared again, handing him a bowl of savory venison stew. Again she smiled at him but made no comment.

The lifelong bachelor watched her as she walked away from the fire, and it was no accident that her hips swayed provocatively, that her short steps gave her a daintily feminine air.

Renno, who quickly became aware of what was happening, said nothing to his old friend. By the next morning, however, when Sun-ai-yee again was served his favorite breakfast by Talking Quail, there was no doubt in his mind that the war chief was rapidly developing a strong interest in her.

Sun-ai-yee was able to put her out of his mind only when the members of the high command discussed the problem of how best to deal with the establishment of the Franco-Spanish fort on Mobile Bay.

"The enemy has planned well," Jeffrey Wilson said. "This base provides him with a secure anchor, and he can be easily supplied from Havana."

"He has a choice, depending on our strength," Ned Ridley declared. "If our forces prove too strong, he can take the defensive and force us to attack him. On the other hand, if he has the greater strength, he can use that base as a starting point for a major campaign against us."

"I believe it is likely he will use the fort as a base

and pursue us," Renno said. "We know for certain he is already stronger than we are. The big question we cannot answer is: how strong is he? Do we dare risk a pitched battle with him?"

"We can do nothing until we find out," Sun-ai-yee growled.

They agreed it was essential to send volunteers to scout the new fort. Scores of men—Indians and militia men alike—promptly offered their services when the situation was explained. But Jeffrey was not satisfied. "Your warriors lack the sophistication to judge the French firepower, Renno," he said.

Renno nodded solemnly. "I know. This situation requires a special kind of scout."

André Cooke, who regularly attended the nightly meetings, but who spoke only when the next day's route was being planned, could keep silent no longer. "It seems to me," he said, "that I am a perfect candidate. Many of the Biloxi warriors know this area well and can guide the column into the delta of the Mississippi River. But I, who speak French as easily as I speak English, am not known by the enemy. There is no need for me to pose, to assume a false identity. I can go to them as myself. I can tell them I am interested in their activities. I can indicate that I might be willing to join them. Surely I can learn all we need to know about them."

Ned Ridley realized that Anne would be badly upset and felt compelled to say, "You'll be taking a big risk, André. If they find out you're one of us, they'll stand you in front of a firing squad as an espionage agent."

"I have taken countless risks every day of every year that I have lived in the wilderness," André replied quietly. "I think my background makes me uniquely qualified for this operation."

"All the same," Jeffrey said, "we can't let you go off alone. We'll need someone else, someone who can speak French without difficulty."

The meeting adjourned on that note, and a short time later André went to Anne at her camp fire and explained his situation bluntly.

She could not hide her concern, but replied courageously. "Do what you must. I can't stand in your way or let my selfishness hamper what Ned and Renno are trying to do."

Kenneth Robinson overheard the conversation as he lingered near Hester at the fire, so he excused himself abruptly and went to Jeffrey. "Colonel," he said, "you had good reason to mistrust me in the past, but I believe I've earned the right to hold up my head on this journey."

Somewhat bewildered by his aggressiveness, Jeffrey nodded. "True enough. The day you saved Renno from almost certain death provides you with solid credentials."

"Then let me go with André Cooke to the French-Spanish fort. I've proved that I can live and take care of myself in the wilderness. You know I can handle firearms. It so happens that I'm also fluent in French and Spanish. It shouldn't be difficult for me to convince the enemy that I'm like André, a hunter and trapper."

"You realize you might lose your life if the deception should be discovered?"

"I lost my soul, but thanks to people like the Jenkins's—and you—and Renno—I've found it again." Kenneth spoke softly. "France is more than my country's enemy, Colonel. She's my personal enemy. The jackals of King Louis forced me to become a traitor and robbed me of what little was left of my pride. I have a personal score to repay, and I don't want to miss this opportunity."

Jeffrey said he would discuss the offer with his colleagues and, finding Renno with Ned, explained the situation.

"I stand in favor of allowing him to go," Renno said

without hesitation. "I have seen nothing in his conduct at any time that would lead me to believe he is disloyal to us."

"He could give the French a full report on our strength, of course," Ned said thoughtfully, "but I'd be astonished if he did. Anne tells me he's smitten with Hester, so he has a great deal to gain by remaining steadfast and everything to lose if he turns traitor again."

They quickly reached a consensus, and Jeffrey told Kenneth. "You'll leave tonight," he said. "We're arranging a rendezvous with André when you return."

The two scouts made their hasty preparations for departure, and then André went to Anne. "Never fear," he said, "I'll come back to you."

"I'm sure you will," she replied, holding back her tears. "When I think of the strange way you and I found each other, I know it was the hand of Divine Providence guiding both of us. I can't believe He would raise our hopes only to crush us."

Others could see them as they stood near the fire, but neither cared. They embraced and kissed without self-consciousness, silently expressing their hopes and fears as they clung to each other. Then André tore himself away and walked to the edge of the forest, where he waited for his companion.

Kenneth tried to be flippant as he said good-bye to Hester. "Be sure you don't get lost in the forest or allow yourself to be abducted while I'm gone," he told her.

Hester replied in the same spirit. "I won't promise, but I'll do my best."

All at once Kenneth sobered. "See to it. I will think of you on this journey, and I will be counting the days that we're apart."

This was his first open declaration of his serious interest in her, and Hester was startled. "I—I will think of you, too," she said, and turned away, realizing it wasn't fair to expect him to say more when he was going off on a hazardous mission.

Kenneth hesitated for an instant, then stalked off to join André, and they disappeared together in the dark forest.

Anne and Hester sat at their fire for a long time that night, and there was little conversation as they stared into the dying flames. Walter remained nearby, sympathetic toward them, as was the militiaman assigned to replace Kenneth as one of their guardians. A corporal, he had a wife and three children at home in Fort Springfield, and he well knew how his family would feel if he were assigned to a dangerous mission.

Meanwhile, Sun-ai-yee had matters of his own on his mind and went in search of Talking Quail. She deliberately had chosen a bivouac only a short distance from his, so it was not difficult for him to find her.

She sat on the ground and peered up at him through her long lashes, smiling shyly. Sun-ai-yee rarely was at a loss for words, as his subordinates had discovered when they had been slovenly in the performance of their duties, but all at once he did not know what to say.

Talking Quail gestured, inviting him to sit, and the Seneca lowered himself to the ground opposite her, admiring her beauty even as he told himself not to dwell on her physical attributes. "Why has the young woman of the Biloxi prepared special meals for Sun-ai-yee?" he demanded harshly.

His tone did not frighten her, and she was well prepared for his question. "The great war chief of the mightly Seneca saves the people of the Biloxi from death at the hands of their enemies," she replied sweetly. "So Talking Quail is grateful to him."

He glowered at her. "Renno is the sachem of the Seneca. Jeff-rey and Ned lead the forces of the English colonists. Why has Talking Quail not prepared special food for them?"

As she returned his steady glare, her shyness vanished, and her expression became bold. "Talking Quail," she said, speaking slowly and distinctly, "has chosen to be of help to the great Sun-ai-yee. That is her pleasure."

It was impossible for him to mistake her meaning. Over a period of more than two decades, Sun-ai-yee had faced countless foes without flinching, and every warrior who had ever gone into battle with him swore he didn't know the meaning of fear. Now, however, beads of perspiration appeared on his forehead and, running down his cheeks, smudged his green and yellow war paint. "Sun-ai-yee is grateful to Talking Quail," he said, speaking with difficulty. "But it is not right that she offer him food and then go away to eat her own meals. Sun-ai-yee will not accept gifts from a free woman who behaves like a slave. Sun-ai-yee will accept the food that Talking Quail prepares only if she joins him and shares his meals with him." His glower became even more ferocious, and he made it clear that he was daring her to deny his request.

Talking Quail was relieved to be able to lower her head in a graceful gesture of assent. Under no circumstances did she want him to see the triumph in her eyes. "Talking Quail will obey the will of the great Seneca war chief," she murmured, her manner docile.

She had agreed so quickly that he was somewhat stunned. Unable to think of anything more to say, he rose to his feet and lumbered off.

Talking Quail realized that her long quest for a mate worthy of her beauty and cunning was ended. Not only would she become the wife of a renowned warrior, but she would leave the inconsequential Biloxi forever and would become a member of the most prestigious of Indian nations. She had to admit she disliked the prospect of spending her winters in a cold climate, but she comforted herself with the thought that when Sun-ai-yee went hunting he would bring her warm furs and a cloak of buffalo hide.

She—as well as the amused Renno—did not have to wait long to see that Sun-ai-yee was becoming entangled even more rapidly than he knew. The very next day he disappeared for a time from the line of march, returning with two wild ducks. At the end of the day's march, he went to Talking Quail, then silently thrust the birds at her.

She murmured her thanks as she took them, and that night they feasted together on roast duck. When the members of the high command began their nightly, informal conference, Talking Quail calmly went off without comment.

In all of Sun-ai-yee's long existence as a bachelor, he had never thought of women except as casual sleeping partners, but tonight the notion occurred to him that he should thank Talking Quail for the best duck supper he had ever eaten. When the meeting ended, he went to her and was astonished to find her sewing green and yellow beads, the Seneca colors, on his spare buckskin shirt.

Her smile of greeting indicated that she didn't believe she was doing anything out of the ordinary, but he was so startled that he bolted.

After they shared breakfast the following morning, he placed himself in command of the official hunting party, and well before noon he brought down a buck. Giving the carcass to his subordinates, he kept only the antlers, and thereafter he went off alone at every opportunity to carve, polish, and whittle.

Renno guessed that his old friend was making a necklace or bracelet for Talking Quail. Without yet knowing it, Sun-ai-yee was making a commitment for the rest of his life.

A few days after returning to the main town of the Seneca, Betsy almost felt as though she had never gone off to England. Ja-gonh and Goo-ga-ro-no resumed their rigorous training, and she herself worked in the fields with the other women; she and the children ate at the house of the Great Sachem, and she shared the cooking responsibilities with Ena and Ba-lin-ta, who was delighted by the family's return and who never tired of repeating in full detail the story of how Walter had gained the power of hearing.

Only a few days after the homecoming, the women had settled into their customary routine. While Ghonka sat in front of the house, enjoying the midsummer weather and telling his grandchildren the true story of their father's friendship as a child with the great brown bear whose name Ja-gonh bore, the women cut up meat, chopped vegetables, and deboned fish for the evening meal.

While they were busily engaged, they became vaguely aware of a commotion in town. Warriors and women were hurrying out of longhouses, talking animatedly. The members of the Great Sachem's family felt as though bolts of lightning were striking them when they saw a bone-weary El-i-chi approaching them, the dust of the trail thick and streaked on his body. Ghonka was on his feet instantly, exchanging greetings with his second son. Ena, Betsy, and Ba-lin-ta continued with their food preparations, even though fear gripped them.

The warriors and women reluctantly returned to their own homes. In due time they would be told whatever it was fitting for them to hear.

El-i-chi shattered the Seneca custom by touching his mother's forehead with his lips and then telling them what they most wanted to hear. "Renno is safe and well," he said. "So is Wal-ter. They have been joined by the sister of Betsy and the red-haired girl who is her friend," Very briefly he told them how Anne and Hester had been found.

Betsy was still enough of a Virginian to have to brush away the tears that formed in her eyes.

Ghonka waited impassively for his son to tell him the reasons he had made the long journey back to the land of the Seneca. It appeared that the Great Sachem was growing more mellow. There had been a time when the nation's business would have taken precedence over any family news.

But there were limits to the advantage that others could take of his calmness. Ja-gonh and Goo-ga-ro-no clung to El-i-chi, babbling delightedly at the sight of their uncle, and Betsy hastily pulled them away as the warrior went to sit beside his father at the front of the house.

Ghonka made no comment as El-i-chi outlined the military situation. Waiting until his son had finished, he wanted to make certain he understood the details. "The Creek have joined the French. The Osage and Shawnee have joined the French. The stupid little Pensacola and Natchez have joined the French."

"That is so. Renno, the sachem of the Seneca, asks that all of the nations of the Iroquois send reinforcements quickly, so he and Jeffrey and Ned are not overwhelmed by their enemies."

The Great Sachem sat motionless, his arms folded as he listened. At last Ghonka stirred and turned first to his wife. "Let the children be fed," he said. "The danger is grave, so our meal must wait."

El-i-chi followed him as he donned his feathered bonnet and buffalo robe, then walked quickly to the council lodge of the Seneca. The members of the council, having anticipated the call, were already waiting. Seeing the Great Sachem's expression the principal medicine man dispensed with the customary ceremonies.

As El-i-chi repeated his account, the members of the council listened in tense silence, and when he was finished no one spoke.

Ghonka said, "The English colonies are in danger. But the danger to the Seneca and the other nations of the Iroquois is even greater."

The others were puzzled. "Why should that be?" one of the war chiefs asked.

Even though El-i-chi was very tired, he could not help admiring his father's keen, sensitive understanding of the constant tug-of-war in the struggle for power among the Indian nations of the continent.

"Why do my brothers think that strong nations like the Creek, the Shawnee, and the Osage have joined the French? Why do they think small vulture-tribes like the Natchez and Pensacola have joined the French? They will be given many firesticks and blankets. But those gifts would not be enough to make such alliances. The Huron and the Ottawa already have French firesticks, but they have not joined. The Algonquian also have remained neutral."

The members of the council listened closely.

"The nations that now have joined the French," Ghonka declared gravely, "see a chance to shame and mock the Seneca. They see a chance to shame and mock the Oneida and the Mohawk. Their numbers are greater than the forces that Renno, sachem of the Seneca, commands. They plan to meet him in battle. Not even the Iroquois can win a battle when their foes outnumber them badly. The Creek, the Shawnee, and the Osage will wear the scalps of Seneca warriors in their belts. The puny braves of the Pensacola and Natchez will wear the scalps of Seneca warriors in their belts. They will strut like the turkeys that roam through the forest."

"That must not happen!" one of the war chiefs cried.

Ghonka looked slowly around the room. "It shall not happen," he said, and there was a note of finality in his voice.

Even though the others didn't know what he had in mind, he had spoken, and they were relieved.

"Swift messengers will carry the word of this planned humiliation of the Iroquois to our brothers in the League this very night. All will call to arms as many warriors as they can spare. The Seneca also will summon every warrior who volunteers."

The principal medicine man interrupted. "What will happen if the French march from Quebec into the lands of the Iroquois?"

"That must not be allowed to happen," the Great Sachem declared. "General Wilson will be asked to stand guard over the lands of the Iroquois with his militia. The militia of New York and Connecticut and Rhode Island will be asked, also. So a great Iroquois army will go to the relief of Renno."

There was a silence, and then one of the war chiefs shook his head. "It would take many, many days for the Iroquois to march so far. By the time they reach the place where Renno will fight, he and his warriors may be dead and scalped."

"That will not be," Ghonka assured him. "The warriors of the Iroquois will not march through the forest. They will go first to Fort Springfield, then to Boston. There a fleet of the ships that brought the Great Sachem home will carry them to the place where they will meet Renno. The ships-that-look-like-great-birds move across water as swiftly as the hawk flies through the sky. It will take only a short time for the many warriors of the Iroquois to arrive at the place where they will meet Renno and his warriors."

His subordinates were satisfied. No one else could have worked out such a sound strategy so swiftly.

Ghonka turned to his second son. "Did El-i-chi hear the new plan of the Iroquois?"

El-i-chi nodded. "I have heard every word said by the Great Sachem. Those words are carved into the mind of El-i-chi for all time."

"No other warrior," Ghonka said gently, "can explain to General Wilson better than the son of the Great Sachem. General Wilson needs time to assemble the ships in Boston. He needs time to alert the sachems of the other colonies so they will provide the militia to guard the borders of the land of the Iroquois."

El-i-chi knew what was being asked of him and tried to shake off his fatigue.

"Come to the house of your father," Ghonka said gently. "There you will eat the food prepared by your mother, your sister, and the wife of Renno. That food will make you strong again. As soon as you have eaten, you will leave this night for Fort Springfield. You will go with the speed of the hawk. Then you will wait in Fort Springfield for the Iroquois to arrive. Also tell General Wilson that the Great Sachem will command the warriors of the Iroquois himself. He and his sons will prove to lesser nations that the Seneca cannot be conquered!"

Strength flowed into El-i-chi's legs and body. Ghonka had spoken words of truth: he and his sons, working and fighting together, were truly invincible, as the nations that had joined the French would learn.

The stockade that surrounded the Franco-Spanish encampment at the mouth of the Mobile River, facing the great natural harbor of Mobile Bay, was substantial, even though hastily constructed. Made of logs fifteen feet high, with pointed tops, it was sufficiently sturdy to prevent an enemy from making a surprise attack on the force gathered there. It also served the useful purpose of preventing the one thousand French troops and two thousand Spanish troops recently landed there from straying into the wilderness. These soldiers, just arrived from Europe, were unfamiliar with the New World and consequently were unfamiliar with ways in which they could make themselves at home in the vast wilderness.

The Indian warriors from the nations allying themselves with the French preferred to remain outside the new fort. They slept in the open, hunted for their food, and happily sold to the Europeans the meat and fowl they themselves did not use.

There were no permanent dwellings inside the stockade. The commanders of the French and Spanish regiments were not thinking in terms of establishing a permanent base at the site. The interior of the fort was a sea of tents, with the French on one side and the larger Spanish units on the other. Each company had its own cooking fire, but the officers preferred to eat in large, pavilionlike tents, where they also gathered during off-duty hours to socialize, drink the wine they had brought with them on their transports, and idle away their free time at makeshift gaming tables.

André Cooke and Kenneth Robinson encountered no problem in acquiring access to the fort. The lieutenant in charge of the sentry detail had taken them to the commandant of the French regiment; and after questioning them at some length, he had accepted their story, believing that only hunters and trappers would be willing to make such a trek through the wilderness.

He urged them to join the French as scouts, in return for generous pay, and suggested they stay at the camp as guests until the return of Colonel Alain de Gramont, who had gone off alone in the hope of obtaining the support of yet another tribe. The pair quickly agreed and were given a tent of their own near the quarters of the French officers.

André and Kenneth planned their movements. The former, who was familiar with the Indian nations and spoke their language, would spend a day or two wandering through the encampment outside the stockade in an attempt to learn the number of Indians and what arms they carried. Kenneth, meanwhile, would familiarize himself with the strength and firepower of the European contingents.

The task proved easier than either had anticipated. They wandered where they pleased, with no one challenging them; they ate their meals with the French officers; and in the absence of the shrewd Alain de Gramont, the commanders of the expedition, ignorant of the New World, saw no reason to question the validity of the two men's credentials.

It did not take Kenneth long to discover that there was one other civilian in the camp, a strikingly attractive young Spanish woman whose hair was cut short and who dressed like a man. He learned, too, that she could not be dismissed as a camp follower. She was treated with great respect by the Spanish officers, including the colonels commanding the two regiments, with whom she ate most of her meals. She slept in a large, comfortable tent equipped with a bed for her convenience, a luxury enjoyed only by the highest-ranking officers, and she seemed to be on familiar terms with no one.

"All I can find out about her," Kenneth told André when they were alone, "is that her name is Beatriz de Bernardo. She has been here for some time, and as nearly as I can gather, she came to the New World before the troops arrived. What puzzles me is that everyone—even the regimental and battalion commanders—treats her with deference. She seems to be someone of authority."

André realized that this was the Spanish woman he, Anne, and Hester had encountered in the forest. Now he remembered what he had heard from Renno and the leaders of the English colonial expedition about Alain de Gramont and his female companion. "I'm sure this is the woman the Biloxi call the she-devil," André said. "She's had a major hand in recruiting the tribes that have become the allies of the French and Spaniards. Maybe we can learn what other nations are likely to join the alliance. We've already gathered enough information to sneak away tomorrow, but we have nothing to lose by trying to become acquainted with her before then. Why don't you try this evening?"

Kenneth hesitated. "She spends her evenings playing cards with some of the Spanish officers."

André smiled. "Well, between us we can scrape

together a few gold louis. It could prove to be well worth our while if you join the game."

Kenneth was unwilling to discuss his past. "I'd rather not become an active player," he replied. "Perhaps I might watch and see if I can fall into conversation with her."

A feeling of dread mounted in him throughout the rest of the day, growing unbearable as evening approached. He had made no wagers of any kind since starting his new way of life, and the prospect of actually sitting at a gaming table filled him with terror. Suppose he found the old lure of gambling too great to resist? All that he had achieved in his struggle for self-respect might be lost. Somehow, he had to force himself to watch others gamble, yet refrain from participating in the game himself. But André was right in suggesting that Beatriz de Bernardo might be in a position to provide them with vitally important information, so he had to take the chance.

His fear making him feel weak, Kenneth nevertheless made it his business to linger in the vicinity of the Spanish high command at sundown. His fluent Spanish and polished manners already had won him the approval of the officers, so it was not surprising when one of the colonels invited him to join the group for supper, which was served by two orderlies at a table set up inside a tent.

Deeply troubled by the ordeal that awaited him, Kenneth had little appetite, even though the food, which came from provisions sent from Havana, was delicious. He studied Beatriz de Bernardo covertly as they ate and concluded that, in spite of her charm, she was hard-bitten. He would be better able to judge her when he watched her play cards.

Beatriz was conscious of the interest of this handsome man, a hunter and trapper with the manners of a gentleman. Bored while Alain was absent from the camp, she was mildly intrigued.

After the meal ended, the dishes were cleared away by the orderlies, and several additional candles were lighted to provide brighter illumination. "It is time for high-low," a Spanish major announced.

A trickle of perspiration moved slowly down Kenneth's back.

"Join us in a friendly game, why don't you?" a lieutenant colonel asked him amiably.

Kenneth forced himself to speak calmly. "I—I'm afraid I don't have the funds," he said, even though he carried several gold coins in his purse and was tempted to squander them.

"I will advance you some money, if you wish," Beatriz told him.

He shook his head as he thanked her, and thought it best to offer a logical explanation. "My partner and I don't yet know what the French will offer us to serve with them as scouts, so I prefer not to go into debt."

Aware of his nervousness, she wondered what lay behind it. The effort to find out would cost her nothing. "Sit beside me, then, and bring me luck," she said.

He was making better progress with her than he had anticipated, but his agony became worse. All he could do was to accept with a polite bow.

As the game began, the orderlies returned with cups of wine, and Kenneth was handed one as a matter of course. He had tasted no alcoholic beverage for months, and his first impulse was to refuse. But his better sense told him to take a cup. He quickly discovered he disliked even the smell of the wine, and he had no difficulty in resisting the desire to drink it. Instead, as the game began and the players became absorbed in it, he slowly dribbled the contents of the cup onto the ground and let the dry earth soak it up. He did the same whenever the orderlies refilled his cup.

The Spaniards played cards passionately, with great gusto, and the stakes rose gradually. Only Beatriz de

Bernardo remained cool and detached, judging her opponents with care and placing her wagers accordingly. She was the biggest winner in the group, and the piles of gold and silver coins on the table in front of her mounted steadily.

Unlike the others, Kenneth noted, she drank sparingly, too, moistening her lips with the wine from time to time, but never taking a real swallow. Consequently, her glass was not refilled.

Beads of sweat stood out on Kenneth's forehead, and he had to wipe them away repeatedly. He yearned to become a player, his heart and soul crying out for the joy of gaming. Never had it been necessary for him to fight temptation so fiercely, and he had to tell himself again and again that he would have no future if he allowed himself to backslide now.

He lost all count of the passage of time, and not until Beatriz turned to him with a bright smile did he come to his senses. "You truly bring me luck," she said.

He knew the comment was untrue. She was winning because she was bold but not reckless, because her temperament was that of a born gambler. He lacked that instinct, and the realization abruptly ended his agony. The desire to demand a card from the dealer faded, and a sense of tranquility he had never before experienced flooded him. At last he knew, beyond all doubt, that he had recovered from his curse. Never again would he be haunted by the fear that he might yield to the temptation to gamble.

The card game was breaking up, and as Beatriz stuffed gold and silver coins into her purse, it occurred to Kenneth that he had scarcely broken the ice in his attempt to gain information from her. "Perhaps you would like to stroll for a time," he said. "The weather is very pleasant this evening."

She measured him behind her smile. "There are tents everywhere," she replied. "They interfere with walks. Come to my tent, and we can chat in greater comfort there."

Kenneth quickly accepted the invitation, and when they reached her quarters, he offered to light the candles for her, but she preferred to do it herself. As he watched her carrying the tinderbox and flint from one taper to the next, he was struck by the feline grace of her movements. She lacked the femininity of Hester MacDevitt, however, and he wondered what made them different. Being an accomplished swordsman, he recognized that Beatriz de Bernardo had the control and balance of a practiced duelist.

Beatriz poured two small mugs of wine, motioned him to an upturned keg that served as a chair, and seated herself on the foot of the bed opposite him. "You do not find the life of a hunter in these North American jungles boring?" She was wasting no time learning what she wanted to know about him.

"Not really," he replied carefully. "The forest isn't as isolated as Europeans think."

"So I have discovered for myself in the time I have been here," she said. "Sometimes the jungles seem filled with Indians."

"It's a fact that there's always one tribe or another in the vicinity."

Beatriz became even more casual. "I wonder if you have ever encountered any of the tribes that have become our enemies."

Was she suspicious of his real identity and trying to trap him? He had to be cautious. "I know very little about such matters. When my partner and I heard that France and Spain were at war with England and that this expedition had landed, we came here to find out what we could. I'm not sure, even now, that I really know which tribes are supporting us and which have joined the English colonies."

"The most important of our enemies are the Iroquois."

Still unable to determine whether she was testing him, Kenneth remained noncommittal. "They are said to be formidable," he replied.

"There are none more ferocious than their principal partner, the Seneca."

This time he merely nodded.

"Do you speak the tongues of the Indians?" she demanded.

The abrupt change of topic was somewhat startling. "I am not as fluent as my partner, but I am learning," he said, adhering to the truth as closely as possible.

"An expedition led by the Seneca is only a few days' march from this camp," Beatriz said.

He raised an eyebrow.

"You do not know them?" she asked.

He shook his head vigorously. "I've never encountered them, and they don't know me, either," he lied.

The light of the candles reflected the sudden glow in Beatriz's eyes. "How convenient."

She offered no explanation, so Kenneth felt he had to ask, "What do you mean?"

"I shall make myself clear in due course. For the moment there is just one fact I wish to know. As a white hunter and trapper you are supposedly neutral in the war. Do I assume correctly that the Seneca would make you welcome in their camp?"

His mind racing, he tentatively concluded that she hadn't guessed he was acting as an espionage agent for the Seneca and English colonial militia, but instead was curious for reasons of her own. "I've made it my business to be on friendly terms with most Indian tribes, so they would have no cause to regard me as an enemy. I don't know that I can answer your question, but I guess they would accept me if I strayed into their camp."

"That discussion can wait until more personal matters are settled." Her smile steady, Beatriz slowly unbuttoned her shirt, exposing her firm, small breasts.

Kenneth was so astonished that he neither moved nor spoke.

"There has been a friendly flow betwen us," she said. "Now we shall find out if we also are compatible in bed."

Even more stunned, he watched her as she continued to undress.

"You struck me as a man of sophistication." She was goading him now. "Do not tell me you are shy!"

He was compelled to remove his own clothes. Still wary of her motives, he nevertheless joined her on the bed when she beckoned insistently. He hadn't been paticularly drawn to her and, in fact, had found her much less appealing than Hester MacDevitt. But she was sure to become antagonistic if he rejected her.

Beatriz literally threw herself at Kenneth, her body pressing against his, her lips already parted for his initial kiss. Still startled by her lack of modesty and unexpected lasciviousness, he nevertheless responded and began to make love to her. But she was so demanding, so eager that he found it virtually impossible to gain the initiative for more than a few moments.

She was insatiable, increasingly frenzied.

Ultimately they became one, and only then did it occur to Kenneth that his release was perfunctory. The young woman's passion seemed overwhelming, and he couldn't help wondering if she was simulating for his benefit. He was experienced, to be sure, but he knew better than to imagine he was a great lover.

For a short time they rested side by side in silence. Then Beatriz dressed as abruptly as she had removed her clothes. He reached for his own clothes, still bewildered by her inexplicable conduct.

"What do you want more than anything else in the world?" she demanded abruptly.

"A peaceful, contented life," Kenneth replied warily.

"If you seek riches, I can do nothing for you. But if

you want to become the owner of a small estate near Valencia, you need only say the word, and it will belong to you. Do you want me as your mistress for as long as I remain in the New World? Do you want both the estate and me? You need only say the word."

He wondered how a man who was not her nation's enemy would respond and tried to reply accordingly. Obviously she believed she had bewitched him. "What must I do in return?"

"Go to the camp of the Seneca, wherever they may be in the jungle," Beatriz said, a throbbing hatred becoming evident in her voice for the first time. "Gain access to it. Find their leader, a man called Renno. Then kill him!"

His flesh crawled, but he managed to recover. "You're not joking," he said.

"I do not jest on that matter, ever," she said. "He escaped from an earlier attempt on his life and must not escape again!"

Kenneth felt positive she had been responsible for the mysterious attack on Renno by the two Creek warriors hidden in the wilderness. Inadvertently, he was gleaning information far more valuable than anything he had hoped to learn.

"Surely," he said dubiously, playacting superbly, "one Indian war chief cannot be the key to victory or defeat in this war."

Beatriz became impatient. "If you prefer a slave girl of your own to me, I will obtain a beauty for you. If you want a commission and a staff post in the Spanish force, with a guarantee that you shall remain in the army after the war ends, you need only say so."

He stared at her. "You promise much."

She opened her purse, removed the letters from the Spanish Crown and the viceroy of New Spain granting her broad powers, and showed them to him. The documents appeared authentic, and he read them with care.

"I do not make idle promises any more than I make idle requests," she said.

He moved swiftly to the heart of the matter. "Why should the death of this Seneca—Renno, I believe you call him—mean so much?"

Beatriz replied through clenched teeth. "He and his warriors set an ambush outside an Indian town that my father, our French colleague, and I were visiting. When we left the town, Renno murdered my father in cold blood. Colonel de Gramont shot at him but missed, and we were so badly outnumbered we were fortunate to escape with our lives. But I will not be satisfied until I have avenged the death of Don Diego de Bernardo, one of the greatest men who has ever served Spain!"

Her anger and anguish were genuine, Kenneth saw, and at last he understood. She had invited him to seduce her—no, she had virtually forced the seduction —in order to place him in her debt. She already had selected him to make another attempt on Renno's life.

"I won't press you now to name the reward you want," she said. "Think about it as you go to and from the camp of the Seneca in the jungle. All I ask is that you bring me the scalp of Renno. Then you shall have anything and everything in my power to gain for you."

Her hatred was so intense that he felt chilled, and he was sure that if he refused her request outright she would turn on him. He had too much to conceal to allow trouble to develop.

"I leave details to you," she said. "As one who has survived in the wilderness of this frightful continent, it is plain you must be a man of many resources. I don't care if you shoot him, knife him, or even strangle him with your bare hands. Just know that I want the murderer of my father killed!"

"I understand your position," Kenneth said, trying to reassure her with a smile.

"Then you will do it?"

"I'll gladly leave this fort tomorrow morning at dawn," Kenneth said firmly. "I'll go as quickly as I can to the camp of the Seneca, wherever they may be. And I won't waste a moment finding Renno. The rewards in this enterprise are truly great, and I have no intention of disappointing those who have faith in me."

Beatriz's smile was radiant.

"But there are complications," he said.

Her smile faded.

"I must persuade my partner to come with me. I'll have to conceal from him my reasons for making this journey, but this is my problem, and you need not concern yourself with it. However, the French and Spanish high command here at the fort will wonder why we've left without waiting to see Colonel de Gramont. And he may not want to hire us as scouts if he believes we aren't reliable."

"Leave all that to me," Beatriz said. "I will think of something that will satisfy the regimental commanders. And I swear that Alain de Gramont will share my gratitude to you."

He hid his elation. She would see to it that there were to be no repercussions when he and André left abruptly, and it was unlikely that either would be suspected of espionage on behalf of the enemy. "You've settled my doubts," he said. "I don't know how long it will take me to do what I must, but I'll see you again as soon as possible." Preferably in battle, he told himself.

Beatriz placed her hands on his shoulders and lifted her face for the kiss that would seal their supposed bargain. "You won't regret this," she said.

He had to use all of his willpower to force himself to kiss her. The Biloxi had been right when they had called her a she-devil.

The hour was late, and André Cooke was growing apprehensive by the time his companion joined him, but he had no chance to ask any questions. "We can't talk here," Kenneth muttered. "I don't want to take even a remote chance that we might be overheard. All I can say is that we'll leave at dawn and that no one will try to stop us."

They slept only a short time, eating a breakfast of cold meat before they departed at daybreak. Four Spanish infantrymen were stationed at the gate, and all saluted the pair with their muskets. Apparently Beatriz already had told the soldiers' superiors a tale they accepted.

Not pausing, André set a swift pace, and the pair quickly made their way westward. Traveling in the style of the Seneca, they marched for long hours at a time, pausing only for very brief periods of rest. Even during these pauses, they kept their voices low and their talk to a minimum, never knowing what Indians might be in the vicinity.

It was apparent to André that his companion had been badly shaken by his encounter with Beatriz de Bernardo, but he refrained from asking questions. It was enough, for the moment, that the major objectives of their mission had been accomplished.

They stayed on the trail day and night, sleeping only in snatches, and after a grueling march they came to the sentry line maintained by the Oneida. André estimated that the new camp of the Iroquois and militia was located about one hundred miles inland from the Gulf of Mexico on the delta of the Mississippi.

Camp had been made for the night much earlier, the evening meal had been consumed, and the fires were burning low by the time the weary pair arrived. André paused just long enough to greet Anne Ridley with a fierce hug and kiss.

"Are you all right?" she asked, searching his haggard face anxiously as he released her.

"Fine. Both of us are fine."

"Have you eaten supper?"

"We've had nothing but jerked meat and parched

corn for longer than we care to recall," he replied, "but we can't stop now for a meal. We have a vital report to make."

As he continued forward through the bivouac area, the determined Anne immediately asked Walter to fetch some venison stew that she could heat for the tired travelers.

Kenneth saw Hester MacDevitt only from a distance, and instead of going to speak to her, he contented himself with waving to her. Just seeing her made him feel unexpectedly guilty because of his brief liaison with Beatriz de Bernardo. He was surprised by his reaction and knew he needed an opportunity to think about what had happened before he spoke to Hester.

Renno, Jeffrey, and Ned were consulting with the Biloxi scouts when Kenneth and André approached them. Sun-ai-yee, who sat at a nearby fire with Talking Quail, finishing the special meal she had cooked for him, hastily joined the group, too.

"We were completely successful," André told the silent, tense members of the high command. "We learned that there are already close to three thousand warriors of various tribes in the enemy camp, and it appears likely they'll be joined by another five hundred to one thousand in the immediate future. They've been given firearms as part of their bargain with the French and Spaniards, but they're not yet proficient in the use of muskets. So I think it likely they'll rely on their bows and arrows, spears and tomahawks when the fighting starts."

Kenneth picked up the report. "The French have landed a full regiment of veterans, who sailed directly to the New World from Brest," he said. "King Louis's generals may need troops to face the Duke of Marlborough, but Paris recognizes the importance of the war on this side of the Atlantic, too. The men carry the latest make of muskets and bayonets. The only bright side of the picture is that neither the officers nor the men have ever engaged in wilderness fighting, and they have no artillery. However, you can be sure that Colonel de Gramont—who was absent from the fort during our visit—will know how to utilize the regiment to the best possible advantage."

Jeffrey Wilson sighed and stared into the fire.

"The Spaniards have landed two thousand men, also well armed," Kenneth continued. "Other than whatever value their sheer numbers may afford, I have doubts about their reliability in battle. Most of them are recruits who were given a minimum of training after leaving their farms in Castile, León, and Andalusia, and their officers are pompous gentlemen who spend their days sleeping and their nights gaming and drinking."

Jeffrey heard the contempt in Kenneth's voice and marveled at the change in him. Lord Symes truly had become a new man.

"They may not be efficient," Ned Ridley said, "but two thousand armed Spaniards comprise a large force."

The discussion was interrupted by the arrival of Anne and Hester, who were bringing the agents large gourds of steaming venison stew. "Welcome home," Hester said pointedly to Kenneth, obviously piqued because he hadn't paused long enough to greet her.

"Thank you," he said, and embarrassed himself by turning scarlet beneath his tan.

The girls would have lingered, but Ned waved them away.

Kenneth was famished but felt compelled to complete his report before he ate. Placing his gourd on the ground, he drew his pistol, then took his knife from his belt and held it in his other hand. "I have learned a great deal more," he said. "With the possible exception of Colonel de Gramont, the most influential person in the enemy camp is the woman the Biloxi call the she-devil. Renno, I wonder if you know how easy it would be for me to kill you right now."

The young sachem's expression remained unchanged.

For an alarmed instant, André wondered if his companion had fallen under the woman's influence. Then Kenneth thrust the pistol back into its holster and drove the knife downward into the ground, where it quivered delicately. He had demonstrated his point, and only then did he tell the full story of his encounter with Beatriz de Bernardo.

Renno continued to sit motionless.

"You say she carries documents from the Spanish Crown and New World viceroy giving her special powers?" the concerned Ned asked.

Kenneth nodded. "Broad powers. And I believe she considers it far more important to see Renno killed than to win the war!"

"All of us are grateful to you for this information," Ned said as Kenneth finally began to eat. "Now that ambush by the Creek makes sense. Renno, you're too valuable to us for this threat to be taken lightly. I propose that we establish a special escort to protect you."

Renno shook his head. "We have more important problems to solve."

"I'll grant you that our overall situation isn't too promising," Jeffrey said, "but Ned is right. You do need protection, Renno."

"Since we are so badly outnumbered, we will need every warrior and every militiaman in battle," Renno said. "It would be wrong to assign men to do nothing but guard me when I already have all the protection I need."

Only Sun-ai-yee knew what he meant. The others looked at him blankly.

"The manitous keep watch over me," he said. "I need no other help."

As Ned knew from long experience when they had faced various grave dangers together, his mind was made up and nothing would be gained by argument with him. Besides, as Betsy had said when telling her family about Renno's faith, he had survived and escaped unscathed from many situations when death had seemed inevitable.

Knowing better than to argue, Ned dropped the subject. He said, "In the light of what we've learned tonight from André and Kenneth, we may have to devise a new strategy to meet the threat of a far stronger enemy. I propose that we think about it overnight and meet again in the morning. It might even be wise to remain at this campsite until we decide how we can best defend ourselves."

"That is wise," Sun-ai-yee said.

Jeffrey, who was keenly aware of Kenneth's growing interest in Hester MacDevitt, had a final word before they adjourned for the night. "I suggest," he said, "that we regard Kenneth's encounter with the she-devil as confidential."

Everyone understood the point he was making, and Kenneth was grateful to him. Bracing himself, the young nobleman walked to the fire to which Hester and Anne had returned.

Anne diplomatically remembered an errand that required her presence elsewhere and asked Walter to accompany her. Hester, sitting alone at the fire, averted her face. "Don't waste your time on me when you're busy," she said.

Kenneth wanted to make a full confession to her but had the sense to realize it was too much to expect her to understand how he had become involved with Beatriz de Bernardo. He lowered himself to the ground, then said, "I missed you far more than you'll ever know."

Hester had no idea why he had virtually ignored her when he had first returned, but she knew he was making amends. The solemn expressions she had seen on the faces of the expedition's leaders had told her that serious troubles loomed ahead, so this was no time to be distant, no time to permit herself to be miffed. "I missed you, too," she told him candidly, "and I prayed for your safe return."

His absence had deepened their relationship, and the time was rapidly approaching when he would need to reveal his true identity to her.

Chapter XI

The commanders of the Spanish and French regiments met in the latter's tent and were joined by the war chiefs of their Indian allies. Since Alain de Gramont alone was able to interpret for all who were present, he assumed the role of chairman of the council of war. Beatriz de Bernardo sat inconspicuously in a far corner of the spacious tent, well knowing that some of the men resented her presence but were powerless to exclude her.

"Our scouts are keeping watch on the movements of the enemy as he marches deeper into the delta country of the Great River," Alain said. "We don't know his intentions, although he can't stay forever in that land of swamps, lakes, and rivers. All we know is that we outnumber his forces heavily. The question to be decided is whether to attack him or wait for him to move against us."

The middle-aged commander of the French regiment, who had distinguished himself in two campaigns against the English and Dutch, was blunt. "I favor an attack," he said. "It is always preferable to taking up a defensive position, especially when the odds are favorable to us. Think of the enemy's situation, gentlemen. His forces consist only of English colonial militiamen —citizen-soldiers who know nothing about the arts of war—and bands of stupid savages."

Alain was glad that none of the war chiefs present could understand a word of French, and he deliberately refrained from translating the reference to "stupid savages."

"With all due respect," the senior Spanish officer said, "I must disagree with my French colleague. In my opinion we would do best to await the enemy here. It is true that the walls of this fort are made of wood rather than stone, but the enemy has no artillery, so we are secure behind our palisade."

The other Spanish colonel nodded. "We should build a platform inside the walls and station our best musket men there. When the enemy advances toward us, we can shoot down his militiamen and savages in large numbers. Meanwhile, our own losses will be slight. I always prefer a defensive stance to an offensive one because casualties are lower."

The war chiefs listened intently to the translation, and the leader of the Creek was the first to speak. "It is wise when dealing with the mighty Seneca to be cautious. Never before have the Creek met them in battle, but they are renowned for their valor."

"It is said of the Seneca," the Osage war chief added, "that the demons of the afterworld enter their souls when they fight. It is said that arrows are turned aside at the last instant and cannot break their skins. It may be that even firesticks cannot kill them."

"The Shawnee," the war chief of that nation declared, "fear no tribe. They win wars. They do not lose wars, as our former enemies well know."

The Osage bristled but remembered that he was dealing with a new ally.

"The spirits of the Shawnee who have won great victories fill the afterworld," the Shawnee boasted. "It is true that there are no warriors in this world who have greater skill and courage." He paused and became reflective. "It is true also," he added, "that the Shawnee have never met the Seneca in battle. Word has come to the Shawnee that the stories told to the Osage are right. A demon enters the body of a Seneca warrior when he begins to fight. The eyes of the demons are sharp, and the arrows of the Seneca always strike deep into the hearts of their foes. The skins of the Seneca become stronger than the skins of the bull buffalo, and the arrows of their foes are blunted so badly they do not even draw blood. It may be also that demons invade the bodies of other Iroquois."

The Creek was quick to agree. "None who are here have ever fought the Mohawk and the Oneida, but it is said they are only a little less ferocious than their brothers of the Seneca. So the stories heard by the Osage must be true. The demons also enter the bodies of all the other warriors of the Iroquois."

The Shawnee was emphatic as he summed up their position. "The nations that will fight beside the men of France and the men of Spain agree with the war chiefs of Spain. Let the enemy come to this fort, and it may be that the strong firesticks will overcome the magic of the Iroquois and destroy them."

Alain de Gramont looked unhappy as he translated. He felt compelled to interject a comment of his own. "I have fought the warriors of the Seneca and those of the other Iroquois in many battles. They are not invaded by demons. They are mortal men. They bleed. They die. In my house, in the land of the Huron, I have the scalps of many Seneca I have killed."

The war chiefs listened politely, but it was plain they did not believe his claims. They thought of him as a fellow Indian rather than as a Frenchman, and just as they themselves willingly lied in order to gain desired ends, they took it for granted that he would do the same.

"I agree with the commander of the French," Alain said vigorously. "Our foes are vulnerable and weak. Let us attack them in full fury with all our troops and all of our warriors. We will finish them for all time." He thought, but did not mention, that the myth of Seneca invincibility would die, too.

The Spanish colonels, however, remained firm in their insistence on fighting a defensive campaign, and the war chiefs were unwavering in their support.

Beatriz de Bernardo became restless. She was already out of sorts because she had neither seen nor received any word from the supposed French hunter-trapper whom she had sent to kill Renno, forcing her to conclude a similar arrangement with a brave of the Natchez in whom she placed little faith. Now the timid conservatism of her fellow Spaniards and their Indian allies annoyed her. "Am I permitted to speak my mind before this council?" she demanded.

Alain was not surprised, and knowing there was no way to keep her silent when she wanted to express herself, he did not bother to check with the colonels as he nodded assent.

The European commanders were irritated by the unwelcome interruption. The French colonel glowered, but the two Spaniards, conscious of the documents from Madrid and Havana that she carried, were afraid to protest.

Aware of their attitude but not caring, Beatriz stalked to the center of the tent, her stride brisk and masculine. Planting her booted feet apart, she hooked her thumbs in her belt. "There was a time," she said, "when I wished I had been a man. No more. I thank God that He created me a woman. Spanish men are cowards, and so are Indian chieftains."

Her hearers bridled, and only the French commander, who began to perceive what she had in mind, stopped frowning, then chuckled.

"A war is not a game," she said. "It is a struggle to the death. Only the strong are winners, and they never allow themselves to forget that they must never shrink from their duty. It is your duty to destroy the citizens of the English colonies who play at being soldiers. It is your duty to destroy their Indian allies. Are you such cowards that you are afraid to attack them?"

The Spanish colonels stirred uncomfortably, and the war chiefs, always afraid of losing face, looked sheepish.

"Just for this one day," Beatriz said passionately, "once again I wish I were a man!" She drew her sword and thrust the point of the blade into the ground. "How I wish that spot were the heart of the enemy! As a man I would force you to attack! I would lead that attack myself! Even as a woman I will gladly lead you into battle if you are afraid to fight!" Plucking her sword from the ground, she thrust it viciously into its scabbard, then stamped out of the tent.

Her abrupt departure, Alain de Gramont knew, was a calculated risk. Now he had to do his part before the spell she had cast was broken. "Let each of you who favors a campaign of attack rise," he said.

The French commander stood at once. The Spanish colonels looked at each other, then reluctantly rose to their feet, too.

The war chiefs of the Creek, Osage, and Shawnee faced a delicate dilemma. Nothing that had been said diminished their dread of the Seneca. But none wanted his tribe to be branded as a nation of cowards. That reputation would be difficult to dispel and, in the months and years ahead, would be certain to invite trouble with neighbors. The war chiefs no longer had a choice, and all three were forced to stand.

The die was cast: every member of the council had

voted in favor of waging an offensive campaign. As much as Alain had come to dislike Beatriz, he had to admit she had no peer as a manipulator.

Two of the Oneida scouts, who had been keeping the enemy fort under observation, were the first to bring the less than welcome news to the high command of the expedition. "The warriors of the Creek, the Shawnee, and the Osage are smoking buffalo meat and venison," they reported.

Wise in all the ways of the wilderness, the four leaders knew instantly that the enemy intended to attack.

"I must admit that's what I would do if I were in their place," Jeffrey Wilson said.

Ned Ridley was grim. "We're going to have our backs to the wall, that's certain."

Renno, as always, remained unruffled. "We can win a defensive campaign, but our needs are special," he said and, offering no fuller explanation, summoned André Cooke. "How well do you know this territory in the delta of the Great River?" he asked.

André shook his head. "I've traveled through these bayous many times," he said, "but they're a maze. What with swamps, cypress, live oak, and palmetto, not to mention bushes and underbrush I've never seen anywhere else, it's easy to lose my way. I've done it more than once in years past."

"How well do the Biloxi know the region?"

André was cautious. "They claim to be familiar with all of it, but I don't necessarily accept their word."

"Take Da-no and three or four of the others," Renno said. "The most reliable of their warriors. Find an area where game is plentiful. We may have to live off the land in one place for a long time."

André nodded. "I'll go at once."

"Wait," Renno said. "I have only started to tell you our needs. We must make our bivouac in an area where there are many trees and bushes. That will prevent the Spanish and French regiments from attacking us in the open."

The others began to see his point, and Sun-ai-yee added a condition of his own. "It would be helpful if we have a large lake directly behind us. We could use it for fishing and for our water supplies, and the enemy could not attack us from the rear."

Renno knew that he and the war chief who once had been his tutor frequently thought in the same manner. "It would be a great help if we settle in a place where there is also a large swamp on each of our flanks." Renno well knew that no enemy would want to make his way through swamps that could not be charted, with quicksand and muddy water that sometimes rose to a height of four feet and where rattlesnakes, water moccasins, and a number of other equally deadly snakes were rife.

André understood the strategy and smiled. "In such a location," he said, "we'd need to keep a close watch only on one side, our front. From what I've seen of the bayous, there must be a place that meets those specifications!"

"One of our many problems," Jeffrey told him, "is that you won't have much time to search. If the Indian allies of France and Spain are smoking meat to eat during the campaign, they'll soon be on the march against us."

André left at once, accompanied by four experienced Biloxi warriors who had hunted and fished in the bayou country. Meanwhile, the expedition made no further move. Large hunting parties went out each day for supplies that could be used during a siege, and the entire Mohawk contingent joined the advance bands of Oneida and Seneca on sentry outpost duty. Now there was virtually no chance that the expedition could be overwhelmed in a surprise assault.

André and his companions returned after searching the primitive wilderness of the bayou country for three days and nights. All were grimy and weary but triumphant.

"Maybe we were just plain lucky," André said, "but we stumbled into an area that appears to meet all of our requirements. I'll tell you this much—the enemy will have hell's own time gouging us out of there!"

The entire company was on the move at daybreak and needed a day and a half to reach the site. At Renno's quiet insistence, Anne Ridley and Hester MacDevitt now marched with the elders, women, and children of the Biloxi. The swamp-infested region through which they traveled, cut by the many streams formed by the splitting of the Mississippi into countless smaller rivers as it ran toward the Gulf of Mexico, reminded him and Ned of the treacherous Everglades they had been forced to travel through several years earlier. He saw no need to alarm the girls, but he knew snakes were everywhere. The Biloxi women, familiar with the area, would be able to stay away from the venomous creatures and could guide the two white girls.

Renno and Sun-ai-yee made a swift but thorough tour of the bivouac area when they reached the site, while Jeffrey and Ned inspected it more slowly. All were delighted with André's find. The lake at the southern end was a deep-water body, abounding with fish, and Ned estimated that the far shore was at least a mile and a half away. Not even the most ambitious of the enemy's Indian allies could negotiate it without first constructing a large fleet of canoes.

The swamp that lay to the east was forbidding, and from Da-no's lurid description it was almost endless. A few senior warriors of the Seneca penetrated to the depth of several hundred yards, and in spite of their undisputed personal courage, they were relieved when they returned intact. They had killed no fewer than five poisonous snakes with their tomahawks and had sighted more than they could count. No foe would dare to launch an attack in that sector.

The swamp on the western side of the natural redoubt appeared at first glance to be far less menacing. It was about half a mile wide and treeless, with tangles of vines and scrub brush that rose to a height of no more than six feet. Large flocks of geese, ducks, and other edible birds had nests there, and the overall appearance was peaceful, but André was able to determine that vast patches of treacherous quicksand lay beneath the tranquil, muddy surface of the water. An enemy force that attempted to penetrate the quagmire would be certain to founder.

The bivouac area itself, which lay on relatively high ground, was about a mile wide and two miles long, most of it heavily wooded. Small game abounded there, but the need for large quantities of meat vanished when one of the Seneca scouts reported the presence of a herd of buffalo several miles away. A party of senior warriors was sent hunting and brought down so many of the animals that an additional one hundred and fifty braves had to be sent to bring back the meat. Fires were lighted, and for the next two days, as the expedition rested, enough meat was smoked to withstand a long siege.

Strictly as a precaution Renno stationed sentries on the sides of the perimeter facing the lake and the two swamps; but the approach to the area to the north, which was certain to be the route the enemy would take, received the most attention. Sun-ai-yee stationed three hundred Seneca and two hundred Mohawk in the forest, and behind them Ned Ridley's marksmen erected barricades of fallen logs. Most were of palmetto; the soft wood, which would halt and absorb enemy bullets, was ideal for defense purposes.

Renno sent a small number of his best scouts out to keep watch on the enemy and report his movements, and the entire company settled down to await the beginning of the hostilities. No attempt was made to hide the presence of the militia, warriors, or the whole Biloxi tribe. Cooking fires were kept lighted, and men openly fished in the lake or brought down birds.

As Jeffrey Wilson succinctly explained to his Massachusetts Bay troops, "If the enemy doesn't already know we're here, it won't be difficult for him to find us. So we're not trying to hide from him. We've come a long, long way from home for this campaign, and we're ready any time the enemy wants to start a fight."

André Cooke had little to keep him occupied and consequently spent most of his days with Anne. They had a long discussion one morning, then went to Ned.

"We understand," André said, "that Sun-ai-yee is marrying the Biloxi woman today or tomorrow."

"Today, I believe," Ned said, grinning. "Talking Quail suggested it, and Sun-ai-yee is willing, so they've decided not to wait."

"We think they're right," Anne said. "We'd very much like to follow their example."

Ned studied the pair, his smile slowly fading. "In the absence of a Seneca medicine man," he said, "Renno has the authority as a sachem to grant Sun-ai-yee and Talking Quail permission to marry. There will be no ceremony. They'll say a few words to each other with only Renno and the sachem of the Biloxi in attendance, and that will be that. They'll be married. Your situation is quite different."

Embarrassed, André knew his future brother-in-law was right, but Anne held her ground. "If Sun-ai-yee and the Biloxi woman can marry, so can we."

"You're a stubborn Ridley for sure," her brother told her. "If you remember, when you first told me of your desire to get married, I said you'd have to wait for our father's permission. For one thing, you're still quite young. For another thing, there's no clergyman in the company who could perform the ceremony. I have no legal authority to do it, and neither does Jeff Wilson. And even if Renno would grant you permission to marry in the Seneca manner, you can imagine what our parents would say when they heard about it."

"Betsy and Renno were married in a Seneca ceremony, Ned!"

"Indeed they were. A full ceremony. Betsy was becoming a full-fledged member of the Seneca nation, and that's what they wanted. But you forget they had already become man and wife in our own Norfolk church, where, if I remember correctly, you were the flower girl."

Anne tried to argue, but her brother cut her off. "Go to Renno, if you wish. But I can promise he'll turn you down."

"He's as conservative and old-fashioned as you are!" Anne said angrily.

André put a hand on her arm to calm her. "I told you there's no way we can marry now," he said. "We'll have to be patient and keep waiting."

She glared at him, then flounced off alone.

"All the women in our family are high-spirited," Ned said mildly.

"Anne is, but I don't mind," André said. "She needs a little time alone now so she can cool down, and then she'll be fine again. I knew there was no practical way we could marry now, but she wouldn't have been satisfied until she came to you. So I had to let her have her way."

Ned grinned at him. "She'll appreciate a real wedding when the time comes."

"I know. Her problem is that she's had so many troubles, and now she has nothing else to think about —until the fighting starts."

"Which won't be long." Ned lowered his voice. "One of the Seneca scouts brought in word last night that the regiments of the enemy are on the move, with the warriors fanning out ahead of them by the thousand. We should get another report later today, and then we'll announce an alert. We're saying nothing too soon to Sun-ai-yee because we see no need to spoil his wedding."

Sun-ai-yee appeared alone at the small clearing where Renno had established his command post, and for the first time in all the years they had known each other, the older war chief appeared nervous. A few minutes later they were joined by the Biloxi sachem, who discussed the problems of food distribution with Renno. But Sun-ai-yee's mind appeared to be elsewhere.

To the surprise of all three men, Anne and Hester came into the clearing, both of them smiling. "I heard about the wedding, and I told Hester," Anne said to her brother-in-law. "We've invited ourselves."

Renno saw the expression in her eyes, which reminded him of Betsy's when she made up her mind. He knew it would be useless to tell her that the presence of outside witnesses was not customary, so he merely shrugged and made no comment.

Then Talking Quail entered the clearing, wearing a garland of tiny wildflowers in her hair. She lowered her head to Sun-ai-yee in a gesture of submission to his will, then greeted the two sachems in a similar fashion. Hester happened to catch her eye for an instant and saw a knowing, happy gleam.

It was apparent to both Hester and Anne that Talking Quail, in spite of her seeming shyness, knew precisely what she was doing. It was possible that Sun-ai-yee never would know that his wife controlled him.

Sun-ai-yee announced abruptly that, in accordance with the wartime tradition of the Seneca, he was making Talking Quail his wife.

The woman responded in an almost inaudible voice. "Talking Quail is no longer of the Biloxi, but becomes a Seneca, the nation of her husband."

"The sachem of the Seneca has heard," Renno said.

"The sachem of the Biloxi has heard," the leader of the small tribe declared.

Hester, who was prepared to become misty-eyed, was surprised that the ceremony, which had lasted only seconds, was completed.

Sun-ai-yee turned away from the witnesses and started to walk off into the deepest portion of the forest, his gait rolling.

Talking Quail meekly fell in several paces behind him, as befitted the wife of a great war chief. Before she disappeared from sight, however, she looked directly at Hester and Anne, mischief sparkling in her eyes. Her expression made it plain that she had planned and won her campaign.

The bride and groom would retreat into the far recesses of the forest and would consummate their marriage. Discreetly placed warriors of the Seneca would see to it that no member of the expedition inadvertently wandered into the area during the next few hours.

"How I wish André and I were Indians," Anne said as she and her friend wandered back to their camp. "Our civilization makes simple things so complicated."

Hester laughed.

"Don't mock me," Anne said. "You'll feel just as I do if you and Kenneth ever make up your minds to marry."

"I've already made up my mind," Hester said, her mirth evaporating. "Kenneth is the one who is holding back."

"That's strange. He's so attentive to you, and he gives every appearance of being a man in love."

"I know, but he keeps making little references to something in his past. He's very mysterious, and all I've persuaded him to say is that I might not want to marry him if I know his background. I've told him it wouldn't matter to me if he turns out to be an indentured servant—he knows I am. But he just frowns and shakes his head, and then he refuses to say another word. He sometimes says he'll tell me everything if he lives through this campaign. I'm trying to be patient, but it isn't easy."

"Patience! How I hate that word!" All at once Anne started to giggle. "But you've got to admit our lives have changed since the days we complained to each other that we couldn't stand Norfolk because our existence there was so dull."

The day passed like so many others that had gone before it. The weather was humid, and as the sun rose higher, the heat became more intense, driving the militiamen into the shade. The warriors, particularly the Seneca, seemed impervious to the elements.

In mid-afternoon one of the scouts came into camp with news that electrified the high command. "The Creek, who are leading the enemy, are drawing close," he said. "It may be they will attack when the daylight ends."

"How many Creek are in the war party?" Renno asked.

"Ten times one hundred warriors."

"What arms do they carry?"

"Many have firesticks, but do not know how to hold them," the scout said.

Renno turned to his fellow commanders. "If they launch a surprise attack," he said, "I am almost certain they will use bows and arrows rather than muskets. One shot would alert us."

"Yes," Ned replied. "They well may believe they can overwhelm us, and silent arrows would be far more effective than muskets."

All militiamen and warriors were placed on alert, and the sentry details were doubled. A number of the Biloxi who knew the bayou country joined the Oneida sentinels, forming a thin line about half a mile to the north of the encampment. Then, as night approached, the Seneca and Mohawk who formed the defense vanguard took up their places in the forest, and the Virginians moved into place behind their barricades of palmetto logs.

Renno's orders to his warriors were sharp and specific. "Let no one send an arrow in the direction of the enemy until the signal is given," he said. "It may be the hope of the Creek that they will surprise the Iroquois. But they will learn that our warriors have cunning."

The men ate their evening meal of cold meat at their duty posts. The bulk of the Seneca and the Massachusetts Bay militia, who were being held in reserve, lighted their fires as usual and ate a hot supper. An approaching enemy would see the glow of the fires and would believe the defenders were unprepared.

Sun-ai-yee and the radiant Talking Quail, who dutifully followed him, came into the camp to eat, and the war chief immediately realized that the defense posts were manned. "I was not told that the enemy draws near," he said to Renno in an aggrieved tone.

"There was no need to disturb Sun-ai-yee and his woman," Renno said. "There is time for my brother to fill his belly with fighting and take the scalps of the Creek."

Food immediately forgotten, the portly war chief sent his bride to join the women of the Biloxi, then moved forward to a place of concealment in the front ranks of the Seneca and Mohawk.

Gradually a silence settled over the camp. Fires were allowed to die down, the children of the Biloxi became drowsy and soon fell asleep. Crickets chirped in the undergrowth near the banked fires. The Iroquois and the militiamen who had traveled so far from their homes to engage in combat on alien soil waited tensely for hostilities to begin.

An owl hooted mournfully in the distance.

"That is the word that the enemy approaches," Renno murmured to Jeffrey Wilson and Ned Ridley, and all three moved forward to a command post in a hollow directly behind the concealed warriors of the vanguard.

A coyote howled somewhere in the depths of the wilderness.

Renno nodded. "Soon," he said in a low voice.

Sun-ai-yee had the authority to start the battle when he deemed the moment appropriate. He peered into the gloom of the forest, pleased that the moon and stars were hidden by increasingly thick layers of clouds. Before the night ended rain would fall; weather conditions were perfect.

Another owl hooted, its cry muted, and the senior warriors of the Seneca promptly notched arrows into their bows.

Sun-ai-yee blinked to improve his vision and was rewarded when he made out a large number of dark shapes creeping forward toward his position. He took a dry stick from his belt, having carried it for this special purpose, and waited until the shadows were no more than fifty feet from his front line. Then, in a quick, decisive move, he snapped the stick.

The cracking sound was distinct, although not loud. Anyone unfamiliar with the techniques of the Iroquois well might have assumed that a small animal had stepped on a twig, but the Seneca had been waiting for the signal. Each of the senior warriors had selected his own target, and fifty arrows sang through the air simultaneously.

Then the Seneca and Mohawk in the second line let fly. The warriors directly behind them moved forward silently, and within moments the air was filled with hails of arrows.

What made the attack eerily impressive was its utter silence. No verbal orders were given, and no Seneca or Mohawk made a sound.

The stunned Creek were overwhelmed before they realized what was happening to them. Their lead warriors dropped to the ground, many of them dead and most of the others wounded. The Iroquois were living up to their reputation for accuracy.

Some of the Creek instinctively fell back several paces. Before they could regroup, however, Sun-ai-yee emitted a soft owl call, and all five hundred of his Seneca and Mohawk advanced toward the foe. They held their fire until they were able to make out their targets clearly, and then every warrior was on his own.

The Creek outnumbered their foes by two to one, but the Iroquois mercilessly reduced the odds, their warriors letting fly now as rapidly as they could fit arrows into their bows.

The war chief of the Creek had made one fatal error, sending his main body forward in a solid mass, and Sun-ai-yee was quick to take advantage of the situation. With a sweep of his arm, he sent one hundred of the Seneca circling to the left, then motioned for an equal number of Mohawk to circle toward the right flank. The remaining three hundred continued to press forward in the center.

The Creek lacked the ironclad discipline of their foes and began to retreat, but they were not cowards and did not panic, starting their fallback in good order. But they were packed into a confined space, and with their foes pressing in against them on three sides, it was impossible for them to spread out. Effectively hemmed in, they presented a solid mass to the Seneca and Mohawk, who abruptly changed their tactics.

Sun-ai-yee, personally leading the direct onslaught, was the first to hurl his tomahawk at the head of a Creek war chief, easily identifiable by the feathers at the base of his scalp lock. Realizing instantly what was required, the Seneca and Mohawk threw their tomahawks, too. Endless hours of practice made them marvelously skilled in the art, and Creek after Creek was felled.

Those who survived lost what little discipline they still retained and began to crowd toward the rear, the only avenue of escape still open to them.

One final tactic remained to be utilized, and Sun-ai-yee, a master in the Seneca science of striking terror into the hearts of a disorganized enemy, timed the move perfectly. Waiting until his followers had thrown virtually all of their tomahawks, he broke the silence with an ear-shattering war whoop, then drew his knife. Five hundred Seneca and Mohawk promptly followed his example.

Renno, still at his command post far to the rear, heard the sound and glanced at Jeffrey and Ned. "We have won," he said.

The Creek gave in to panic at last and, throwing away their weapons as they ran, raced off into the forest in disgrace. Without exception these survivors were convinced that the stories they had heard through the years were true: the Seneca were not only ferocious, but were indeed invincible.

The night's work was not yet done for the Iroquois. They methodically collected their tomahawks, carefully retrieving the weapons discarded by their enemies, and then began the task of finding their spent arrows. When necessary, they hacked the shafts from the bodies of their victims. The dead were scalped, the wounded were given a death blow, and then they were scalped, too. No quarter was shown, as that was not the Iroquois way. They had emerged victorious in a fair fight, and there were no Creek survivors.

Finally the dead were counted, and as the successful warriors returned to the principal bivouac area, many of them with scalps dripping at their belts, Sun-ai-yee went to the command post to report. "Nearly four hundred Creeks have gone to join their ancestors," he said, displaying no emotion.

"How many Seneca and Mohawk were killed?" Renno asked.

"None."

"Wounded?"

"None."

The results were astonishing. The Creek had lost almost forty percent of their assault force, but the defenders had suffered no casualties.

"I can scarcely believe it," Jeffrey said.

"Let us not rejoice too soon," Renno said. "Now the enemy know what the Iroquois can accomplish in battle. But they still outnumber us, and when they resume the fight, they will attack in great force. We may not fare as well in the next battle."

314

The dismal failure of the Creek surprise attack caused the commanders of the French and Spaniards to revise their tactics. The scouts of their Indian allies reported that the English colonial militia and Iroquois were holding a virtually impregnable position, with a large lake to their rear and dangerous swamps on their flanks. So it was decided that, for the present, siege tactics would be adopted.

The troops of the French and Spanish regiments put aside their muskets, picked up their shovels, and threw up breastworks of the heavy, black bayou soil. The Shawnee and Osage took up positions to the rear of the European musketmen, and the Creek, discouraged by their defeat, were granted a temporary respite and allowed to withdraw for a time. Well aware of the shame they had suffered, the war chiefs of the Creek plotted vengeance against their foes.

The scouts of both sides met in brief, occasional skirmishes, but there was no other contact between the foes, and Renno was pleased. "The warriors of the Osage and the Shawnee share the fears of the Creek," he said. "All are afraid of the Seneca, and that is good."

"Plainly they hope to starve us out," Jeffrey Wilson said.

"Well, we anticipated a siege," Ned Ridley replied, "but I can't say I enjoy the prospect. It isn't easy to maintain the spirits of fighting men when they're cooped up day after day."

Renno shrugged. "The food we have on hand and the food we can acquire will make it possible for us to stay here for many weeks," he said. "It may be that the enemy will become discouraged before we lose heart."

In order to conquer the inevitable boredom, he wisely rotated the scouting assignments, giving all of his warriors regular opportunities to roam through the area that separated the defenders from the enemy and to stand sentry duty in the forest. These tasks, combined with the patience that the Iroquois had acquired through years of unrelenting training, resulted in their continued high morale.

The same was not true of the Biloxi, however. Their warriors, even though kept busy in such mundane activities as fishing, hunting, and collecting firewood, became restless. The women and elders suffered even more severely and began to make up songs and chants about the day when they would return to their own homes.

Many of the older militiamen had taken part in the long siege of the great French fortress of Louisburg years earlier, when their present commanders had won their first laurels, so they understood what was at stake and resigned themselves to a long wait. But the younger soldiers, officers and enlisted men alike, found the passage of time maddeningly slow. The weather remained hot and sultry, and after each frequent rainfall they fought off mosquitoes that rose in swarms from the swamps. Each new day was like the last, tempers grew short, and even the closest of friends quarreled over trifles.

With no activity and nothing to occupy their minds, men from Massachusetts Bay and Virginia thought of the wives, children, and parents waiting for them at home. These men had participated willingly and cheerfully in the long trek that had brought them so many hundreds of miles from their farms and towns, but they had come to loathe this strange, almost junglelike wilderness. They knew that forces many times their size were lying in wait for them, and with their own leaders content to let the siege drag on indefinitely, they regarded their outlook as bleak.

It did not occur to them that their commanders had to overcome personal problems, too. Ned Ridley had left a pregnant wife in Virginia, and he knew that by now Consuelo had given birth. He could only pray that she and the baby were safe and well. In addition, he had the responsibility of somehow seeing to it that

Anne reached home safely. Jeffrey Wilson, too, had a family waiting for him, and he wondered if he would ever see them again. Even the stolid Renno was worried about Betsy, Ja-gonh, and Goo-ga-ro-no, as well as his parents. He hoped they had survived their return crossing of the Atlantic Ocean. By now, he knew, El-i-chi either had been killed or had safely carried the request for help to the land of the Seneca, but in the absence of any news he found it increasingly difficult to believe that his plea would be answered.

As the younger officers and men felt more and more sorry for themselves, they discussed their plight openly, then gradually came to conclusions of their own. They decided to take their thoughts to the high command. The Virginians elected a lieutenant and a corporal to represent them, each of the Massachusetts Bay battalions did the same, and believing that André Cooke and Kenneth Robinson could exert a measure of influence, they were invited to join the petitioners. The pair agreed, although both made it clear that they did not necessarily share the views of the troops.

Jeffrey, Ned, and Renno, suspecting what the men had in mind, readily consented to meet them at the command post. "They'll feel better after they've spoken freely," Jeffrey said.

The emissaries sat in a circle on the ground, facing the three commanders, and a sergeant from Massachusetts Bay was the first to speak. "This ain't a mutiny," he said, "but we're tired of doing nothing except getting eaten alive by the damn mosquitoes. We've been doing a heap of talking among ourselves, and we wonder why we can't just plain break through the enemy lines."

"We know we'll suffer casualties," the Virginia lieutenant declared, "but we'll break the siege."

Kenneth was the most articulate member of the group. "As André and I understand the plan of the petitioners," he said, "the Iroquois and the small body of Biloxi warriors would advance first and soften the

317

enemy. They'd be followed by the Virginia sharpshooters. The civilians would march in the midst of the Massachusetts Bay regiment, and the troops would blast a path to freedom."

"Too many would die," Renno said, his manner sympathetic but firm. "It would not be possible to blast such a path with only two thousand fighting men and take along the many people of Biloxi. Our foes are too numerous."

The representatives listened to him glumly.

"But there is something even more important to consider," he said. "The Iroquois and the militia have not come to the mouth of the Great River just to escape from our foes. That is not our goal. The regiments of France and Spain must be defeated. Their Indian allies must be beaten so badly that those who survive will return to their homes. If we fail, our enemies will be doubly strong. They will invade the English colonies and the lands of the Iroquois. The Huron and Ottawa will join them, and so will the regiments at Quebec. They will win the war. All of our towns and farms and hunting grounds will belong to Louis of France, who is a tyrant. This must not be allowed to happen. We cannot permit it!"

Suddenly, as he spoke, a tomahawk was hurled at him. It grazed the side of his head, leaving him momentarily stunned but otherwise unharmed.

Before anyone else could move, Kenneth Robinson drew his pistol and fired. A figure tumbled from the thick branches of a tree at the side of the hollow, and a warrior smeared with the crimson paint of the Natchez sprawled on the ground. He was bleeding heavily.

Renno recovered swiftly and was the first to reach the brave's side, his knife in his hand. The dying Natchez mumbled something. Only Renno heard him, and when the man expired, he rose. "He spoke of the she-devil," he said.

No one caught the significance more rapidly than

Kenneth. Beatriz de Bernardo had sent yet another assassin to kill the Seneca she held responsible for her father's death.

Renno grasped the young nobleman's forearm. "Twice you have saved my life," he said, "and now I cannot repay the debt to you. Not ever." He gestured toward the dead warrior. "His scalp belongs to you, so take it before the body is thrown into the swamp."

The petitioners, badly shaken by the incident, dispersed without further ado. Renno, who remained calm after this latest attempt on his life, had demonstrated the fallacies of their plan, so it was plain that the siege would continue.

The troop transports, most of them commercial brigs borrowed from ship owners in Boston, Newport, and New Haven, slowly rounded the southern tip of Florida and headed into the Gulf of Mexico. They had not been built for speed, and they lumbered awkwardly through tranquil seas, fortunately aided by a following breeze.

Their decks were crowded with warriors of the Iroquois, who lined the rails as they stared in silence at the low-lying coast of Florida. Never before had they traveled by ship, never before had they been so far from their own homes. Many were bewildered, and some were apprehensive, but they were united in their determination to do their duty. They were under the command of the Great Sachem himself, and they would follow wherever he led.

Shepherding the convoy was a squadron of sleek sloops of war, their lookouts constantly on the watch for alien sails that might prove to be French or Spanish warships. A similar watch was maintained on the powerful frigate that led the procession, the flagship of the commodore in charge. Indian braves were everywhere on his decks, too, but the commodore no longer resented their presence. One of his passengers was the Great Sachem, and the senior Royal Navy officer, struck by his innate dignity, had discovered they had much in common, including a fierce determination to win the war, no matter what the cost.

Ghonka stood near the prow, looking straight ahead as the wind ruffled the feathers of his bonnet. His arms were folded across his chest, his eyes were fixed on the horizon as he stood unmoving. Beside him, equally unmoving, stood El-i-chi.

Ghonka had studied many crude maps of the Mississippi River delta and of the territory that lay north of it. He knew better than anyone else how difficult it might be to locate Renno, his warriors, and the English colonial militia units. By now, certainly, they had traveled far from the place where they had halted when El-i-chi had started northward on his mission.

Some leaders might have found the problem of finding and joining the expedition insurmountable, but Ghonka remained tranquil, and he began to explain to El-i-chi his plans. "The ships will stop in two days, maybe three, and the warriors will stay on them and wait," he said, "El-i-chi will go to the land. He will take with him as many of the most clever and cunning scouts of the Seneca and Oneida as he needs. He and his warriors will not rest as they search for Renno. It may be they also will find our enemies. El-i-chi will send word when his work has been done. Then Ghonka will come to the land with the warriors of the Iroquois, and they will march to the side of Renno."

El-i-chi marveled at his father's faith in him. The young warrior had just been given the most difficult and hazardous of assignments, that of finding Renno either in the maze of the bayou country or the vast wilderness beyond it. Ghonka had made it clear that he was supremely confident his second son would succeed, regardless of the obstacles that lay ahead.

His mind spinning, El-i-chi calmed himself as he concentrated on the best method of accomplishing the task. He would need fifty warriors—no, seventy-five.

Each would march alone, with the brave on either side of him no more than a mile away, making it a relatively simple matter to communicate when there was news to be passed along. Each man would march precisely the same distance every day, maintaining the same pace as that of his fellow scouts. This could be accomplished only by the most seasoned warriors.

Ultimately this human net, like the nets made by the Cayuga to scoop fish from their lake, would yield results. Renno was sure to be somewhere in the bayou country or on the Great River itself. And by now it was possible that he and the enemy were close to each other.

El-i-chi was not in the least afraid that Renno had been defeated. Had that tragedy occurred, the Huron and Ottawa would have swarmed across the Iroquois borders and would have been joined by the soldiers of the French from Quebec. So it was probable that Renno's force was still intact.

How good it would be to rejoin him! How good it would be to fight beside him again, under the wise leadership of their father! El-i-chi straightened, the problems of dealing with his new responsibility settled in his mind.

"El-i-chi," he said quietly, "has heard the words of the Great Sachem. That which the Great Sachem has commanded will be done."

Ghonka's nod was casual, but a fierce pride welled up within him. The gods had given him the most competent of sons. Perhaps he, too, could claim some of the credit for them because he had always made it a principle that they had to make their own plans and work out their own techniques for performing the deeds he demanded of them.

El-i-chi would find Renno. Then he, his sons, and Walter, who would become his son-in-law, would fight together against the most hated of foes. Still outwardly immobile, Ghonka inwardly rejoiced.

General Wilson spent the better part of his time at his Boston headquarters, where he received regular reports from his own Massachusetts Bay militia scouts and from Royal Navy sloops of war on the military state of affairs in Quebec, the capital of New France. A close watch on the enemy was maintained by land and by sea, and the English colonies were prepared to increase their defensive posture at once if the French regiments and their principal Indian allies, the Huron and Ottawa, showed any sign of movement that would herald an attack.

Occasionally Andrew Wilson seized an opportunity to return for a few days to his Fort Springfield estate, and he arrived unexpectedly one night when his wife, daughter-in-law, and granddaughters were finishing supper. He played with little Patience and Margot for a time, until they were sent off to bed, and then he braced himself for the inevitable questions with which Mildred and Adrienne would bombard him.

Hoping to curb their anxiety as they sat with him on the open veranda, he spoke soothingly. "We've had no word from the expedition other than El-i-chi's arrival in the land of the Seneca. As you already know, Ghonka is personally leading substantial reinforcements. I was able to provide him with transportation by sea, and he should be arriving in the operations area very soon, if he isn't there already. So, for the present, there is no other news."

"For all we know," Adrienne said, "Jeffrey may have been killed or wounded."

"We live in dread from day to day," her mother-in-law added.

General Wilson had to be honest. "I'll admit that anything is possible," he said. "And you know as much as I do. But it isn't likely that Jeff is dead or has been hurt."

Adrienne looked hard at him, wanting to believe him and waiting to be convinced.

"The French in Quebec are our weather vane," he said. "If they launch a major campaign against us, we'll know our expedition in the south has been defeated. If that should happen, I'll be far from certain that Jeff has survived. But the French regiments are still in garrison. The Huron and Ottawa have made no move to mobilize. That means the French are still counting on their own expedition to beat our lads."

"How can you be so sure of that?" Mildred demanded.

One of the servants appeared with a platter of cold meats and bread for the general and poured him a mug of steaming tea. He waited until the serving maid had gone before he replied. "The enemy's overall strategy is very simple. If they win in the south, that expedition will start to move north and will attack the Carolinas, while the Quebec forces will move south against us. Until that happens, it's reasonable to assume they haven't defeated our lads." He began to eat his late supper and tried to look more confident than he felt.

"I know Jeffrey is not easy to kill, and neither is Renno," Adrienne said. "I'll happily pit them against any commanders the French have sent against them. But I'm still haunted by my uncertainty."

"Of course you are, my dear," her father-in-law said soberly. "On nights when I can't sleep, my imagination runs wild, too. That's when I'm forced to use basic military logic to conquer my fears. But I'm positive of one thing—if no decisive engagement has been fought before Ghonka and his warriors reach the combat area, the odds in our favor will increase sharply. I'd hate to be the commander of the French and Spanish army that faces Ghonka. Jeffrey and Renno are exceptionally able commanders, as is young Ned Ridley, but Ghonka is almost unbelievably formidable. I'll never forget him during our siege of Louisburg. His instincts are remarkable, and he's had so much experience that no general in the New World is his equal." He finished his meal, then wiped his mouth and hands with a linen napkin.

"We live on hope as well as fear," Adrienne said. "That's about all we can do."

Andrew stood and patted her shoulder. "I won't insult your intelligence by telling you not to worry, my dear," he said. "I worry, too. Now you'll have to excuse me until tomorrow morning. I had a long ride today, and my lack of stamina is an unfortunate reminder that I'm not growing any younger."

"I'll come upstairs shortly," Mildred called to him as he went into the house.

Adrienne waited until he was out of earshot. "What do you think, *Maman* Wilson?"

"Andrew and I have been married for almost forty years, and in all that time he has never lied to me," Mildred said. "He can't reassure us any more than he's done because he simply doesn't know the situation."

Adrienne tried in vain to stifle a sigh.

"Until we find out whether the campaign has been won or lost, we must rely on his judgment. He feels we have cause for optimism, so we've got to hope harder that Jeffrey will be victorious and safe."

They smiled at each other somewhat tremulously and without another word walked arm in arm into the house.

There were reasons to rejoice in the Ridley house outside Norfolk, and the atmosphere was buoyant. Consuelo had given birth to a healthy boy, and both she and the baby were thriving. As she had vowed, Consuelo named the baby for Linnick, the Indian who had risked his life for her, Ned, and Renno a few years earlier.

The day after the baptism the family received a letter from Betsy, written in the land of the Seneca and forwarded by way of Massachusetts Bay. To their infinite relief they learned that Anne was safe, as was

Hester, and that El-i-chi also had reported that both girls were accompanying the military expedition under the protection of Ned and Renno.

Mary Ridley could not speak, and tears ran down her face.

Consuelo hugged her baby. "Anne and your papa are coming home and will see you," she whispered to her son.

Austin Ridley sat in silence for a time, then grinned. "I can think of no better escorts for Anne than Ned and Renno," he said. "Our prayers have been more than answered. This is a miracle!"

After the baby was placed in his crib, the Ridleys and their daughter-in-law had a festive dinner, but gradually their euphoria began to fade. Consuelo was the first to mention the other news that Betsy had scribbled in haste.

"If Ghonka has gone off with warriors from all of the Iroquois nations to join the campaign, the expedition must be in trouble."

"It is," Austin replied. Although he had not yet heard from the expedition's messenger, he had just received a full explanation of the campaign from General Wilson. Still, he did not want to tell the women any more than was necessary.

Consuelo shook her head. "I can't imagine Ned and Renno being in serious difficulty," she said. "They're the most competent fighting men anywhere."

"Indeed they are." Her father-in-law did not elaborate.

Mary knew her husband too well to be fooled by his uncommunicative response. "You know more than you're telling us, Austin," she said accusingly.

General Ridley realized his wife would give him no peace until he revealed the whole truth. "There was a letter from General Wilson in the same packet that brought Betsy's letter," he said. "It's true that Ghonka has gone off with a large number of warriors to join our sons."

"What does it all mean?" Mary demanded.

"Well," he said, "the New England colonies and New York are far more vulnerable now if the French launch an attack from Quebec. The Iroquois warriors who have been left behind would give a good account of themselves, you may be sure, but the Massachusetts Bay militia are forced to accept an even greater burden of responsibility; and I'll be caught in the middle if we're attacked simultaneously from the north and from the south. I haven't had time to study the situation in depth yet, so I don't know whether I'd take my own brigade down to the Carolinas or to New England. The problem becomes quite complicated." He tried to speak calmly and display no emotion, but he gave away his concern.

Consuelo was quick to grasp the meaning behind his words. "If there should be an attack from the south," she said, "Ned and Renno will have failed."

"I didn't say they have failed or that the Carolinas will be attacked for sure. We must prepare for the possibility, that's all."

"Well, you can be sure it's a remote possibility," she replied fiercely. "Ned and Renno will never give up. Never! They were wise to ask for help when they needed it. Each of them, by himself, is resourceful, and together they're unbeatable."

Austin knew the young woman's views were colored by the experiences she had shared with Ned and Renno in the West Indian islands and Spanish Florida, where they had outwitted the forces of New Spain against heavy odds. But the situation his son and son-in-law currently faced was far more dangerous than any they had known previously, and the success or failure of their current campaign would determine the fate of the English colonies.

In short, they were engaging in the fight of their lives. Not wanting to frighten Consuelo or Mary, however, Austin managed to sound cheerfully optimistic as he said, "You have great faith in them, Consuelo. So do I. Mark my words. They'll win a victory that will end the war in the New World!"

Consuelo wanted to believe him and smiled in relief.

Austin Ridley silently prayed that his predictions would come true. He had not mentioned his principal concern: neither he nor Andrew Wilson knew how many troops had been mustered by France and Spain in the south, and Ghonka's warriors, no matter how great their number, would find it difficult to defeat experienced soldiers armed with the most modern muskets and cannon.

Ja-gonh moved from the house of his parents into one of the lodges of the Bear Clan to begin his pre-warrior training. Though he was younger than the other boys in the group, it was right that the son of Renno and the grandson of Ghonka should begin early. For years to come, Ja-gonh would lead a harsh life. He would be taught to shoot with a bow and arrow, to wield a tomahawk, a spear, and a knife. He would learn the countless secrets of the wilderness and ultimately would be able to survive alone in the forests for long periods. His stamina would be developed, and he would absorb the proud traditions of the Seneca. He would be granted no favors because he was the grandson of the Great Sachem of the Iroquois and son of the Seneca sachem. On the contrary, because of his ancestry he would be subjected to disciplines even more demanding than those his peers would know, just as his father was before him.

Goo-ga-ro-no was still too young to leave home, but on her third birthday a major change took place in her daily existence, too. According to the ways of the Seneca, she was placed in the custody of her grandmother, whom she accompanied into the fields each day. Ena was a strict taskmistress, never spoiling the child. The women of the Seneca, like the men, set exceptionally high standards and lived up to them.

327

Betsy had known what was in store for her children, and in spite of her very different background, she approved of their treatment. They were Seneca, after all, and only the strong, the courageous, and the cunning could survive and flourish in the hard, primitive society of a wilderness people.

More than two-thirds of the total number of warriors who lived in the main town of the Seneca had gone off to war, some having accompanied Renno and an even larger contingent having marched with Ghonka. Those who remained behind served double duty as hunters and as sentinels, never complaining as they worked long hours, rarely enjoying respites.

On the surface, at least, the nation's life was unchanged. The women worked in the fields, growing the corn, beans, and squash that would be the staples of fare after the growing season ended and wild fruits and vegetables were no longer available. They fished, cured the skins of the animals the hunters brought home, and then fashioned the skins into clothes and moccasins. Occasionally, at night, they watched the dances and joined in the chants of the medicine men and elders.

At no time did any of the women mention the current military campaign in public. It was enough that the manitous guarded their sons and husbands, and it was believed that any woman who talked about an absent loved one might arouse the anger of the manitous and consequently subject that warrior to even greater dangers.

Only at night, when the women gathered with relatives in their own homes, was it permissible for them to share their fears and seek at least some measure of relief by expressing them aloud. But constant restraint was shown in the dwelling of the Great Sachem because of the standards set by Ena.

As far back as she could recall, the men of her family had gone off to war, and through the long years of her marriage to Ghonka, she had hardened herself, enduring the trials and agonies of their frequent separations in stoical silence. Ena had more at stake than most in the current campaign. Now her husband had gone off to join her two sons and future son-in-law. But she never mentioned them as she sat in front of the fire, cutting and sewing a new dress of doeskin for Goo-ga-ro-no. Stiff-backed and quiet, she was willing to chat only about inconsequentials.

Betsy tried hard to emulate her mother-in-law. She never worried aloud about Renno, but rather prayed for him in silence, just as she thought about him in silence. Displaying remarkable skill with the curved knife of Seneca women, she concentrated on the task of making a new pair of moccasins, which she subsequently would decorate with dyed porcupine quills.

"It is said," Ena declared, "that huge numbers of wild red berries that are sweet to the taste have been found a quarter-day's march from the town."

"Who found them?" Betsy asked.

"Two warriors of the Fox Clan. Tomorrow," Ena added, glancing at Ba-lin-ta, who was cutting thongs of rawhide, "they will ask for volunteers from the ranks of the unmarried women to pick the berries. Sentries will escort the girls because the berry patches are far from the town."

Since earliest childhood Ba-lin-ta had been something of a rebel, frequently showing her impatience with the nation's long-established customs. She knew, of course, that her mother was suggesting that she volunteer for the berry picking and that it was her place to announce that she would act accordingly. Instead she said, "Ba-lin-ta does not think of herself as an unmarried woman."

Ena's lips tightened. "She is not yet married to Walter."

Betsy attempted to warn the girl with a look not to try Ena's patience, but Ba-lin-ta had never appreciated the values of silence. "In my heart I am married to him," Ba-lin-ta said. "If he dies in battle far from home, I will mourn for him as a widow would mourn and will smear ashes on my face. I will live as his widow, and I will never marry another."

Ena's frown deepened.

"It isn't fair!" Ba-lin-ta cried, throwing aside all restraint. "For many winters Wal-ter could not speak or hear. Then the gods relented, and he became like other warriors. But no sooner was he healed than he marched off to war with Renno and El-i-chi. I think of him every day and every night. I am so afraid he will be killed and that we will never know a happy married life together."

"It is you who tempt the ire of the gods with such loose talk," Ena said primly.

"It is easy for you to remain quiet, my mother," Ba-lin-ta said. "You and my father have been married for more than five and thirty summers. It is easy also for Betsy to be silent. Renno's children remind her of the years they spent together. But Wal-ter and I have no such memories. We have not even slept together!"

Betsy spoke quickly, before Ena could reprimand Ba-lin-ta. "It may seem to you that those who are married part more readily. But that is not so, Ba-lin-ta. Each year Renno and I have been married we have drawn closer together. So it must be with your mother and Ghonka. There must be a terrible hurt in their hearts when they are separated."

"It is so," Ena acknowledge curtly, then turned to her daughter. "If Ba-lin-ta wishes to mourn aloud like a coward while her warrior yet lives, let her go alone into the fields. There her tears will serve a useful purpose by feeding water to the soil and making the corn grow taller. Let her not weep like a woman of the Huron or Erie!"

No insult was worse than that of being branded a Huron or Erie. Ba-lin-ta fought long and hard within herself and ultimately managed to recover her poise. "When I go tomorrow to pick the berries," she said, "it may be that I will also see some of the wild herbs that my mother uses when she cooks venison stews. If I do, I will bring some to her."

Ena accepted the apology with a nod. "That will be good," she said, "because tomorrow Goo-ga-ro-no will begin her lessons in cooking. I will begin to teach her about herbs."

Betsy sympathized with Ba-lin-ta. Her own heart ached unceasingly, and she would not know happiness again until the day Renno returned to her.

Chapter XII

The ten war canoes, built hastily but carefully, stood on the south bank of the lake, and the two hundred and fifty warriors assigned to participate in the initial move filed into them silently, freshly applied war paint smeared on their faces and bodies. They observed strict discipline, as did the braves who would make the journey across the lake after them, and the silence was broken only by the quiet dipping of paddles into the still waters.

On the other side of the lake, in the bivouac area occupied by the English colonial militia and Renno's warriors, the evening was seemingly like any other. Repulsed by the unrelieved diet of buffalo meat, the warriors, soldiers, and members of the small Biloxi tribe nevertheless sat around their campfires forcing themselves to eat because they knew they would become ravenous otherwise.

333

Only Sun-ai-yee, who sat apart from the other commanders with his bride, seemed to be enjoying himself. Talking Quail had found an herb that she had crushed and sprinkled on the war chief's meat, and he liked his meat so much he promised her that, when the campaign ended, he would shoot a deer and an antelope for her in order to provide her with the new clothes she wanted.

Renno, Jeffrey Wilson, and Ned Ridley were silent as they ate. All three realized that the siege was corroding the spirits of their men and that sooner or later they would be forced to take the extreme risk of trying to fight their way through the strong lines of the enemy. There seemed to be no other choice.

Then a sentry of the Oneida, one of the few assigned to sentinel duty at the lake, ran to the fire. "Many boats cross the water," he said. "In them are many warriors!"

So the Franco-Spanish forces and their Indian allies were growing tired of the siege, too, and were going to launch an attack on the rear!

Leaving their forces on the northern side of the perimeter in place, the commanders immediately sent the better part of the Massachusetts Bay regiment and the Iroquois who had no other assignment toward the lake. The warriors took up positions nearest the water, lying on the ground, while the militiamen formed their lines to the rear.

"Don't fire until Renno's warriors let fly with a flight of arrows," Jeffrey told his subordinate commanders. "We want the enemy to believe they're succeeding in surprising us, so we'll hold our fire as long as possible."

The women and children were evacuated from the area in which the fighting was expected to develop, and then Jeffrey joined Renno behind a high tangle of bushes near the water that would serve as their joint command post. After the brief flurry of activity, the camp seemingly was quiet again.

Renno pointed grimly.

Jeffrey's eyesight was not equal to that of his old friend, but after some moments he could make out the vague shapes of the canoes. He counted ten of them, and all appeared to be crowded with warriors.

All at once the clear, high trill of a cardinal floated toward the compound from the water. Renno stiffened.

Jeffrey was puzzled. He had seen no cardinals of any kind in the bayou country.

Renno raised two fingers to his lips and, to Jeffrey's astonishment, he emitted a similar bird call. Again a trilling sound came from the lake, and again Renno answered it, then called aloud to his warriors, "Do not fire! Those who approach are not enemies!"

The bewildered Jeffrey, at his friend's urgent request, issued a similar command to his militiamen.

Renno walked alone to the water's edge. A few moments later the lead canoe came toward the shore, and a number of warriors leaped out of the craft in order to haul it up onto dry land.

A majestic figure in a feathered bonnet and long buffalo robe stepped ashore, and an impassive-faced Renno raised an arm in salute to his father. An equally expressionless Ghonka returned his son's salute, and then they grasped each other's forearm, with only the tightness of their grips revealing the emotions seething within them.

The warriors of the Seneca came ashore, and the canoes returned to the far bank for more braves. They would ply back and forth through the better part of the night.

Ghonka immediately went into conference with his elder son, the delighted Jeffrey, and the equally elated Ned. The Great Sachem explained succinctly that he and nearly three thousand Iroquois had come ashore from their transports and had marched about fifty miles through the bayous. Then they had built their canoes and had initiated the move across the lake.

Renno deeply appreciated his father's stealth. "The

enemy does not know, then, that we have been reinforced!"

Sun-ai-yee joined the group, while Talking Quail, overawed by the presence of the legendary Great Sachem, remained in the background. The sachem of the Biloxi was presented to Ghonka, and the war chiefs of the other Iroquois nations came to the fire as soon as they landed.

There was no need for the Great Sachem to take formal command of the forces. Everyone present automatically deferred to him. He listened, making no comment as Renno, Jeffrey, and Ned, speaking in turn, told him in detail about the state of the siege.

"We will attack," he said at last, "before the French and their allies learn that the defenders here have grown stronger."

Wasting no time, Ghonka made a tour of the sentry outposts with Renno. There he learned that the Pensacola and Natchez were manning the enemy's sentinel positions, with the Osage stationed in the vanguard, supported by the Creek. The French and Spanish regiments, with the Shawnee split into two groups on their flanks, formed the core of the besiegers' stand.

This information enabled him to determine the order of attack, which he did without hesitation. "Renno, the sachem of the Seneca, will lead all of the Seneca," he said, assigning the warriors of their own nation who had accompanied him to his son.

Renno was pleased. Not only would he have the honor of leading the assault, but he would command a formidable force of Seneca. He would be followed by the Virginia sharpshooters, and then the Massachusetts Bay regiment would advance. In the meantime, according to the cunning tactics devised by the Great Sachem, Ghonka himself would lead all the other Iroquois, with the relatively few warriors of the Biloxi, who were most familiar with the bayou country, acting as this powerful unit's guides. The principle to be followed was simple: the enemy would be concentrating on the force trying to break the siege, so Ghonka and his Iroquois would rely on stealth, hoping to remain undetected as they attempted to loop around to the rear of the enemy. Thus, if the maneuver succeeded, the European regiments and their allies would be pounded simultaneously from front and back.

The element of surprise, Ghonka emphasized, was all-important. The enemy would be confronting a force twice the size of what they had anticipated.

The newly arrived Seneca joined those who had previously been under Renno's command, all of them happy to be going into battle together. The young sachem explained the situation to them in a few words. It was their right, as the most renowned warriors in the New World, to act as the spearhead of the attack. They, together with the militiamen who would follow them into combat, would be expected to keep the far larger enemy force completely occupied until Ghonka had the time to conduct the other Iroquois to the rear. The odds against the Seneca would be overwhelming in the initial stages of the fight, but they accepted that fact with their usual calmness, confident they would accomplish the task assigned to them.

Sun-ai-yee, concentrating on the work that awaited him, spoke curtly to his bride. "Talking Quail," he said, "will join the women, elders, and children of the Biloxi. She will wait with them until the battle ends."

This was the young woman's first taste of what the Seneca expected of their wives in an hour of crisis, and she became flustered. "Where will Talking Quail search for her husband if we lose?"

"If we lose," the war chief said, "Sun-ai-yee will be dead. But we will not lose."

El-i-chi came to Renno and said simply, "I have earned the right to march beside my brother."

"You have earned that right," Renno replied.

Walter stood nearby in silence. He, too, wanted to march at the head of the column, but as a junior warrior it would have been unseemly for him to make such a request.

Renno saw his expression, knew what he was thinking, and beckoned to him. "Wal-ter will follow close behind me," he said. "He will act as my messenger and will take word to the Great Sachem of the progress we make."

Walter was overjoyed. Ordinarily that difficult assignment would have been given to a senior warrior because, with thousands of men in motion through the junglelike wilderness of the bayou country, it would not be easy to find Ghonka.

André Cooke had no formal place in the battle order, so Ned Ridley extended an invitation to him. "You can handle a musket as well as any of my sharpshooters, if not better," he said. "So march with me. I can use your help as a guide, too."

"You will not be sorry," André promised him.

Kenneth Robinson would have preferred to join the Seneca, but he lacked their ability to make no sound as they advanced through the forest, and he was at loose ends until Jeffrey Wilson summoned him. "I had my doubts about you for a long time," the commander of the Massachusetts Bay regiment said, "and with good cause. But your loyalty has been consistent, and you've more than proved yourself by twice saving Renno's life. I'll be proud to have you march with me."

Overcome by a rush of emotion, Kenneth was unable to speak and silently gripped Jeffrey's hand. Now he knew where his future lay if he survived the battle; he would settle permanently in the frontier country of Massachusetts Bay.

His most pressing personal problem remained to be settled, however, and he went in search of Hester MacDevitt. She and Anne Ridley had been instructed to stay behind with the women, children, and elders of the Biloxi when the battle began, and he found the two young women in their bivouac area. "I must speak with you alone," he said, tight-lipped, to Hester.

Hester walked with him a short distance and at Kenneth's invitation sat on a tree stump.

He sucked in his breath. "I'm not what you may think I am," he said. "I was a gambler who lost my entire inheritance and was tricked into becoming a French spy. I disgraced a title that goes back to the time of William the Conqueror."

Hester stared at him in astonishment. "A title, Kenneth?"

"I am Viscount Symes," he said.

"Then you've been fooling me all this time!" she shouted, leaping to her feet. "What pleasure it must have given you to persuade a penniless indentured servant that you've been interested in her!"

Kenneth caught hold of her shoulders before she could flee. "I'm as penniless as you are. I've been afraid you'd react just as you're doing, or I'd have told you the truth long ago."

Hester tried unsuccessfully to free herself. "What would a lord want of a girl who was sent to Newgate Prison for stealing food?"

"What would an honorable and decent young woman want of a man who was a traitor to his country? Damnation, Hester, I'm trying to tell you I love you! I want to marry you, and I'm willing to starve—for as many years as may be necessary—to buy off your indenture!"

She stopped struggling and looked at him in wonder. "You mean that, milord?"

Kenneth looked hard at her. "This is not a time for jesting. In the next twenty-four hours I may be killed—"

"I—I couldn't bear it," she cried, interrupting him.

"If I live through the battle—and all I know is that we'll be fighting against heavy odds—there isn't much I can offer you. I'd like to settle in the neighborhood of Fort Springfield. I know nothing about farming, and I have no idea how I can earn a living. But I'm willing to work hard for you for the rest of our lives. And I'll gladly assume the price of your indenture if the Ridley family will allow me to pay them off a little at a time."

He was so intense that Hester felt giddy. "General and Mrs. Ridley are wonderful people," she said. "The settlement of my indenture will be the least of our worries. As for the rest, I don't care what work you do. I'm willing to work with you, but there is a problem. I—I'd feel ridiculous if people started calling me Lady Symes."

Kenneth's tensions evaporated suddenly, and he laughed. "I've already planned to renounce my title, which will go to a distant cousin. All that matters is that you're willing to become Mistress Robinson!"

"For a man who is going into battle in a few hours you squander time like—like a gambler. Aren't you ever going to kiss me?"

Anne, surreptitiously observing them from a distance, could not hear what they were saying, but smiled when she saw them embrace. She realized that the obstacles that had kept them apart had been removed.

The Iroquois who had accompanied the Great Sachem were briefed by their war chiefs on what would be expected of them. Then, like all the others in the camp, they settled down for a few hours of sleep. Only Renno and Ghonka remained awake. Their planning for the coming day had been completed, and they sat together at a small fire, bringing each other up to date on all that had happened since they had last been together. Renno felt infinite relief when he heard that Betsy, Ena, and his children were well.

"Betsy," Ghonka assured him, "is even more of a Seneca than she was before she went to London."

Renno knew how his wife felt. He had reacted in precisely the same way after being exposed to the alien ways of life in the glittering British capital.

The Great Sachem told him in detail about the success of his mission. Although Ghonka could neither read nor write, his memory was remarkably sharp, and he knew precisely how many cannon each of the warships assigned to the New World squadron carried and how many muskets and bags of gunpowder had been sent for the defense of the English colonies.

Then it was Renno's turn to speak, and he related the highlights of the long march to the bayou country from the land of the Seneca.

Ghonka did not interrupt, and only when his son had finished speaking did he ask, "Is Golden Eagle in the camp of the enemy now?"

"If he is," the young sachem replied, "the manitous will lead me to him before the battle ends. They will preserve his life so Renno may be the one to take it from him."

His father's faint nod indicated that the reply was what he had expected. "What of the woman who is called the she-devil? Does her tent stand with the tents of the French and the Spanish?"

Renno shrugged. "Only once, for no more than a moment, did I see this woman. And in that moment I looked only at Golden Eagle, whose manitous shielded him from me. I do not know that I would recognize the she-devil if I saw her again. And I could not force myself to harm her. Renno of the Seneca does not harm women."

Ghonka gently contradicted him. "She who has tried to take the life of Renno cannot be allowed to go unpunished. It may be she will hire others to murder him."

"It may be," Renno conceded. "But I cannot kill a woman."

His father sat motionless for a long time before he asked, "What weapons does Renno carry into battle?"

"The weapons of the Seneca."

"He will carry no firesticks?"

Renno shook his head.

Ghonka reached beneath his buffalo robe, then produced the gold-handled pistol he had brought with him from London. "This was a gift to the Great Sachem from the woman sachem of the English," he said. "Renno has used firesticks. The Great Sachem does not like them. This firestick is loaded. Carry it into battle, and it may be the son of Ghonka will find need for it."

Although he didn't want to be encumbered unnecessarily, Renno could not refuse the offer from his father. The gold-handled weapon meant nothing to him, but his father's generosity was important, so he took the pistol, slid it into his belt, and inclined his head in a gesture of thanks.

There was no need for further conversation, so they sat in silence, and never had either felt closer to the other. The tactics they would employ in battle would be exceptionally difficult to execute and would require exact timing, with each depending on the skills of the other. Renno's confidence in his father was absolute, greater by far than what he would have felt for any other colleague on whom he and his warriors depended. It was gratifying to know that Ghonka returned that sense of faith in full, a compliment he had never before paid anyone. Regardless of the outcome of the pending battle, this was a moment of total rapport to be remembered and treasured.

About an hour before dawn, the pair rose with one accord, bathed in the lake, and then daubed themselves with fresh war paint. Other Seneca in the vicinity saw what they were doing and followed their example, as did the Iroquois and the Biloxi, and the militiamen made a last check of their muskets. The whole force was stirring, and everyone followed the Seneca custom of eating a few strips of smoked meat and a handful of parched corn.

Sun-ai-yee paid a very brief visit to the bivouac of the women, where Talking Quail awaited him. Demonstrating her right to be regarded as a true Seneca wife, she stood erect and dry-eyed as she bowed her head to her husband. The portly war chief inclined his head in return, then stalked off without touching her. They would have violated one of the nation's most sacred traditions if either had spoken a word of farewell.

André Cooke came to Anne Ridley, and they followed the traditions of frontier dwellers. Unwilling to voice their hopes and fears aloud, they kissed and parted. Anne did not weep until André vanished from sight.

The farewell of Kenneth Robinson and Hester Mac-Devitt was shattering. Having just revealed their mutual love, they found it difficult to part, and they embraced repeatedly.

"Well," he said gruffly, "the battle won't wait."

"I'll pray for you," Hester whispered, her gaze following him as he walked rapidly toward the bivouac of the Massachusetts Bay regiment.

Before Ghonka went with his Iroquois to the extreme left flank, the Great Sachem made a swift inspection of the Seneca. He moved silently through the ranks of the warriors, each of whom raised an arm in salute to the leader whose very presence increased their confidence. At last he moved to the front of the loose formation.

Sun-ai-yee, who had served as his principal lieutenant in so many battles and was now fulfilling a similar function for Renno, exchanged stiff nods with the Great Sachem. They understood each other, and both were eager for the fight to begin. Ghonka paused in front of El-i-chi, then unexpectedly grasped his younger son's shoulder in a rare gesture of affection. Turning quickly to Walter Alwin, the Great Sachem took hold of his shoulder in the same manner.

Walter was deeply touched. Never in all the years he had lived with the Seneca had Ghonka so clearly indicated what he thought of him. The gesture meant that Ghonka was accepting Walter as a man and would welcome him as Ba-lin-ta's husband.

At last Ghonka came to Renno, and for the first

343

time he spoke. "The Seneca," he said, "will fight through the ranks of the Osage by the time the sun rises."

"The Seneca," his son replied firmly, "will obey the command of the Great Sachem." They grasped each other's forearms, then parted, and a moment later Ghonka disappeared into the predawn gloom.

Without further ado Renno moved forward at a silent trot toward the sentry lines, and the entire column was in motion. Never within their memory had so many of the Seneca warriors taken part in a single battle.

As the leaders came to the most advanced sentry line, Renno veered sharply to the right, and Sun-ai-yee, at the same moment, went to the left. The warriors spread out behind them, and although the braves of other nations would have reduced their speed to a cautious crawl, that was not the way of the Seneca. They were in the midst of the Osage vanguard before the startled warriors of that nation realized they were being challenged.

Walter won the honor of being the first to bring down an enemy. An Osage loomed up no more than a dozen paces in front of him, and before the startled brave could react, Walter's arrow pierced his throat. Renno promised himself that he would remember the incident so he could tell Ba-lin-ta about it. If Walter continued to conduct himself in this manner, he would be certain to win promotion to the rank of senior warrior before the day ended.

The stunned war chiefs of the Osage made a basic mistake. Thinking that an enemy patrol was engaging in a sally merely for the sake of creating a disruption, they were too proud to raise a general alarm. By the time they recognized their error, it was too late. Wave after wave of Seneca advanced, cutting deep into the core of the Osage position.

More accustomed to fighting in open prairies than in

the thick tangle of deep forests, the Osage suffered a natural handicap in combat with foes who seemed capable of seeing through trees and bushes. The Osage chiefs made a gallant effort to rally their forces, but Renno and Sun-ai-yee were wielding their tomahawks and knives with precise, deadly efficiency, literally chopping their way through the Osage lines, and the ferocious warriors who followed them also scorned the use of their bows and arrows. Ever present in their minds was Ghonka's order to slice all the way through the Osage position by sunrise. Dawn had already broken, so there was no time to lose.

The Osage finally sounded the alarm, their drummers beating a hasty tattoo that carried through the forest and alerted the Creek, who were stationed directly behind them. Still conscious of the disgrace they had suffered when they had fled from the field in the earlier heavy skirmish, the Creek braced themselves.

The Seneca warriors' momentum continued to carry them forward. Renno notched an arrow into his bow as a signal that hand-to-hand combat with the Creek was to be avoided at the outset, and the warriors behind him instantly followed his example.

In one of the miracles of silent communication that made the Seneca unconquerable, Sun-ai-yee either sensed the change in Renno's tactics or reached the same decision at the same time. Whatever his motivation, he switched to a bow and arrow, and the warriors in his charge immediately did the same.

The Creek sent their arrows high into the air in arcs, hoping they would rain down on the unseen enemies moving through the forest toward them. But the Seneca utilized a far more direct and effective technique. Wasting no ammunition, they waited until they actually saw a foe, then shot at him. Those in the forward ranks never paused, knowing their comrades behind them would continue to advance, too, so more and more Creek were forced to reveal themselves. As they did, the expert archers of the Seneca brought them down.

Outnumbered by the combined forces of the Osage and Creek, the Seneca nevertheless pressed their attack with the ruthlessness born of experience in countless wilderness wars. Their enemies, fearing them, regarded them as reckless, but were mistaken. Every member of the band, from Renno and Sun-ai-yee to the youngest junior warrior, was coldly efficient. Trained from earliest boyhood never to allow emotions to sway him in battle, each Seneca did what was expected of him and did it well. Occasionally a warrior fell, but no one in the column paused. The rear guard would attend to the wounded and carry the dead away so the enemy could not scalp them.

The sun was rising by the time Renno had slashed through the ranks of the Creek and had come into the open. Directly ahead lay a large, soggy plain, interspersed with swamps and rivulets. There were no trees anywhere, and at the far side of a vast field, more than half a mile away, he could see the French and Spanish regiments hastily moving into battle formation.

Calling a halt, Renno instantly sent El-i-chi to the rear, instructing him to tell the Virginians to move forward. Then he turned to Walter. "Find the Great Sachem," he said, waving toward the left. "Tell him the Osage and Creek are meeting their masters. Tell him the Seneca have reached the place they were ordered to reach. Tell him also that ahead lies open land where warriors cannot hide with ease."

Walter sped away on his mission.

Ned Ridley and André Cooke, the Virginia militiamen behind them, required little more than a quarter of an hour to reach Renno's side. In the meantime the Seneca were continuing to assault the Osage and Creek in the forest behind them. Renno silently pointed through the last fringe of trees across the open space.

"Ah," Ned said. "The French and Spaniards are assembling." He studied their formations for some moments. "It appears they're only mustering some of their regiments."

"That makes sense in the light of the information they've gleaned about us," André said. "They think they're facing only one regiment and a separate battalion, units they easily outnumber."

Again Renno sent El-i-chi to the rear, this time to summon the Massachusetts Bay troops and lead them forward as quickly as possible. "The pressure on the enemy must be kept up," he said. "The Great Sachem must make a wide detour to escape detection, so it will take him much time to reach the rear of the enemy position."

Sun-ai-yee came to join them as Ned asked, "How much time do you estimate Ghonka will need?"

Never having learned the way men of European civilization marked the passage of time, Sun-ai-yee could only shrug.

"At least an hour," Renno said. "Perhaps as long as two hours."

"I see." Ned made an immediate decision. "We'll engage the infantry in combat while your warriors finish taking care of the Osage and Creek," he said, then ordered his battalion forward.

Instead of marching in formation as though on parade, as Europeans would have done, the wilderness-wise Virginians spread out, moved slowly, and, when they came within range of the French and Spanish muskets, lowered themselves into the waist-high grass of the plain, which offered them ample concealment.

Watching from the edge of the forest, Renno admired his brother-in-law's techniques. The sound of musket fire erupted for the first time as the French and Spaniards, holding their stiff formations, sent round after round at their foes. But the Virginians made poor targets and, using their ammunition sparingly, took careful aim before returning the fire. Soldiers began to drop here and there in the ranks of the Franco-Spanish contingent.

A breathless Colonel Jeffrey Wilson reached the edge of the forest at the head of his regiment, and Renno quickly explained the situation to him.

"I understand," Jeffrey said. "We've got to make the French and Spaniards believe we're trying to break out of the siege. We've got to keep them engaged while holding our own casualties to a minimum in order to give Ghonka time to swing around to their rear."

"It will not be an easy task," Renno said.

Jeffrey grinned at him. "You and I have yet to win an easy victory," he said, then sent his regiment forward. The militiamen from Massachusetts Bay followed the example of the Virginians and lowered themselves into the high grass as soon as they came within range of the enemy's muskets.

The Osage and Creek were scattering, unable to withstand the relentless Seneca attack, and the remnants of their bands fled across the right flank to the safety of the enemy position.

Renno's warriors would have pursued them across the open plain, but he halted them. "We will rest here for a time," he told his war chiefs. "Let the militia keep the enemy engaged. The hearts of the French and Spanish would be filled with joy if they could kill Seneca with their firesticks."

The sounds of heavy musket fire increased, with the Virginians and Massachusetts Bay troops doing far more than holding their own.

Breathing heavily, Walter returned to Renno's position. "The Great Sachem even now is moving to the rear of the enemy," he said. "He tells the sachem of the Seneca to hold firm. He reminds the sachem of the Seneca that the Shawnee, the best of the enemy warriors, have not yet entered the fight."

"Has the Great Sachem or any of his Iroquois seen the Shawnee as yet?"

Walter shook his head. "I looked for them myself as I came to you, but I saw no trace of them."

"The Great Sachem is wise," Renno said to Sun-ai-yee. "The enemy is planning to use the Shawnee in some trick against us, but we will be ready." He called his warriors together and assembled them in the forest near the edge of the plain.

"The battle is progressing well," the commander of the French regiment said, smiling at his Spanish colleagues and at Alain de Gramont and Beatriz de Bernardo, who was wearing the uniform of a Spanish officer, complete with a plumed brass helmet. "I must congratulate you, Colonel de Gramont. So far the enemy is doing exactly what you predicted."

Alain was far from satisfied. "The Osage and Creek together heavily outnumber the Seneca who led the advance against us. I can't understand why they became panicky and fled."

"Either they are cowards or the Seneca are better fighters," Beatriz said.

Even now, as the battle was being waged, this interfering woman could not resist the urge to inject her opinions into a high command conference, and Alain was annoyed. Rather than become embroiled in another argument with her, however, he raised his spyglass to his right eye and studied the field that lay beyond the embattled French and Spanish regiments. His common sense, combined with his knowledge of Indians, told him that more than fifteen hundred Seneca, Mohawk, and Oneida had taken part in the swift, bloody dispersal of the Osage and Creek. The tactics they had used had been those of the Seneca, and he had to admire them for utilizing them, but he couldn't imagine how they could have received reinforcements of warriors familiar with their method of fighting. Perhaps the mystery would be solved before the day ended.

The French regimental commander also watched the progress of the battle through his glass. "The enemy has committed all of the forces at his disposal," he said. "The time draws near for us to launch our counterattack."

"Not yet," Alain replied.

"Why not?" Beatriz demanded angrily. "The sooner we attack, the sooner we will force their survivors to surrender."

Alain studiously ignored her and addressed himself only to the three colonels. "If this were a battle being fought in the European style, it would be right to counterattack now. But the Seneca are gathering their forces again at the far side of the field, and soon they will join the militiamen, hiding themselves in the grass even more effectively than the colonists are doing. This is a time for patience."

"I do not necessarily dispute you," the senior Spanish colonel said, "but I would appreciate an explanation. It seems to me that this is the time to send the Shawnee savages forward."

"Every militiaman," Alain said, "carries his own bullets. You will note there are no carts and wagons in the field with extra ammunition and powder. So my approach is the only right one for a New World style of fighting. I say we allow the enemy to exhaust his ammunition. It is true that our regiments are suffering some casualties, but they are light. It is unlikely that any of those militiamen carry more than two horns of powder or more than thirty or forty bullets apiece. So I recommend—urgently—that we hold our present position. We allow them to use all of their ammunition. They will not retreat because they know we will drive them back into their siege camp. Instead, they will stay on the field. Not only will we send the Shawnee against them first, but I hope we can rally the Osage and Creek, too. They will be eager for revenge. Then, when the time comes for our regiments to advance, the enemy will already be defeated."

Beatriz protested, but none of the commanders listened to her.

"You make great good sense, Colonel de Gramont," the French commander said. "Our casualties would be much worse if we advance now. Paris will appreciate our victory far more if our casualty lists are small."

"So will Madrid," the junior Spanish colonel added.

Alain continued to study the action on the plain, gratified that the young woman at last was remaining silent. The Indians who called her a she-devil were more accurate than they knew.

A sudden flash of light rising high into the air from somewhere to the rear and to his right caused Alain to turn, and his blood chilled when he saw a flaming arrow soar behind the French regiment. To the best of his knowledge, that burning arrow was a signal used by the Seneca. He scrambled onto the highest boulder in the pile behind the command post and through his spyglass studied the underbrush and trees of the woods behind the plain.

For an instant, no more, he caught a glimpse of a burly figure in a feathered bonnet, his face smeared with green and yellow war paint. Only one warrior in all of the New World could be wearing such a bonnet and the colors of the Seneca. Could it be possible? he wondered.

Another flaming arrow rose behind the troops in the rear line of the French regiment before plummeting to the earth. It was true, then. Somehow Ghonka, the Great Sachem of the Iroquois, had come to this remote land and was about to enter the battle. Alain's original guess had been all too correct; Renno had been able to defeat the Osage and Creek because his Seneca force had grown larger.

"Call out the Shawnee at once!" Alain shouted. "Rally the Osage and Creek! I don't know how they did it, but the Iroquois have assembled a large force behind us! Now we're in a battle for our lives!"

When Renno saw the first flaming arrow rise behind the lines of the French regiment, he felt deep gratification, but was not surprised. He had expected the near impossible, which only one man on earth could have achieved. No one but his father could have led a large body of warriors into an attack position behind the enemy without being detected.

He immediately alerted his Seneca, who spread out as far as they could just inside the outer fringe of trees. When the second flaming arrow shot skyward, Renno exchanged a quick glance with Sun-ai-yee. Both knew precisely what was expected of them, as did their warriors. The Seneca were about to execute their primary, classic maneuver, a pattern that had been perfected in centuries of wilderness warfare. Now, for the first time, European foes would be subjected to simultaneous assaults from front and rear.

More than two thousand Seneca waited in tense anticipation behind their young sachem and principal war chief. When a third burning arrow rose into the air, the entire Seneca force went into action together, the warriors trotting at an even pace behind Renno and Sun-ai-yee. Soon they reached the deliberately stalled rear lines of the Massachusetts Bay militiamen, who were concealing themselves in the tall grass. The warriors, aware they were within musket range of the enemy now, also threw themselves to the ground and began to wriggle forward on their bellies.

The troops from Massachusetts Bay and Virginia held their positions and made no attempt to advance. They formed the anchor for the Seneca, and their turn would come later.

Renno moved closer, then closer still to the French and Spanish regiments, whose musket fire passed harmlessly overhead. When he judged that he was close enough for the arrows of his warriors to be effective, he let fly at a French captain in the front rank, an officer whose white and gold uniform, burnished helmet, and polished boots made him a perfect target. The captain staggered backward and dropped.

The warriors of the Seneca had received their order

to fire at will, and they instantly opened a murderous attack. The air was thick with arrows, their effect all the more terrifying because of the disciplined quiet as well as the accurate marksmanship of the warriors releasing them.

Meanwhile, the Iroquois under the Great Sachem's command were performing an identical maneuver at the Franco-Spanish rear, and entire companies of soldiers who had thought they were being held in reserve suddenly found themselves in the thick of the fight. As they turned to open fire on the Iroquois, another error made by their high command quickly became apparent. The forces of the Shawnee, along with the Creek and Osage who had regrouped, were stationed a considerable distance from the scene of active fighting. Had they been nearby and instantly available, they might have been effective in neutralizing the grave threat, but their delay in coming to the aid of their European allies forced the French and Spaniards to face the fury of the Iroquois alone.

No army could long withstand the flights of arrows, and as Renno watched he detected signs of spreading panic in the tightly formed ranks of the French and Spanish regiments. Officers in glittering uniforms tried to keep their men in formation, their hoarsely shouted commands becoming increasingly frantic as they used the flats of their swords to prevent their men from bolting.

Renno realized that, since he was in the best position to determine when to open the next phase of the battle, his father was granting him that privilege instead of deciding it himself. He halted, shooting two more arrows, then leaped to his feet, emitted the high-pitched war cry of the Seneca, and raced toward the enemy with El-i-chi and Walter directly behind him. In a moment the entire Seneca force followed him, their war cries rising above the rattle of musket fire. Ghonka took his cue from his son, and the Iroquois at the rear of the Franco-Spanish position were also on their feet, the warriors of each of the brother nations proudly shouting their own war cries.

The French and Spanish regulars, already bewildered by the unfamiliar tactics of their savage foes, were completely unnerved by the sight of howling, painted, half-naked barbarians racing toward them from front and rear, all brandishing tomahawks. The lines of the regiments were shattered.

Now every warrior was on his own, giving no quarter and expecting none. Every brave wanted to participate in the rich harvest of scalps, and within moments individual fights developed all over the field.

Jeffrey's and Ned's troops continued to hold their places, temporarily forced to hold their fire for fear of hitting their allies in the surging masses that were moving in every direction on the confused battlefield.

With great regret Renno abstained from direct participation in the hand-to-hand combat. As the leader of the Seneca, he had a greater obligation, even though he might not add to his collection of scalps. He realized that the Shawnee had not yet appeared, and he knew, too, that the Osage and Creek were almost certain to reenter the fray in an effort to redeem themselves. So, as he roamed the field unceasingly, he kept a sharp watch for the Indian allies of the Europeans. Sun-ai-yee was doing the same, and both knew that Ghonka was similarly engaged. When an Indian leader reached a top command position, he had to sacrifice his personal desires for the common good.

Renno was mildly surprised when he saw a young, very slender Spanish officer racing toward him with sword upraised. Gripping his tomahawk, he intended to hurl it at this enemy who was being foolish enough to seek personal combat with the Seneca sachem.

To his astonishment the Spaniard halted, and in pantomime made gestures that indicated beyond doubt that he was inviting Renno to participate in a duel. Such a request could be ignored only at the cost of a warrior's honor. Very well, Renno thought. He would fight a duel, dispose of the officer, and then concentrate again on his larger mission.

He picked up the discarded sword of a dead officer that lay on the ground a few feet from him and saluted his foe. During his visit to England years earlier, he had taken lessons in swordplay and, since that time, had fenced with Jeffrey for sheer sport from time to time. He had no lack of self-confidence because he knew he held several decided advantages: his physical strength was great, his eyesight was keener than that of anyone he had ever encountered, and he enjoyed the benefit of remarkably quick reflexes.

Several of the Seneca who were nearby were on the verge of hurling their knives or tomahawks at the Spaniard, but Renno waved them away. His honor was at stake, and he neither needed nor wanted help.

The young officer's eyes gleamed with venom as he initiated the encounter with a wicked thrust. Deflecting the blow with only a fraction of a second to spare, Renno instantly realized he had miscalculated. In spite of his lack of weight and height, this Spaniard was a superb swordsman. Realizing he was badly outclassed, Renno retreated slowly, parrying thrust after lightning thrust.

Only his instinct for survival, his reflexes, and his eyesight were saving him. But he knew, as steel clashed repeatedly against steel, that sooner or later this foe would break through his guard.

Renno had no time to lose. His talents were inferior, so he had to rely on his greater strength and speed. He decided to shift to the offensive and knew he could not afford to miss. A swordsman as deft as this Spaniard would take immediate advantage of even the smallest error and would impale him.

Tightening his grip on his blade, Renno beat aside his foe's sword, then lunged hard. His thrust was so unexpected that he took the officer by surprise, and his sword cut deep into the Spaniard's body. A crimson stain spread rapidly over his tunic, and as the officer toppled to the ground, astonishment and deep chagrin on his face, his helmet was jarred from his head.

Renno was so stunned that he could not move for a moment. This Spaniard was a woman, not a man. Then he realized that this woman had to be his implacable personal enemy, the she-devil.

Sprawled helplessly on the ground, Beatriz de Bernardo, knowing she was dying, tried to speak. Unable to hear her, Renno dropped to the ground beside her, making certain that she held no knife in either hand.

Again she spoke, but he still could not hear her, and oblivious to the combat raging around them, he cradled her in his arms.

"You have conquered me," Beatriz whispered. "My hatred for you was so great that I allowed it to destroy me."

Renno amazed himself by feeling deep pity for the life she had wasted, and as he held her he gently brushed a loose curl off her forehead.

A faint smile touched the corners of her lips as she closed her eyes and died in his arms.

Renno rose to his feet and beckoned to Walter. "See to it that two of the junior warriors remove the body of this woman from the field," he said. "Later we will bury her according to the custom of her people. And let the order of the sachem be known. No one will scalp her."

As Walter hurried away, Sun-ai-yee approached at a run. "The Shawnee are coming," he said. "So are the Osage and the Creek."

Renno, anticipating what his father expected of him, ordered his warriors to retreat across the open field to the forest, then requested that Jeffrey Wilson and Ned Ridley withdraw their troops to relative safety, too. Although they were startled by the unexpected development, the militiamen joined the Seneca in the pullback.

Again Renno summoned Walter. "Go to the Great

Sachem," he said. "Tell him what the Seneca and their allies have done. Tell him also we await his orders."

As Walter raced off, the Shawnee began to appear on the field, followed by the bulk of the Creek and Osage forces. In all, several thousand warriors were gathering, and Renno felt his throat tighten when he saw Golden Eagle directing them into forming a battle order, and he silently asked the manitous to allow him to meet his foe face to face.

The French and Spanish regiments, although badly battered, were heartened by the appearance in full strength of their Indian allies, and they, too, regrouped. The Iroquois to their rear had broken off contact with them, as had the Seneca, and the French commander voiced a cautious hope. "Perhaps the enemy warriors have exhausted themselves," he said.

"It may be," Alain replied, "but I doubt it. The Iroquois, particularly the Seneca, have never been known to leave a field of battle before a final decision has been reached."

The Shawnee boldly sent reinforced patrols in strength to test the defenses of the Seneca and militia.

"Hold your fire," Renno told Ned and Jeffrey. "Save your bullets and let the Seneca take care of them."

Sun-ai-yee took charge of the limited operation. He knew it was as important to stall for time until instructions were received from Ghonka as it was to prevent the enemy patrols from learning too much about the strength of the forces that had taken up new positions in the forest. So he ordered his warriors to wait until the last possible moment, and then they inundated the Shawnee braves with arrows. The Shawnee were far more courageous and resolute than the members of the other enemy tribes had been, but they could not match the skill of the Seneca archers, and after making repeated sorties, they were forced to withdraw.

There was a complete lull on the field now, after a

long morning of fighting, and the quiet seemed strange. But the peace of the moment was only an illusion. Renno and his comrades well knew that the climactic phase of the battle would soon begin.

Walter returned, his chest heaving as he fought for breath. Two Shawnee arrows had grazed him, but he paid no attention to his minor wounds. "The Great Sachem tells the sachem of the Seneca we will use the hammer," he said.

Jeffrey and Ned exchanged puzzled glances, but Renno and Sun-ai-yee knew instantly what Ghonka meant. "Who will provide the hammer?" Renno asked.

"The Great Sachem." Dismissed with a nod, Walter threw himself onto the ground to snatch a brief rest.

"When corn is ground," Renno said to the militia commanders, "a hammer pounds the grain that rests in a bowl. The hammer must be strong, and the bowl must not crack or break. The Great Sachem is the hammer. We are the bowl."

Jeffrey and Ned, grasping the principle at once, aligned their musketmen behind the Seneca in the forest, with the Virginia sharpshooters in the vanguard. Ghonka's Iroquois would attack, hoping to drive the enemy across the field in the direction of the Seneca and militia, and it was the duty of these units to hold firm. Badly outnumbered, they nevertheless were expected not to yield one inch of ground. If the Shawnee managed to move into the forest, the task of repelling them would become infinitely more difficult.

The enemy unwittingly aided the new tactics that Ghonka had devised by moving across the field in force. It was obvious that the Franco-Spanish high command had decided to eliminate the militia and Seneca before turning on the other Iroquois.

The long lines began to move across the open area. The sturdy Shawnee were in the lead, with the Creek and Osage directly behind them, and the European regiments, drawn up in their customary close battle formations, brought up the rear.

Ghonka made no move against them, and Renno could imagine his father's delight. The enemy was saving him considerable effort. Now, however, the young sachem had to put Ghonka out of his mind. His warriors were well concealed in the forest and would hold their fire until he gave the signal. Although the sun was directly overhead and they had been fighting for almost six hours, they were still fresh and resilient.

The Shawnee demonstrated that they, too, understood the principles of discipline as they spread out, trotting cautiously, then dropping to the ground and concealing themselves in the grass. Unfortunately for their sakes, much of the grass had been trampled in the earlier fighting, and it was not easy for them to hide effectively.

Renno decided to wait until the last possible moment before opening fire. As the Shawnee crept toward the fringe of trees, they sent shower after shower of arrows at their unseen foes, but the fire was not returned.

Only men with nerves of steel could have waited so long to return fire that they were able to count the stripes of war paint on the faces of their foes. The wait was agonizing, and Ned Ridley, who had never lacked courage, turned to André Cooke beside him and muttered, "Good Lord! The front lines of the Shawnee are no more than ten yards from Renno's front line!"

At that moment Renno let fly, and his subordinates did the same. It was almost impossible for experienced archers to miss, and the Shawnee suffered heavy casualties. Nevertheless, they continued to advance doggedly.

In a discussion of generalship in London, Ghonka had agreed with the Duke of Marlborough, who had said that the supreme commander of an army could not be forced to follow rigid rules. Instead, Marlborough had declared, a general's instinct told him when to launch a major assault. The Great Sachem's genius, honed by years of experience, told him that moment had come.

His Iroquois hurtled forward into the open, attacking the French and Spanish regiments from the rear and creating hole after hole in the long, rigid lines.

Again Renno was forced to admire the Shawnee, who had been given an objective and did not deviate from their pursuit of that goal. They still pressed forward, with the Creek and Osage gaining courage behind them, and soon the entire Seneca force was engaged.

Renno sent Walter to the rear. "Tell Colonel Ridley to open fire above our heads," he said.

Within moments the crackle of the Virginians' musket fire made the forest come alive. The Shawnee were halted but held their ground firmly.

Meanwhile, the Iroquois were wreaking havoc in the ranks of the Europeans, who were again confused by the New World tactics of their savage foes. The lines of the Spanish regiments buckled, and the French, afraid of being isolated, were forced to withdraw with them across the open area. The tactics the Great Sachem had devised were effective, but ultimate success depended on the ability of the Seneca and militia to continue to hold firm.

"Tell Colonel Wilson to engage," Renno instructed Walter.

Soon the troops from Massachusetts Bay were crowding on the heels of the Virginians as they, too, opened musket fire. The Seneca, in the front ranks, rained arrows on the Shawnee, who were equally determined not to retreat.

When Ghonka told his Iroquois to start using their tomahawks and knives, fresh hand-to-hand encounters swiftly developed. The Osage and Creek realized they were trapped between the Seneca on one side and the bands of the other Iroquois behind them. Although many of the Osage and the Creek fought with courage and determination, they lacked the disciplined fervor of their enemies, and soon they were unable to maintain even their loose formations.

The time had come, Renno realized, for the bowl to be transformed into a hammer. Sending Walter to the rear for the last time to alert the militia to his abrupt change in tactics, he waited until the musket fire behind him died away, then led his Seneca forward in a wild surge into the open. The colonists were equal to this last challenge, and they, too, raced forward in loose formation, moving into the open and firing at the enemy.

Not even braves as resolute as the Shawnee could withstand the ferocious charge of the Seneca. Throughout their lives they had heard stories about these furious attacks that no tribe could survive, and now they faced the truth of those tales. Slowly, continuing to fight, they moved toward their rear. But they quickly discovered, as did the increasingly frightened Osage and Creek, that their fallback was blocked by the retreating Europeans.

Ghonka and Renno met on the field, each raising an arm in a quick salute, and the Seneca were united with their brother Iroquois. Now they were engaging in the type of combat they liked best, and they killed and scalped ruthlessly. The enemy ranks disintegrated, and the senior Spanish commander ordered a white flag raised.

As Renno sent his last arrow at a Shawnee war chief, he felt a bullet crease his cheek. He whirled and at a distance saw Golden Eagle, who had just fired at him.

The Frenchman-Huron well realized that Renno had no more arrows, and he knew, too, that they were separated by too great a distance for Renno to throw a tomahawk or knife at him. Grinning in grim satisfaction, he continued to watch his adversary as he calmly began to reload his pistol.

Renno's pride was too great for him to consider

seeking cover just because he was helpless. He could not give in to cowardice, and in this moment of supreme crisis he preferred to be killed by his lifelong enemy so his spirit would be forever free in the afterworld.

He prayed to the manitous to give him strength, and suddenly he remembered the gold-handled pistol that had been Queen Anne's gift to Ghonka. Snatching it from his belt, he was well aware that he had only one bullet.

The Frenchman-Huron, astonished when he saw that Renno had a pistol, quickly completed his reloading, raising his own weapon.

Renno fired first, and his bullet drilled a hole between Golden Eagle's eyes. As he crumpled to the ground, Renno raced toward him. By rights the young sachem could have taken his scalp, but in a final, gallant gesture he refrained. In their dealings Golden Eagle frequently had been two-faced and tricky, but he had always fought with distinction, and Renno preferred to salute his memory by leaving his scalp untouched.

The commanders of the Spanish regiments surrendered to Colonel Jeffrey Wilson, the senior English colonial officer on the field, and the French commander was forced to do the same. Surrendering to a civilized man was better than permitting their troops to be hacked to pieces by savages who continued to give no quarter.

The Osage and Creek fled from the field in wild disorder, never to return. The Shawnee, finally outnumbered, had to pull back, too, and somehow managed to maintain some semblance of discipline. They were compelled to leave their dead and wounded behind, realizing, of course, that the scalps of their comrades would become the trophies of the Seneca and their brothers. The Shawnee had learned a lesson they would not forget, and before nightfall they would send a delegation forward to present to the Great Sachem six strips of sacred white wampum, one for each nation of the Iroquois, as a pledge that they would never again take up arms against the mightiest of Indian Leagues.

The Franco-Spanish campaign had ended in total disaster, so Jeffrey Wilson and Ned Ridley could afford to be generous in the surrender terms they granted their foes. The troops of the defeated regiments would give up their arms, but their officers would be permitted to retain their swords. The fortress on Mobile Bay would be dismantled. The Spaniards would go to Cuba, the French would proceed to Martinique, and every man in the defeated force took an oath not to engage in combat against the English colonies again.

Some of the Biloxi warriors went off to the bivouac area to fetch the women, elders, and children, and the commanders of the militia sat at a camp fire with Renno and Ghonka to decide what would be done in the immediate future. No one looked forward to a long march home across half a continent, so it was agreed that the entire force would proceed to the transports still riding at anchor at the mouth of the Mississippi. The ships would be almost unbearably crowded, but a few days of discomfort at sea were far preferable to weeks of marching through the wilderness. The Biloxi, who had served so courageously, could return to their own homes, free of fear.

In spite of the severity of the fighting, the Indians' and colonists' casualties were relatively light. The dead were buried and the wounded attended to, with the commanders making the rounds of the new campsite. Among the injured was Kenneth Robinson, who had been knocked out of action when a Shawnee arrow had cut deep into his thigh. Two Seneca adept at the art cut out the arrow, and Jeffrey poured some of his dwindling supply of brandywine into the wound to prevent infection.

While the wound was being bound, Kenneth lay on the ground, his eyes closed, gritting his teeth and clenching his fists. He felt rather than saw someone hovering near him, and he opened his eyes to see Hester, her face only inches from his. She kissed him, then wiped perspiration from his forehead.

"Colonel Wilson swears you'll be whole again," she said. "I've told him we want to settle in Fort Springfield, and he's promised to do all he can to help us. Oh, yes. Ned has already given me a free release from indenture on behalf of his family. I've also made arrangements for you to be carried to the ship in a litter. Like it or not, sir, your future is settled."

In spite of his pain Kenneth managed a weak smile. "I love it," he murmured. "As much as I love you."

André Cooke and Anne Ridley were reunited joyously and went together to Ned. "We've decided to settle in Norfolk," André said. "We won't even return to my cabin to pick up the few belongings we left there."

"I'm sure my parents will be as pleased and proud as I am to welcome you to the family, André," Ned said. "And rest assured there's a place in Norfolk for a man of your talents. I place just one condition on your marriage."

Anne bristled. "What's that?"

He chuckled. "I insist on the right to stand up with André at your wedding," he said, then embraced both of them.

At the camp fire of the Great Sachem, Renno performed a pleasant duty: he promoted fifteen juniors, among them the proud Walter, to the rank of senior warrior, and he gave additional feathers as scalp lock ornaments to senior warriors who had distinguished themselves in the battle. El-i-chi won two, one for his conduct in battle and the other for saving the campaign by carrying the request for help all the way to the land of the Seneca.

When the brief ceremonies came to an end, Sun-ai-yee brought his bride forward and presented her to the Great Sachem. Talking Quail was properly demure, but there was a sparkle in her eyes, and Renno knew, in spite of his father's severe manner, that Ghonka approved of the war chief's choice.

The warriors of the other Iroquois who had distinguished themselves in battle came forward to receive their rewards from the Great Sachem, and then everyone went off to sleep. The march to the waiting ships would begin at dawn.

At last Ghonka and Renno were alone at the fire. "My son fought well," the Great Sachem said.

Renno inclined his head in a gesture of thanks, then removed his feathered bonnet. "The war has ended," he said. "Renno is no longer sachem of the Seneca."

Ghonka studied him. His eyes were like live coals. "Ghonka," he said, "will remain the Great Sachem of the Iroquois until he goes to join his ancestors. That is the custom of the Iroquois. But he grows too old to be sachem of the Seneca as well. Our people require a new leader. The son of Ghonka has earned that place in the long campaign. He has led the warriors of the Seneca as only Ghonka could have led them when he was younger." He picked up the war bonnet and replaced it firmly on his son's head.

Renno was too full of emotion to speak. But his father understood his silence, and they continued to sit, weary but happy after winning the greatest victory in the history of the New World.

The entire Ridley family was on hand when the troop transports put into Norfolk to discharge the Virginia battalion and take on additional supplies that would be needed to feed the many men who would continue on the voyage.

Anne was surrounded, and her mother embraced André. Ned saw his son for the first time, and Renno, who would spend the night at the Ridley house with

Ghonka before the voyage was resumed in the morning, was presented to his nephew and Linnick's namesake.

"He is a strong baby," he told Consuelo. "Bring him often to the land of the Seneca, where he can learn the ways of a warrior with my son."

Ample food was taken on board, and Renno carried letters to Betsy from her parents and Anne. Anne's wedding would take place in three days, but Renno was too eager to see his own family to remain behind for the ceremony.

Thousands of citizens of Massachusetts Bay crowded into the waterfront area to greet the conquering heroes when they disembarked in Boston, and as the militiamen came ashore they were cheered. The Iroquois were given an equally warm reception, although the presence of several thousand warriors in the city made some people nervous.

"No words can fully acknowledge the magnitude of your accomplishments," a proud Major General Andrew Wilson told his son, Ghonka, and Renno in a brief ceremony at the dock. "You have preserved our freedom and destroyed the French invader. The people of the English colonies, their children, and their children's children will forever be in your debt."

The militiamen and Iroquois refused the offer of a banquet in their honor and left Boston that same day, marching to the west. Another welcome awaited them at Fort Springfield, where the members of the regiment were reunited with their families. Obadiah and Deborah Jenkins insisted that Hester MacDevitt and Kenneth Robinson stay with them as house guests, and plans were immediately made for their wedding. By now Kenneth had decided he wanted to become a land surveyor, and General Wilson, after hearing all he had accomplished, promised he would secure the post from the colonial government for him.

Walter spent the night at his mother's home, and Ida Carswell had the joy of talking with her son, knowing he could hear her for the first time. It no longer mattered to her that he was now more at ease in the tongue of the Seneca than he was in English. All of her prayers had been answered.

The Iroquois resumed their journey the following day, with the Mohawk soon leaving their brothers to return to their own homes in the immediate vicinity. The others marched together for several days before taking separate paths, and finally the Seneca went on alone.

Drums heralded the approach of the column through the wilderness, and every man, woman, and child in the main town of the Seneca was on hand as Ghonka and Renno led the proud procession through the gates. Goo-ga-ro-no almost spoiled the solemnity of the occasion by breaking away from her mother and hurling herself at the father she had not seen in many months. Renno picked her up, hugged and kissed her, and then handed her to Ghonka, who greeted his granddaughter with equal affection.

Ja-gonh showed the effects of his training and inclined his head, then raised his arm in salute as his renowned father and distinguished grandfather marched past him. Renno smiled inwardly and gravely returned his small son's salute.

Ba-lin-ta trembled with excitement when she saw Walter, but she recovered sufficiently to race home so she could greet him there in private. She noted from his scalp lock feathers that he had been promoted to senior warrior, and she was positively giddy by the time he came into the house and swept her into his arms.

Betsy, noting that Renno still wore a sachem's bonnet, maintained the dignity of a leader's wife as she stood in stony-faced silence beside her mother-in-law. But both were inwardly rejoicing because all the warriors of the family had been preserved.

Like Ba-lin-ta, Betsy went off to her own house to await her husband. He came into the main room and halted, his reserve melting as he studied her. "You are even lovelier than you have been in the images that have filled my mind every day and every night since we have been apart," he said. Tears of joy streamed down Betsy's face as they kissed.

That night the entire family ate at the fire outside the house of the Great Sachem, and custom was relaxed so that El-i-chi and Walter could tell the women and children about the successful campaign.

Ghonka and Renno preserved their usual silence as they ate. Betsy had already gleaned the essentials of Anne's romance from the letter her sister had written her, and later she would ask Renno to fill in additional details. She wanted to know, too, about his own seemingly permanent promotion, but she told herself that talk would have to wait. Above all else she wanted to make love to Renno, and she knew that he wanted her badly, too.

The following day the Seneca council was called into session and confirmed Renno's permanent promotion to the position of sachem. Not in twelve generations had a father been succeeded in that high post by his son.

A scant twenty-four hours later Ba-lin-ta and Walter were married in a ceremony attended by everyone in the town, and that same day they moved into a small house of their own, his new rank entitling him to that privilege. Sun-ai-yee and Talking Quail also settled in their own house.

Gradually the excitement over the return of the victorious warriors subsided, and the Seneca returned to the even tenor of their ways. Autumn was approaching, so the men ranged far into the wilderness on hunting trips, while the women were busy beginning to reap the rich harvest. Renno attended a council meeting each day and met frequently with the war chiefs and medicine men of the smaller towns and villages of the nation. Betsy, although she enjoyed no special standing because of her husband's rank, was more content than ever before, and went off each day to work with the other women. Goo-ga-ro-no returned to her training under her grandmother's tutelage, and Ja-gonh, after spending a few days with his parents, went back to the lodge of the pre-warrior boys for the special schooling he received there.

Summer became autumn, and a letter from Jeffrey Wilson, delivered by a messenger from Fort Springfield, brought news that heartened Renno and Ghonka. Word had just been received, Jeffrey wrote, that the Duke of Marlborough and Prince Eugene had won one of the most decisive battles in European history, defeating the finest French divisions and the forces of their continental allies at Blenheim, in Bavaria. It seemed likely that the war in the Old World might drag on for a long time, but Louis XIV had been placed on the defensive now, and his threat to the freedom and security of his opponents was vastly reduced.

One day was very much like another until the morning that Ghonka came to his elder son's house shortly after breakfast to say, "The time has come to go into the forest for a day."

Renno knew what he meant, and they went together to the lodge of the pre-warrior boys. There they summoned Ja-gonh, who was puzzled by the break in his normal routine, but he took his knife and the small tomahawk his father had fashioned for him, and they walked together past the fields where the women were gathering the harvest.

When they came to the edge of the forest, Renno said, "Ja-gonh will lead us."

Proud of their trust in him, the child asked solemnly, "Where do the Great Sachem and the sachem want to go?"

"Ja-gonh will lead us," Ghonka repeated.

The boy struck out on his own. His father and

grandfather followed him in single file, taking turns bringing up the rear and carefully matching their pace to his short steps.

Ja-gonh knew they were testing him, so he took great care to tread silently, as he had been taught. He pushed deeper into the wilderness, where the sweet scent of the pines was strong and the leaves of the oak, maple, elm, and ash were turning from green to brilliant reds, browns, and yellows.

He penetrated farther than he had ever gone on his own, and Renno and Ghonka neither halted him nor directed him. At last he saw a hollow ahead, its grass still green, its far side overlooking a lake he had never before seen, and there he stopped. Neither warrior protested when he sat down to rest, and after exchanging a quick glance, they sat cross-legged, too.

All at once they heard a faint, rustling sound in the underbrush nearby, and Ja-gonh looked questioningly at his father. Renno nodded, and the boy drew his tomahawk, waited until the sound grew a trifle louder, and then hurled the weapon. His aim was true, and he was pleased when he discovered he had killed a large rabbit. He needed no one to tell him to build a cooking fire, and after he skinned the rabbit, he began to roast it. The aroma of cooking meat made him realize that he was very hungry, so he found a vine and a certain kind of thorn, then went to try his luck at fishing.

Obviously the manitous approved, because he soon caught a surprisingly large fish. Packing it in clay, he placed it in the fire and sat again, pleased that he had provided enough food for a meal.

The twinkle in his grandfather's eyes encouraged him.

After the food was cooked, they ate in a companionable silence, drank from the waters of the lake, and then sat again in front of the dying fire.

"Ja-gonh has done what was right," Renno said. "He will become a true Seneca warrior."

The rare praise made it difficult for the boy to refrain from revealing his elation.

A gentle breeze rustled the leaves, the odor of the wood smoke mingled with the scent of the pines, and the early afternoon sun was warm. Thoroughly enjoying the outing, Ja-gonh wondered why his father and grandfather had chosen to make the excursion.

Ghonka answered the boy's unspoken questions. "This wilderness is the home of the Seneca," he said. "The father of Ghonka brought him here, as did his father before him."

"The day will come," Renno added, "when Ja-gonh will bring his son into the forest." Gently he placed a hand on the boy's shoulder, and Ghonka grasped his grandson's other shoulder.

Now Ja-gonh understood. He and his father and grandfather were filled with the same spirit. He had been taught that all Seneca were brothers, and at this moment he realized that, in a very special way, these two from whom he was descended—the wisest and most powerful men in all of the Iroquois League— were admitting him to their brotherhood.

"The manitous who guide and guard us may be unseen," Renno said, "but they are everywhere."

Ja-gonh sat very still, scarcely daring to breathe, and little by little he came to feel the presence of the manitous. His heart was light within him, but he was aware, too, of the new sense of responsibility.

"The manitous brought Ja-gonh to this place on this day," Renno said. "It is no accident that when Renno first came into the forest with Ghonka, he brought his father to this same place."

A chill crept up Ja-gonh's spine. The manitous, who had protected his grandfather and father for so long, now were extending that protection to him.

Renno and Ghonka looked at each other over the head of the boy, whose hair recently had been shaved for the first time on either side of his scalp lock. With one accord they laughed aloud. Seneca warriors seldom laughed, but the sound was joyous, an expression of their mutual love and respect, a reflection of their pride in their family and their consciousness of their Seneca heritage.

Ja-gonh found himself laughing with them. They were demonstrating to him, as they could not do with words, that they had faith in him. He silently vowed to live up to that confidence. When his turn came, he would carry on the great traditions of family and nation that were personified in his father and grandfather.

There was no need for Ja-gonh to tell Renno and Ghonka what he felt. They knew it from his proud bearing, the light in his eyes, the way he held his head high. It was not too much to hope that, far in the future, he, too, might earn the high rank of a sachem of the Seneca.

FROM THE PRODUCER OF WAGONS WEST AND THE KENT FAMILY CHRONICLES— A SWEEPING SAGA OF WAR AND HEROISM AT THE BIRTH OF A NATION.

THE WHITE INDIAN SERIES

Filled with the glory and adventure of the colonization of America, here is the thrilling saga of the new frontier's boldest hero and his family. Renno, born to white parents but raised by Seneca Indians, becomes a leader in both worlds. THE WHITE INDIAN SERIES chronicles the adventures of Renno, his son Ja-gonh, and his grandson Ghonkaba, from the colonies to Canada, from the South to the turbulent West. Through their struggles to tame a savage continent and their encounters with the powerful men and passionate women in the early battles for America, we witness the events that shaped our future and forged our great heritage.

☐	22714	White Indian #1	$3.50
☐	22715	The Renegade #2	$3.50
☐	22716	War Chief #3	$3.50
☐	24476	The Sachem #4	$3.95
☐	22718	Renno #5	$3.50
☐	20559	Tomahawk #6	$3.50
☐	23022	War Cry #7	$3.50
☐	23576	Ambush #8	$3.50

Prices and availability subject to change without notice.

TALES OF BOLD ADVENTURE AND PASSIONATE ROMANCE FROM THE PRODUCER OF WAGONS WEST

A SAGA OF THE SOUTHWEST
by Leigh Franklin James

The American Southwest in the early 19th century, a turbulent land ravaged by fortune seekers and marked by the legacy of European aristocracy, is the setting for this series of thrilling and memorable novels. You will meet a group of bold, headstrong people who come to carve a lasting place in the untamed wilderness.

- ☐ 23170 Hawk and the Dove #1 $3.50
- ☐ 23171 Wings of the Hawk #2 $3.50
- ☐ 20096 Revenge of the Hawk #3 $3.25
- ☐ 22578 Flight of The Hawk #4 $3.50
- ☐ 23482 Night of The Hawk #5 $3.50

Prices and availability subject to change without notice.

★ WAGONS WEST ★

A series of unforgettable books that trace the lives of a dauntless band of pioneering men, women, and children as they brave the hazards of an untamed land in their trek across America. This legendary caravan of people forge a new link in the wilderness. They are Americans from the North and the South, alongside immigrants, Blacks, and Indians, who wage fierce daily battles for survival on this uncompromising journey—each to their private destinies as they fulfill their greatest dreams.

☐	24408	**INDEPENDENCE!**	$3.95
☐	22784	**NEBRASKA!**	$3.50
☐	24229	**WYOMING!**	$3.95
☐	24088	**OREGON!**	$3.95
☐	23168	**TEXAS!**	$3.50
☐	23381	**CALIFORNIA!**	$3.50
☐	23405	**COLORADO!**	$3.50
☐	20174	**NEVADA!**	$3.50
☐	20919	**WASHINGTON!**	$3.50
☐	22925	**MONTANA!**	$3.95
☐	23572	**DAKOTA!**	$3.95
☐	23921	**UTAH!**	$3.95

Prices and availability subject to change without notice.

Buy them at your local bookstore or use this handy coupon:

Now Available!
The Complete Sackett Family Saga in a Boxed Set

THE SACKETT NOVELS
OF LOUIS L'AMOUR

$39.95   (01379-3)

Now, for the first time, the 16 novels of the Sackett family have been collected in four handsome large-size volumes with a beautifully designed gift box. Each volume has a special introduction by L'Amour.

These best-selling L'Amour novels tell the story of the American frontier as seen through the eyes of one bold family, the Sacketts. From generation to generation, the Sacketts conquered the frontier from the wild forests of the East to the dust cattle trails of the Great Plains to the far mountains of the West. Tough and proud, the Sacketts explored the wilderness, settled the towns, established the laws, building a mighty Western tradition of strength and courage.

You can enjoy all these exciting frontier stories of the Sacketts by ordering your boxed set today. And remember, this boxed set is the perfect gift for a L'Amour fan.

SPECIAL
MONEY SAVING
OFFER

Now you can have an up-to-date listing of Bantam's hundreds of titles plus take advantage of our unique and exciting bonus book offer. A special offer which gives you the opportunity to purchase a Bantam book for only 50¢. Here's how!

By ordering any five books at the regular price per order, you can also choose any other single book listed (up to a $4.95 value) for just 50¢. Some restrictions do apply, but for further details why not send for Bantam's listing of titles today!

Just send us your name and address plus 50¢ to defray the postage and handling costs.